The Bohemian Girl

The Bohemian Girl

Kenneth Cameron

FELONY & MAYHEM PRESS • NEW YORK

All the characters and events portrayed in this work are fictitious.

THE BOHEMIAN GIRL

A Felony & Mayhem mystery

PRINTING HISTORY
First UK edition (Orion): 2009
First US edition (Minotaur): 2010
Felony & Mayhem edition: 2018

ISBN: 978-1-63194-148-1

Manufactured in the United States of America

Library of Congress Cataloging-in-Publication Data

Names: Cameron, Kenneth M., 1931- author.
Title: The bohemian girl / Kenneth Cameron.
Description: Felony & Mayhem edition. | New York : Felony & Mayhem Press, 2018. | Series: A Felony & Mayhem mystery
Identifiers: LCCN 2018017514| ISBN 9781631941481 (trade pbk.) | ISBN 9781631941641 (ebook)
Subjects: LCSH: Novelists, American--Fiction. | Americans--England--London--Fiction. | Bohemianism--England--London--Fiction. | City and town life--England--London--Fiction. | GSAFD: Mystery fiction.
Classification: LCC PS3553.A4335 B65 2018 | DDC 813/.54--dc23
LC record available at https://lccn.loc.gov/2018017514

To
Bernard Weisberger
For all the years and all the miles

ACKNOWLEDGEMENTS

I am indebted to my editor, Bill Massey, for both his expertise and his having put up with me in the first place. As well, this book and several others owe much to Tim Waller, whose linguistic knowledge and sense of period slang seem boundless, not to mention his ability to move back and forth with ease between British and American styles while I am floundering in the middle.

Several works were also useful to me: the Grossmiths' *Diary of a Nobody* and Robert Machrae's *The Night Side of London* for details of the period; Michael Holroyd's biography of Augustus John and Alison Thomas's *Gwen John and Her Forgotten Contemporaries* for details of artistic life, and, less so, Virginia Nicolson's *Among the Bohemians*; *Yesterday's Shopping: The Army and Navy Stores Catalogue, 1907*; Frank Harris's *My Life and Loves* and *My Reminiscences as a Cowboy*; and, as always, Baedeker's *London and Its Environs* (in this case, the 1902 edition) for details of the city, including such trivia as the address of Kettner's restaurant in that day and 'Old St Alban's Church' for what is now called St Alban's Old Church. Finally, two websites: The Museum of Menstruation and Women's Health, at www.mum.org; and the Metropolitan Police, at www.met.police.uk.

The icon above says you're holding a copy of a book in the Felony & Mayhem "Historical" category, which ranges from the ancient world up through the 1940s. If you enjoy this book, you may well like other "Historical" titles from Felony & Mayhem Press.

For more about these books, and other Felony & Mayhem titles, or to place an order, please visit our website at:

www.FelonyAndMayhem.com

Other "Historical" titles from

FELONY&MAYHEM

ANNAMARIA ALFIERI
City of Silver
Strange Gods
The Idol of Mombasa
The Blasphemers

FIDELIS MORGAN
Unnatural Fire
The Rival Queens

KATE ROSS
Cut to the Quick
A Broken Vessel
Whom the Gods Love
The Devil in Music

CATHERINE SHAW
The Library Paradox
The Riddle of the River

LC TYLER
A Cruel Necessity
A Masterpiece of Corruption

LAURA WILSON
The Lover
The Innocent Spy
An Empty Death
The Wrong Man
A Willing Victim
The Riot

The Bohemian Girl

CHAPTER 1

The room in sunlight was not half bad, everything too heavy, of course, but so was every other middle-class room in London. Denton's chair was too heavy; the curtains were too heavy; the air felt heavy, but the sun that poured in was bright and cheerful and lightened everything. And, after six months away, two of them in a Central European prison, his own house would have looked wonderful in pouring rain.

'Well,' Denton said, luxuriating in his own chair at last, 'we did it!' He was more than six feet tall, lean, fiftyish, with an enormous Mr Punch nose and an unwaxed moustache that hung down over the ends of his mouth. Even in a Jaeger robe and pyjamas, he carried an air of the American West.

Atkins made a face. 'Yes, though I'm not at all sure what we done, except go on a fool's errand and come out with nothing we took in but our skins.' He eyed a very large dog whose forward end resembled a bull terrier's. 'Rupert'll never be the same.'

'Thank God.' Rupert had lost thirty pounds during the imprisonment, thanks to a diet of cabbage and potatoes, and little enough of those. They had all lost weight, but Denton still thought the trip had been a triumph. After a month in Paris learning how to take a motor car apart and put it back together, they had driven a Daimler 8 across France, Germany and Austria-Hungary and into the Carpathian Alps; then, after several adventures (including thirty-one tyre repairs, a tow over a mountain pass from eight draught horses, and a wait of three weeks for petrol), they had gone into Transylvania, where they had been arrested as spies. The motor car and Denton's guns and a mostly finished novel were still there, seized as 'military contraband'. But it made a great story, and it had made a great series of articles in England, America, France and Germany, and it would make (as it was supposed to, for that was the object) a popular book: *Motors and Monsters: From Paris to the Land of Dracula by Automobile*. Denton banged his hands on the arms of his chair and shouted, 'By God, we did it!'

'I never want to see a cabbage again.'

'On the other hand, look at the taste you've developed for bread made out of sawdust.'

'Rupert's skin and bones.'

Denton stuck out a hand, and Rupert licked the open palm from fingertips to wrist. 'I wish he hadn't bitten that customs officer.'

'Fool threatened us; what'd you expect? Bloody tyrants, them Central Europeans.'

'You shouldn't have said "get him".'

'Who was to know Rupert was trained to attack?'

They were both drinking coffee, Atkins standing from some ingrained sense of protocol, although he was wearing a seedy velvet robe, napless in many places—he was a small man, and the original owner had been large—and munching a piece of

Denton's toast. Denton poured himself more coffee and, looking up at Atkins with a smile that didn't quite hide his sincerity, said, 'I'd never have made it without you.'

'Likewise, I'm sure, General, except that of course I'd never have made it without you because I'd never have been daft enough to undertake such a jaunt in the first place.' Atkins shrugged himself upwards into the robe as a means of avoiding more thanks and said, 'We're in the morning paper. *Noted Novelist Returns.* I'm included as "faithful soldier-servant Harold Atkins". Faithful, my hat. You done with me?'

Denton was starting to rip envelopes open, the accumulated mail of six months, throwing crumpled paper towards the fireplace and missing. He was hoping to find a letter from a certain woman but failing. 'Hold on.' He tore the end off an envelope of a particularly heavy paper, noted that it was addressed from 'Albany', the once-fashionable 'single gentlemen's flats' (correctly 'Albany', no 'the', although most people said *the* Albany, as had Oscar Wilde), found inside a note on the same heavy paper with some sort of embossed thing and a smaller, lighter, plainer envelope. He read the few words on the heavy paper and then looked at both sides of the smaller envelope but didn't tear it open.

'Got steam downstairs?'

'Nothing that'd run a ship, if that's what you're after. Goose the kettle, if that'll do.'

Denton handed over the small envelope and muttered that he didn't want the envelope damaged, to which Atkins answered that of course he was in the habit of damaging everything that came into his hands, and he vanished back into the darker end of the long room and clumped downstairs, Rupert in tow. Denton dealt with the rest of his mail by glancing at it and throwing it away—invitations that he threw towards the fire unopened, both because he didn't go anywhere and because they were months out of date; the usual letters from people adoring his books and wanting something, often to sell a 'sure-fire idea for a best-selling book' of their life stories, sometimes to borrow money. The only new thing among this lot were four—no, six; there were two more at the bottom of the pile—from somebody named Albert Cosgrove, proclaiming boundless enthusiasm for his books and profound awe at his genius. The first, sent a month before, was a request for a signed copy of one, 'please to inscribe To Albert Cosgrove', no offer to pay for the book, of course. The others were hymns of praise, one beginning 'Dear master', another 'Cher maître'. Two had been written on the same day, only three days ago, one saying 'I long for your arrival that will return the English language's greatest literary artist to our land' and asking for signed copies of *all* of Denton's books.

Albert Cosgrove went into the fire, too.

Denton was American. He wrote grittily realistic novels about American sod-busters and the demons that tormented them, and he didn't think of himself as a literary artist. He preferred to live in London, and he preferred living well to living like his characters. For that reason, his only regret about the Transylvanian trip was that most of the new novel—already paid for by his publisher and expected soon, as the editor's letter showed—had been taken away when they were arrested and not returned when they escaped. Or were allowed to escape, as he believed had been the case.

By the time he had disposed of the mail, Atkins was back beside him with the steamed-open envelope on a salver.

'The silver thing's a nice touch,' Denton said.

'It's called a salver. In the best houses.'

'This isn't one of the best houses.'

'Mmm.'

Denton extracted the folded paper that was inside, teasing it out with the end of the letter-opener, and let it fall to his lap, where he prised the folds apart with the same tool and held it down so he could read it. When he was done, he said, 'Read it?'

'I didn't presume.'

'That'll be the day.' Denton turned the paper over and searched the other side and only then picked it up with his fingers and handed it over. 'See what you think.'

Atkins read it. 'Woman.'

'Good. Most Marys are women.'

'Fears bodily harm.'

'So she says.'

'You know what she's doing, don't you, Colonel? It's the same old song and dance—somebody sees spooks or hears burglars under the bed, what does she do? Write a letter to the sheriff!'

'I wasn't a sheriff; I was a town marshal.'

'And then they expect you to come riding on your faithful horse Fido with six-guns blazing! That's what she's on about. Another hysterical female, wants a bit of the thrilling.'

'You should be writing novels, not me.'

'Well, what you going to do?'

'Nothing.' Denton turned to look at the servant. 'Look at the date.'

Atkins studied the paper, suddenly saw the light. 'Oh, my heart, it's two months old.'

'Two and a bit.' He picked up the heavy notepaper that had enclosed the small envelope. '"Dear Mr Denton, I found this missive behind a recently purchased little Wesselons. As it is addressed to you, I send it on like a good postman. Yours most sincerely, Aubrey Heseltine."' He handed the note to Atkins. 'Pretentious—"little Wesselons"! Some Albany idiot who wants everybody in London to know he bought a painting.'

'A Wesselons is a painting?'

'Don't play the dunce, Atkins! What's got into you?'

'My mind's on higher things.'

Denton sighed. Atkins had had some sort of religious experience in prison, the source of a new dourness. 'Does piety have to be humourless?' he said.

'I don't think humour comes into it.'

'Surely there are jokes in the Bible.'

'I certainly hope not!'

'God ought to be allowed to laugh, surely. Jesus laughs somewhere, doesn't he?' Denton thought of telling Atkins an American joke—a rabbi and a priest are almost run down by a carriage, and so on—but he wasn't sure it was relevant. 'Is this about a woman?'

'Now you're offending me.'

'It's like you to have been led into the tent by a female. Was it Katya?' Katya had been some sort of hanger-on at the prison (actually, Denton thought, Colonel Cieljescu's—the commandant's—mistress), but Atkins had been much taken with her.

'I'll give notice if you keep this up.'

'There's nothing wrong with hearing a call to God just because the voice is a woman's. Read *Adam Bede.*'

'Who's he?'

'That's the title. Upright man who falls in love with a lady preacher. Not your usual, however.' Atkins was a great reader of Charles Lever. 'George Eliot.'

'I thought it was Adam Breed.'

'The author.'

'Never heard of him.'

'It's a her. England's greatest novelist.'

'I haven't had your advantages.'

'You've had exactly my advantages; you just made different use of them.' This was only roughly true: both men had been in the army, both had been poor, but one was English and one American, and one was a servant and one was a figure of some notoriety, even fame. Denton indicated the notepaper. 'Wha'dyou think?'

'I think he's a gent who's coming it a little high, as you say, but I don't see nothing suspicious. He buys a painting, finds an envelope, sends it to the person it's intended for. Trail's cold after so long; female has either had harm done to her or not by now.'

Denton read the woman's letter aloud. '"Dear Mr Denton, I should like to come by one evening to seek your advice. I believe that someone threatens harm to me and I do not know quite what to do. If I may, I will call and if you are not in I will return. Mary Thomason."' Atkins had been pouring coffee and now put it down next to him. Denton said, 'No salutation—simply "Mary Thomason". Suggestive. Have some more coffee yourself.'

'Don't mind if I do. Suggestive of what?'

Denton shrugged. 'Unconventionality?'

'Ignorance, more likely.'

'No, it's a good hand, trained, and she says "I should like". Mm-mnmh. Maybe in a hurry or maybe wanting to seem businesslike, but maybe unconventional.'

'You're off on a hare because the thing was found behind a painting—arty stuff. You think, "Art, Bohemians, unconventionality, that's for me!" Rushing your fences, Colonel.'

'And how do you find something "behind a painting"?' Denton sipped his coffee. By now, Atkins was sitting in the other armchair. 'He can't mean on the wall behind a painting, because he says he bought it, and I can't believe he bought the wall, too. What he probably means is "in the back of a painting".'

'Not my line of work.'

'Nor mine, but we've both turned paintings over.' There were four or five on the walls, two more in the downstairs hall, both stinkers he'd bought because they were big and he was trying to fill a lot of space. 'I suppose Aubrey Heseltine could tell us.'

'You're intrigued.'

'I am. I'm guilty, or bothered, or something. A woman thinks she's appealed to me for help, and I don't hear her cry until too late.'

'Hardly your fault, is it? She never sent the letter, did she? There wasn't no stamp on it, was there? The back of a painting isn't exactly the Royal Mail, is it? No on all counts. She thought better of it; you're free and clear.'

'Why did she put the letter in the back of a painting?'

'Did she? You got no evidence.'

'Well—you have me there. But the letter didn't put itself in the back of a painting. Hardly "thinking better of it" to put it there, was it? The trash would be the likelier place.'

'But you don't know she did it. It's moot.'

Denton studied him, or seemed to; he was really thinking of the woman and the somebody who might have wanted to harm her. 'I think I'd like to know where Mr Heseltine bought the painting.'

Atkins put his eyebrows up and rose, gathering the cups and putting them with the ruin of Denton's breakfast. 'I'm off, then,' he said.

'What are you off to do?'

'Stack this lot for Mrs Char and then read my Bible. Going to look for jokes. You've got me thinking.'

'Good.'

Atkins got to the end of the room and put the tray into the dumb waiter and then said from the gloom, 'Mind, I'm not to be got at with secular reasoning. I'm a saint by revelation.'

'Nice, having a saint for a servant.'

He went on down the stairs, the door banging behind him. Denton didn't want to rob the man of his religion if it was a genuine comfort to him, but he liked Atkins better when he was doing what amounted to a music-hall turn as a comic servant. After thirty-one years in the British army, Atkins was an accomplished batman, liar, thief and entertainer; he could cook, press, argue with creditors, give points on etiquette and do imitations of every officer he'd ever served. Denton was sure he did imitations of Denton, too, or at least had until Calvinist humourlessness had revealed itself to him. Atkins needed to be shaken out of his dumps, Denton thought; he needed to be seized by a new interest.

Well, maybe the outdated letter from Mary Thomason would fill the bill.

He went upstairs to the room that served him as both bedroom and office, littered now with the relics of life after the prison. He kicked aside the worn boots in which he'd walked out of Transylvania, the straw suitcase that had been all he could afford in Cluj, the canvas jacket he'd worn as a deckhand on a Danube steamer, and sat at the dusty desk.

It hurt him that there had been no letter from *her*. Maybe she didn't know he'd got out. Maybe she thought he was dead; she lived in a world of prostitutes and want, read few newspapers, knew nobody. He sighed. They had corresponded throughout the trip; even in prison he had written to her, for the last weeks almost every day. Letters from her had reached him until he'd been arrested; then he had got nothing from her, hadn't expected to, but he'd sent her a cable as they had come through Paris on their way back and had thought—hoped—he'd find a note asking him to come to see her. Maybe the cable hadn't reached her. Maybe—

He tried now to write her a note to tell her he was alive, that he was in London, hesitating at once over 'My dearest Janet', settling for 'My dear Mrs Striker', then 'Dear Mrs Striker', then writing a page about not receiving letters from her at the prison and then being on the run, about missing mail, all of that, then pitching it out and writing simply, 'I'd like to see you. May I visit?' He sent an unhappy Atkins out to find a Commissionaire in Russell Square to carry it to the telegraph office, reply prepaid.

He sat on, head on one hand, elbow on desk, staring out of the unclean window at the back of another house forty yards away. He sighed again. The happiness of the early morning couldn't last; left behind were Janet Striker's silence, the mystery of the woman who had left the note in the painting, the irritating knut at the Albany who had found it.

He decided to write to him: 'I must thank you for forwarding to me the envelope you say you found behind a Wesselons. May I call on you to discuss this matter briefly?' Mr Heseltine, he thought, would say yes, because he suspected that Mr Heseltine was the sort of pretentious ass who would have pitched the envelope into the coals if he hadn't recognized that it was addressed to a well-known author.

The question was, why did Denton want to discuss the matter with him at all? As so often, his own motives seemed rooted in a guilt about something he hadn't done. His gloom deepened. The only antidote he knew was work. He would go to work; he would try to recover the novel that he couldn't bring out of Central Europe. He had written an outline of it before he had left London six months before. It was in a drawer in the desk.

He pulled the drawer open. It was empty. He was going to shout for Atkins when he found that Atkins was standing at his door. Denton said, 'Have you been cleaning up my desk?'

'Not likely. You know somebody wears a black bowler and has a red moustache?'

'Did you find a Commissionaire?'

'''Course I did.'

'I'm missing something from my desk.'

'I haven't been home long enough to pinch it. You know a bowler and a red moustache or don't you?'

Denton was going through the other drawers. 'I hope not. Why?'

'Looking at us from the window of the house behind.'

'Lives there, I suppose.'

'Housemaid two doors up says the house is empty and to let. Then, coming back from finding the Commissionaire, I see him skulking across the way. Have yourself a look.'

They both went along the corridor to the front of the house, on this floor a small bedroom he never used. Side by side, they looked down into the street. 'Gone,' Atkins said. 'I knew it.' He sniffed. 'Suspicious.'

'What's suspicious about it?'

'He had a rum look.'

'Probably what he'd say about you.' Denton went back to his desk.

Atkins followed. 'As long as I've come this far, I might as well get your clothes.' Denton's blank look made him add, 'Air them out. Six months in the clothes press. Eh?'

'Well, hurry up, I'm working.' He began again to search the drawers he'd already looked through.

'Could have fooled me.' Atkins loaded his arms with wool suits. Going out, he said, 'That fellow was a bad actor, I'm telling you. They know you're back, Colonel.'

'Who?'

'Your enemies.'

Denton put on an old shirt and hugely baggy corduroy trousers, stuffed his feet into leather slippers and went up another flight to the attic. Could he have left the outline up there? The unfinished wood smelled the same as it had six months before—

dusty, dry, resinous—and his exercise contraption seemed the same, his dumb-bells, his Flobert parlour pistols, locked in their case and hidden under his massive rowing machine. The old Navy Colt that had been with him since the American Civil War, however, wasn't there; like his novel and his Remington derringer, it hadn't made it back from Transylvania. The outline wasn't to be found, either. Denton hoisted a hundred-pound dumb-bell, thought he'd lost strength in the prison. He sat in the rowing machine, looked up at the skylight to make sure that nobody had tried to break in, went back downstairs. Checking his domain, like a dog pissing at corners.

Then he sat again, trying to find if he could recall, word by word, the novel that the Romanians had thought too dangerous to return.

CHAPTER

2

The outline was nowhere in the house. Nonetheless, the novel was mostly there in his head, still his if he hurried to get it down on paper. He had seen the phenomenon before when he had lost a page or two of something and had had to do it over, then had located the original, and, comparing them, found that the second reproduced the first almost exactly. Writing was concentration; writing was thought: what came hard stayed in the brain. And pulling it back out, setting it down on paper, blotted out everything else—Janet Striker, the little Wesselons, the somebody who might be looking at them from the house behind, although that was an idea of Atkins's he thought overblown, nonetheless offensive: he hated being spied on. Even having somebody read over his shoulder irritated him.

At two, he threw the pen down and rubbed his eyes. The left one stung. He supposed he'd need glasses soon. Distance vision was good—he could still shoot the spade out of an ace at twenty yards, as he'd proven to the sceptical officer who'd run the Romanian prison. But reading and writing made the eye hurt. The idea of eyeglasses piqued his vanity, reminded him of Janet Striker, brought back his feeling of deflation.

'I'm going out!' he shouted down the stairs. He'd walk, he thought, clear out his brain. At the very least, he could carry the pages he'd written up to his typewriter in Lloyd Baker Street. He wouldn't trust anybody else to do it, anyway—the only copy, its loss not to be risked a second time. He started to pull on a different shirt and trousers, then went to the stairs and bellowed down, 'Are we still wearing black?' Victoria had died in January; they had left London in March, the city still in mourning.

Atkins was two flights down. He bellowed back, 'What?'

'Are—we—still—in—black?'

'No—we—are—not!' Atkins padded up to the first floor, his head appearing at the bottom of Denton's stairs. 'New king said three months' mourning was enough. Wear the brown lounge suit.'

The brown suit was the only one left in the press. Atkins's revenge for the Commissionaire, he thought: Denton disliked the suit, and Atkins knew it. Passing through his sitting room on the floor below, he automatically reached out towards a box on the mantelpiece, drew his hand back. He had been used to taking the derringer from the box and carrying it in his pocket, but the derringer hadn't got out of the prison. Still, he flipped up the lid, as if the little pistol might have materialized there. It hadn't.

He walked to Gray's Inn Road, then up it to Ampton Street and so across to Lloyd Square, now and then stopping to look behind him, seeing nobody. The idea of being followed by a man in a bowler and a red moustache, of being *known*, troubled him.

His typewriter was flustered to see him, as always; they embarrassed each other somehow, as if they had some intimate past or future they didn't dare discuss. He handed over the papers and fled to Pentonville Road where, on an impulse, he swung himself up into a Favourite omnibus—except it wasn't an impulse, for he was still thinking of Atkins's 'bowler and red moustache' and wanted again to watch to see who climbed aboard. Several bowlers boarded, none interested in him and only one with a moustache, that yellow. Atkins was seeing spooks, he decided, the product of a morbid interest in religion.

The ride invigorated him. London invigorated him, the day sunny and not quite cool—that tremendous sense of bustle that the city had, of pulsing, as if it were a live, growing thing that was always bursting a skin and emerging in a new one. He would visit a friend, he thought—an acquaintance, at least—at New Scotland Yard and report Mary Thomason's letter, and that would be that matter out of the way. Let the police handle it. Guilt made him add that first he would stop at his publishers to go through some likely unpleasantness about the novel, which at best was going to be two months late.

He got down at London Bridge and got on a Red 21 and rode it to the Temple and in a light drizzle walked into the twistings of little streets north of Temple Bar—Izaak Walton's London—to the somewhat ramshackle offices of Gweneth and Burse. His editor was a dry, thin man named Diapason Lang (his father an organist of some reputation), at once severely agitated to see Denton. There was no welcome back to London, no polite chit-chat about the trip.

'I'm *awfully* glad you've come,' he said, '*at last*. Awfully glad.' Lang was older than Denton, apparently sexless, in love with books. 'You've brought the new book?' He sounded hopeless; he must already have seen that, unless Denton's overcoat had a hidden kangaroo pocket, the manuscript hadn't come with him.

'The manuscript is in Romania.' Denton tried to make a light story of it—Colonel Cieljescu, a novel in English as military contraband. 'I'm putting it down again as fast as I can, Lang.'

'Oh, dear. Oh, dear. Gwen will be beside himself.' He looked at Denton as if appealing for help. Gwen was Wilfred Gweneth, the publisher; the Burse of the firm's name seemed not to exist. Lang picked at his blotter. 'Gwen's *most* unhappy about the motor car.'

'It was seized, too.'

'Gwen's terribly upset. He's said quite unkind things.' The publisher had bought the motor car in which Denton had made the trip to Transylvania; it was in the contract, part of the deal. When Denton brought it back to London, it was to have been turned over to the firm. 'Gwen even suggested you *sold* it over there.'

It had occurred to Denton that Cieljescu had let them 'escape' so he could keep the Daimler, but he wasn't about to say that to Lang—right now, it would sound too much like having traded it for freedom. He smiled and pointed out that the vehicle had been insured.

'Yes—yes—but the insurer is balking. They want proof. They want to know if you reported it to the police.'

'Colonel Cieljescu *was* the police.'

'Well, it's all *very* awkward. Gwen is terribly upset. He blames *me*.' The original idea for the book had been Lang's, although it had been Denton who had added, in fact demanded, the motor car. Lang inhaled so suddenly the sound vocalized. 'He'll be in a state about the novel's not being done, too.'

'I'm working as fast as I can. A month. Lang, you've got the book on the Transylvanian trip; it's going to make lots of money! What's the problem?' He had written the travel book as a series of articles as he travelled.

Lang looked at him with sick eyes. 'He's talking about taking the cost of the motor car out of royalties.'

Denton needed those royalties to live. He felt anger coming but pushed it back. 'He can't do that, as you well know. I'll sue.'

'I know, I know!' Lang's voice was a wail. He looked at a print on his wall—Elihu Vedder's *The Nightmare,* a demon looming over a sleeping woman with much exposed flesh—and said to it instead of Denton, 'We're having a little party. *Please* come. It may mollify him.'

'I hate parties.'

'It's to launch the collection of ghost stories. *Henry James* will be there!' Lang, who loved horror in any of its forms, had put together stories from twenty authors, not all of them from the house. Denton was one, James another. 'It would look *so* well if you came.'

'And brought the motor car with me?'

'It isn't a laughing matter.'

'I'll send Gwen a letter explaining everything. Gwen will be delighted.'

Lang groaned, sure that he wouldn't.

'Everything will be all right, Lang.'

Lang leaned his narrow head on one dry hand and looked at the Vedder. 'No, it won't,' he said.

Denton gave it up and headed for New Scotland Yard.

'Well, well, by the saints! How's the Sheriff of Nottingham?'

'I wasn't a sheriff; I was a town marshal.'

'You've lost weight.' Detective Sergeant Munro of the CID grunted. 'I haven't.'

Munro had come limping towards Denton across the lobby, outpacing the porter who'd gone to him with Denton's card. He was big, as most detectives now were big, with a massive head that seemed to grow into a huge pair of jaws as it went downwards from his hairline, becoming almost Neanderthal. He could be brusque, acid, hard, but he was as dependable as anybody Denton had ever known. And he was good at his job.

'I was in the clink,' Denton said with a grin.

'So I read in the press. Come on upstairs. Cup of tea?'

'You've moved.'

'I'd moved before you left town—thanks to you, and I do mean thanks, Denton. You got me back into the CID.'

Denton muttered something. Munro had got part of the credit for finding a murderer whom Denton had killed.

'How's the lady?' Munro said.

'I haven't seen her yet.'

'She forgiven you for shooting a bullet past her ear?'

'She hasn't said.' Janet Striker had been held as a shield when Denton had shot the man holding her, who had already slashed her face once. It was true, the bullet had had to pass just above her ear to hit his eye.

They went up a flight of stairs and turned into a corridor where any trace of marble ended and a scruffy look of police business began. At the end was a huge room filled with wooden desks—and men. Denton saw at least a dozen, many in shirt-sleeves; a fug of pipe smoke hung in the room, which smelled of the smoke and nervous sweat and damp wool.

Munro waved at somebody and caused two white mugs of tea to appear; he motioned to a chair by a desk that was like all the others. 'Sit.'

'No guns here,' Denton said.

'This isn't the Assiniboine.' Munro was Canadian and had been in the Mounties—the second intake, early days in the Canadian West. 'We investigate, not shoot it out.'

'You like it?'

'It's heaven, compared to pushing paper like I was. This lot here do nothing but complain; I tell them that a week at the Annexe untying bundles of paper and tying them up again in a ribbon, and they'd sell their wives to get back here.' He drank tea, looked at Denton, sat back so that his patent chair squeaked on its big springs. 'All right, what is it? You didn't come to see me on your first day back in London because you're in love with me.'

'I was in the neighbourhood.'

'Tell that to some sailor on a horse!' Munro laughed. 'You're all business, Denton—I've watched you. Don't tell me you've got another corpse for me.'

'Only a letter. Maybe a missing girl.'

Munro slapped the desk. 'How do you do it? Twenty-four hours home and you're making trouble for me! Look, we don't do missing girls here. We investigate. We—'

'She sent me a letter just after I left. Months ago.'

'And she's actually missing?'

'She said somebody was trying to harm her.'

'And she's missing?'

'I don't know.' Denton leaned forward to cut off Munro's response. 'The letter reached me kind of roundabout. I don't want to make a lot out of it.'

'Good. Don't. Drop it.'

'I thought you'd know how to find if anything bad had happened to her.'

Munro stared at him. His jaws bulged even more. He said, 'Do you know what "gall" means?'

'I thought maybe you thought you owed me a favour.'

Munro tipped his head back so he could study Denton down the length of his fleshy nose. He stuck his lips out. He pushed out his chin. 'You got a name?'

'Mary Thomason.'

'What division?'

'She didn't give an address.'

Munro made it clear he thought that that was the last straw. He muttered that Denton was going to give him heart failure one day. He gulped down his tea and stamped off through the room to a bank of three telephones on the wall at the far end. When he came back, he seemed better humoured.

'Two days,' Munro said. 'Hope you can wait two days.'

'Beggars can't be choosers.'

Munro began to fill a pipe. 'Beggars, my arse! Well, you're right I owe you one—wouldn't be back here if not for you. I've put a query in train at the divisions, anything they have on Mary Thomason, same at the coroner's. If she's made a complaint or died, you'll hear of it.'

'I don't remember you smoking.'

'Self-defence in this place. Go home stinking of it, anyway; the wife complains. You don't have a wife.'

'Indeed.'

'Thought there might be something with the lady whose ear you almost shot off. Mmm?'

'Unlikely.'

'Oh, well, take that line if you must. How'd you like prison?'

'I'm taking up your time.'

'Slack hour. The prison?'

So Denton gave him a sketch of life as a political prisoner in a country that was still squirming out of the mire of the Middle Ages. Munro filled out paperwork and grunted. When Denton was done, Munro said, 'Been in prison before?'

'I was a guard once.'

'Dear heaven. Almost as bad.' He pushed his papers aside and laid both forearms on the desk. 'Ever think about joining the police again? I could use a partner with some brains.'

Denton smiled. He liked Munro. 'I write books,' he said.

'A waste and a shame.'

'Get Guillam.'

Munro made a face. George Guillam was a Detective Sergeant who had accepted a false confession in the crime that had led to Denton's shooting the real criminal; Guillam and Denton had started off on the wrong foot and got worse. Munro said, 'Georgie's in a bit of a funk just now. Not saying much to me.'

'The business last spring?'

'Aye, that and me getting some credit. And there's you.'

'I didn't strike on his box.'

'You might say you weren't his favourite fella.'

'He still want to be a superintendent?'

'In a funny kind of way, he is—acting like a super, anyway, but without the title. They kicked him sideways after the business with you. He's "on leave" from CID and acting as super of a division of odds and sods—Domestic, Missing Persons, Juvenile, a lot of stuff. Georgie has pals upstairs, but he put his foot in the dog's mess with that false confession he accepted. There's some talk it was got with some physical persuasion, too. Georgie did what was right for him, not for the law, and he's going to be in bad odour for a while. Serves him right, although I don't say that to his face.'

'Maybe I should have a word with him.'

'Maybe you should and maybe you shouldn't. Georgie don't forgive easily.' Munro dropped his voice to an almost inaudible rumble and leaned closer. 'Georgie piles up grudges like bricks. Says all's forgiven and then can't resist the knife when you turn your back.' He raised his voice to its normal boom. 'Mind what I say.' He put a finger next to his nose, an antiquated and strange gesture that made him seem like an actor playing Father Christmas. 'Now I've got work to do.'

Denton found his way back to the lobby and was about to leave the building when he realized that postponing a meeting with Guillam was stupid; Denton didn't mind being disliked, didn't mind even being hated if the hater was of the right contemptible kind, but he had once wanted Guillam's respect and he didn't see that things had much changed. If Guillam had a bean up his nose, better to face him than skulk away.

The porter led him to where Guillam could be found. Denton climbed the stairs again, went up a second flight this time, followed the man into more barren corridors and stopped by a door that the porter held open. Inside were four men, each at a desk, electric lights burning overhead, a smell like burnt toast mingling with the tobacco and wet wool. All four looked up. Three swept their eyes over him and went back to their work. The fourth stared at him, frowned, got up as if he were in pain and came around the desk.

'I thought we'd let bygones be bygones,' Denton said. 'I was in the building.' He put out his hand.

'What bygones are those?' Guillam ignored the hand.

'We had some differences a while back.'

'News to me.'

'I thought there might be some—feeling—over—you know.'

'Can't say I do. No idea what you're getting at. I got work to do.'

And he turned his back and headed for his desk.

Denton tried to find his way out, got lost, felt the sting of Guillam's rejection turn to rage. Where was the buoyant mood of the morning? He wanted to kick something. Somebody. A young constable finally had to lead him down to the lobby. Denton steamed through it and aimed himself at the door.

A bench stood next to the porter's lodge. Several sorry specimens were sitting on the bench. Denton merely glanced at them, details in the landscape to be forgotten, until one detail caught his eye: a raised newspaper, folded almost to the size of a book, the newspaper lowered to show a pair of eyes. And then a hairless face, no red moustache, although his upper lip had a gleam that could have been gum arabic. The newspaper was raised again. On the bench, upside down, a black bowler.

'The moustache could be false! But who'd be stupid enough to put on a red moustache if he was going to follow somebody, unless he wanted to call attention to himself?'

'You've lost me.' Atkins put on his deliberately stupid look.

'Wear the thing, you're the most memorable man on the street!'

'Yes, but take it off, the most memorable thing about you is gone, you're nobody!'

Denton had started in on it as soon as he had come through his front door. 'He could have been following me all day. Probably was!'

'Master of disguise, you mean? Popping in and out of beards and Inverness capes? Bit *Strand Magazine,* isn't it?'

'You're the one who said he was a rum one!'

'So he was. But like you pointed out, General, black bowlers is tuppence a hundred.'

'Well, red moustaches aren't. And at New Scotland Yard! Hell's bells, that's brazen.'

He had shouted his way up the stairs and into the sitting room, had shucked himself out of his overcoat and tossed it at Atkins, thrown his hat at a table and flung himself into his armchair before Atkins managed to say, 'You got a telegram. Telegram from *her,* eh? On the sideboard.'

'Why the hell didn't you say so?'

Atkins muttered something that sounded like 'Just listen to yourself' and wandered away with the coat. Denton tore the telegram apart and read:

TOMORROW 5 PM ABC BARBICAN STOP
JANET STRIKER

His heart jumped, even though the message was as impersonal as a military order. He tried to remember his own message to her. Had it been as heartless? Had he started them off wrong? He threw himself down again. He remembered her choice once before of an ABC—a shop of the Aerated Bread Company, cheap and faceless. Five tomorrow—twenty-four hours more, good God.

Returning, Atkins said, 'You've a parcel, too.' He was standing now behind Denton's chair; next to him, Rupert was cleaning his private parts. Atkins handed Denton a battered package. 'From the garden of Central Europe.' He had been holding it with both hands; Denton took it, found why: it was heavy. Atkins wasn't leaving, his posture said; he wanted to see what was in the package. To make sure that he did, he held out his pocket-knife, already open.

The package was tied with heavy string that had been stuck down with sealing wax in six places; the paper, brown, cheap, had been so battered in its travels that it looked like lizard skin, but the string had held everything together. The stamps were triangular, green and purple, now peeling. Denton cut the string, then enlarged a tear in the front of the package to reveal something like a tea box, which the knife made quick work of—the small nails in the lid could be prised up—and Denton dumped the contents into his chair: a tied packet of envelopes with British stamps, the name Striker in the upper left corners (his heart lurched); two objects wrapped in the same brown paper and tied with the same string, one long, one short, both heavy; and, in a separate envelope, a photograph and a sheet of embossed notepaper. 'From Colonel Cieljescu,' he said.

'The Transylvanian Napoleon.'

'Now, now—' Colonel Cieljescu had subjected Denton to long, almost nightly monologues about 'culture', most of which Denton hadn't understood because he didn't know Central European history, but the gist of it had been that English was a barbaric language and America was a desert. 'I think it was the Colonel who got us sprung from that hole.'

'Katya said it was God's will.'

'Yes, but the Colonel had the keys. Somebody left the doors open, and if you tell me it was an angel, I'll fire you.' He pocketed the letters from Janet Striker, then tore open the two heavy wrappings: one was his Navy Colt, the other his derringer.

'Must be he don't fancy antiques,' Atkins said.

Denton pulled out the note. Under an embossed double eagle and the name of the prison where they had almost starved was the date in blue ink—three weeks before, a month after their 'escape'—and a message:

> *My dear American friend Denton,*
>
> *Now you read this I am believing you are in your own bed. I am desolated to not have you my guest any more for our long chats anent art. For remembrance, herewith is new photo of me for you. Also I am forced by duty to keep your writings which you say is fiction but may be espionage, one day you must read Alfons Duchinatz a real author. Plus some letters I am sending you were overlooked in giving to you during your stay with us. Your vehicle I have with gratest regret empounded for military contrabandage. Hoping you are found good in health, Your esteemed friend, Cieljescu, Anton-Pauli, Colonel, Imperial Corps of Mounted Infantry and Guards, by the Grace of His Imperial Highness, Franz Joseph, Archduke of Austria and Hungary...*

Denton picked up the photograph. A large man in uniform, recognizably the Colonel, was sitting in the passenger seat of a motor car, recognizably Denton's Daimler 8. The man was smiling. Beside him, a driver, less clear, sat with both hands grasping the wheel as if to keep it from flying away.

Denton burst into laughter. 'It's our motor car! He sent back my guns and he kept the car!'

Atkins looked over his shoulder. He groaned. 'That's Katya beside him. That's *Katya*!'

'God works in mysterious ways.'

Atkins snatched his knife from Denton's hand and turned for the stairs. 'I'm sure there's an explanation. She was to me an angel!' He strode away, and Denton heard him mutter as he closed the door, 'The bitch—'

Denton found himself filled again with something that felt good—contentment, perhaps, even happiness. At once, with the two pistols in his lap, he read Mrs Striker's letters. Written weeks before, they were about trivia—her job with the Society for the Improvement of Wayward Women, her alcoholic mother, the weather, her piano—but they delighted him. More than that, the *fact* of them delighted him. The last letter was dated well after they had left the prison, so she had gone on writing even when he hadn't. Never intimately, never warmly, always signing herself 'your friend', but *she had written.*

He loaded the derringer—.41 black-powder Remington, wildly inaccurate but horrific at a foot or two—and put it in its old place in the box on the mantel, then took the Colt up to the attic and laid it in its case. Somebody in Transylvania had screwed the balls out and dumped the gunpowder and cleaned it. Closing the lid on it now, he thought, was like closing a coffin— the pistol, which he had picked up on a Civil War battlefield and carried through his early years in the West, which he had used to kill the man who had been threatening to slash Janet Striker's throat only six months before—the pistol had earned a rest. Obsolete, big, it had become a relic. He loved the Colt, but senti-ment has its limits.

Downstairs again, he clapped his hands together and walked up and down his bedroom. It was all right. Everything would be all right. Her message had seemed curt because that was the nature of telegrams. The ABC could be quickly got over. Or out of. He was back, he was free, he was going to see her. What were twenty-four hours after all these weeks?

He put the photograph and Cieljescu's letter in an envelope to go to his publisher, Gweneth; if that didn't settle the matter of the motor car, the hell with him.

CHAPTER

3

On the second morning back, Atkins said as he presented his coffee, 'Garden's a jungle.'

'What, out back?'

'Yes, that one. I thought I'd hang your suits out there. What a hope! Need a map to find the garden wall.'

'Start weeding.'

'My hat.' Atkins was many things but not a gardener. He poured Denton's coffee and said, 'Find us somebody with a strong back and a deal of patience.'

'Aren't there gardening agencies?'

'There's everything; this is London. You want an egg? I had one. Quite good. Or a kipper.'

'Why do you buy kippers? You know I don't like them.'

'I do.'

'Poached, on toast, bacon.'

'If you care, the parlourmaid next door but one says the madam there complains that the seeds from our weeds are spoiling her garden.'

'I'll get somebody—dear God, we just got back!'

'Middle-class respectability. Weeds not respectable. Preserve with your toast?'

'Is that the same as jam? Yes, jam.'

Atkins padded off downstairs—he affected Prince Albert slippers in the house—with Rupert puffing behind him. Until his breakfast came, Denton worked on the novel, a writing tablet in his lap, the words coming faster than he could move the pen. It would be all right now: the book was still in his head, perhaps with a vividness it had lacked when first created, needing only to be set down. He hurried because he didn't want to forget it, yes, but he hurried also because money, finally, was the issue, not art: without the novel, he would come on hard times in eight or ten months. With it, he could look ahead a year and a half, time to write something else.

Atkins brought the first mail of the day at ten—bills (how could there be bills when he hadn't been there?), four dinner invitations he'd refuse—then lunch at twelve from the public house next door, the Lamb. At two, he was back with more mail, this time including an answer from Aubrey Heseltine: *Would Mr Denton care to drop by Albany 134-B tomorrow between two and five?* Mr Denton supposed he would.

At four, he stopped. He had written thirty-seven pages. If it hadn't been Janet Striker he was stopping for, he'd have gone on. And on, although he knew it was better to stop, better to leave some water in the bucket for tomorrow.

He accepted Atkins's advice about clothes. Atkins of course knew without his saying so that he was going to meet Mrs Striker; Atkins wasn't above doing archaeology in his wastebasket. A dark frock coat, grey waistcoat, subdued necktie. He rejected lavender although told the colour was 'immensely fashionable'. A soft hat, but with a narrower brim than he really liked.

'This ain't the Wild West, General.'

He walked again to Lloyd Baker Street and dropped off the day's work. As he had the day before, he behaved like a guilty man (what was it about the typewriter—she was a mouse), stopping to pretend to look at houses, trees, birds, then covertly looking back down the way he had come. Had he seen anybody? He couldn't be sure. Nobody he saw twice, certainly—nobody he could run after. He told himself he was still disoriented from the trip and fled from the typewriter's, first down Goswell Road, then Aldersgate, finally to the ABC on Barbican—fifteen minutes early, even though it was no good being early; she would be on time. He didn't fancy sitting in the tea shop alone. He walked, thinking about the novel, about her, about Mary Thomason, who had sent him a letter and might be dead or married or living at home by now. Nobody following; he'd checked again and again. When he finally got to the ABC a second time, he was ten minutes late.

She was, of course, there. She was sitting at a far table, wearing as always an unattractive black hat, a dress that even he knew was years out of fashion—something about the widely puffed sleeves. She turned her head and saw him and he felt a pang of sadness for her: the knife slash down her face was now a red ribbon that seemed to have escaped from her hat. It was nothing she could or did try to hide; seeing him, she even seemed to turn the left side of her face more towards him as if to display it.

'I'm late. I'm sorry I'm late. I didn't want to be early.'

'I was early.'

'I came by before—maybe you were already here.' It was a ridiculous conversation. He had known they wouldn't pick up where they had left off six months before—that grudging and hard-won, only partial intimacy—but this was worse, almost like a first time. He sat, then got himself tea at her urging, some kind of supposedly edible bun, put it down on the table, where it sat, uneaten, for as long as they were there. He thanked her for her letters, explained about the package that had come the day before.

She hardly spoke. It became terrible—long silences, questions that got one-syllable answers. The trivial and the obvious. He said, 'And your mother?'

Her mother had in effect sold her when she was seventeen; the husband was older, brutal, had put her in a mental institution when she had rebelled. She smiled with one side of her face—the unscarred side. 'My mother is being seen to.' She looked up from the teacup she was using to make overlapping rings on the tablecloth. 'She is senile, and, as you know, a drunkard. I stood it as long as I could. She's in a house with three other old women and a matron of sorts who cares for them.' She put the cup down in its saucer. 'She's dying.'

'I'm sorry.'

'Oh, don't say things like that, Denton! I can't be sorry; why should you? I'm sorry *for* her, but not *sorry*.'

He told her about Mary Thomason. She seemed uninterested. Her life was spent counselling prostitutes in how to get off the street, find work; she hadn't much use, he supposed, for nice young women. She had been a prostitute herself, 'never a very good one'. He tried to think of funny stories from his months away, but they fell flat. Out of nowhere, she said, 'I'm going to be fairly well off.'

'Money?'

'The suit's being settled.'

He remembered. She'd sued an Oxford college for her share of her husband's estate after he'd changed his will and shot himself. The case had been going on for fourteen years. She said, 'They tried to wear me out, but I got too expensive. I'm to get half the estate plus the pension that should have been my mother's payment for turning me over to him.'

'You can stop working.'

'Can I? And do what? Become one of the women I despise? Go to live in Florence?' She stared into the teacup, rubbed the rings she'd made with her finger. She said, 'I'm sorry, Denton. I'm being unpleasant.' She looked up. 'You thought it would be different, didn't you?'

'I thought—' She made him angry when she was like this. 'Yes, I thought it would be different.'

'So did I. I thought we would—' She got up. 'Let's walk.'

It was still light outside, full daylight but of a colour that seemed ominous, a yellow-green; the air was sultry, wrong for late September. He wondered what he had done to spoil things; it couldn't all be her doing. 'I'm sorry,' he said.

She put her hand in his arm.

They turned into Aldersgate and walked towards St Paul's, then diverted towards the tangle of Little Britain. He suggested dinner but she said she couldn't. She never gave explanations. 'Couldn't' might simply mean that she wouldn't. He had thought that he might be able to whisk her off to the Café Royal, a place he liked and in which he felt comfortable, but of course she wouldn't. Perhaps it was the scar, which ran from cheekbone to chin, that was behind that 'couldn't'.

As if tuned to his thought, she said, 'You saw the scar.'

'Of course.'

'The doctors wanted to operate again and hide it somehow. I don't think they really knew what they'd do.'

'Now you'll have the money.'

'That isn't the point.'

'No, of course. But don't you—'

'The women are afraid of it. It's got hard for me to talk to some of them. They see it and they think, "That's what could happen to me, some man," and they don't want to be reminded of that part of their lives, and they stay away from me. If I were going to stay, I'd tell the doctors to have a go, but I'm not. I don't give a damn what other people think.'

'Least of all men.'

She hesitated. 'Most men.'

'Me?'

'You're always the exception. That's why I—' She teetered on the edge of saying it, and he stopped so that she'd stop, too, but she pulled her hand away from his arm and he saw that he'd lost the moment.

'Janet—'

'Don't—please—'

'Janet, I want—'

'Don't tell me what you want!' She backed away. A man going by had to veer around her, looked at them angrily. She paid no attention. 'You're moving too fast.'

'For God's sake, Janet, I've been away six months! Things didn't just stand still for me; I—'

'Don't tell me!' She looked her worst then—red-faced, gaunt, absurdly dressed. She had told him once that she'd been a pretty girl, the reason her mother had 'got a good price' for her, but nearly five years in a prison for the criminally insane had worked on her like a holystone. Now, in her late thirties, she could never be thought 'pretty', seldom even handsome. But her face was passionate and intelligent, contorted now with her fear of him. 'Don't draw me in!'

'Janet, I want to be with you.'

She made an impatient gesture with her right hand, as if she were pushing away a child or an animal. 'Oh, I wish I'd never met you!'

'You don't mean that!'

Two people coming towards them separated and went around, both pretending not to see them. She waited for them to go on and said, sagging, 'No, I don't mean that. But I wish I did!' She started off in the direction they had come. 'Don't follow me! I mean it. Give me a day—two days—'

'I don't even know where you live.'

He had followed her a few steps despite what she'd said; they had both stopped again. She waited, looking down at St Paul's as if expecting the dome to tell her what to say. 'I'll write to you.'

'If you write, it'll be too easy to say you don't want to see me. I want us to meet.'

'Yes. Yes, that was cowardly of me.' She held up a hand as if to push him off. 'I'll write to you where and when.'

And she strode away.

He looked after her. He was enraged and saddened, the two feelings wound together. She was ugly, he told himself; she was cold; what sort of hold could such a woman have over him? But it was no good. The hold was real.

He turned his head back towards St Paul's in time to see a figure change its course and disappear into what seemed a solid wall. The movement had been furtive, he thought; Atkins's 'rum type' came to him. The change of direction, the movement could have been those of somebody following him, thinking himself seen and dodging into a doorway.

It was what his anger needed. Feeding on it, he charged down Little Britain Street and found a gap where the figure had disappeared. He came into a wider lane, blue-grey sky darkening overhead. He saw openings to his left and ahead, chose the second, plunged on, his long legs like scissors cutting up the distance.

Ahead was a cul-de-sac; another opening, barely an alleyway, opened to his right. He turned into it and found his way blocked fifty feet on by a wooden gate higher than his head. It was another small courtyard, grimy windows looking down on him, a single doorway up two feet off the pavement with no steps to it, above it a gallows-like beam meant to hold a block and tackle. The place felt unused and dusty, as if he'd opened a door on it that had been locked for decades. Not even a pigeon.

Chasing spooks.

He decided to take his ghosts to some place that served alcohol.

CHAPTER 4

He woke from troubling dreams to taste the once-familiar sourness of hangover. A voice was calling. The bed shook and he realized it was he who was shaking or being shaken. He opened his eyes.

'Profuse apologies, General, but you like to be up by half-seven.'

'What time is it?'

'Pushing eight. I brought tea and a headache powder.'

'I was out late.'

'Hardly news.'

Denton heard the tray clatter on the desktop. His breath was foul; his head ached, but not at that level that suggested real calamity. He sat up—the room didn't swim.

What had he done? In fact, he remembered it quite well. The Criterion, the Princess Louise, the Lamb. He reviewed the evening: no gaps, no horrors, a certain amount of sordid boozing.

'There was one thing,' he said aloud.

'Only one?' Atkins handed him the cup of tea.

'Don't be cute when I'm like this; my temper's short. Yes, only one. When I got home, I could see a light in the house beyond the back garden. Where you saw the red moustache before.'

'Certain fact?'

'Not the drink nor the lateness, no. It was a quarter of one—I remember looking at my watch.'

'House's supposed to be empty. Somebody looking this place over for an entry, could be.' Atkins had been given a bad knock on the head by somebody who had broken in the year before. 'I think I'd like the derringer until this is settled, if you don't mind.'

'Mmm.' He did mind, but he understood. 'Time I bought myself another pistol, I think.'

Later, Atkins presented a raw egg with Worcester and lemon, which he dutifully drank down despite feeling better by then. The headache remained—to have lost it entirely so early would have been to miss the point of the lesson—and a slight imbalance if he moved too fast, but he could work and think. And worry about Mrs Striker, who might well send him a note saying she never wanted to see him again.

In the middle of the morning, he broke from his work to go up to the attic, where he pushed the hundred-pound weight off his chest fifty times and rowed on the contraption for fifteen minutes before shooting twenty shots with the Flobert pistols. When he was done, he unlocked the skylight and put his head out. He meant to look down at the rear of the house behind his own. Regrettably, the roof was in the way.

He had a panic fear of heights that was not quite great enough to keep him from going out. Last year, somebody had got into his house this way; now, going out, he saw how reckless the man had been. The centre of the roof was flat, but around it were cascades of slate down to the eaves, interrupted only by four multi-flued chimneys. He all but crawled to the edge of the flat part, then held a chimney as a child holds its mother and looked down. To his relief, he could see what he wanted: the house behind had a cellar entrance that was reached by a door seemingly flat on the ground, actually angled down from the foundation wall. There was also a rear entrance at ground level, probably giving directly on the kitchen and pantry.

Not a problem getting in for anybody with some tools. He meant himself as well as the man Atkins had seen; he was thinking of breaking into the house and looking for signs that somebody had in fact been there. A moment's thought showed him what a bad idea he had had. If he found anything, he would then have to tell the police; they would have him for breaking and entering—enough to test even Munro's indulgence of him.

He crawled back to the skylight, slipped in and locked it, his heart pounding.

The morning's letters were on his desk when he reached it: two more invitations he would refuse, another letter from a publisher promising better terms than he was getting from his current firm, one from somebody who offered 'to increase his income substantially by representing his works to publishers in a competitive fashion, for a small percentage'. That was new, he thought—every writer he knew made his own arrangements. Or took what was on offer; few were in any position to bargain.

And another letter from the man (or woman?) calling himself-herself 'Albert Cosgrove':

Carissimo maestro

What a delight and comfort to know you are back with us again! I exult to see you in good health! How I long to sit in your drawing room with you and 'chew the fat' as they say in your country like two old friends sharing the communion of literature and mutual creativeness. I think of our conversations on all topics of interest to men of letters. The city hums again with your presence! Even

*though I am not fit to clean the pens with which you
create in so masterly a fashion, I entreat I beg you to send
me your books suitably inscribed.*
I am yours for ever.
Albert Cosgrove

No return address.

'Mad as a hatter,' Denton said.

When Atkins came upstairs again, Denton showed him the
letter. Atkins said, 'Raving lunatic.'

'Man or woman?'

'Man, of course. Not a woman's hand.'

'Some of it sounds a little, mmm, romantic. Excessive.'

'That's the lunatic part. Along with the conversations,
which it sounds like he thinks he's already had.' Atkins looked at
the letter again. 'The bit about seeing you in good health—that
sounds like he's been looking at you.'

'You mean you think he's your man with the red moustache?'

'I don't like him, Colonel.'

He wrote until two; by then he had set down forty-one new
pages as if he had been taking dictation. He was reluctant to stop,
but he was at the point again where to do more was to put tomorrow's work at risk. Better to use the time to accept Mr Heseltine's
invitation to the Albany.

He wore one of his American hats, decidedly too wide in the
brim for London, the choice deliberate to counter the snobbery
he thought he was going to find in Aubrey Heseltine. So were
the boots—old, polished but deeply wrinkled, brown rather than
black, what he supposed Henry James would call 'louche'. Going
out, he opened the box to take the derringer without thinking, but
the box was empty, and he remembered that Atkins had wanted it.

Atkins stopped him at the front door. 'Going to rain.' He
held out an umbrella.

'I'm not English.'

Atkins draped a mackintosh over his left arm. 'The rain
will be.'

The Bohemian Girl

He walked quickly to Russell Square (he'd take today's writing to the typewriter with tomorrow's), strode along beside the Museum, ducked into Greek Street and down to Old Compton Street, then zigzagged into Brewer Street and so behind the Café Royal at the Glasshouse Street end, giving a regretful glance at the café, where he wanted to be sitting with Janet Striker, drinking the milky coffee. He dodged across Regent Street to Piccadilly, a cacophony of horse-drawn buses and cabs and a surprising number of motor cars (many more, he thought, than a year ago—the world was speeding up), and strolled to the entrance to Albany Court. Only men lived in that odd collection of buildings called the Albany. Denton, as an American, thought that he would never understand such places, where men sequestered themselves in gated and guarded byways that had for him a feel of monastic sterility. 'Here,' these places said, 'lives masculine Privilege; avert your eyes and pass on.' Maybe it was a residue of their (irrationally named) public schools. Boys together, and so on. Perpetual boys?

'Heseltine,' he barked at the attendant. 'I'm expected.'

'Name, sir?' The man looked old enough to be Denton's father, frail enough to be on sticks; he moved with a maddening slowness. If he was the guardian, the Albany could have been easily breached—except that this was Piccadilly, and the real guardian was respectability, and habit, and the horror of 'scenes'.

He was passed in and directed, and he strolled down the court, feeling its sense of comfort and pleasant isolation, disliking it for the same reason that he disliked having a servant. He was a democrat.

To his surprise, then, Aubrey Heseltine opened his own door. There was no mistaking him for a servant—wrong clothes, wrong manner. Aubrey Heseltine was younger than Denton had expected, shyer than he had expected, pretentious—if he was—out of unsureness. He was a type: almost emaciated, not much chin, prominent cheekbones with cheeks like planed surfaces, high colour, tall. Handsome in his way. 'Neurasthenic', to use a fashionable word.

'Oh, do come in,' he said as soon as he understood who Denton was. Denton's wide hat and old boots seemed to have no effect on him. He moved about, muttering and making quick, incomplete gestures, said his man was out, apologized, said the place wasn't his, only borrowed, stammered, blushed, then stood in the middle of the room and looked stricken.

Denton found himself pitying him. Something was very wrong with him. *Damaged,* Denton thought, not knowing why he thought so. He looked away to relieve the younger man's embarrassment. The room was almost shabby, much lived in, Georgian without being distinguished: a fireplace with a simple mantel, two deeply set windows in one wall, what had once been called 'Turkey' carpets on the floor, a great many books that filled three walls, and a single framed picture between the windows.

'Is this "the little Wesselons"?' When Heseltine looked puzzled, Denton said, 'That's what you called it in your note.' It didn't take much to puzzle Heseltine, he thought; the young man was either injured somehow in the mind or terribly distracted.

'Did I? How affected that must have seemed to you. Oh, I am sorry. It's what the chap, Mr Geddys, in the shop called it—"a little Wesselons".'

'Well—it *is* little.' Denton went to it. Inside a tarnished gold frame almost three inches wide was an oil no bigger than his hand. 'Is it a Wesselons?'

'Oh, yes, yes—he assured me. There's a signature. Of sorts. There in the corner. And the name on the brass plate—Andreas Wesselons, 1623 to 1652. It's a sketch, really, an oil sketch. Of a lion. In a menagerie.'

'Dutch?'

'Yes—all that brown. Somebody important at the time had a menagerie. Wesselons made these sketches—the animals— quite a famous painting, one of them—of the lion, actually. This is a sketch for it.'

The brushwork looked as if it had been quickly laid on, the tracks clear in the thick paint, yet the animal was almost alive. Enormous vigour. Denton said, 'And the envelope you sent to me was in the back.'

'Yes, yes—behind.'

'Could you show me exactly where?'

'Oh, yes, yes—' Heseltine snatched the painting from the wall and turned it over. Denton thought his hands were shaking. The twisted wire by which it hung was almost black with corrosion. 'In this corner,' Heseltine said. He pointed at the lower left. 'Tucked in between the canvas and the stretcher. There's room, you see.' He sounded hurt, as if Denton had suggested that the envelope couldn't possibly have been there; in fact, Denton could see that the small envelope could have easily been tucked way down where most of it would have been masked by the wide frame.

'Odd that somebody in the shop didn't find it.'

'I thought that, too! Yes, oh, yes. But they didn't. If they had—well, it wouldn't have been there, would it?' He stood there, staring at Denton with his hurt eyes, the painting in both hands, and he said as if it had just occurred to him, 'Won't you sit down?'

Denton picked an overstuffed chair with a worn red cover. He put his hat on the floor next to him. Heseltine, after replacing the painting, sat on the edge of a straight chair. He said, 'Should I not have sent the envelope to you?'

'No, of course you should.'

'It was addressed to you.'

'Of course. But you didn't open it.'

'No!' It was like a groan of pain. 'No, I swear I didn't!'

'I didn't mean to suggest you had. I just wondered if you knew what was in it.'

'No!'

Denton was afraid the young man was going to weep. He became gentle. 'Could I ask you a question?'

'Yes. Of course. Should you like tea? Coffee?' Heseltine looked around vaguely. 'My man is out.'

'The date on your note to me was some weeks ago. How long had you had the painting then?'

'Oh—oh, let me see—I got to London in August. The twelfth.' He gave a sudden, unexplained laugh. 'The Glorious Twelfth. Do you shoot? I used to. Now I can't—The noise upsets me.'

It came to Denton slowly: the twelfth of August was the opening of grouse season, a very big event in the lives of sporting people. He waited for the young man to go on; when he didn't, he murmured, 'So you got to London on August twelfth.'

'Yes.'

'And bought the painting? I mean, how long after did you buy the painting?'

'Oh—The date would be on the receipt. If I still have it. They could tell you at the shop. In the arcade. It was—oh, a while ago.'

'It's now the twenty-sixth of September. You sent me your note and the envelope on August twenty-ninth.'

'Oh.'

'So, it must have been pretty soon after you bought it.'

'Yes, it was while I was hanging it. My man was hanging it, I mean. He, mmm, brought it to my attention. I put it in an envelope and wrote that silly note the same day. "Little Wesselons"!' He laughed a bit hysterically. 'Ass.'

Denton waited several seconds for him to get calm. 'The letter inside the envelope was dated more than two months ago.'

'What did it say?'

'It must have sat in the back of the painting—or somewhere—for several weeks before you found it.'

'I was in the war.'

That meant South Africa—fighting the Boers, a war that had gone on far too long and had reached a vicious stage where the British army was building concentration camps. It probably explained Aubrey Heseltine. Denton had seen young men like this after the Civil War, young men who were never the same, young men whose lives had been taken over by war. 'Are you on leave?' he said.

'No, I've been—I'm invalided home. You reach a point—
Then it's no good going on. You're no good. They don't trust you
any more.'

'I was in the American Civil War.'

'Then you understand.'

'A little, maybe.'

'You've seen it, then. You've seen them.' His face twitched.
'Boys. Men with families. My sergeant said we'd get them out. He
told them that. Then he was dead.' The right side of his mouth
pulled down in a tic. 'They shelled us. Our own guns. The line
was cut. I sent a runner back—A boy, one of mine, he was eighteen, then he was just a tunic, you know, and one leg. A nice boy.
Lancashire. I pulled them back. Against orders. I admitted it at
the investigation. Why should they die like that from their own
guns? That isn't right, is it, Mr—Denton? Is it?'

Denton shook his head.

'I'm on medical leave.' The side of Heseltine's face pulled down
again. 'But they're going to court-martial me. For pulling back.'

The soldier in Denton wanted to judge him harshly; on the
other hand, his older self said, nothing was proven yet. 'Is it bad?'

Heseltine gave him the half-smile again. 'They'll cashier me.'

'You have dreams about the war?'

'Yes.'

'You remember all their names.'

'Yes, yes—'

'You don't want to go out.'

'No.' He hardly voiced the syllable.

'I shouldn't have bothered you.'

'I'm glad you came.' Heseltine put his face in his hands, then
sat up very straight. 'I'm afraid you must think me weak.'

Denton stood. 'Thank you for your help.'

'I thought there might be—something—'

Something what, Denton wondered. Something more?
Something for me? Something to be done? He said, 'The envelope had a note asking for my help.'

'I'm so glad I sent it on, then.'

'Was there a woman at the shop where you bought the painting?'

'Only the man in the front, but I think in the back—where they framed and so on—I think there was someone else. But I—didn't—'

'I wanted to see if the sender of the note was all right.'

'Yes, oh, you must! Yes, it's so important to help people when they ask you for—protection—help—' The side of his face pulled down. 'Will you keep me informed?'

'It's been so long, I'm not sure it's worth pursuing.'

'But you must! Yes—please. I'd like to feel I had a part.'

So Denton took the name of the shop in Burlington Arcade where he'd bought the painting and promised that he'd report back, and each of them said again how important it was to follow things through and to help when help was asked for. As Denton was leaving, he said, 'Why did you buy that particular painting?'

'The Wesselons? Because—it was a bargain, he said; somebody else had put down money on it and then not taken it—and—It was the idea of the menagerie, the animal so far away from his own kind—' He was looking at a bookcase, not at Denton, frowning in concentration. 'He must have been a wretchedly unhappy animal, but he looks so stalwart! As if he'd come through. Do you know what I mean?'

Outside, the day was close. A dull sky suggested rain. The air smelled of horse dung and urine. The city's clatter and hum filled Albany Court.

The old man let Denton out to Piccadilly. He made his way to Burlington Arcade and strolled through, looking at the shops and seeing nothing, wondering how many horrors and sufferings there were just then in London, and how an attempt to resolve one simply led to another.

He hadn't intended to push things any farther that day. Or any day—he had enough without a possibly missing woman. He felt sluggish since he had seen Heseltine, drained of the hangover-derived energy that had driven him when walking. But, because it was raining and he was standing outside a shop that said in dull gold letters on black, 'D. J. Geddys Objects of Virtue', he went in.

The public part of the shop seemed small, over-filled with things that even Denton sensed were good—Oriental vases, Wedgwood, Georgian silver, several shawls, many enamelled and decorated surfaces, antique lace, mahogany end tables and tapestry fire screens; on the walls, oil paintings large and small, either safely pre-Victorian or intensely Royal Academy. Denton's experience of art had been only with big Scottish paintings of sheep and hairy cattle—he had bought by the yard, not the artistry—and had left him indifferent to all of them.

'May I help you, sir?'

The man had materialized from a dark corner. He was small, so hunched that he was barely five feet, his neck dropped forward and down so that his face had to be turned to the side and up to speak. He had very thick glasses, a beard cut short, the upper lip shaved. He might have been sixty, suggested some near-human, faintly sinister creature, gnome or troll, with a nasty sense of humour kept bottled in, perhaps to come out as practical jokes. His voice was hoarse and very deep, coming out of his pigeon chest in a bass rumble.

Denton debated pretending to be a customer. What might he have been looking for? He knew nothing about 'objects of virtue'. Not a field in which he could pretend.

'Mr Geddys?'

'The same.'

'I'm trying to locate a woman named Mary Thomason.'

The name had a strange effect on Geddys, as if he'd been bumped. He rolled his head as if to get a better look at Denton, but the movement might have been a cover for something else. There *was* something wrong with his neck, Denton thought, almost as if he had been hanged. Unlikely, however. There was also something wrong with his expression—a false disinterest, perhaps. Geddys said, 'Yes?'

'I believe that perhaps she worked here.'

Geddys looked away from him. 'I can hardly be expected to talk to a stranger about employees.' He glanced over his shoulder at Denton. '*If* she worked here.'

Denton produced a card. 'Did she?'

'I don't understand your interest.'

'I want to know if she's missing.' He was irritated; he said deliberately, 'I've already been to the police.'

Geddys looked at the card. He flicked it with a finger. 'This is simply a name. You could be anybody. Are you a relative?'

'Mary Thomason wrote me a letter, asking for my help. She missed an appointment with me.' That wasn't quite true, but he found himself wanting to squelch Geddys. 'Is she missing?'

Geddys put the card down on a table. 'She left us.'

'But she did work here.'

'For a while.'

'What did she do?'

Geddys got cautious again, argued privacy, said that Denton could be anybody, his real feeling perhaps exasperation that Denton wasn't a customer. Then they got as far as Geddys's saying that Mary Thomason was young and naive and had framed prints and drawings for him when they were interrupted by a genuine customer, a lavishly got-up woman dripping ecru lace as if it were a skin she were shedding. Denton had to retire to a safe zone between two virtuous objects while they murmured about a 'sweet bit of pavé' in a case. But she didn't buy, and she swept out with a vague promise to look in again, and Geddys smiled his ironic smile, twisting his head at Denton.

Then Denton had to go through it all—the little Wesselons, the note, his absence—leaving out only the things he didn't see any point in telling. And Geddys admitted he had been annoyed that Mary Thomason had left him without notice, only a note instead of coming in one day in August pleading 'a family crisis at home'. He was almost too voluble now, too helpful.

'Where was "home"?'

'I've no idea. She seemed more or less genteel.'

'You didn't know where she lived in London?'

'Ask at the Slade.'

'What's the Slade?'

Geddys stared at him. 'The Slade School of Art.'

'She was an art student?'

'So she said.'

He persuaded Geddys to find the precise date when Mary Thomason had gone away. Geddys had in fact kept her note. It was dated the same day as the letter to Denton that she or somebody had tucked into the back of Heseltine's painting.

'I don't understand about the painting,' Denton said.

'Neither do I. Most irregular. If I'd known, I'd have stopped it.'

'But why would she do it?'

Geddys sighed. 'People, especially young people, do things beyond the comprehension of the mind of man. I hardly knew the young lady.' He didn't look Denton in the eye when he said that.

Other questions got only repetition, as of a well-rehearsed story, and the information that Mary Thomason had been clean, prompt, shy and inarticulate. No, she seemed to have no young men, no 'followers'. No, he had no idea where she had lived, and would Mr Denton forgive him, but he had a business to manage.

Mr Denton didn't forgive him, because Mr Denton didn't entirely believe him, but Mr Denton left. Outside the arcade, it was still raining.

He took a cab to Victoria Street, was surprised to have the doorman at the Army and Navy Stores recognize him, the more so because he was only an associate member, and that because Atkins—an actual veteran of the British army—had got him in. He went directly to the gun department and bought a Colt New Pocket revolver in .32 nitro. It didn't have the feel of the old Colt, but he knew it was quicker and more powerful, far faster to reload. It was smaller and with a shorter barrel, but it weighted his overcoat pocket like a bag of coins.

Munro had the reports for him from the divisions. They had nothing about a Mary Thomason. He complained that Denton should be getting all this from Guillam's Missing Persons office, not from him.

'I get along better with you,' Denton said.

'Hmp.' Munro gave him a rather dead stare. 'Coroner's office has three unidentified corpses for the day the "missing" woman wrote you the note, seven for the week following, five for the week before. Five female, ten male. Autopsies performed on two—suspicious causes—and the lot buried after the statutory period because you can't keep dead bodies indefinitely.'

'Foul play on any of the women?'

Munro shrugged. 'Two of them taken out of the river, ditto five of the men, all but one been in too long to know much. Nothing caught the eye.'

'What does that mean?'

'Didn't strike anybody as justifying investigation.' Munro folded his hands on his desk. 'Fact of life, Denton—some folk are worth the trouble, some aren't.'

'You mean they were poor.'

'I don't make those judgements. If a middle-class house-holder with two kids and a wife and a job as a senior clerk turns up in the Thames, we investigate. If somebody in rags with no way of knowing who she was washes up, well—'

'So if I dress the householder in rags and throw him off a bridge, you bury him without an autopsy?'

'I'd assume the wife would either raise a stink or the neighbours would. *Respectability,* Denton. It drives the world. You know how it goes—respectability is never being noticed, isn't it? Never wearing the wrong necktie or saying the wrong word, or suddenly living without a husband when the neighbours know you ought to have one. It comes to our attention. But those who aren't respectable to start with—'

'The poor—'

'You sound like a reformer. Come off it, Denton—you're respectable, I'm respectable, we read what's respectable and we think what's respectable and we don't go into some parts of London because they aren't respectable. It's a not a perfect world out there. A lot gets left to God to sort out.'

'Mary Thomason maybe wasn't respectable?'

'An art student? How would I know? It would help if you could tell me something about her and weren't just passing gas. Anyway, she should be reported to Missing Persons, which you'll do posthaste, right?' Munro slapped his hands on the desk. 'Tea? Look, Denton, CID aren't here to find missing shop girls, all right?'

'Neither am I.'

'Then give it up. It's daft, anyway. She probably got a bun in the oven and went home to Ma, or she met some darling artiste and is living in a gypsy caravan someplace.'

Denton accepted a mug of repellent tea. 'You could be right.'

'Thank you.' Munro sipped the tea and made a face. 'Bitter as a tanner's pee. My God, why can't they make it fresh once in a way!' He pushed several sheets of foolscap across the desk. 'Keep that, if you like.'

Denton looked it over. Of the list of corpses gathered in after the date of the note to him, one caught his eye, pulled from the Thames—'Female, slender, hair long, age unknown because of water and decomposition, contusions on head'—he thought of bodies he had seen in the war. At the end, he had been in Louisiana; there had been a skirmish, hardly a battle, nothing that would get into the history books, but a dozen bodies had floated down a small river to where he had been camped, three or four catching in a slow eddy; at night, they could hear the alligators tearing at them, their tails splashing the water as they tried to spin pieces off; finally, unable to stand it, he had ordered his men to pull the bodies out and bury them. The faces were ghastly. Was that how Mary Thomason had ended—bloated, unrecognizable, inhuman? 'Nobody ever heard of Mary Thomason, then. Well—' He folded the sheets and put them in a pocket. 'If I'd known what the tea was like, I'd have gone to Guillam.'

'Try Sewer and Water Authority. Their tea's capital. They're not much on crime, though.' He smiled, the deliberately false smile that merely lifts the corners of the lips. 'We investigate when we get evidence. There's no evidence.'

Denton stood. 'Maybe I'll find something where she roomed.'

'If you do—' Munro pointed a pencil at him, his huge head lowered as if he were going to charge—'you report it to Missing Persons. No inspirations, right?'

'I wouldn't dare.' Denton grinned. 'It wouldn't be respectable.' He tried the tea again and gave up on it.

It was still raining at nine o'clock that night, when, encased again in the mackintosh, he stepped out into his 'back garden', actually a tangle of weeds that he had never bothered himself with before. He had the new Colt in one pocket and a patent 'Ever Ready' electric tube light in the other. 'The very latest thing, and the light lasts as long as twelve seconds,' the American sender had written. Called it a 'flash light'. He hadn't turned it on yet when he tripped over something and almost fell headlong; he caught himself on his right hand and felt loose earth: there were a small hole, a small pile of soil and a spade. Atkins's imitation of gardening.

The rain poured down, windless and incessant. The nearby houses showed only as shapes against the dull reflected city glow, their masses broken by rectangles of gaslit windows. The garden was a black pit within head-high brick walls. The dead weeds, stiff as sticks now, stood almost as high, and their feathery ends dripped with water as he brushed through them. He and Atkins had once talked about sowing grass and restoring the borders, still a mare's-nest of old climbing roses, the remains of an espal-iered fruit tree, and shrub-like eruptions that may once have been meant to flower. Atkins wanted a kitchen garden, herbs and lettuces. Nothing had come of the talk: the back garden remained a jungle.

Making his way in the dark down what was left of a brick path, Denton found himself thinking about Heseltine. The young man's anguish had stayed with him. His own response to the hell of war had been delayed and had come out as a failure of sympathy, an isolation from his young wife and then his sons. And it had appeared still later as imaginings and fantasies that had turned into the novels that his English editor called 'masterpieces of horror'. Now here was young Heseltine, living through a horror of his own, but hard on the heels of the horror itself without the cushioning of delay or metamorphosis into fiction.

He stumbled, cursed, moved on by sliding his feet over the wet bricks and the grass that grew between them. The mackintosh covered him to halfway between his knees and his boots, but his trouser legs were already wet. The broad hat kept the water out of his collar but would soak through, he knew. He was in for a miserable hour or two, because he meant to wait to see if the man in the red moustache—or Albert Cosgrove—went in or out of the vacant house.

He felt the brick bulk of the former privy, once discussed as a possible garden shed. Weed trees surrounded it, gripped it; he had to fight his way through them, head down to keep twigs out of his eyes. When his reaching fingers felt the rear wall of the garden, he shuffled left, flattening against the bricks to escape the densest of the growth. Once behind the privy, he dared to try the 'flash light', which showed him rain, branches and, surprisingly, a wooden ladder against the rear wall. He lifted his finger from the touch ring that was the light's only switch, careful of his batteries.

Up the ladder, belly on the curved top of the wall, he felt downwards and found another ladder on the other side. Grim discovery: somebody seemed to have made himself a route between Denton's garden and that of the house behind.

And if into the garden, therefore into the house? He felt the sickening lurch of disgust at the idea of somebody's invading him.

He was clumsy going over. He felt the ladder's fragility as he put his weight on it but got down to find a real garden shed on that side, wood not brick, and no tangle of weed trees—a true garden that had been the real thing until a couple of months ago. Crossing it was easy—something rigid and crotch-high, a sundial or a statue, was a temporary discomfort—and then he leaned against the back wall of the house between the cellar door and the back door and waited for his man.

And waited.

And waited.

At half past ten, a distant church bell sounding, he felt his way along the house wall to the back door and tested it, found it locked. No such luck.

He gave up at half past eleven. The lights were out in the adjoining houses. The rain still fell; the city glow burned on; the city's growl was muted.

He went home the way he had come, wet, angry, like a cat who's been shut out in the rain.

CHAPTER 5

'Anything?' Atkins said, not without scepticism.

Denton was in his own entrance hall. Atkins, wearing the bedraggled robe, pyjama bottoms visible between the hem and the floor, was standing in the doorway to his quarters. A staircase ran up the wall on Denton's left to his own part of the house. Around them, the oversized Scottish genre paintings were inscrutable in the dim light.

Denton shrugged himself out of the mackintosh and handed it over, hat to follow. 'Your intruder's either a figment of your imagination or he's got another home.'

'Figment? Who chased somebody because he thought he was being followed? Who saw a man with a funny upper lip at New Scotland Yard?'

Denton grunted. 'Maybe we're both seeing things.' He stopped partway up the stairs. 'I almost tripped over a shovel in the back. Was that you?'

'Ha, ha. I hired a layabout that was recommended by the ice-man; he started digging and half an hour later told me the back garden was concrete, not dirt, and I could take my spade and put it in a certain place. Which reminds me, I mean the ice-man does, the ice-cave is leaking again, and I'm sick of mopping up around it.'

'We just had it soldered.'

'Well, it's leaking. We need a proper modern ice-box. Ice-caves went out with the bustle.'

'Keep mopping.'

He went up to the long sitting room, walked its length without turning up the gas and looked out of the high window at the back. The house behind was mere blackness, a peaked hole in the night. It was almost midnight—no, four minutes to; there was the bell of Holy Trinity, never on time.

He went back to his chair by the near-dead coal fire, tossed on a pitchy stick or two and several chunks of coal and sat in his chair. He opened a book but didn't read, sat instead with his fist against his lower lip, thinking of Janet Striker.

Later, Atkins came up to clear things away. Putting glasses on a tray, he said, 'Jesus never laughs.'

'"Jesus wept."'

'Exactly. I been through the gospels and through them. He don't laugh. He weeps, as you say—the miracle of Lazarus. Wouldn't hurt him to laugh, would it?'

'Blasphemous remark.'

'We're told he's the divine made flesh, aren't we? Flesh laughs!'

'Katya losing her hold?'

'Don't get personal, please—not in our contract.'

'Go to bed.'

'I was *in* bed, and then you come back and now some of us have to wash up the glasses that others have used. Go to bed, my hat.'

Denton smiled at his back. He closed the unread book, turned down the light and walked again to the long window. The rain was a cold drizzle now, holding the reflection of the city in a low yellow blush, against which the houses were uncertain silhouettes. The house behind was only deeper blackness—until a small dot of light moved along it, a will-o'-the-wisp doing a slow dance from right to left.

'He's there!' Denton pounded up his stairs for the new revolver, then down again. 'Call a constable!' Another glance out of the back window showed nothing, the moving light now gone.

Atkins was at the bottom of his stairs in pyjamas, his hair tangled. 'What do I tell the copper?'

'I saw a light in the rear garden of the house behind, what d'you think you tell him?' Denton was running down the stairs towards him.

'I'm ready for bed. Look at me.'

'Throw on my mac.' He went around Atkins. 'I'm going out the back way.'

'You've not even got boots on!'

Then he was in his own back garden again, the tall, wet weeds brushing his face and hands. He should have worn a coat, but there hadn't been time. His old velvet jacket was already soaked, as were his thin-soled slippers. He pushed his way through the weeds, found the brick path, made better headway. Halfway up the ladder, he realized he'd forgotten the flashlight. He hesitated, one foot up, one on a lower rung, told himself it didn't matter and went on up and over the wall. Going down the other side, he felt exposed, his back now turned to that upper window where Atkins had seen the figure and he had seen the light. He shivered, told himself it was the wet, and dodged around the obstacle (sundial? statue?) to cross the grass. Far away, he heard a police whistle, like a thin bird's cry, infinitely lonely—perhaps Atkins calling the constable.

The ground-level door was closed and locked, but the sloping door to the cellar was raised, leaned back on a support so it was held safely beyond the vertical. In the wet air, light from the city glow was diffuse, dim, but less than blackness to his now-adjusted eyes. The hole below where the door had lain—surely there were stairs there—was real blackness, however. He knelt and put a hand down, found the first step—stone, cracked, cold. He lifted his head and listened for Atkins, for a policeman.

Somebody was inside the house now, he was sure. The cellar door had been left open for a quick escape; it seemed to him a stupid, even childish thing to have done—if a policeman with a lantern came into the garden, it would be the first thing he saw. But the mind at work here was not normal. Childish, perhaps. Less than sane? Denton squatted there in the rain and thought about the face he'd seen at New Scotland Yard. Childish, but—clever? Not stupid, perhaps. And cautious. *So if I'm childish but clever, what would I have done here?* He thought that a clever child might have put something down there in the darkness to trip an intruder or to sound a warning.

Denton lay in a puddle and felt down the top step, then the second. Across the third step, about six inches up, a rope had been stretched, one end tied to a nail and the other to a cluster of used tins that, as he leaned his head down, smelled of old meat and older fish.

An alarm system. Like something from Boy's Own.

He felt his way down and stepped over the rope and down another step, then felt ahead of himself to the crumbling wood of an old doorway. A broom had been leaned across it.

The cellar smelled of earth and cat piss and old fires. Low windows at ground level were pale yellow rectangles. He went on hands and knees across the floor, feeling his way towards where he hoped a set of stairs would go up to the door that stood on the other side of the house. He was off by about five feet but found the stairway well enough because of the light coming in a window at the top, a streetlight throwing yellow-green patterns through it. He went up.

The space above was some kind of corridor, doors opening off it, windows down one wall. Feeling ahead for more *Boy's Own* alarm systems, he made his way forward towards Millman Street, through a doorway, the door open, and so from what would have been the servants' part of the house to its public self—a large space, dark, more spaces opening beyond it—an entrance hall? To his left, a stairway up. At the top, sound.

A voice, the words unintelligible. Then another voice, different, no more understandable than the first.

Denton felt with his fingers and then put his left foot on the first stair tread. He pulled himself up, waiting for a creak, got none. He felt for the next tread.

The first voice murmured again, went on. Male, he thought. He went up another step. The other voice, incantatory, sing-song—female?

He was raising his right foot to the fourth tread, off-balance, when a loud noise of knocking racketed from the front of the house—*bang-bang-bang-bang*. 'Police! Hullo? Police!'

Startled, Denton stumbled momentarily, caught his balance and leaned back against the wall. Above him, there had been a quick sound of scurrying movement, then nothing.

The knocking came again.

Denton charged up the stairs, turned at a landing and started up again and saw something hurtling down at him, big, flying, unreal, and he raised the Colt, flinching away from the thing, his thumb reaching for the familiar big hammer of the old revolver and not finding it. The pistol was too new, too little tried; he forgot that it was double-action and fired simply by pulling the trigger; his thumb fumbled over the smaller hammer, and before he had it cocked and could fire, the thing was on him, smothering him, stinking of mould and mice. He pushed it off, feeling its damp softness, small weight, cocked the revolver at last, and found himself alone on the stairs. He looked up into more darkness.

The pounding came again.

'Go to the back!' Denton shouted. 'The back!' He charged upstairs and, making the turn at the top into a corridor, felt movement, saw the darkness in motion around him, raised his left arm to shield himself and his right to fire and felt a whack on his shoulder that glanced off and struck his head. He stumbled, dropped to his right knee, points of light in his eyes like sparks. Something shoved him hard on the left side of his head, and heavy footsteps clattered down the stairs.

Denton stayed. He tried to stand and fell to a sitting position against the wall.

The front door opened and slammed shut.

'Can you walk?'

'It's only my arm. I'm all right, Sergeant.'

'Was it him?'

'It was somebody—had a bar or a club or something—'

'Oh, crikey.'

The shrill bleat of a police whistle came from behind them—the constable arriving with reinforcements. They were in the back garden of the house behind his, Denton seated on the ground at the top of the cellar stairs. The rain had stopped. He was thinking that he had underestimated their man, and maybe that was his own fault because he hadn't taken somebody who'd wear a red moustache seriously. He was also thinking that he'd been an idiot.

'Dr Bernat's on his way.' Dr Bernat had a surgery at the corner of Lamb's Conduit Street and Guilford Street, only steps from Denton's house.

'Stop fussing over me.'

Then a constable came up behind Atkins, and Dr Bernat came the long way around and found the route into the garden from Millman Street. The policeman had a dark lantern, which Atkins held trained on Denton's arm while the doctor examined it and the constable took 'the victim's statement'.

'It is not broken, only bruised,' Bernat said. 'I need more light. I think a cab and the hospital—he protests, but—'

'No hospital, absolutely not.'

'You are hurt.'

'I'm embarrassed! And I've been hurt lots worse. All I had was a knock on the arm and a knock on the head. I made my own way down through a dark house. I'm all right, doctor! I was shaken up, that's all.'

The policeman said, 'A bit peculiar.'

'Which part of it?'

The policeman cleared his throat. He was older than many of them, not brilliant. 'Them ladders, to start with.'

'On the garden wall? Yes, well—'

Denton stood, refusing Atkins's help. Atkins was wearing Denton's mackintosh, which was so big on him it dragged on the ground. From their own back garden, Rupert was objecting in single, well-spaced barks to being kept away from the action. The policeman shone his dark lantern down the cellar steps. Denton told him about the voices, the attack, the front door. 'I thought you'd come when I shouted, Constable.'

'Question of entry, sir. You said to go to the back. I got to the back and didn't see nothing. Thought it important to get some help.' He had Atkins hold the lantern while he made notes. 'About them ladders,' he said.

'We found them that way.'

The policeman cleared his throat and took the lantern back and walked over the grass to the rear wall. He aimed his light at the ladder and pulled it down to study the end. 'Been sawed.'

'Is that significant?'

'Something you did yourself, sir?'

'Of course not.'

'Not your ladder?'

'I don't own a ladder.'

The policeman replaced the ladder and then climbed up it and stood there, looking down into Denton's back garden. He came down. 'Ladder on the other side's also been sawed. Two ladders sawn from one, if you follow my meaning.'

'I do.'

'Deliberate.'

'That sounds right.'

The policeman paced back and shone the light around. 'This is a matter for a detective.' He stood straight. 'Get one here in the morning.'

He came closer to Denton. It was cold in the garden. Denton shivered and remembered that his clothes were soaked. Still, there was something perversely pleasant about the moment—the darkness, the quieter city, a star that he could see above them—a sense that things could easily have been worse. 'Now, sir,' the policeman said.

'This isn't a good place to give a statement. Why don't we go into my house? There's tea.'

The man considered that. 'If your man will just remain here at the scene, sir, I'll fetch another constable to keep guard, and we'll proceed.'

It took him fifteen minutes. Denton got quite cold.

He got to bed finally. The story of the man with the red moustache, the figure in the window, the glow Denton had seen there, were more than the policeman wanted to hear. He said several times that Denton would have to tell this to a detective. Denton's having waited over there himself earlier that evening made him frown; Denton's actually going into the house made him frown even more. He was a stolid copper with a balding head that had what seemed to be a permanent red crease where his helmet rode. The hairs at the sides of his head, some grey, were damp from the sweat of it. He shook his head several times but didn't say outright that this was a strange tale.

'Matter for the detectives,' he said once more, and left.

'Now you're for it,' Atkins said.

'Me?'

'Police'll have you the guilty party for breaking and entering, before they're through.'

'Go to bed.'

'I ain't been staying up because I like it, General.' Atkins looked at him with suspicion. 'You sure you're all right?'

'My arm hurts, but I can use it and wiggle the fingers. The knock on the head had me seeing stars, but they're gone and all I have is a headache. Mostly, my feelings are hurt for being such a dub. You'd think I'd never fired a pistol before.'

In the morning, his arm was bruised but his headache was gone. The embarrassment was still there, perhaps more acutely. Wanting to erase it, he went around to Millman Street and looked at the front of the house and found a 'To Let' sign, not very large, by the front door. On it in a small, neat handwriting was the name of an estate agent in Russell Square. Neither the sign nor the size of the writing suggested that anybody was very hopeful about Number 14 Millman Street. Denton looked at the house and thought he saw why: too small, too old, too poorly maintained. Had he ever known whoever had lived there before? He didn't think so.

At nine, cursing the time off from his work, he was at Messrs Plumb and Angevin in Russell Square. Plumb, an eager, smiling, rabbity man too young to be so familiar, was astonished that somebody had been attacked in one of his houses, shocked that the house had been invaded.

'That's breaking and entering,' he said. 'You should have apprised us!'

'There was nothing to apprise you about.'

'You have a duty under the law!'

'Don't be ridiculous.'

'That's a valuable property!'

'And I'm the King of Siam. Now look, Mr Plumb, it appears to me this man was spying on me from that house.'

'You admit it's your fault, then.'

Denton considered taking Mr Plumb by his revers and lifting him off the floor. However, at that moment, a detective walked in and showed his credentials, and Denton backed off a step and said, 'Is this about Number 14 Millman Street?'

The detective, who was young and clearly afraid he didn't project enough authority, rapped out, 'Who're you?'

'I live in the house behind Number 14. I'm the man who was attacked.'

'Oh, are you?' He glanced at some notes. 'You Mr Denton?'

'I am.'

'We want to talk to you.' He touched Denton's arm as if he were going to seize him. 'My name's Markson. Detective.'

Twenty minutes later, Denton was answering questions in the back garden of Number 14, and Mr Plumb was standing against the house, looking cold and worried. A policeman who had been standing there part of the night looked dour. After some minutes of answering Markson's questions, Denton was relieved to see Munro, who hove into view around the corner like some large animal. He was carrying his hat—he had been hurrying, he said—and his hair was plastered down as the policeman's had been last night. He nodded at Denton and loomed over the young detective. 'What've you got?'

'Just examining the man Denton.'

'In aid of what?'

'He was the victim of the attack.'

Munro rolled his eyes. 'Have you been inside the house yet?'

'Proceeding deliberately. I was told to be alert for fingerprints.'

Munro exhaled noisily and glanced at Denton. Munro and the detective walked quickly over the turf near the cellar door, which Markson called 'the crime scene', Munro saying 'Yes, yes,' every few seconds as if he'd heard it all before. Then Munro grabbed Denton's arm and walked him towards the back of the garden. 'You think somebody's been watching you from this house, that true? Didn't see anything for a couple of nights, then this—true? Saw somebody at a window once *maybe,* then a "glow" at night, *maybe*—true? That it?'

'The ladders.'

'Ah, ladders.' Denton led him to the ladder, which Munro mounted and from which he looked down into Denton's garden. 'You going to do something for those roses?' he said.

'Hadn't given it a thought.'

'Roses are the thing. Now, they're difficult, mind, but they give great satisfaction. Looks as if the soil would be all right. I could give you some slips—cuttings, you know. Rather pleased with my roses.'

'Atkins wants to grow vegetables.'

'He has no soul.' Munro looked at a notebook. 'Yes, the ladder's been cut in two and propped like that—not your doing or your man's, true?' He sniffed. 'The notes from the first copper on the scene were on my desk at seven with a note from Georgie Guillam—"Look what your pal is up to now." I thought I'd best get over here before somebody decided you were a vicious criminal.' He put his hat on and lowered his voice. 'I told you that Georgie could be trouble. This isn't even his manor, but he must have had somebody looking for paper with your name on it.' He took Denton's arm again and steered him back to the young detective. 'You're doing a fine job here, Markson, but we don't want to spend time running the wrong fox. Mr Denton is a well-known man of good reputation, rather a friend to the Yard—I'm sure you remember the Stella Minter case last year—so, a word to the wise from an old hand: don't spend too much time on him. Right? Right. Let's go inside.'

Munro raised the cellar door by its U-shaped handle. The estate agent jingled some keys but Munro ignored him. He stood staring down the stone steps at the door in the foundation wall. 'Modern alarm system, I see.' He kicked the rope and the tins aside and turned to his right, surprisingly light on his feet, and tiptoed down the edge of the steps, then felt along a ledge up at ground level and grunted. He took out a handkerchief and reached up to the ledge again and came down with a big key. 'One of those old locks you could open with a hairpin, anyway.' Holding the key in the handkerchief, he waved it at the detective. 'Fingerprints, I know.' He looked at Denton. 'We just got a directive on fingerprints. Our newest fad. We now have a Fingerprint Branch, as of last August.' He wrapped the key in the handkerchief and gave it to Markson. 'I want that handkerchief back.' He looked up at Denton, still at the top of the stairs. 'Of course, we can't get fingerprints off objects unless the person conveniently has paint or mud or dog turd on his fingers, but it's important that we handle everything with "gloves or clean cotton wool".' He growled.

'I've got a key to the front door,' the estate agent said.

'Good for you.'

The cellar, Denton now saw, had a stone floor and the smell of cats and mould and wood that had been too long damp. Dimly seen, a huge fireplace in the far wall proclaimed that this had once been the kitchen. The wooden stairs he had felt his way up led to a corridor, a more recent kitchen now to be seen opposite, a pantry to the left. The house itself was narrow and unfurnished, with mouldings and fireplaces that seemed to Denton old-fashioned, more like those of his childhood.

'Closed houses're always colder than your mother-in-law's breath,' Munro said.

He led them to the stairs, where Denton recounted what he had done and what he had heard. A soiled mattress for a narrow bed lay partway down the stairs—the shapeless thing that had attacked Denton first. In the daylight, it and everything else looked small and mean and harmless. At the top of the stairs, a fireplace poker without a handle lay against the wall—the thing with which Denton had been struck. Markson used a handkerchief to pick it up.

They went into the room in whose window Atkins thought he had seen the man with the red moustache. The window gave an excellent view of the back of Denton's house.

'Could be a tramp. Stood here and watched?' Munro said. He looked at Denton. 'Why?'

Denton thought of telling him about the man he had seen at New Scotland Yard, the possibility that had occurred to him that there might be some connection with Guillam, but thought better of it. He said, 'I wish I knew.'

'You said you heard two voices.'

'I thought I did—a man and a woman—but I think only one person went past me down the stairs—I'm not sure—'

'Enemies? Been getting threatening letters?'

'Rather the opposite.'

Munro looked as if he was about to say something but turned away. He sent the detective off for somebody to start searching the house. Plumb, the estate agent, was looking uneasily about as if expecting to find that the ceilings had fallen in. Munro warned him to touch nothing and sent him downstairs to open the front door for the police. Then he paced up and down by the window, studying the floor, and got down and put one side of his face against the boards.

'Been somebody here, all right. Marks in the dust.' He got up. 'If you were spying on yourself from here, would you sleep here?'

'That would be one way to do it.'

'But the water and gas are off. You'd need a bed and a chamber pot and something to drink and probably something to do. Boring, surveillance is. Done my stint, I can tell you.' He had taken his hat off again, now put it on. 'Listen, while there's just the two of us—what makes you think this had anything to do with you?'

'Atkins saw somebody. I saw a light—'

'Yeah, yeah, you told us all that. Could be a tramp. What else?'

'I've had some kind of, mm, strange letters. The last sounded as if he'd been watching me. Had seen me, anyway.'

'What's the connection?'

'I don't know.'

Munro shook his head. 'You look in the closets for signs somebody's spent time here. I'll be back.' He started out, turned around. 'Don't touch anything unless you use your handkerchief. Upper brass are nuts on fingerprints. I already said that, didn't I?'

Denton went up another flight to the bedrooms and started going through the rooms. On the floor above that one, in what had been meant as a maid's room, he supposed, he found two blankets rolled up together in a small cupboard under a stair, along with a chamber pot and a stack of writing paper. He wrapped a pocket handkerchief around one hand, lifted the pot's lid, got its stink, saw it needed washing.

Most of the paper had been written on in green ink, a cramped hand that couldn't keep a straight line. The first page was rather elaborately decorated with calligraphic scrolls and tiny faces, impish, like something in a medieval manuscript. In the middle, in half-inch-high decorated letters, it said 'The Demon Inside His Head', and below that in smaller letters 'A Novel. By Albert Cosgrove.'

He lifted the pages with the tip of his pocket-knife. He read words, phrases, saw interleavings and scribbles at angles, what seemed to be a loss of control as he got deeper into the pile. Then pages with only a few words on them in huge letters, then drawings—grotesque faces, penises and balls, an eye. Then a page of incoherence, mere words, illegibility. Then relative coherence, even a sense of starting again—and the names and actions of the characters in the outline that was missing from Denton's desk.

Then Munro came back and said that the intruder had been emptying his po down the privy in Denton's garden, and Denton felt sudden queasiness: *He's being me.*

Sitting in his own room again with coffee, Munro opposite with his overcoat open, Denton pondered the question—was it the menace?—of Albert Cosgrove. Down towards the far end of the room, the doors to the dumb waiter stood open—Sergeant Atkins's means of eavesdropping on what was said. Denton didn't mind; he'd want to discuss it with him later, anyway.

'I'm losing a day's work,' Denton said.

'And me? I'm on my hols? I'm not even supposed to be here, Denton; CID have better things for me to do.'

'Run off, if you must.'

'Markson, that young detective, is a good lad. This is his case; he'll be the one you talk to. But bear in mind that he's young and on the make and he don't necessarily know better than to let Georgie Guillam sniff around his tail.'

'What's all that about fingerprints?'

'You know what they are? Of course you do. No two alike, and so on.' He grunted. 'Let's pass over whether that's proven.

What matters is the Home Secretary and other powers that be want us to collect fingerprints at crime scenes. Will they help us find criminals? No, because we don't have anything to compare them with. Will they help us in ten or twenty years if we get enough of them? Maybe, if the theory is correct. Right now, all they'll tell us is if somebody whose prints we already have may have been at a crime scene. Which is why you're to come down to the Yard today and get your prints taken.'

'I've better things to do.'

'Fingerprint fella goes off at six; get it done before then. All right?'

'Look, Munro—'

'You're not hearing me! The nicer you are, the quicker it'll go away.' He leaned forward for emphasis. '*I want you to give your fingerprints today.*' He held up a hand. 'And another thing.'

'My God, what now!'

'You had no business going into that house. You should have called a constable.'

'I sent Atkins to call one.'

'While you went inside a house that wasn't your own, in the dark, and forced the hand of somebody who might have really broken your crown.' He shook his head. 'It wasn't wisely done, Denton.'

'All right, all right. It wasn't wise.'

'You're a man that attracts trouble. Last year, it was a murderer; a few days ago you came to me about some girl who'd disappeared—How is that, anyway?'

'Stymied.'

'And now there's this—somebody—shadowing you and breaking into a house to do it.'

'It isn't my fault that some lunatic wants to spy on me.'

'Who says he's a lunatic?'

'Did you look at that manuscript?'

'Little faces on the front, yes, seems a bit peculiar. Fairies, were they supposed to be? That a fairy tale he was writing?'

Denton looked grim. 'The first paragraph is a word-for-word theft from the first paragraph of one of my books. Partway through, his scribbles start to use the outline for the book I'm working on. That outline was in my desk when I left London!'

'He's been in your house? What else is missing?'

'Nothing that I know of. But—goddamnit, Munro, he's been *in* here. He's sat in my chair, he's lain down on my bed, I'll bet anything he took a crap in my WC because he couldn't control himself!'

'Burglars do that, it's true—often in the middle of the carpet.'

'Munro, I thought this was some harmless booby. Now I think otherwise. It's—it's "creepy"!' A British reviewer had called Denton's second book 'an American fantasy of the creepy variety'. Now the word had come home to roost.

Munro's stolid face seemed to become wooden. He stared at Denton. 'I don't see what it's about.'

Denton got up and took a few steps down the room, then back. 'I think it's about imitation.'

'You lost me.'

'"Imitation is the sincerest form of flattery." Would-be writers imitate writers who've made it—"playing the sedulous ape", Stevenson called it. I think "Albert Cosgrove" may have gone a few miles beyond that.'

'So you make him out a loony.'

'I don't know. But it's creepy, finding something of my own that somebody else has taken over lock, stock and barrel. He may even believe he made it up himself.'

'You mean, if he knows it's yours, he's an honest thief; if he thinks it's his own, he's mad—that it?' Munro tapped the crease in his soft hat lightly with the side of a hand. 'He dangerous, you think?'

'How would I know?'

'Well, he hit you with a poker. I think we'd best put some minders on you—see if he's following you about.'

Denton didn't like the idea of minders. 'He may just be some kid who's wild to be somebody.'

'The somebody is you?'

'I certainly hope not.' Denton was no enthusiast of the new pseudo-science of psychology, but he'd read enough—Krafft-Ebing, James—to know that there was a form of fantasy that merged into obsession. He sometimes wrote about it, in fact, although differently, expressing it as a ghost or a demon instead of an aspect of personality. He wondered now if Albert Cosgrove had used 'demon' in his title as a deliberate imitation. Or was it identification? 'Maybe he wants to hide in somebody else.'

'From what? You're off in fairy-land, Denton.' Munro got up. He jiggled his hat on a finger inserted into the crown. 'Sending you love notes, sort of, was he?'

'You make it sound female—like a schoolgirl's crush. Atkins said something like that.'

'Well?'

'Yes, it could be like that.'

'You have any of his letters?'

'Burned them the night I got home. No, maybe I have the one that came yesterday—' He knelt by the grate, saw only ash and dying coals. 'I'll look for it. Maybe it's in the waste bin.'

'And you've forgotten the address.'

'I'm not even sure there was one.' He jammed his hands into his pockets. 'I get letters like that, maybe not as excitable, all the time. It comes with the profession.'

'The trials of the famous. You ever answer them?'

Denton huffed. 'These had been here for a while. Of course I didn't answer them. My God, in one he wanted a copy of each of my books, signed, with a personal inscription!'

'But there wasn't an address?'

'I don't think so. He isn't rational.'

'Mmp.' Munro buttoned his overcoat. 'Anyway, you're to be a good citizen and take yourself down to New Scotland Yard before six tonight. And we'll put somebody to trail you. And you're going to let us know anything else that happens. Aren't you.' It wasn't a question.

'Anything related.'

Munro gestured with the hat, holding it so its brim was vertical and waving it up and down. 'And you're not to go off on this by yourself! I don't care if you were once upon a time the Lord High Sheriff of America, *we're* the police authority here.'

'My main concern is to finish my book.'

'Good. Keep that in your head and we'll be all right.' He put his hat on. 'You ever report that girl as a missing person?'

'I never established that she was missing.'

'Albert Cosgrove is police business enough for you for this year, anyway.' He stood, bear-like, by the door, turned abruptly. 'Dammit, I know it isn't your fault, Denton, but you're a bleeding magnet for loonies and misfits! I'll see myself out.'

And he did. Denton heard the rumble of Atkins's voice mingle with the sound of the front door's opening.

When Atkins came up, Denton was back in his chair. 'You heard?' he said.

'Couldn't help myself. Dumb waiter left open through oversight.'

'The bastard was in here. He took my outline. God knows what else he did.'

'Kind of makes you want to give everything a wash, don't it.'

'What d'you think?'

'I think you've put your foot in a bow-wow's mess. Best take a few weeks in Italy.'

'We just got home.'

'Awfully nice, Italy.' Atkins pursed his lips. 'I think I'll hang on to the derringer for a bit. You really think this Cosgrove is mental?'

'*I* don't know. I don't need these distractions just now!'

'Say it louder, General. Maybe they'll go away.'

Dr Bernat came in towards noon and looked at his arm and his head and told him he was a very hard nut. When he was done with the back of Denton's head, Bernat came around to the front, stepped closer, lifted his spectacles to look at Denton's eyes. He had to stand on tiptoe to do so, a short man with a beard, stocky, rather handsome. 'Your eyes are not happy, Mr Denton.'

'I've been working.'

'Eye strain.' Bernat backed away and picked a book at random from the shelf and opened it. 'Read.' He held the book at eye level several feet from Denton.

'Uh—no, too small—'

The doctor came a step closer. 'Now?' He moved again. 'Now?'

'It's blurry.'

Bernat closed the book with a clap. 'You are needing eyeglasses for the close work.'

'I haven't got time to go someplace and go through a lot of rigmarole!'

Bernat was writing on a pad. 'You can go to Harley Street and pay several pounds and then go somewhere else and pay several more for eyeglasses.' He handed over the paper. 'Or you can go where I am going and where Whitechapel people are going and pay very little. You just try on glasses until you are finding a pair you like. Very nice people, also Jews like me, helpful—I am recommending it.' He looked over his glasses. 'Go today.'

'I'm already supposed to go to New Scotland Yard to have my fingerprints taken.'

'That sounds interesting. Good for you!' He reached up to put a hand on Denton's shoulder. 'Splash cold water on the eyelids when there is pain or, what is the word—stinging. Also rest once each hour. Also look away from the work at some distant beauty—' He waved a hand. 'Maybe a pretty girl. But only at a distance!' He laughed and headed for the door. 'Don't be putting too much strain on that arm. Meanwhile—look at a pretty girl.'

Denton was off at two towards the typewriter's with more manuscript; then he took the underground to Whitechapel because his eyes were on fire and he thought that if he didn't get relief, he wouldn't be able to go on with the book. Far behind him, a fat man in dark clothes seemed to appear, then be replaced by a thin man in brown, then reappear. These were his police minders, he supposed.

He found his way to Newark Street and the Fancy Modern Imperial Spectacles and Eyeglass Emporium, where dour young men in business suits and pince-nez behaved as much as possible like doctors, helping the clientele pick glasses from shallow trays that covered twenty or so long tables.

'Short-sighted, is it?' a youth said.

'For reading.'

'Fuzzy? Not clear?'

'That's it.'

'No tunnelling? No like looking through the keyhole? No black around the edges?'

He left, the possessor, for one and six, of spectacles with thick rims the motley colours of a cat ('best artificial tortoise'). He thought he looked comical in them but decided he'd let nobody see them except, perhaps, Atkins. With the glasses in his pocket, he went back to New Scotland Yard, where a man who smelled like a navvy held each of his ten fingers one by one and pushed them into an inked pad as if he meant to break them.

He fell into bed at ten and was asleep almost at once.

CHAPTER

6

It was raining again the next day as he made his way down the Embankment to meet Janet Striker. A telegram had come from her at noon:

BANDSTAND GARDENS CHARING CROSS
BRIDGE 5 PM STOP STRIKER

Not immediately clear, the meeting place had been sorted out with the help of a Baedeker's, the sense that her knowledge of London was better than his, awareness that she too was a walker; he had wondered if she walked the city at night when she couldn't sleep or when she had to escape (her mother, her life).

Then the connection to streetwalker, her past, although she had told him she had tried the streets only once, too naive to know how or where, and had been pulled towards Mrs Castle's whore-house on Westerley Street.

He had set down almost forty pages that day. Work blotted out concern.

He was walking on the river side and crossed over the street when he reached the plaque that celebrated the engineer who had tamed the London sewers and built the Embankment. Ahead, he could see the bandstand, white and a green that was turning black in the gloom, a pointed roof with a flagpole where no flag was flying. An omnibus clopped by in the roadway, water splashing around the horses' hooves; he saw movement on the bridge, shapes, but little that suggested life, rather some city of shades, that Homeric hell where there is no fire but only the absence of what we take to be human.

He saw her first as a black blot in the shadow of the band-stand. The blot took on a shape, skirted and therefore female, something widening it above—a rain cape. Another hideous black hat. He felt anger at her: she seemed to offer so little for him to have come this far for.

'You're here,' he said. He had come up three wooden steps. Under the white ceiling, no rain fell, but the floor was wet, puddles lying in low places.

'Of course.'

She was leaning against a white railing; a furled umbrella stuck out at an angle. 'You're very wet.'

'Aren't you?'

'I took a cab. It's a poor place to have picked for a rainy day. I thought we'd walk.'

'Well—'

'No. It was raining when I sent the telegram; I knew better. Maybe I thought you wouldn't come.'

He leaned one shoulder against a post. The bottoms of his trouser legs were drenched. He shook water off his hat and put it back on.

'Have you been working?' she said.

'All day.'

'Something new?'

He told her about Cieljescu and the novel.

'What's it about?'

'Oh—' He wanted to hurry things, caught himself. 'A marriage. A man and a woman.'

'Are they happy?'

'Of course not. What sort of novel would that be?' She didn't smile. He said, 'They destroy each other, but they don't see that that's what they're doing. They're always—undermining—it's worse than undermining, it's going to each other's weaknesses. It's like a long mutual siege.'

'What's it called?'

He chewed his lips. He didn't like titles, which always sounded stupid to him. 'It used to be called *The Machine*. Now it's *The Love Child*.'

'You didn't say they have a child. More than one?'

'No, no, no children. It's a—it's what they, mmm, nourish in each other. Books always sound so stupid when I talk about them.' He looked away down the Embankment, chewing his lower lip. 'What I saw was that when things go bad, it isn't one of them or the other. It's both of them. A bad marriage is a conspiracy between two people to destroy themselves. So it's something they give birth to and then encourage and—nourish. So the husband begins to see—he thinks he sees—a child, a boy. He sees him out a window. Then the boy is older; he sees him again. Then the next time, the boy is nine or ten, there's something wrong with him, some look, some expression—he seems sly, his eyes too wide apart. And so on. They're raising a monster child and they don't know it.'

'Does she see it?'

'Oh—' He tried to smile away his embarrassment. 'At the end, he thinks she does. She sets fire to herself and he thinks something made her do it. The trouble with talking about a book when you're working on it is that then you don't want to work on it. It sounds so foolish!'

She waited several seconds and then said, 'I've been thinking about what you said. And what I said. Like you and your book, I don't like talking about it.' She drew a pattern with the tip of her umbrella. 'I went to see Ruth Castle.' Ruth Castle was the madam who owned the house on Westerley Street where Janet had once worked. 'Ruth is a wise woman, a good woman. She's drinking a lot now, but she has a good head on her shoulders. We talked for ages.'

'Well?'

She looked up at him. It was the first time really since he'd come up the steps. 'You frightened me, Denton. You wanted too much all at once.'

'Six months?'

'People don't pick up where they left off after six months.'

'I'm sorry if I hurried you. But, you know, I didn't want to pretend. To court you, woo you, all that—degrading stuff.'

She played some more with the umbrella tip. 'What are we talking about?' Before he could say anything, she raised the umbrella as if to parry something he was about to do. 'Don't use that word. Don't sentimentalize. I'm not sentimental; neither are you. Neither of us knows what "love" is.'

'I was going to say—we could get married.'

'Never. Never, never. I'll go on the street again before I'd do that. You've picked the wrong woman, Denton. I need space around me. I need emptiness—nobody else with me. It's the only way I can deal with—perhaps with myself, much less the rest of you.'

'Then—what?'

'Then whatever we make of it. Time, Denton, it takes time; don't hurry me and don't hurry yourself. It'll come clear or it won't. You said you want to be with me; yes, I want to be with you, I saw that yesterday, I saw the possibility of it—I never thought I would, never thought there was room for anybody but myself. But I'm not going to promise you anything. I can't promise you anything. I don't want to trick you.'

'I'm not going to court you, Janet.'

'Thank God for that, then.' She straightened. 'Let's walk.'

'So what you've said is that you're not shutting me completely out.'

'Denton, I've let you in deeper than anybody in my life! Don't you understand?'

He put a hand out, touched the rain cape. It was the tentative move a man makes to see if he can go further; she must have recognized it for what it was, but she neither protested nor encouraged him; their eyes locked; he kissed her; she surprised him with a kiss that was passionate but short, and she said again, 'Let's walk.'

When they came down the few wooden steps, he saw a solitary figure farther along the Embankment turn away and look at the river.

'Man's following me,' he said. 'He's a policeman. I know the rubber raincoat.'

'What have you done?'

He laughed without humour. 'It's a long tale.' He began to tell her about Albert Cosgrove.

They walked for an hour, then, finding themselves in Oxford Street, went on and turned into Church Street and to Kettner's. She surprised him again by making no objection to dinner; he had thought that she didn't want to be in public with him, but there was nothing to that. They were both hungry, ate hugely of the French food, drank a bottle of wine, laughed. It can be like that, first a kind of ultimate talk on which futures hang, then lightness, even light-headedness, an emotional exhaustion, even with things left unsaid.

They talked about other things. She told him she was leaving the Society for the Improvement of Wayward Women. She was going to put her mother in a better home; she wanted to find herself a new place to live. She would remain, however, aggressively independent: his hint that she might live with him made her briefly angry.

So much had happened that he was confused about what he had told her and what he hadn't. He realized only afterwards, when she looked confused by something he said, that she knew nothing about the mystery of the letter found in the Wesselons. He told her now about the note in the painting, the young woman named Mary Thomason; about Aubrey Heseltine, the art dealer, Geddys.

'What have you done about the woman?'

'Went to see Munro—it seems like weeks ago. It's not his bailiwick.'

'Did you go to the Slade?'

'Where Geddys said she was a student? No. I'm sure they wouldn't talk to me—give information about a woman to a man who isn't a relative, even a friend?'

'They'd give it to me. I'd tell them she had applied to the Society for clerical work and we lost her address.'

'Would you? When?'

'Tomorrow. Tomorrow?'

'Yes, tomorrow, yes—'

'Off on another wild hare together, Denton?'

'The last one did all right, didn't it?'

She touched the scar on her face. 'Is there a monster this time?' She had told him once that she believed that all men hated all women.

'I hope not.'

She smiled. 'Well, it's something we can do together while we're—coming towards each other.'

She wouldn't let him see her home. There was no repetition of the kiss, which, he was sure now, had been a mark of punctuation, not a statement. He saw her into a hansom and watched it roll away into the rain. So, he saw, did his police follower, now a thin man in a baggy tweed.

Time, she had said. Taking their time was ludicrous for two people of their ages. It was all of it ludicrous—men, women, kissing, emotional exhaustion, waiting. But probably inescapable.

Next day, he met Janet Striker in front of University College in Gower Street on a walk in the now-flowerless gardens near the college entrance. People, most of them students, were going around them. She had already been to the offices of the Slade.

He said, 'I had a talk with Munro about her. The divisions and the coroner have never heard of Mary Thomason. That means she didn't report anybody trying to hurt her, and her corpse hasn't turned up.'

'Good, because we're going to talk to her landlady.'

'You got her address?'

'The Slade people wanted to be helpful. It wasn't easy—the fact is, it was months ago, and she seems to have made very little impression, and students leave all the time. I did learn that she was on a list to do modelling, so she probably needed money.'

'In the—Without her clothes on?'

Janet Striker laughed. 'No, clothed. Nude models are a separate species, it seems.'

'Why did they think the Society for the Improvement of Wayward Women wanted her? Did you suggest she was wayward?'

'No, I suggested we were interested in starting an art class for our women. They didn't question that—even gave me the names of other students who might want to teach.'

'Had she told them she was leaving?'

'A note, purportedly after she'd gone home. Somebody brought it by, they thought—they didn't remember. I asked about her friends. They knew nothing, of course—it's only an office. They suggested I see a man named Tonks who teaches drawing. Of course he isn't here just now. Shall we go?'

'You seem eager enough to enter into my project.'

'I told you, it's something we can do together.'

That sounded encouraging. 'You can enter into my life, but I can't enter into yours?'

She looked away as if something had caught her attention along Gower Street. 'Maybe there's something in that.' She clutched his arm. 'Let's go—it's raining.'

'Not like last night.' He was glad for a cue to mention it, afraid that the emotional intensity, the kiss, the dinner, would be allowed to slip away. She glanced at him, grinned, flushed. She squeezed his arm. 'We're going to Fitzroy Street. Do you know Fitzroy Street?'

'Why did you smile just now?'

'Because we're both thinking about last night.' She laughed. 'What a pair of fools we are.'

Number 22 Fitzroy Street was a tall house that came right to the pavement, its brick blackened, a sign advertising rooms in a front window. Despite the remains of a broken urn that had fallen off the doorstep and lay next to it, and despite the roar and horse-piss smell of Euston Road hard by, the house had a look of stubborn respectability in the blind face it turned to the street—no wrappings of food put out on the windowsills to stay cool, no broken panes patched with paper, no views through uncurtained windows into student squalor. Beside a bell, a handwritten slip of paper said 'Mrs Durnquess'.

'The Slade keep her name on a list. She's some sort of preferred haven for new students—her record is good, I suppose. The woman I dealt with said that Mrs Durnquess was "trusted by the parents", whatever that means. I can't imagine that parents with a girl at the Slade know much of what goes on, unless they live in Euston Square.'

She rang the bell. Thirty seconds after a second ring, an adolescent with an Irish accent opened the door. Without waiting to hear what they wanted, she said, 'No rooms—all gone.'

'I want to see Mrs Durnquess, my girl.' Janet Striker's voice could have gone through steel.

'Oh, yes, ma'am. Didn't look properly at you, I'm so sorry, ma'am. I'll git her direct.'

'May we come in?'

'Oh, oh, sure you may, ma'am, I'm all to sixes and sevens today—forgive the mess the students make please, ma'am—and sir—I'll just git—' She was off down the corridor that ran the depth of the house. A door on their left had once led to a front parlour, Denton supposed, now rented to somebody trustworthy enough to keep the front window curtains closed. On their left, a staircase ran to the upper floors, once-figured carpet climbing it wearily, held back from collapse by tarnished rods. The banister and newel showed signs of many collisions. The place smelled of boiled meat.

'I've seen worse,' Denton murmured.

'I live in worse.'

The Irish maid appeared again at the far end of the corridor, waving them towards her. Her hair hung down in sweaty curls from a grubby cap. She was fastening her sleeves, which had been unbuttoned when she opened the door, as if they had been rolled up. 'Miz D will see you in her parlour,' she said, and, pointing at the last of the doors, vanished.

A voice answered his knock. The open door showed a room chock-a-block with furniture, perhaps all the 'good' pieces of the entire house, the rest left for the tenants. A chesterfield sofa was assumed to double as a bed. The walls were covered with paintings, cows much in evidence, the frames jammed against each other. On the shore of this sea of clutter, a vast woman sat where she could get the light from a window. Her black dress and cap aimed for austerity; her huge excess of flesh argued indulgence. 'I am Mrs Durnquess,' she said. 'I don't get up.'

'Not at all.' Janet Striker walked into the room as if she owned it and presented a card. 'I am Mrs Striker of the Society for the Improvement of Wayward Women. This is one of our patrons, the well-known man of letters, Mr Denton. Our business is beneficent, Mrs Durnquess: we seek the whereabouts of one of your tenants.'

'My tenants' whereabouts are here, or they aren't my tenants. I am ever so particular.' Her accent suggested to Denton a forced gentility, but he was poor on the English of the English; anything with a dropped H was to him 'Cockney', most else 'genteel'.

'We hoped you could help us.'

'I'd be ever so happy to help you, Mrs—mmm—Strickers—I don't have my right glasses on—and at once when I am apprised who the person might be.'

'A young woman named Mary Thomason.'

The fat face pouted. Some delicacy had been denied it. 'Gone,' she said.

'Ah.' Janet sounded to Denton as forced as the landlady; he'd never heard her put on the full gloss of the middle class before. 'As we feared. Gone from our ranks, too—oh, not as one of our clients, not one of *the* women. Rather, a volunteer. A helper.'

'Gone.' Mrs Durnquess sighed. 'Not like some, not folded up her tents like the Arabs in the middle of the night and as quietly stole away down Fitzroy Street. No, she was a good and honest girl; she paid her rent and a week ahead, but she has gone.'

'May I ask when? We have missed her since August.'

'It *was* August. Won't you sit down, Mrs mmm, and you, sir. I stand so little any more, but I know it is fatiguing. The Queen Anne side chair is quite comfortable, or the Récamier. Yes, it was August. She left me a note and a shilling, and she disappeared.'

'Do you know why?'

The head, topped with grey sausage curls that might not have been entirely real, bobbed up and down. 'Her father. An accident at the works. I have only the haziest idea of what a works may be, and it suggests a level of society not of the best, but she was a good, sweet girl with manners well above that station.'

'She told you in the note that her father had had an accident? And so she was going home to be with him? And where was home?'

Mrs Durnquess waved an arm from which flaccid muscle hung like dough. 'The west.'

'Cornwall? Devon? Wales?'

'Mary was an artist and suffered the artist's flaw of inspecificity, though it is inspecificity that makes them artists. Many of my tenants are artists, or artists in embryo. When the late Mr Durnquess passed away—also an artist, twice accepted annually at Burlington House but not, alas, an RA—I was left with only this house and his paintings.' A fat little hand waved at the walls. 'I survive by renting rooms that were formerly my domestic haven to students in that great cause—Art.'

'Ah.' Janet glanced at Denton. 'Mr Denton has spoken with her employer.'

'The man Geddys? Hmm-hmm. I never approve of older men and younger women. Not to suggest that there was anything. I disapprove of speculation, especially on that score. But—' She raised her tiny, blackened eyebrows. 'He saw her home from work more often than perhaps a *gentleman* ought to have done.'

'Could she have run off with him?'

'Oh!' It was a breathy little yelp. The thought of running off had a very strong effect. 'To Gretna Green? I hardly think. I had required to speak with him in January and reminded him that we must appear to be upright and to *be* upright. People, I said, must not be given cause for scandal. I required to know what his seeing her home meant.' She pulled herself up a little, sniffed. 'He was—is—a very *smooth* man, if made somewhat unattractive by a physical affliction. I told him I was not subject to flattery or sham. He took my meaning and said quite forthrightly that he saw Mary home because she was in his employ and she was a naive, sweet creature in a city full of risks. I gave him what I refer to as the benefit of the doubt. It is true, after all, that a child like Mary was vulnerable, to put a point on it.'

'And that was the end of it? A note and a shilling?'

'Why, no, there was her brother. Next, I mean. In her note, she said that her brother would come for her things, and the brother would bring another note from her as his bona fides. And so he did.'

'And what sort of man was he?'

'Why, somewhat like Mary. One could see the family resemblance. Bigger, to be sure, manly, rather poorly spoken, I fear—taking after the father, I suppose. Mary spoke like a gentle-woman. But he had the aforementioned note, and he gathered up her things, and that was the end of it.'

Denton leaned forward. He was sitting on a chair with a horsehair seat, very high in the middle, and he risked sliding off if he didn't keep his balance. 'And her things?'

'She wasn't wealthy in the things of this world. He brought a little trunk and a man to carry it, and he put her things in it and away they went.' She waved the other arm towards Euston.

Denton asked more questions about the brother, but she had told them what she knew. As for the man who carried the trunk, she said, 'My maid, Hannah, dealt with him.'

Mrs Durnquess said she was fatigued then and would she excuse them, and she pulled on a tasselled cord that hung from a cast-iron arm up near the moulding. Janet Striker tried one or two more questions, but they'd got what there was to get; half a minute later, they were out in the corridor. Slow, thumping footsteps announced the Irish maid, who appeared in a narrow doorway, sleeves pushed up again, face red. 'Going, are you,' she said.

Denton gave her a shilling. 'We're looking for Mary Thomason.'

'Who's that, then? Oh, the little thing that was up in Seven. She's been gone for ages.'

'Going on three months, I think,' Janet Striker said.

'And me the only servant in the place, it seems like years.'

Denton gave Janet a look that meant that he wanted to do this one himself, and turning back to the maid he said, 'Your name is Hannah.'

'And what if it is?'

'Hannah, Mrs Durnquess says you dealt with Mary Thomason's brother.'

'Sure, there was no "dealing with" him. He come, he got what he wanted, he left.'

'What did he take?'

'And how would I know? He brought a box with him; I suppose it was heavier when he left than when he walked in. He didn't fill it with nothing of *ours*, you may be sure.'

'Did you stay with him while he got the things?'

'Not me. Haven't I got plenty else to do than watch somebody fill a box? He emptied the room of her stuff, that's all I know. Little enough she had, poor thing. A lot of art stuff. When the brother was gone, it was gone. I got the work of cleaning the room, of course, but she'd left it pretty good.'

'Did she have friends in the house?'

'If she did, I never saw them. Madam don't like visitors, and she don't like to-ing and fro-ing between the rooms. She hears the footsteps over her head, she raises the roof. Of course, I'm the one's supposed to set it right.'

'Did you ever have to set Mary Thomason right?'

'Her? No, she wasn't the sort. Quiet.'

'And the brother? Did he ever visit her?'

'Never saw him before. Little cock o' the walk, if you take my meaning. Fancied himself, I thought—couldn't be bothered to carry the box, but brought a man to do it.'

'And where did they go?'

'You think I have the time to watch folk off the premises? They went, that's all, and good riddance. He give me tuppence. A *great* gentleman, I don't think.'

'And the man? Did he help the brother pack up her things?'

'Not him. Half drunk he was, and the brother wouldn't have him in the room at all. I had to take him to the kitchen to keep him from skulking about and doing who knows what. He wasn't a bad sort, oney in my way, and a bit deep in the beer for the time of day.'

'Do you know the man?'

'Me? Know some layabout that pushes a cart? I'm a decent girl.'

'He didn't give you a name.'

'Oh, he did, like he expected me to shine it up and put it on the mantel for a keepsake. "Alf". If he'd had more front teeth and a clean shirt he'd have been about half the man I'd care to spend five minutes with.'

'Old or young?'

'Born old and got older quick, would be my guess. A lot older than me, I can tell you.'

'Did he say where he could be found?'

She laughed. The laughter transformed her; he could see the robust farm girl she had been a year or two before. She pushed some hair back from her forehead. 'I give him a cuppa tea and one of me scones and he tried to—' she glanced at Janet—'to what you'd call take a liberty with me, and he said if I was lonely I could always find him in the arches behind St Pancras station. I laughed in his face! I'd have to be dead lonely because there was nobody left on God's green earth before I'd go prowling for the likes of him!'

Denton said she had a hard row to hoe, and he gave her another coin. She showed them out, and he heard her footsteps clumping back towards the rear of the house. On the pavement, he said to Janet Striker, 'Well?'

'My very thought.'

'At least we know that Mary Thomason's gone.'

'To "the west". Not very helpful.'

'I think I'll go looking for Alf.'

'My very intention.'

They were walking towards Euston Road. At the corner, Janet Striker swung round and looked back at the house. 'At the Society, we tell girls who've taken to the street that they'd have a better life in service. You see a girl like Hannah, you wonder.'

'She'd be better off back on the farm.'

'Oh, aye, except for the starvation.'

They crossed Euston Square and turned towards the Midland Railway station. The great medieval bulk of the station hotel loomed above the other buildings, its towers and walls like one of Ludwig's wilder fantasies. Denton said, '"The arches behind St Pancras". Where the rail lines cross St Pancras Road, I think.'

She took his arm. 'I go to Old St Pancras Church sometimes. Bits of it were put up not so long after the Romans left.'

'I didn't know you go to church.'

'No, I expect not. You don't?' So they talked, wading painfully through their ignorance of each other. Church-going, the war news, did he have old friends, 'being political'—were these issues worth testing each other on? Odd and unpredictable, the doors one opens to try to find the other person.

He told her more about Albert Cosgrove, muted the encounter in the dark house, the knock on the head. Reminded, by a roundabout linkage, of his back garden, he said, 'Dammit—I promised Atkins I'd get somebody to dig. Sorry—not your concern—'

They turned down St Pancras Road, and the crash and rumble of Euston Road fell away. Here, the traffic was mostly carts and wagons, the odd bus, a cyclist dodging in and out. She said, 'Do you really need somebody to do physical work?'

'I don't think a woman would do.' He thought she meant her Society.

'Would you take a Jew?'

'I'd take a Hottentot.'

'If a man named Cohan shows up at your door and says I sent him, put him to work.'

The street seemed to grow older as they walked, brick changed here to stone. Denton was aware of the plain-clothed policeman following them. Felt a stab of annoyance, wondered if it was because of something to do with Mary Thomason— hardly, as he'd gone to the police about her—or Janet Striker, or simply the fact of being watched. For whatever reason, he was tired of that presence always back there.

Ahead, the railway tracks crossed above them on a stone roadbed held up by massive arches, the central one open for the road itself, the others turned into small factories, machinists' works, the odd rag-and-bone shop. They asked at only two of them before a red-faced man in a soft cap shouted 'Alf the carter?' over the rumble of iron tyres on macadam. 'Cross under, third arch on the right. Though he might be out jobbing.'

He was. The arch was boarded up; set into the boards were a window that might have come out of a demolished house—six over six, the glass wavy, one pane replaced with wood—and a door with six panels and the remains of a fanlight over it. Next to it, a bell that also might have come out of a house had been nailed to an upright; it had been made to jingle when a rope was pulled—thoughts of Mrs Durnquess and Hannah inescapable here—but was now sounded by grasping the flexible metal of its support and giving it a shake.

'Alf's out jobbing,' she said. She took out a card, wrote on the back. 'Let's see what that brings.' She put the card in the crack between the door and its frame.

'You're taking over my pursuit of Mary Thomason?'

'You said you were trying to finish a book.'

'I didn't mean for you to get pulled in.'

'I've pulled myself in.' She turned him back towards Euston Road. 'Really, I think the one we want is the brother, not toothless Alf.'

'Easier said than done.'

'There are the directories.'

'And a thousand Thomasons, I'll bet.'

'Hannah didn't like him.'

'He didn't tip her enough.'

'More than that. Odd. Mrs Durnquess thought he was common; Hannah thought he was—what, getting above himself? Although he wouldn't be the first to be common as dirt and treat a servant as if he were the Prince of Wales.' They walked along, almost back to Euston now. 'Still—'

'What?'

'I don't like the brother somehow.'

'He's a man.'

'There is that.' They walked on a few steps and he said, 'I don't like Geddys.' He looked aside at her. 'He lied to me.'

'How?'

'Saying he didn't know where she lived. Mrs Durnquess said he'd seen her home and was "interested" in her. You deal with Alf; I'll tackle Geddys again.'

Opposite the corner of Judd Street, she said, 'I'll leave you here.'

'Dinner?'

'Not tonight.'

'I feel like one of those knights in an old tale who's being set a test to prove himself.'

She shook her head. 'I'm the one being tested. You don't understand.' She walked away towards Euston station.

CHAPTER

8

He was at work again next morning by eight, hard at it still at three that afternoon, grateful for the eyeglasses that made hours of writing possible. He felt harried by the need to get the book out of his head and on paper—the more so because of Cosgrove's theft of the outline, as if irrationally he believed that Cosgrove might replicate it. Atkins, when he had first seen the glasses—Denton, of course, had forgotten he had them on—had blinked once and raised his thin eyebrows a fraction of an inch. Joker though he was, Atkins had a sense of tact. Later, when Denton, in pacing around his bedroom, passed the mirror, he saw the strange face, its huge nose topped by the spectacles that enlarged the eyes behind them. He looked like somebody on the stage. Somebody definitely comic.

At four, when his back hurt and his wrist was sore, Atkins appeared in the bedroom door.

'Mrs Striker's below with a box. Cab waiting at the door.'

Denton jumped up, struggled into a coat. When he turned to Atkins, the soldier-servant tapped between his own eyes. When Denton didn't get it, Atkins made circles around his eyes with thumbs and fingers.

'Oh—dammit—' He pulled the glasses off, threw them on the desk and started out of the door.

'Collar and tie, Colonel,' Atkins murmured from the stairs.

Why did it matter? Why did such trivialities matter? But he put on a collar and tie.

Of course.

She was standing at the far end of the long sitting room, wearing the same or another equally awful hat and a dark coat. At her feet was a small trunk. She smiled when she saw him. 'I've found Mary Thomason's trunk.'

He stared at her. 'How?'

She laughed. 'It's rather a tale.'

'Atkins—take her coat, Mrs Striker's coat— Want tea? Or coffee? There's sherry—' He had thought he would never get her here; now she was here under her own steam, and he didn't know how to behave.

'I have a cab waiting,' she said as she handed over her coat. She kept the hat on.

'Send it away. We can get another when—'

She shook her head. 'It's one thing for a woman to go to a man's house and leave the cab waiting in front. It's another for her to send it away. I don't give a damn, but you're a public sort of man.'

'You know I don't care about that—' he hesitated, finished lamely—'stuff.'

'Then you've lost whatever common sense you had. I'll stay twenty minutes, no more.' She glanced at Atkins. 'Tea, if you can have it here in ten.'

'At once, madam.'

Denton frowned, aware that Atkins was doing his perfect-servant turn, waved him away. He went closer to her. 'I'm having a hard time realizing you're really here.'

'Do you want to hear my story or don't you?'

'Have you opened it?'

'All in good time.' She sat in the chair across the small fireplace from his; he perched on the arm of his own. She said, 'Alf found me last evening. You remember Alf, the carter—St Pancras Road? Well, I'd written "To hear something to your advantage" on the card I left for him, and my address—'

'You never left *me* your address.'

'Perhaps I had nothing of advantage for you. At any rate, he turned up last evening. Alf lacks teeth and had been into gin somewhere, and he looked as if he might have been carrying sacks of coal—a sort of overall and a cap with a flap down the back—not awfully well washed, shorter than he ought to be, perhaps from bending. But agreeable in the way of men who say what they think you want to hear.

'So I asked him if he remembered picking up a box from a house in Fitzroy Street in August. He didn't, nor did he remember the brother, but he remembered Hannah well enough—mostly her scones—and then it came back to him. More or less. The long and the short of it was that if he sent the box off somewhere, he'd have a receipt for it. So back to St Pancras Road we went.'

'You didn't!'

'I did. What have I better to do? He lives there, under the railway arch. It was as filthy as you'd expect. I've seen worse. He keeps his receipts impaled on a nail driven in from the outside—several nails, actually—and he went through them pile by pile, as apparently there's no order to them—he smashes one on whatever nail he's near. He found it at last, by the date. The signature was illegible—presumably the brother's—intentionally so? But there it was, a receipt for one small trunk sent by rail to Biggleswade, "Hold until called for."'

'My God, you're a wonder!'

'It was getting on for dark by then. I stepped outside where I could see and asked him if he'd let me have the receipt for a few days. Alf was shocked at the very idea. Could I *rent* it for a few days? Alf said it would upset his record-keeping something fierce, not to mention morality, but two-and-six turned out to be the price of his record-keeping *and* his scruples. He was casting about for something else to sell me by then, but I had the receipt and I simply walked away to the telegraph office at St Pancras station, where I sent a telegram to the left-luggage office at Biggleswade to ask if the item number of the receipt had been picked up.' She grinned. 'They wired back this morning that it hadn't.'

Denton slid down into his armchair. 'Mary Thomason never got there.'

'The trunk hadn't been retrieved, at any rate. So this morning, I went and got it.'

He looked down at the trunk. It was shaped like a loaf of bread, perhaps two feet long, cheap wood partly covered with pressed tin and held together by oak slats. 'What's in it?'

'I stopped at a locksmith's on my way here and had it unlocked. But I haven't looked inside.'

He tried to smile at her, but the smile was crooked and unconvincing because he was thinking she could be in trouble if somebody eventually came looking for the trunk. There was, too, a hesitation about looking into somebody's privacy—more pointed, perhaps, because somebody had been looking into his. 'You're a wonder,' he said again.

Atkins came in with a tea tray, which he put on a folding cake stand that he produced from the shadows of the room like somebody doing a magic trick. He put it down near Janet Striker with a perfect-servant flourish, poured her a cup of tea, and then faded back down the long room, hardly pausing as he opened the doors of the dumb waiter before disappearing down his stairs.

Denton took a cup of tea, then put it aside and bent forward and pulled, using the trunk's hasp as a handle. Inside, a folded dress was visible, filling the interior, white with a narrow yellow line in the fabric, wrinkled bits of ruffle and lace showing; the fabric looked much washed. When he didn't move to take it out, Janet Striker lifted it in both hands and put it on the chair in which she'd been sitting, then thought better of it and shook the dress out, turning it so that it fell from her hands as if it were being worn. She held it against herself. 'Rather *jeune fille*. Appropriate, then. Summer dress, cotton, not awfully well made. She wasn't as tall as I.'

Smudges of something black marked part of the skirt. She held it up. 'Charcoal, don't you think? From drawing. Meaning she'd worn it and not laundered it. Or it didn't wash out.'

Under the dress were a couple of petticoats, a very plain nightgown with long sleeves, a small hat, also white, fairly new. 'Rather virginal,' Janet Striker said.

'Maybe her mother bought her her clothes for her.'

'I'd say they almost look too young for a woman going somewhere like the Slade. But who knows.' She pulled out three pairs of drawers, the sort that tied at the knee. Unembarrassed, she said, 'The new style, anyway.' She tossed them aside to reveal a brown cloak very worn around the bottom, also a pair of grubby wool mittens and a heavy cardigan, much ravelled at the cuffs and stretched and bagged all over. Janet fingered a few pairs of white stockings. Denton leaned over to see to the bottom—a single pair of shoes, very worn; a stack of handkerchiefs; a narrow box about six inches long; a pasteboard box that the shoes might have come in; and an imitation-leather folder so wide that it had had to be put in at an angle. Denton took the narrow box and pulled off the lid. 'Why does a young woman have something called "The Princess Depilatory"?'

'Women have hair, like men. Sometimes they want to get rid of it.'

He looked up at her. She was smiling. Underarms and legs, he supposed she meant; women were still so completely covered that, despite a tendency for skirts to creep up an inch or so, no hair was ever seen except on their heads. One famous writer was supposed to have abandoned his wife on their wedding night when he'd found she had pubic hair.

'Is it something she'd want with her?'

'She left in a hurry, didn't she?'

He lifted out the imitation-leather folder. It was made to hold prints or drawings, tied with a limp cotton ribbon. 'What's in the shoe box?'

She had it in her hands. 'Drawing pencils, India ink, charcoal—a soft eraser—pen nibs, some metal thing with a plunger, like a perfume atomizer—some reddish sticks of something, also white—'

The folder held about twenty sheets of what artists called 'cartridge paper', cheap stuff used for sketching. Most of the drawings were, he thought, classroom work: a clothed model, a still life of jugs and dishes, hands and noses and heads; a male nude, his privates hidden in a sort of sling; a piece of statuary. Three of the sheets were different—one a drawing of a house with rather formal shrubbery, one of a front door with urns and an upside-down cone that had once been used for extinguishing torches. The third was on different paper, heavier and textured, a drawing of a female head. Two much smaller drawings, one in ink over the original pencil lines, took up the two lower corners. The paper was wrinkled, as if it had been crushed and then smoothed out again.

'What are the little ones?'

'I don't know. Don't you see that on etchings sometimes, little scenes like that?'

He wished he had his new glasses. What he could make out was some sort of arched stonework on the left side and a male head on the other. 'What's he doing?'

'Screaming? Shouting? Not enjoying himself, certainly.' She was standing next to his chair now. He was acutely aware of her, a smell of soap. She reached across him and took the drawing to turn it over. On the back had been written in pencil, now smudged, 'Mary 3 aug 01.' Janet said almost eagerly, 'It has to be her!'

'Lot of Marys out there. Self-portrait?'

'The style's very different from the other stuff. Somebody else drew it, I think. Denton, it has to be her.'

They wrangled over it. Finally Denton put the drawing back in the trunk and said, 'Is that everything?'

'There's a sketchbook.' She leafed through it. 'More Slade stuff, I expect. Half of it still unused.'

'I think it's a self-portrait. She didn't have much money for models. Look at the clothes. One dress.'

'And one she wore when she went away. Two dresses—wealth, to some people.'

'Starving artist?'

Janet picked up the drawing, studied it and put it down again. 'She, or whoever did it, must have thought better of it—balled it up and then tried to smooth it out.'

'Didn't like it, maybe, but couldn't part with it. Because it was her own face? Or because somebody else did the drawing and she valued the person?' He picked it up again. The face was pretty, young, the hair almost unkempt, rather shaggy over the forehead and down the sides of the face. 'Is the hair "Bohemian"?'

'I don't meet many artists in my line of work.' She moved away from him. 'I have to go.'

'I know you got the box for me, but—It wasn't wise. There could be trouble if anybody ever comes looking for it. Promise me you'll never do such a thing again.'

She was putting on her coat. She turned her head and looked at him. He knew instantly that he'd said the wrong thing. She said, her voice low, 'Don't ever tell me what I should and should not do. And don't tell me what's "unwise".' She had her hand on the doorknob. 'I shall take it back late on Monday and say it's the wrong trunk.'

He had moved to her. 'Stay,' he said. 'I'm sorry—'

She shook her head. Going down the stairs, she said, 'Please get a photo of that drawing made on Monday, and perhaps I can show it at the Slade. I'm going on half days at the Society now—dwindling down to the end like a candle.' He told her he wanted to talk more to her, but she had rattled him and he babbled. She, on the other hand, was calm, seemed to have forgotten her flare-up.

Atkins was already standing by the lower door. Denton said, 'I'll see Mrs Striker into the cab.'

When she was inside the hansom, he held it by putting his hands on it and leaning in. 'Janet, I want to *see* you.' He waited for some response, got only her steady eyes and then a turn away. He backed to the pavement and called up 'Drive on!' to the man behind.

Denton lingered in the cold lower hall, angry with himself. He stared at his dreadful Scottish paintings. *Fool, you damned fool, you treated her like a woman!* Atkins was in the sitting room when he went up, collecting the tea things; he must have been doing so for several minutes—rather a long time for two cups—so as to talk.

Knowing what was expected, Denton said, 'Well?'

'Resourceful lady.'

'I meant the trunk.'

'Well, the brother did his part, else the box wouldn't of got to Biggleswade.'

'Biggleswade's north. The girl told her landlady she was from the west.'

'Girls lie.' He made a face. *Like Katya,* he meant.

'Granted, but why? She has her studies; she has a room; she writes me a note but doesn't send it; then she leaves London. That all makes sense, more or less. Her brother collects her things; all right, that's sensible. Then the trunk goes north instead of west and she never collects it.'

'She's dead. I mean, that's what's likely, let's be honest. Somebody done her the harm she feared. Not a cheerful thought, but a sensible one.' Atkins grinned. 'Maybe Albert Cosgrove did her in.'

'Oh, shut up.'

He woke during the night feeling at first feverish and heavy, then anxious. The bedcovers were like lead, and he pushed them back, then used his drawn-up legs to shoot them to the foot. It had got warm. He pulled off his nightshirt and lay there naked, feeling the air on his hot skin.

A dream had made him anxious. Worse than anxious—near panic. He knew the dream. Back in the house he'd built in Iowa. Seeing his wife through the window, walking towards the pasture. The horrifying sense of the inevitable, the terrible. But the dream hadn't gone on to his finding her body as it usually did, the lye jug beside her. That was the way it always ended, but not tonight. Tonight's had ended with seeing her through the window, as if seeing her that way was seeing it all, suffering it all, leaving him to wake with the anxiety of knowing what was to come and not being able to stop it.

He got up and walked to the window. The dream wasn't all of it. It was also that damned man, whoever he was, Albert Cosgrove, who had written him the letters, broken into the house behind, broken into even his own house.

With more coming—that was the sense of the dream: *There's more to come.*

He saw his own reflection in the glass, a double laid over the dim bulk of the house behind. There was a man out there who wanted to be his double—to *be* him. That was it. Circling, watching, stealing bits of him, trying to become him.

Denton shuddered.

He knew what it was to concentrate on someone else so fiercely that the mind seemed to detach itself and fix. But his 'someone elses' were inventions—the characters in the unfinished novel. He knew that he partly lived in it. He carried on conversations in his head, saw faces, rooms, vistas. But he knew that that world was not real. And this novel was about his own marriage, his dead wife, their harrowing of each other, so it was that much more like inhabiting a second self. But he was—he smiled in the darkness—*sane.* The man who wanted to be him, he was sure now, was not. Denton himself was Albert Cosgrove's novel, or at least the central character in the novel Cosgrove apparently couldn't write, couldn't create, and so Cosgrove's concentration went into imitating—*stealing him.*

And it would get worse. And when it didn't succeed, because it couldn't, would Cosgrove do what Denton had done with a book that went wrong—turn on it and destroy it?

He pulled the nightgown over his head and pushed his arms into the sleeves of a robe. He lit the gas and sat at his desk and tried to write.

He slept a few hours in the early morning, woke and went back to his desk. The mood of the night, somewhat dissipated in daylight, faded as he bored in on his work.

Atkins, who was going to church (Denton was surprised to find it was Sunday) and apparently thought Denton should, too, made disapproving noises with dishes and clothes hangers.

'Stop that racket.'

'Being as quiet as I can.'

'You're making noise fit to raise the dead. If you've something to say, say it!'

Atkins lifted Denton's empty plate to the tray with the care of somebody taking an egg from a nest. 'My grandmother banged the pans about when she was crossed,' he said.

'What's that supposed to mean—you come by noise-making honestly? Go to church!'

'It isn't church, it's chapel.'

Denton looked at him over the tops of his new eyeglasses. 'Katya went to *church*.'

'I've moved beyond Katya. I don't want to hear about her.'

'Give my regards to the saints.'

Before Atkins could do so, Denton heard a knock at the front door; a minute later, Atkins was beside him again.

'You know anything about a Son of Abraham's on our door-step saying he's come to dig up the garden?'

Thinking of his work, Denton stared at him. 'No. Don't bother me. Wait—yes. Mrs Striker said something about—Hell, she gave me a name.'

'Cohan. Sounds Irish to me, but he looks about as Irish as the Levite that crossed over the road. Right, he mentioned Mrs Striker's name.'

'Why didn't you tell me that?'

'Thought I'd get right to the point. You want him to dig up the garden, or not?'

'Yes, yes, put him to work. Have we got a spade?'

'Probably. We had good intentions back there, once.' Atkins put on a pious face. 'You sure you want him working on the Lord's Day?'

'If he's a Jew, that was yesterday. Go away!'

Denton worked until noon and could do no more. The penalty for having worked part of the night. Atkins, by his own choice, had Sunday off until late evening. Denton found a couple of eggs, scrambled them on the gas ring in the alcove off his sitting room: part pantry, part kitchen. A year before, somebody had waited in there to kill him. He wondered if Albert Cosgrove had been in there, too, handled the cutlery, opened the cupboard, inhaled the air.

Denton prowled his house, restless now. He tried to read and found nothing interesting. He thought he would go out, but where? Not to find Janet Striker, certainly; he didn't know where she lived, and she wouldn't be in her office today. Munro wouldn't be at New Scotland Yard. He looked out of the rear window, saw a dark-haired man, foreshortened, digging up the weeds. He went at them as if they were his worst enemies. Denton went down and introduced himself.

'All one to me. I got lots of this muck to keep me busy.' He was overweight, shorter than Denton but broad, with shoulders and arms that filled his threadbare coat like a sausage its skin. He wore a cloth cap, filthy rat-catchers; his nose was mashed to his face, his ears battered. Small eyes glared at Denton as if the world were a perpetual challenge.

Denton said, 'You're a prizefighter.'

'I was, and proud of it! Never knocked off my feet I wasn't. I may not have won every time the bell rang, but nobody ever knocked me down. Just you ask! Ask them wot the Stepney Jew-Boy did.' He had a definite accent.

Denton flinched. 'Jew-Boy?'

'Jew-Boy. When I started fightink, they'd shout "Jew-Boy" at me to insult me, they did. I thought, I'll give you Jew-Boy, I will, so I called myself Jew-Boy and beat the livink tar out of the first six gentiles I fought. Then I was the Stepney Jew-Boy for good.'

Denton studied him. 'What's a prizefighter want to spade up a back garden for?'

'Am I still a prizefighter? Do I look twenty again? Or do I look canny enough to've got out with my brains intact when I was thirty-five? How old you think I am?'

'Forty.'

'And four. How many prizefighters you think are still at it at forty-four without they're hearink bells nobody else can hear? Judas Cripes, give me some credit for intelligence, please do. I'm forty-four and I ain't fought in nine years and I got no job! That's why I'm diggink up your back bloody garden!'

Denton asked what he was to pay him, and he said he and Mrs Striker had settled on three shillings a day, for which she'd paid two days in advance because he'd been 'caught short' when he talked to her.

'So you'll be back in the morning.'

'You think I'd take money for work I wasn't goink to do? Yas, I'll be here in the mornink. And I don't steal and I don't lie and I didn't kill Christ. Good day to youse.'

The day yawned ahead of him—a Sunday, little doing. He decided to go out, if only to walk himself into exhaustion.

The air beyond his front door was cool, clear—he thought that if he could have got up high, he could have seen all the way down the Thames to the North Sea—with a sky the clear blue of a bottle with the sun behind it. The light was glaring, but even so the day was too cool for sitting about, perfect for walking. Stopping often to look back for Albert Cosgrove, he walked, first to Holborn and Chancery Lane, then along Fleet Street and Cannon Street, turning west again along the river at Billingsgate Market, now only residual fish smell and gulls and a great many cats, and a memory of the days when the fishwives had been there and 'Billingsgate' was a term for creative insult. He picked his way through small, silent streets to Soho, turned along Old Compton Street and, on an impulse, having nowhere to go, found his way again to the Albany, where he lingered at the entrance before going in and walking slowly to the door of Heseltine, the man who had found Mary Thomason's letter. If he objected to be called on on a Sunday, he could always turn him away.

He offered his card to the bottle-nosed man who opened the door.

'Mr Heseltine isn't well, sir.'

'Oh—I'll call again—'

'It might—Let me ask him, sir. It might do him good.'

The man was Denton's age, grave, rather like a doctor who always had bad news. When he came back, he said, 'Mr Heseltine asks if you'd forgive him not dressing.'

'Of course.'

'He hasn't been well.'

'I understand.'

Closer to, the man gave off a mixed odour of bad teeth and sherry. He kept his sombre bedside manner, however; Denton supposed it was the main reason for employing him.

'Mr Denton.'

Heseltine was wearing a dressing gown and slippers, as if he'd just got out of bed.

'I'm sorry you've been ill.'

'Not ill. Just out of—' Heseltine tried to smile, shrugged.

The man came in with a tray of glasses and a decanter and a plate of mostly broken biscuits—Atkins would have fed them to the dog. There was a slight rattle of glassware as the tray was put down, something like a hiccup, perhaps a grunt. 'Sherry, sir?'

'I'll take care of it, Jenks.'

The man turned slowly and made his way out. Denton realized now that Jenks was thoroughly boiled. So, apparently, did Heseltine. 'Jenks drinks anything that doesn't have the cork cemented into the bottle. He's quite incorrigible. I should let him go, but I'd have to find somebody else, and I just don't have the go.'

'Better than no man at all?'

'In the morning, yes. After noon, no. But I—What do I care, really? If I had the taste for it, I'd spend my days like him.'

'I only came to tell you about Mary Thomason—the woman whose note you sent on to me. I won't stay.'

'Oh, do! I don't have many visitors.' The wry semi-smile again. 'What about the Thomason girl?'

Denton told him what had happened, ending with the fact that the trunk had never been collected; he didn't say that he had it and had been through it.

'So something terrible has happened to her.' Heseltine looked as if he might burst into tears.

'It's nothing to do with you. It was all over, probably, before you ever found the note.'

'Yes.' Heseltine was looking at his full glass of sherry, which seemed to puzzle him. 'I saw your name in *The Times*,

Mr Denton. At least I supposed it was you. About somebody assaulted behind your house?'

'I didn't know it had been in the papers. Yes. Kind of a strange tale. Somebody seems to have been watching me.'

'Why?'

'I wish I knew. Or, I think I know, but I wish I understood.' He told him in a few sentences about Albert Cosgrove, the letters, the man with the red moustache.

'And he was in that house, writing some sort of thing that used your words?'

'One of my paragraphs, anyway. "Imitation is the sincerest form of flattery." But I don't feel flattered.'

'Soiled, rather, I should think. And he wanted all your books.'

'Signed copies.'

'Does an author sign many copies?'

'To friends, sometimes. I'm not much for sending them to people to impress them.'

'They'd be rather rare then, wouldn't they? Maybe he's tried to find them at the rare-book shops. You might try there to see.'

Denton grinned and got up. 'I've promised the police I won't go poking my nose into their business any more.' He held out his hand. 'I don't think "Good luck" is what I should say, but I hope things work out.'

'Oh, they'll work out, I'm sure!' Heseltine's laugh suggested a state near the edge.

Denton got his coat and hat and said he could let himself out. He said from the door, 'You've got a lawyer and all that?'

'Counsel? Oh, yes. They provide that. Plus my father's hired somebody to advise the military man.' He smiled. 'It will be done with full legal pomp.'

'It may not be as bad as you think.'

'I think they mean to parade me in front of the regiment with my buttons torn off. Did they do that in the American army?'

'War makes people bloodthirsty. You'd think it would do the opposite.'

'Only to those of us who are "sensitive, snivelling women".
My CO's words.'

Denton stood in the cold sunshine at the entrance to Albany
Court. He knew the machinery of military law, its grinding-up of
anybody who seemed weak. War likes blockheads, he thought—
those too stubborn to turn aside. It dislikes nuance, hesitation,
compassion.

Insofar as he was capable of feeling pity, he felt it for
Heseltine. He also felt anger and the decisive man's contempt
for the half-hearted. The military, as he had seen too well, could
always find a desk for incompetence, but it drove weakness from
the room: it feared that weakness was catching. Heseltine, he
thought, was both incompetent and weak. The system was going
to grind him into cat's meat.

There was a light under Atkins's downstairs door when Denton
let himself in that evening. The soldier-servant would be reading
the newspaper, he supposed, or possibly his Bible if his enthusiasm
still ran to it. The truth was, he had almost no idea of Atkins's
private life, his sex life least of all. Atkins treated a nearby pub
as a club, had what seemed a considerable popularity among
the nearby housemaids. The social system, however, was rigged
against them, Denton knew: occasions were few, privacy almost
impossible, the women's fear of losing a place extreme. Atkins,
he guessed, did what soldiers—Denton included—did: found a
whorehouse, perhaps the cheap one near Pentonville Road.

Settling in his chair, Denton mused on the difference
between Atkins and Heseltine. How easily Atkins would have
dealt with whatever mistake Heseltine had made—called in
favours from the sergeants and the sergeant major, half-black-
mailed his officer (about whom he'd always have known juicy
bits), got the company orderly to mislay whatever paperwork
implicated him. Heseltine, on the other hand, probably hadn't so
much as objected.

Denton read one of his psychological books about obsession and impersonation. None of it seemed to apply to Albert Cosgrove. About ten, Atkins put his head in and asked if he wanted a carob drink—an affectation he'd picked up in India.

'I'm having a whisky.'

'Oh well, carob isn't in it, then.' He started away.

'How was chapel?'

'Rum—absolutely rum. Saddest place I ever was. People with grey faces and no smiles singing about hope and heaven in the hereafter. I think I'll concentrate on my secular interests for a bit.'

'How did the pugilist do in the garden?'

'Demon worker. Strong as an ox. Did you know he's descended from Moses's brother? Says he is, at any rate—you can never tell if people are pulling the wool. Brings the Book of Exodus alive, I must say.'

'He calls himself the Stepney Jew-Boy.'

'Told me that—in a voice that made me think I'd better not use the term meself.'

'Wise. Is his first name Aaron, then?'

'Hyam, last name Cohan. Peculiar names they have.'

'Did you ask him what he thought of the name Atkins?' Denton turned around in the chair to look down the room. 'Can you take something to be photographed tomorrow? There's that place on Oxford Street—'

'Barraud's.'

'That's the one.' He rummaged in Mary Thomason's trunk and took out the drawing of the female head with the little sketches in the corners. 'I want a good copy of the head—size of a sheet of writing paper or thereabouts is all right—and then photos of the little drawings in the corners. Oversized, if they can do them. And one full-size of the whole thing.'

Atkins had come down the room and was leaning over him. 'I thought we agreed she's dead.'

'"We" speculated she was *probably* dead. I'm not ready to go that far. I want a picture I can show around.'

'You don't even know it's her."

'That's what I'll find out.'

'Why?'

Denton looked at him, amused and annoyed. 'Because like you I'm nosy.'

'Oh, well—if you're going to take that line—' Atkins picked up the drawing. 'One face-only, one each the little squiggles in the corners, one the lot.'

'Fastest service. The drawing has to be back by noon in case Mrs Striker comes for the trunk.' Atkins looked blank. 'She's going to take it back where she got it.'

'I'd pitch it in the Grand Union canal.' Atkins moved off, grumbling to himself. Rupert, his stump of tail going like a metronome set on Presto, followed.

❀ ❀ ❀

Denton wanted to take a day away from all of it—the novel, Albert Cosgrove, Mary Thomason, even Janet Striker—and he had a fleeting notion of going to Hammersmith and rowing on the river, then a cut off the joint or something even rougher at the Dove. He didn't do it, of course, but pushed himself to his desk before eight the next day and made himself write. His brain didn't want to work—it, too, wanted to be on the river, being washed clean—but he bullied it and began to put words down on the paper as if he were trying to gouge them into it. He wasn't well into it until ten, and then things started to flow, and he heard the bell pulled by the front door. He muttered a curse, got up and closed his own door, and minutes later was interrupted by a knock.

'No!'

Another knock.

Denton wrenched the door open. 'What now?'

'Policeman below name of Markson. Wants to talk to you.'

'Oh—! Damn him and damn Albert Cosgrove!'

He heard Atkins mutter, 'For all the good it does,' and he made himself more or less presentable and went down. Markson, whom he had last seen after the scuffle in the house behind, was standing by the sitting-room door, a bowler in one hand and a black box tucked under the same arm, looking straight down at Rupert, who had his chin planted in the detective's crotch. Denton took that in, but what he was focused on was Mary Thomason's trunk, which was about three feet from Markson's left leg.

'I see that Rupert's found you. You've been told he's friendly?'

'Telling me so himself, isn't he?'

Atkins was behind Denton now, over by the fireplace. Denton looked towards him, made a face and rolled his eyes towards the trunk before saying to the detective, 'Ah, I'm working, you know.'

'Yes, sir, but so are most people. No good time to talk to the Metropolitan Police, is what it comes down to.'

'Is this about Cosgrove? Why are you coming to talk to me *now*? All that happened last week!'

'Yes, sir. It won't surprise you to hear that the police have been busy, too, I'm sure.'

While this had gone on, Atkins, with one smooth movement, had picked up a travelling rug from the chair opposite Denton's and draped it over Mary Thomason's trunk, then brushed the chair seat as if that was what he had meant to do all along, and thrown nonexistent dirt into the coals. 'Beg pardon, sir,' he said now in a voice that made both men look at him. Atkins had put on a stern expression. 'You expressly wanted the sweep in this morning while you wasn't in this room. If I may, I recommend you repair to your study so as not to suffer the discomfort of the chimney.'

'Oh—ah—yes, I'd forgotten. Detective Markson—if you don't mind—upstairs—?'

Markson murmured apologies for upsetting the whole house, but by the time he'd finished they were on their way up to the next floor. Denton's bedroom-study looked sufficiently workmanlike, Denton thought—Atkins had long since made the bed and hung up the clothes—and he pulled out a chair for Markson as he sat at his desk. 'As you see—I was working—'

'I'll make this quick, sir. Only two things, really. First, a question or two.' His questions were the ones Denton had already answered—why he'd gone into the house behind, was there any possibility that 'the man Cosgrove's' letters were still about somewhere. Had he received any more letters from the man Cosgrove? When they were done with those, Markson opened the black box and held up the manuscript that Albert Cosgrove had left in the other house.

'You've seen this, sir?'

'Some of it.'

'Which you allege is lifted from a book of your own, is it?'

'I thought so.'

'Which one?'

'It's the opening paragraph of *The Demon of the Plains*. Then I thought there was some from my outline for the book I'm trying to finish.'

'Left in this house while you were away, sir?'

'In a drawer of this desk.' He pulled open the drawer as if to prove that, there being a drawer there, it must be where the outline had been left.

Markson sniffed. Munro had said Markson was capable; Denton would take his word for it. The questions seemed to him repetitive and obvious, but Markson was perhaps the dogged kind who dotted every i. Now, he said, 'We'd like to have your reading of this manuscript, Mr Denton.' Before Denton could say anything, he went on, 'Literary criticism isn't common at New Scotland Yard. We'd like to know what you see in it—if there's anything more of your own, for one thing. And what you find in it—what sort of mind this chap has, what he thinks he's doing.'

'Detective, I'm trying to finish a book!'

'And we're trying to catch a criminal that attacked you, sir.'

'He didn't hurt me.'

'Also broke into the house over there and, it looks like, broke into this house as well. Anything else missing, by the way?'

Denton stared at the desk. 'I think a pen.' It sounded absurd. He'd noticed only that morning that a pen he sometimes used wasn't there.

'Yes, sir. That sounds right. Anything else? How about clothing?' He raised his eyebrows. 'Underclothing?' The question surprised Denton, suggested a sophistication he hadn't expected in Markson.

'You'd have to ask Atkins. I don't keep track.'

'Yes, sir. You'll read the manuscript?'

'Oh—if I have to—' He reached for it.

'At New Scotland Yard, I'm afraid, sir. Evidence. I had to sign for it, myself. This afternoon?'

Denton allowed himself the luxury, later to be the cause of self-flagellation, of blowing up. It had no effect. One of the qualities Munro may have been thinking of when he'd said that Markson was capable was a calm stubbornness. When Denton's tantrum was over, Markson said, 'Yes, sir. What time would be best for you?'

Denton had another, lesser eruption. When he had subsided, he was aware of voices downstairs, then that one was a woman's, which he sorted out as Janet Striker's. He was out of the chair and down the stairs in seconds. She was standing at the far end of the room with Atkins and the dog. The trunk, which he'd feared Atkins would already have uncovered again, wasn't there.

'I've just come for the—' she began.

'Detective!' Denton shouted. 'I'm with a detective from the Metropolitan Police. Uuuhhh—' He was aware of Markson's coming up behind him.

Janet Striker smiled and held out her hand. 'How nice to see you again, Mr Denton. I've just come for the donation you promised us.'

'Aaahh—' He was shaking her hand. 'This is Mrs Striker of the Society for the Improvement of Wayward Women. Um— Detective Markson.'

Then Denton said he'd write a cheque; she said that would be very fine of him; Atkins took the dog away; and Markson said he would go. 'Three o'clock today, sir?'

'Oh, if I have to. Yes, all right—all right—'

Markson went down the stairs quickly, seeming light on his feet. Moments later, Denton heard Atkins close the front door on him.

Janet Striker was giggling. He'd never heard her giggle before; it was a minor revelation. He said, 'I was afraid you'd mention the damned trunk.'

'I know!' She went off into laughter again, this time more boisterously. He thought perhaps he was seeing some sort of metamorphosis in her, the result of leaving the Society—maybe of leaving an entire way of life. 'Is he gone?'

Denton looked out, didn't see Markson, glanced up and down out of habit for Albert Cosgrove. 'You brought a cab.'

'I'm not about to carry the trunk to Euston station on my shoulder. Well!' She laughed again. 'That was fun.'

'I have to go to New Scotland Yard at three to read that damned lunatic's scribbles.'

'I'll be on my way back from Biggleswade by then. Did you get the drawing photographed?'

'Atkins did, I hope.' He turned to bellow for Atkins, found him standing ten feet away with the trunk in his arms.

'Of course I did,' Atkins said. 'Prints ready tomorrow.'

'Where's the drawing?'

'In the trunk.'

She interrupted, 'We found it under most of the other things.'

'I put it towards the bottom, with the sketchbook, madam.'

'You're a pearl of great price.'

Atkins smiled the gracious smile of royalty receiving tribute. 'I'll just put it in the cab.'

When he was gone, Denton said, 'I'm losing my mind, between the book and these interruptions.'

'No you're not. You're the sanest man I've ever known— also the best. There! You see what comes out when I'm contented.'

'So I'm forgiven? Will you have dinner with me?'

'Can't—I'm having dinner with my solicitor. It's all about money, mostly about when I get some from the lawsuit. I'm as poor as a church mouse, Denton—getting that money is important to me. What did Geddys say?'

'Geddys. Geddys? Oh, dammit—I forgot—' It seemed weeks ago that he'd said he'd talk to Geddys again about the man's apparent lie about knowing where Mary Thomason lived.

'No harm done. I'm off, then.'

'Tomorrow?'

'Yes, tomorrow, absolutely tomorrow.'

'Kettner's again?' They were going down the stairs. Atkins, coming in, held the door for her. They made their arrangements and then she was gone. Denton went back to work.

Albert Cosgrove's manuscript was a painful, sometimes bewildering thing to read. There was a story—or there had started out to be one—that had been infected by Denton's outline, which the writer had apparently tried to blend with his own tale. The result was like a crossing of radically different strains, producing a monstrosity.

Or perhaps it would have been a monstrosity anyway. Denton guessed that Cosgrove wasn't able to concentrate. This seemed contradictory in somebody obsessed, but the obsession, he thought, was not quite the same as what he was writing: that is, the story—novel, novella, whatever it was meant to be—was about obsession but it was not the object of obsession.

In the story with which Cosgrove had started, a young violinist who wants to know the 'secret' of greatness steals a violin bow. It belongs to a famous violinist who becomes a menace—never explained or defined—that looms over the young man. The bow does make him 'great' but it comes at a cost—a demon, who appears each time he plays. The demon takes a payment each time—first, the ability to sleep; then boils that appear on the violinist's face; then the use of a foot. However, by that point (which, for Denton, happened far too soon—Cosgrove was having the non-writer's problem 'making it long enough') Denton's outline had been forced in, and a wife appeared, domestic scenes that had no connection to anything else were added, attempts at Denton's sort of realistic detail were tacked on. Then the demon announced that he wanted the wife for himself, and then a page—the last—seemed to suggest that the demon and the 'great' violinist from whom the bow had been stolen were the same, or somehow connected, or at least in communication.

The prose was bad. Too many words, Denton would have said, too many long words, too much pretentious pseudo-philosophy. Some of it reminded him of Wagner, whom he despised. When Munro put his head in—Denton was reading, as promised, at New Scotland Yard—Denton groaned.

'Not delighting you, is it?' Munro limped in. 'Getting anything?'

Denton held up a list he had jotted down. Munro took it, raised it towards the gas, tipped his head back. '"Intelligent, incoherent, educated—Latin, Greek? reads books—knows mine well, also Shakespeare, poets; young—doesn't know real life; never poor, never hungry, never married." Sounds like most of the lads at our great universities.'

'I think he's unbalanced.'

'I could have told you that without reading his slop.'

'You've read it?'

'Tried. That's why we called on you.'

'I think he's trying to make a fable about himself and Art with a capital A—something about having ability but not making it because of some older fellow who's in the way, the older one being there through magic. Except the magic is also the Art—he's pretty confused. The idea might make it as a kind of horror tale—my editor's speciality—but Cosgrove can't do it. He wants to be a great writer—or thinks he wants to be—but people like me use our magic to keep him unknown. Does that make sense?'

'He might try some honest work.'

'He doesn't know what work is.'

'Well off?'

'There's a sinister female who wanders through it. I think she represents something, but I'm damned if I know what it is.

But she's always "richly dressed" and "glittering with jewels". He hates her, but there's no reason why.'

'So you're Harlequin, with the magic wand.'

'Violin bow, in his case—not so far off.'

'So, he's spying on you to find your magic wand.'

'He may have stolen a pen, in fact. Sort of like a wand.' Denton stood and stretched. 'He doesn't really believe all that, at least not yet. I mean, he's writing a tale he knows—has to know—is fantasy. So he's sane, in that sense. But doing the other things he's done—spying on me, following me, breaking into houses—they aren't sane.'

'We've an entire category of criminals who do nothing but break into houses.'

'But they're after things of value. Things they can sell for money. They're sane—criminal but sane. We understand the motive—it's the basis of society and the Empire, right? Make money. But not Albert Cosgrove.'

Munro put the paper in a pocket. 'You done, then?'

'Hell will be having to read that thing again.'

'I'll have your list copied, give it to Markson.'

'It won't help.'

'What would help is an arrest. He hasn't followed you, I take it.'

'Ask your people. I see them behind me all the time. Call them off, will you? I'm sick of having somebody always looking over my shoulder.'

Munro laughed. 'They were walked off their feet yesterday. One of them told Markson he was going to take up a collection to pay you to take a cab—hadn't walked so much since he was a constable. I'll talk to Markson about pulling them off—may be too soon yet.'

They trudged up the long corridor that led past the CID offices. At the stairs, Munro asked again if he'd reported 'that missing girl'. When Denton admitted he hadn't, but it was a dead issue, anyway, Munro walked him back to the corridor where Denton had had the unsatisfactory conversation with Guillam, what seemed like years ago. Munro pointed at a door. 'You want that one. Take you three minutes.'

'You said to stay away from Guillam.'

'Yes, but best to do things by the book.' Munro walked away.

Inside the office was a young man with spots, wearing a thick wool suit that had belonged to somebody else ten years before. He looked up with what first seemed to be fright, then a stern expression that was ridiculous on his soft face—practising to be a bureaucrat, Denton thought. He explained what he wanted; the young man threw several imagined obstacles in his way; Denton got over them; the young man sighed and took out a form and a pen.

'Name? That the given name or the family name? Given name? Wot d'you mean, you don't use your given name? Address?'

They got as far as 'relationship to the MP'. When Denton said there was no relationship and he hadn't even known the young woman, the clerk looked around the little office as if help might be there somewhere, then bolted through the door. Munro's three minutes became fifteen, and then the door opened again and Guillam came in. The clerk lingered behind with a look of 'now you're for it' on his face.

Guillam said, 'Oh. It's you. What's this, then?'

'I'm reporting a missing person.'

Guillam looked at the form, on which of course he must already have read Denton's name. 'No relation? Not even a friend?'

Denton stayed dead calm and explained about the letter.

'We're the police. We have serious work to do. We don't have time for you spinning tales out of nothing.'

'Munro told me this is the right thing to do.'

'Oh, it's Donnie Munro, is it. I should have known. He cuts no ice here. This is my bailiwick.' He handed the form to the clerk. 'Finish it and file it with a note, "awaiting more information".' Guillam's brutal face was red, perhaps only from bending to talk to the seated Denton. He said, 'Don't bother us with a lot of questions about it,' and he slammed out.

The clerk went quickly through the rest of the form, almost sneering now, and said, as if he were dismissing a pensioner, 'That'll be all.'

'I can go?'

'Yes, you can go.'

'You're sure?'

'What?'

'I want you to be sure.'

'What's that?'

'If you aren't sure, I'd feel better staying here until you are.'

'If you're having me on, I'll make trouble!'

'So long as you're sure.'

The clerk stared at him. The bureaucrat and the little boy in him struggled. Finally he said in an unsure voice, 'I'm sure, then.'

'Good. Then I'll go.' Denton went out.

On his way home, he stopped to talk to Geddys. Only a woman was there. She told him Mr Geddys had gone away on a buying trip and would be back in two weeks.

At home, Atkins greeted him with a dour face and 'You've a letter. From *him*.'

Denton groaned.

He teased the paper out of its envelope with his pocket-knife and opened it without touching anything but the edges. It said:

You have disappointed me most terribly, and just when we were approaching an understanding. I read in the press that you were in the confederacy against me with the police, I cant comprehend how this can be as we share our profound feeling for Art. Now I must ask you to return what of mine has been stolen, I mean my BOOK, which is not now in the place where I had secured it. I will not stoop to believing that you are using my work on which to model something of your own, much less purloin some

of my actual words, but only the return of my MS will
assure me that all is well between us and you mean no
theft. DO NOT TEST MY RESPECT FOR YOU. I am
heartbroken and abject that you have chosen to treat me
in this way.
Yours in sorrow.
Albert Cosgrove

'Rather got the shoe on the wrong foot, hasn't he,' Atkins
said. He had been reading over Denton's shoulder.

'He's turning.'

'Turning what?'

'From adoration to dislike. You see it in hero-worship.
What's constant is the lack of balance.'

'Loony, as I've said a hundred times now.'

'This'll have to go to the police.' He laughed, a single bark
that remained humourless. 'I asked Munro to pull the followers
off me. Just in time.' He looked at the letter again. '"I must ask
you to return what of mine has been stolen, I mean my BOOK—"
He didn't read about *that* in the newspaper. The bastard's been
back in that house!'

'I thought the coppers were watching it.'

'One posted in the front. How difficult would it be to get
into that garden from Lamb's Conduit Street—come along our
passage and through our garden, for that matter?'

'Rupert'd have heard him.'

Denton looked at the letter again. 'Check over the garden first
thing in the morning. He's not above leaving something poisoned
for the dog, just out of spite—or he won't be in a little while.'

CHAPTER

10

'You think he's getting worse?' Janet Striker said. They were gathering themselves together to leave their table at Kettner's after a long meal full of talk and an increasing mutual understanding. She liked to eat, he found; her affection for the ABC shops was, it appeared, entirely economic. 'I've been living on twenty-six shillings a week for the last ten years,' she had said at one point, 'and fed and clothed my mother on it, as well.' Without bitterness, she had added, 'The drink, she bought herself.' When he had asked how her mother was, she had said, 'She's dying. I want to get her into a better place before she does—it's another reason I want my money so soon. Poor old bitch.'

He was counting out money to pay the bill. 'I knew a man in a prison camp who started acting like a guard.' He looked up at her to see how she would take it. 'I was the officer in charge of the guards. This fellow started pushing other prisoners into line at meal time. He wound up killing one of them with a club he'd made from a broken branch.'

'I didn't know you'd been at a prison in the war.'

'It was after the war. Right after. Only for a couple of months. But long enough.' He got up. 'Shall we?'

The rain was coming down on the streets in a steady fall, more than drizzle but less than a downpour, umbrellas hurrying through Soho with legs scissoring under them. Denton started to say 'I'll put you in a cab,' but amended it to 'Do you want a cab?'

She said, 'I'd like to go to your house for a bit, if I may.' She smiled. 'I like your house.'

'But—'

'What I said the other day, I know. It's dark and it's raining, so nobody will see me—how is that?'

'"Consistency is the hobgoblin of little minds." An American said that.'

With the horse clip-clopping along, they were both silent for the first several streets. Then, as if the darkness allowed her to say certain things, she began to talk about her life in the 'hospital' for the criminally insane. Her husband had put her there to crush her, but none of her hatred of him showed. She simply told him about other women she'd known. The 'mad', the despairing. She had a point to make. 'Lunacy isn't always what we're told it is. Lunacy depends on who gets to define it.' By then, the cab had pulled up in front of his house. She said, 'I'm not through. Have him wait.'

They ran to the front door; inside, he shook his hat and then his overcoat; she was shaking out the ugly cape-like thing she had had on over her unbecoming dress. Atkins appeared, said 'Good evening, madam,' as if he had known her for years, and took their things.

'I shall want my coat shortly,' she said. 'Just leave it out here.'

'Of course, madam.' He hung the cape on a monstrosity that combined mirror, hooks and seat.

Upstairs, she refused drink. She kept her hat on. He sat in his chair; she walked up and down, slowly and silently, beating the palm of her left hand on her upturned right fist. 'Do you know what I was talking about in the cab, Denton?'

'You think I should be careful when I say that Cosgrove is insane.'

'I want you to understand what it's like to be called insane—and to be *helpless*. To have "normal" people look at you with that *look*. To have them laugh at you. Because you're "insane".'

She put her right hand on his left shoulder from behind. He was staring into the coals, thinking about what she'd said; unconsciously, he put his left hand up and over hers. 'You feel sympathy for him,' he said.

'I feel sympathy for you.'

'You don't want me to be cruel.'

They were silent. He could feel the pulse of his own thumb where it rested against her hand, under it the heat of her skin. She said, 'Why do you live in England?'

He was silent for many seconds. 'I suppose I prefer to be an outsider.' He turned his head a little towards her. 'Like you.'

'I'm not one by choice. Or I wasn't to begin with, anyway.' She put her left hand on his and traced the big veins with her fingers. 'Did you really kill four men?' she said.

'Yes. Plus the one you saw last year.'

'Do you think about them?'

'I killed them because I wanted to. Or I chose to—I chose to be marshal in that little town. I chose to be there when he tried to hurt you. I don't have regrets, if that's what you mean. My regrets are that somebody has to make such choices.'

'Why do you mind Albert Cosgrove so much?'

'Because I hate being spied on! I hate—somebody pushing into my life. It isn't that I have something to hide—everybody has something to hide. It's that—it's like having a room where nobody is supposed to come, a place to retreat to. And that's where *I* am. Nobody else is supposed to go in there.'

'Then why can't you understand when I say the same thing to you?'

'I'm trying, Janet. It's as hard for me as I suppose it is for Albert Cosgrove.'

She let her hand rest on his for several seconds. She said, 'Would you like me to spend the night?'

He spun in the chair. 'You know I would.'

'Well—' She was pulling out the long pins that held her awful hat. 'You'd better pay off the cab, then.'

Waking, his dream stayed and could be captured: it was the house he had built in Iowa again, the environment of the bad dreams, but this was different, somehow radiant. He woke with a great feeling of contentment, almost triumph, perhaps triumph over the bad dreams of the past. He had been in that house, looking out of the window where he always saw her walking to her death, but this time she wasn't there. It was his pasture, but it was full of horses; he'd owned only one horse back then, and it had never been in the dream, but here was a field of horses that ran, a kind of joy in their trailing manes and kicked-up tails. He went out—always in these dreams he went out, down to the pasture gate, over the slight rise, and there she would be with the lye jug beside her. But he felt no dread this morning. He walked over the rise and the herd of horses pounded by him, and where she had lain there was only the bleached, clean skeleton of a horse. And he was so grateful.

'Janet?' he whispered.

She was there, her bare hip an astonishing presence under his hand. She moved but stayed asleep. Denton lay next to her, revelling in the dream. The surprise of it. Then he heard Atkins coming up from the basement level with the morning tray; he scrambled out of bed, pushed his feet into slippers, realized he was naked—usually, there'd have been a nightshirt—and grabbed a shirt and trousers. Closing the bedroom door behind him, he heard her stir.

He met Atkins halfway up the stairs. He said, 'Mrs Striker has spent the night.'

Atkins looked at him. He showed no expression. Handing Denton the tray, he said, 'You'll need another cup, then,' and turned and went down the stairs. When Denton went back to the bedroom, she was gone, sounds coming from the bath next door. He put the tray down, ran his furry tongue over his teeth, made a face. Pouring himself a cup of tea, he went down the hall to the extra room and hid there until she came out, then went into the bath and made himself more or less presentable. When he went back into the bedroom, she was standing at the window with a cup of tea, wearing an almost floor-length dressing gown of his over her long body. She said, 'This is the first time I've done this with a man I like. It's very nice.'

'"Very nice" doesn't catch it.'

'No.'

He stood behind her, pulled her lightly against him, aware that any of the usual behaviours—joking, talking about it, trying for more—were unwise. She said, 'I don't know what we do now.'

'We could marry.'

'Never. I've told you. Not even you.' The tone was light. 'I won't be put in bondage again.'

'Live together?'

'It wouldn't work, Denton. You can't keep it a secret, and people won't tolerate what they'd call a scandal. I don't know why it's a scandal, two people our ages who like to be together, but it is. People you like would drop you, wouldn't speak to you.'

'Do you think I care?'

'I would, and then you would.'

'We could go somewhere else.'

'Yes, Florence is favoured for that sort of thing. Or Deauville. A little expatriate colony of the unchaste. We'd disgust ourselves and each other. Who's that in your garden? Oh, good heavens, it's Cohan. I thought for a moment—'

He craned his neck and looked past her. 'You see how it is when you have an Albert Cosgrove? Always looking behind you.'

She folded her arms over the one of his that was around her waist, then shuddered.

'What is it?'

'You and me.' She broke away. 'Now I must dress and find a way to face your servant. Can he be trusted?'

'He's made his living being trusted.'

'Let's hope so.' She kissed him lightly. 'Go away while I dress.'

He almost said something about the dress, about all of her clothes—something about his buying her new ones—and wisely stopped himself. His grandmother had often told him to mind his own beeswax. The way Janet looked, dressed, acted, talked, was her own beeswax. The beeswax was in fact, he thought, her poverty, but she would let him into that room only when she was ready.

Anyway, he wanted to think over what she had said about insanity and Albert Cosgrove.

Atkins, of course, was perfect with her. They breakfasted; Denton kissed her; she left.

Two more letters came from Albert Cosgrove that day. The first apologized for the one of two days before; he'd been 'nervously agitated' and not himself. Denton wondered what it meant to Albert Cosgrove to be 'himself.'

The second letter was quite the opposite—angry; it returned to the earlier tone.

> *I trusted you, I respected you, and now you have turned on me in this treacherous manner. I know what you are doing! You are worn out; your mind has got rusty and slow; you want my novel as new blood to freshen your own. You have become degenerate. GIVE ME BACK MY*

BOOK!!!!! If you do not return it, I will have recourse to English law. Or worse. There are quicker ways to the recovery of what is mine than the lawyers.

Denton turned the letters over to Atkins. 'Send them to Sergeant Markson at the Met. I can't be bothered now.' Albert Cosgrove was more right than he knew, Denton thought—having tried to rewrite his novel too fast, he did feel worn out, rusty and slow.

Atkins was reading the letters. 'How does he suppose you'd return his slop, even if you had it? He never gives an address.'

'Maybe it never occurs to him. He wants the book; it should be made to appear.'

'Like a kiddie with the tit—bawling until it gets stuck in his maw. Bloody loony!'

Denton waved a hand at him to get him out of the room. When Atkins was gone, he sat on, his head leaned on his left hand, staring down at the manuscript—*portrait of the author at his desk, by our artist,* he thought. The morning's contentment was of course gone. The novel had reached the worst of the marriage, deeply personal scenes that came in good part from his own life and were preserved in the ambers of guilt and humiliation. The morning's dream, its sense of release, made the writing harder, even the memory of contentment a distraction. And Janet Striker was a distraction, too. Instead of working, he sat and wondered why he was so drawn to her: she wasn't pretty; she was sometimes distant; she went out of her way not to be compliant. Yet he wanted her—more than any woman in a long time, perhaps ever. She didn't intend that it would be easy, he knew—although she had asked to stay, had said she wanted to, and had proved so during the night.

I think that I don't want it to be easy, either.

CHAPTER

11

When he finally stopped in late afternoon his knees cracked when he stood. He felt dimly light-headed, as if he'd drawn in lungfuls of tobacco smoke. He expected to totter when he walked. It was almost five o'clock.

'I'm thinking of going out later,' he said to Atkins. The soldier-servant had picked up the photographic copies of the drawing that they'd found in Mary Thomason's trunk; despite his telling Munro that the Mary Thomason business was over, he wanted to find somebody to identify the drawing. Ever hopeful, or stupidly persistent? Or obsessed? Or cracked?

'Best do, unless you want supper from the Lamb.'

'You could do eggs.'

'Now, Colonel, we've been through this. I don't mind the odd rasher and eggs at breakfast or a light lunch, but we agreed I don't cook in the evening.'

'We did, yes. I thought you might take pity on me.'

'Got to draw the line somewhere. Give an employer an inch, he'll take a you-know-what.'

Denton stretched, then bent to touch his toes. He poured himself sherry, sat, said to Atkins, 'Have some yourself, if you like.'

Atkins shook his head. 'I'm thinking. Might have stumbled on a new business interest.' He had been standing there since Denton had come downstairs; pretty clearly, he had something on his mind. Denton hoped it was not about Mrs Striker; he didn't have time for morals just then. He needn't have worried, however, because Atkins surprised him by saying, 'What d'you know about the kinema?'

'Nothing. What's there to know? And isn't it cinema?'

'We say kinema.'

'We?'

Atkins cleared his throat and looked at the ceiling. This was a learned behaviour, the source East End melodrama—Making a Reluctant Suggestion. 'Pal of mine has bought himself a kinema machine.'

Denton made a face at the sherry. He could guess what Atkins was leading up to. Atkins had a weakness for new technologies, what he called 'business opportunities for a chap with vision', into which he'd put small amounts of money, hoping for a big return that never materialized. 'What happened to the vacuum cleaner?'

Before they had gone off to Transylvania, Atkins had got involved in a hand-pumped machine that looked like an oversized clyster and had been supposed to replace the broom. Now, Atkins said, 'The enterprise died while we was away and I wasn't here to manage it. Boon to women, but they complained they was getting muscles like a barrel-lapper from using it. Two housemaids developed elbows and had to have medical attention. Under threat of lawsuit, the firm dissolved.'

'So now it's cinema.'

'Yes, well, yes—chap has a first-class Polish picture-taking machine, needed a bit of cash to grease the skids, as it were. Him and me are thinking of making what's called a kinema picture.'

'You're going to make a moving picture?'

'Something up to date and educational, yes.'

Denton put his chin in his hands. 'What?'

'The war. The Boer War, that is.'

'It isn't over yet.'

'As good as. Anyway, it don't have to be over. Point is to show it. Thrilling.'

'The war's been on for more than three years. How long will your picture last?'

'I say five minutes, but my pal says we can't get that much film in the machine, so maybe it'll be two. *I* think five would be a sensation.'

'Makes the war a little compressed.'

'Well, the high points. You know.' Atkins cleared his throat again. 'We thought we'd borrow some uniforms here and there, pick up some rifles at the markets. Can't tell a Martini from a Baker at any distance, after all. Blank charges. Dozen men, maybe, let them run about, shoot off the rifles, they can be British troops one day, Boers the next—put the Boers in old clothes and Oom Paul beards and soft hats, can't beat that for convincingness.' When Denton said nothing, he added, 'We're looking for a cannon. Put a quarter pound of black powder in the snout, let the Boers run about, huge explosion—that's the siege of Mafeking. Well?'

'There's a reason you're telling me this.'

'I, mm, thought you might allow us to, ah, make use of the front door.'

'As what? Pretoria?'

Atkins chuckled the way adults chuckle at small children. 'As the scene of the housemaid and the soldier. Idea of my own. Stunned my pal. I said, let's put in something that the people watching will understand is like themselves. Well—The Soldier's Farewell, eh? Our front door—pretty housemaid—there's one

up the street who'd be a marvel for it—soldier in his uniform—
she waves—off he goes—eh? Then all the scenes of the
war. Then—The Soldier's Return! Our front door—the maid,
looking out—he appears!—has a stick—limps—embrace! I call
it a frame—around the picture. What d'you think?'

Denton stared at him. 'You mean you're telling a story!' he
said.

'We are? Well, now—'

'I'm impressed. I'm more than impressed. Atkins, you really
thought of that?'

'Well—It isn't as if I haven't heard you talk about such
things. A frame, I mean. Well, yes, I thought of it. Can we use
the front door or can't we?'

It was both the daftest idea Atkins had so far had and the
likeliest, Denton thought, to work. It was laughable—Hampstead
Heath was to be South Africa—and neither Atkins nor his pal
knew anything about acting or photography or saying things
with pictures, but the 'kinema', so far as Denton could tell, was
a rough-and-ready thing that was being shown in empty shops
and rooms, the pictures projected on a bedsheet and the audience
paying a farthing to stand behind a rope. 'Where are you going
to show your picture, if it gets made?'

'We're looking at a butcher's shop that went bust in Finsbury.
I say we ought to go south of the river—more people, less competition—but my pal says closer is better.'

'You'd be wise to buy some insurance.'

'Whatever for?'

'Running around shooting off guns, things could happen.
Not to mention some householder who says he was so frightened
by what he thought was a Boer invasion that he fell off the step-
ladder and is suing for a painful neck.'

Atkins put his lower jaw to one side. After some seconds, he
said, 'I'm glad we had this talk. Makes me think.' He started for
the back, turned around, thanked Denton again. 'I'm grateful.
The scales are falling from my eyes. You've got a head for these
things. Invaluable.'

Denton thought he'd best take advantage of Atkins's mood. 'One thing.'

'Sir?'

'The lady who was here—Mrs Striker. A very private matter.'

'I never thought otherwise.'

'Not a word.'

'I'm hurt you'd think it of me.'

A little later, Atkins brought up an almost high tea, lavish by the standards he usually set. 'This'll hold you until you get to the Criterion or some such posh spot for dinner.' It was Atkins's way of saying that Denton had told him something useful.

It was in fact to the Café Royal and not the Criterion that he made his way. He liked the Café Royal, its rather disorderly Domino Room, whose high-styled decor was so at odds with many of the patrons. Gold and blue-green, with caryatids near the ceiling and gilded pillars that evolved into acanthus trees as they grew upwards, it expressed an already dated idea of French archness. Upstairs, the Café Royal was fairly grand; down here at ground level, it was part bistro and part Bohemian hangout. The chicken pie and the milky coffee were famous, as were the shouting matches, the models, the touts, the odd fistfight, the philosophizing and pontificating that came and went through the place like a tide.

The waiter knew him. Or seemed to know him. The waiters were mostly Italian, rather cynical, given to ironic facial expressions. He never knew what they were really thinking.

'Has Mr Frank Harris come in yet?'

The waiter eyed the room with one raised eyebrow, then shot out an arm. At the far end, towards Glasshouse Street, Denton picked out the dark head of Frank Harris. Harris was an editor, the magazines changing every few years under him like post horses, his notoriety remaining constant—hard-drinking, sensual, bellicose. Denton kept looking at him until his moving gaze—Harris always seemed to be looking for something better than he had—came his way. Denton waved. He said to the waiter, 'The chicken pie and the red wine.'

'A bottle, sir?'

'A glass.'

The Café had been founded by a Continental. It had gone through a number of managers; the most recent, disgusted with the low tone of the Domino Room, had left it and opened what he thought a proper restaurant next door. The Domino Room, impervious to elevation, had gone its disreputable way.

'By God, you're back.' Frank Harris had a loud voice, a shrewd eye and a moustache almost as big as Denton's. He banged his own drink down on the table as he sat. 'Why didn't you join me up there?'

'I don't like that end of the room. Always seems cold.'

'Yah! I hear you made a lot of money on your trip to wherever it was.'

'Transylvania. Whoever told you that?'

'Writing about motor cars, really! I heard you cleared a thousand pounds on the American serial pub.' In fact, he'd got more than that for the articles, expected still more now that they were collected into a book, but he wouldn't tell Harris that.

The chicken pie appeared. Denton cut into it. Inhaled, ate. Harris said, 'I know that dish is famous, but I'm damned if I can see how hard-boiled eggs and chicken can go together. It's like an English idea of French food. Speaking of money, want to invest some?'

'No.'

'I've an idea for a new mag. Make a fortune.'

'I'm looking for a girl.'

'Who isn't? I could introduce you to Lotty over there—she's quite nice, if you don't let her talk.'

Denton, chewing, took from a pocket a photographic copy of the drawing that had been in Mary Thomason's trunk. 'That girl.'

Harris studied it. 'The ethereal type. Missed her moment— would have been perfect for the Pre-Raphaelites. Although you never know, sometimes it's these apparently angelic little females who just want to do it like rabbits. '"There is no art to find the cunt's construction in the face."'

'Is that a quotation? You English are always throwing quotations at me.'

'I'm Irish, and it's Shakespeare. I know more about Shakespeare than any man in England, were you aware of that? Truth.' Harris put the photo of the drawing down. 'Who is she?'

'Student at the Slade.'

'Why didn't you say so?' He turned almost completely around and shouted, 'Gwen!' The room's growl of talk, counterpoint to everything that went on, continued. 'GWEN!' He turned back. 'Gwen John—know her? Her brother's Augustus, the rising star of English art.'

Denton allowed that he knew Augustus John by sight, had once had a desultory conversation with him.

'Gwen's twice the painter her brother is, but he's got flash, and people get blinded by it. Ah, Gwen, me darlin', here you are.'

A frowning, rather small young woman in multi-coloured scarves and kerchiefs was standing by the table. 'I don't like to be shouted at,' she said in a husky voice.

'Of course you don't. The Café Royal's rather out of your milieu, isn't it, Gwen?'

She looked as if she might not answer him, then reluctantly said, 'One of my friends wanted to come here for his birthday.'

'Must have got a cheque from home. Gwen, this is Mr Denton, famous writer, trying to get a line on this face.' He spun the drawing so that she could see it. 'Ring any bells?'

Without bending, she looked down at the drawing. She seemed to have smelled something bad.

'Slade girl, he says,' Harris prompted.

'Well, it isn't Slade work, is it? Hard to find drawing that bad these days. You're asking the wrong person.'

Before she could turn away, Denton said, 'Why isn't it Slade work?'

'It's *stumped*. Try Burlington House.' She swirled away.

Harris looked after her and said in a musing sort of way, 'You know, under all those rags, there's quite a fine body? Not that that's any more a sign of accessibility than the face. Mind, I've known skinny little things with no more tits than a tinker who wanted to be pounded like a piece of tripe. I once walked into a bookshop on a rainy day, nobody there but this animated broom-handle of a female about thirty; it took me about ten minutes to be fucking her on a collected works of Richardson. She had a bush like——'

'Harris, has it ever occurred to you that there's more to life than sex?'

'Good Christ, I certainly hope not! Where did you hear a thing like that?'

'Made it up myself.'

'What an idea!'

'I wanted to know if you recognized the drawing, not to hear your sexual autobiography.'

'Well, I don't know her.' He tapped the drawing. He sounded grumpy.

'What's "stumped"?' Denton said.

'Hmm? Oh, drawing technique—use a screw of paper to push the charcoal around, rub it out, get lights and shadows. Slade teaches the use of the line—stumping not allowed.'

'And Burlington House?'

'The RA—the Royal Academy. Really, Denton, you've lived here long enough to know that.'

'I don't understand art.'

'Nobody does—except me, of course. Gwen and her crowd believe the RA's the work of the devil. No telling them that thirty years ago the people who now hang their crap in Burlington House were sitting here and saying the same things about *their* betters. Today a rebel, tomorrow an academician. The awful truth is, none of them is awfully good—not good as the really good are good. Britain hasn't produced a first-rate draughtsman since Rowlandson. You see, the trouble is——'

Denton concentrated on the chicken and let the words drown in the general hubbub. He glanced towards the table where Gwen

John was sitting with several other young women and a couple of young men—late-adolescent boys, really—all the women swathed like her in gypsy-like bits and pieces of colourful cloth. The young men expressed themselves in long hair and collarless shirts with scarves; one wore the blue cotton jacket of a French working-man, possibly the badge of a summer in Paris. They certainly looked unconventional, he thought, probably the reason for the costume, at least among the women—the gypsy look just then was the Bohemian uniform, to judge from the young women he had seen near the Slade—but there was also the possibility that they dressed like this because it was cheap. Like Janet Striker, perhaps they didn't have money for clothes: the problem was the same, the solution different. Theirs, he had to admit, was more attractive.

'Ever hear of the Russian ballet?' Harris was saying. Denton had no idea how he'd got there from Rowlandson.

'Can't say I have.'

'You're impossible. Like talking to a cow. Did you know I was a cowboy once? In Kansas?'

'I've heard you say so.'

'Don't you believe me? I was in Chicago, and these four cowboys came into a hotel where I was—'

Denton looked at the young artists again. Gwen John was looking at him, her right hand making quick movements over a small sketch pad. When she saw him looking, she gave an automatic, close-mouthed smile and went on.

'So I left the hotel business and went into cattle-driving. Many adventures. I was younger then. You aren't listening, are you?'

'I'm tired.'

Harris got up. He was perfectly amiable. 'I need an audience. If you have some extra money, let me know—I'll put you on to a good thing.' He strode away, heading back towards his end of the room.

Denton finished the last of the chicken pie, then the wine, and ordered coffee. A couple of minutes later, to his surprise, Gwen John came and stood by the table. 'I want to apologize for being so abrupt,' she said.

'Oh—you weren't. It was nothing.'

'I can't stand Harris. He's wetter than a water meadow. Is he a friend of yours? I'm sorry if he is. I say what I think.'

She might have been all of twenty-two or -three, he thought, yet she had the settled sombreness of a middle-aged woman. She was not pretty, didn't seem to care. He said, 'Won't you sit down?'

'I'm with people.' She looked back at them.

'Would they recognize the girl in the drawing?'

'Not if she's at the Slade now. We've all been out for a while.' She sat down. She didn't want anything to drink. She looked at the drawing again and shook her head. 'I was quite serious, actually, just didn't say it very nicely—this was done by somebody with academic training. It's good of its kind—quite good of its kind—but I don't like the kind.' She became suddenly almost accusing. 'What's your interest in her?'

'She wrote me a letter, said somebody might hurt her. People write to me like that—they have an idea I'm some sort of—The newspapers have given people the wrong idea.'

'Is it the wrong idea? You seem to be trying to help her.'

'It's a kind of obligation. I was away when she wrote—her letter was waiting for me—' He wanted to change the subject. 'I saw you drawing me. Was it the nose?'

'You have a strong face.'

'A strong nose.'

She shrugged. 'I don't care about pretty or handsome or that blather. It's character I like.' Then her friends came over and surrounded the table and said they were moving on. To his surprise, Gwen John said to him, 'Why don't you come? Some current Slade people will be there. Maybe they'll recognize your drawing.'

He glanced at the others; they weren't paying any particular attention to him. *I'm too old, too different.* 'I'd be intruding.'

'No, you wouldn't. Mark says you're a serious writer.' Mark was apparently one of the young men, 'serious writer' apparently a ticket to their world. She stood. 'Coming?'

Well, he thought, maybe it would be an adventure, although he didn't need an adventure. He'd just got back from an adventure.

Thinking of Janet Striker, that a love affair is also an adventure, venturing into the landscape of her, her unmapped territory.

Out on Regent Street, there were introductions of a sort—this is Edna, this is Ursula, this is Gwen (a different Gwen), this is Tony, Mark, Andrew. They all began walking. They had pulled on an assortment of capes, outdated military overcoats, one bearskin coat so worn the pale hide showed through in patches. The boy in the French working-man's jacket was now seen to be wearing rope-soled shoes, as well.

'Is it a party?' Denton said.

One of the young men—was it Andrew?—turned and said, 'The Duchess of Devonshire's evening salon.' There was laughter.

Denton spent little time with young people. These seemed to him rather puppyish, innocent, the women apparently more mature than the men. There was no sense of who belonged to whom, if such arrangements in fact existed. They seemed rather jolly overall.

Gwen John walked next to him as if he had become her responsibility. Denton said, 'I expected to see your brother at the Café Royal.'

'He's in Liverpool.'

Despite himself, Denton laughed. It seemed a strange place for Augustus John, with his earrings and his gypsy hats. She said, 'He took a job teaching. He got married, you know.' It seemed to make her cross; perhaps this was simply her manner, as she and her brother's wife were, she said, old friends. Still, she said, 'Ida's had to give up her painting. I could never do that.'

'Gave it up to be a wife?'

'She's going to have a child.'

They were heading for Charlotte Street. They were all good walkers, and, despite their sometimes overstated idea of themselves as 'different', as decorous as the middle class they despised but from which they'd sprung. They stepped aside for other pedestrians, shushed each other when somebody got boisterous, guided an old woman through the Oxford Street traffic. Their goal was a big house that must have once been somebody's prize.

Now a rooming house, it had a studio at the top, he was told, although they weren't going that far: their destination was a big, seemingly unfurnished room on the third floor.

A cheer rose as they came in, the dozen or so people already there clearly eager for these older, *real* artists to validate their gathering. The room, he found, was not quite bare (his first sense had been that it was empty except for the dim figures), the walls partly covered with pinned-up drawings 'from the life', the floor with pillows made from the sort of bright scraps the women wore. Two crates were holding up a board with a jug of beer, a large bottle, and a dozen or so mismatched cups and glasses. Denton found it politic almost at once to pay for a second pitcher of beer, which somebody fetched from 'the Fitz', apparently the local. He was offered a glass, only slightly grubby, with something from the bottle that was brown, sweetish and disgusting, ostensibly Madeira.

'Are you the chap looking to identify a girl from some dreadful drawing?' a plump young woman said to him after he'd been around the room once.

'News travels fast.'

'Gwen's told us. I'm Caroline. This is my room.'

'You're at the Slade?'

She guffawed. 'Can't you tell?' She waved at the walls. 'Let's see your horrible drawing.'

She didn't recognize it, but she put her hand through his arm and led him through the crowd, now pretty well filling the space. One or two of the young men were lolling on the pillows now (in the left ear of one of them, a glint of gold—homage to Augustus John); other men and women were sitting on the floor with their backs against the wall, most of them smoking cigarettes. There was a lot of talk, some laughter. Denton found himself bending down, then squatting as people looked at the drawing. There was only one gas lamp, but candles seemed to be everywhere, the photographic print gaining several spots of wax.

'Oh, I know her,' a small girl with a cat's face said. She had furry eyebrows and light-brown hair that was very like a mane.

'She was in first-year drawing. Tonks made her weep. Of course, Tonks makes everybody weep.'

From across the room, a young man called, 'He never made me weep!'

'You just turned white as a sheet instead, Malcolm.'

'My sheet's grey.' More laughter.

Three other girls crowded around. He had lost Caroline. They remembered Mary Thomason—called by one of them first Thomas then, no, was it Tomkins?—but they knew nothing about her. She had been 'very private', 'young, that's what I kept thinking, she seemed like a child', 'really quite stand-offish—you'd never have found her at something like tonight'.

'Well, nobody ever invited her.'

'She was stand-offish.'

Denton said, 'Has anybody seen her in the last two months?'

They talked that over, decided they hadn't, although they were vague about the idea of two months. They were sure she hadn't come back for the new term, but most of them had been gone for the summer. They called to others in the room. Nobody had seen Mary Thomason for a long while. One rather languid young woman got up off a cushion and came over to him. She had a cool, appraising stare that he decided was really laziness. 'She was doing some modelling, if that matters.'

'Posing?'

They laughed. 'We call it modelling. It's extra money.'

'How did you know she was doing it?'

'We used to chat. She had something new—a hat, I think. She said she'd made some money modelling for a painter and bought the hat. She didn't say which one. There are hundreds.'

'Thousands!' another girl said. People laughed again.

The languorous girl leaned against the wall. 'She said she'd been modelling for an RA. She said he was "good". I don't think she knew good art from fried plaice.'

By then, Caroline had brought out a parlour guitar and was singing in some other language, sitting on the floor. This evolved into a form of charades when one of the men draped a shawl over himself and said he was John Singer Sargent's Spanish dancer. People started to make references that Denton didn't understand. He knew it was time to go.

'I want to thank you,' he said to Gwen John, whom he found near the door.

'Did you learn anything?'

'A little. She was modelling for somebody.'

She shrugged. 'We're going to get thrown out soon.' The charades had got noisy.

'I'm going.'

'Wise man.'

He put out his hand. 'I hope we meet again.'

'Perhaps.'

Her steady, genderless gaze reminded him of somebody else. Only when he was in the street did he realize the somebody was Janet Striker.

'Actually, they were kind of sweet—more like a church social than an orgy.'

Janet Striker chuckled. 'What on earth is a church social?'

'My God, don't you have those here, either? They're gatherings, socializings, in the church or arranged by the church so people can meet.'

'I don't think the Church of England do that sort of thing.'

'We were Congregationalists. Sometimes there were box lunches—each woman would make a lunch and then they'd be auctioned off—you got to eat with the woman, sort of a picnic— Why are you laughing?'

'I can't picture you at such a thing.'

'Well, I was a kid. In Maine, before the war.'

'It sounds so awful!'

'Well, they weren't. Anyway, the wild Bohemians were nicer to me than most of the toffs I've met, and a good deal more innocent.'

'Not as clean, I'll wager.'

'It was dark. But they did give me that one fact—Mary Thomason had modelled for an older man, an RA.'

'"Man", they said man?'

'RAs are men, aren't they?'

'Oh, of course. Naturally. And they said "RA" and didn't mean just any older artist, but somebody actually with the initials after his name?'

'No, she didn't say that, and it was only the one woman, no "they". And she was about half-asleep and not, I think, the brightest star in the firmament. It isn't much, is it?'

'Every bit helps.'

'But what does it help?'

They were eating in the Three Nuns in Aldgate High Street because she had insisted she wanted to work late despite being on half days. He thought she was trying to avoid him, not see him every day. Something would have to be worked out soon, he thought; he hated running after her, hated more not being with her. 'Why won't you live with me?' he said.

'Because I'm not a whore any more.'

'Oh, Jesus, Janet—!'

'Don't ask me, then.'

'Playing around with trunks isn't enough!'

'That's too bad about you.' She smiled. 'That's what an Irish maid used to say to me when I was little.'

'You mean I'm not thinking about your side of it.'

'That's part of what I mean. What did you mean, "Playing around with trunks"?'

'You're changing the subject.'

'I'm glad you noticed.'

'I meant that trying to find Mary Thomason is a mug's game. I'm grateful to you for going after the trunk, but it's all too distant and too long ago, and while it's something we do together, it isn't like the real thing! Plus Mary Thomason is a distraction; I've got better things to think about.'

'Your book. And me, I suppose. I should be flattered that I'm one of your worries, Denton, but I'm not. I don't want to be a worry, least of all yours.'

'And then there's Albert Cosgrove. I had another letter today—three, all told. One pleading, two threatening. He's come entirely unglued.'

'Threatening what?'

'Oh, mostly noise. Having a tantrum.'

'You'd think the police could find him.'

'The police have better things to do. They're keeping their watchers on me because of the letters, but the truth is they don't know where to look for him. Or how.' He hesitated, pushing a rather grey-looking green bean around his plate. 'I think he saw us together,' he said finally.

'You and me?'

'I think when you took the trunk away in the cab. He mentioned the cab and the house in the latest letter.'

'But the police were supposed to have been watching!'

'"The Lady Astoreth likes not rivals."'

'Don't talk mysteries to me, Denton.'

'That's what he wrote in his letter. Something about seeing me at my door with—pardon me—my "painted harlot", and then, "The Lady Astoreth likes not rivals."' He speared the bean. 'My grandmother used to read the Book of Revelation. Cosgrove sounds like it.'

'And the Lady Astoreth?'

'Something he's invented or heard about.'

'One of his demons?'

'Maybe.' He chewed the bean. 'I bawled Markson out for not finding him. I wanted him to put a guard on you. He says they don't have the men. I told him to take them off me; he wouldn't do it.'

'I can take care of myself perfectly well.'

'You could put Cohan to watching you.'

'I'll do nothing of the kind.'

'He could take care of Albert Cosgrove with one hand.'

'Denton, it isn't me your man is after. It's you.'

'We don't know that. *I* don't know it, anyway. He's unpredictable. To say the least.'

She put a hand over his. 'I'm sorry—but I won't have somebody trailing about after me. Concentrate on your book. When it's done, we'll worry about him. He's more pathetic than dangerous. You can't blame him for wanting his manuscript back. Why not give it to him?'

'It's police evidence now. Anyway, I don't know where to find him. Atkins suggested an ad in *The Times*—"Will Albert Cosgrove please give Mr Denton a place to return his novel?" A child wouldn't fall for that one.' He put his free hand on top of hers. 'I don't like his knowing about you.'

'He doesn't know my name or anything about me.'

'He's a clever bastard. I don't like it.'

She smiled at him. '"That's too bad about you."' She squeezed his hand. 'You do your work. Forget everything else.'

That was Tuesday. He didn't see her the next two days and didn't hear from her. He had four more letters from his nemesis, but there was nothing in them that helped the police. Denton tried to do as she had said; he worked the entire day, blotting out Mary Thomason, blotting out Albert Cosgrove. The Thomason business was pretty well over, he thought. It galled him that Guillam would do nothing, but it was finally not worth fighting.

Thursday evening he was alone in the house. It was Atkins's half day; he was off somewhere pursuing his moving-picture idea. Denton ordered what proved to be a soggy supper in from the Lamb, ate it with his own wine for contrast, and fell asleep in his armchair afterwards.

At nine, somebody was at his front door.

He woke, groggy, displeased, waited for Atkins to get the door, remembered the man was out and fumbled in an overcoat pocket for the new Colt before going down himself. He cursed his own caution: Albert Cosgrove had made him afraid in his own house. *Clever little bastard.* He backed off the night bolt and turned the lock and stayed behind the door as he opened it a few inches, willing it to be Cosgrove so that he could end things.

'Telegram, sir.'

Denton looked around the door. A bicycle was leaned against the railing. An almost toothless man the size of a large child was standing on the top step. 'Telegram for Denton.'

He shifted the revolver to his other hand and took the envelope, realized he had no money and made the man wait on the step while he ran up the stairs, then up to his bedroom; he swept coins from his bedside table, ran down again, passed too much money out of the door.

He ripped open the envelope as he went more slowly back upstairs. Leaning into his sitting room, he held the yellow oblong to the gaslight.

AM AT WESTERLEY STREET PLEASE COME
TO ME STOP
JANET

He pulled his braces over his shoulders as he ran again to his bedroom, pulling on the old jacket in which he had been working. The Colt went back into his overcoat pocket, a hat—any hat—on his head. Rupert was in the lower hall when he went out.

'Hold the fort,' he told the dog.

The ride to Westerley Street seemed interminable, the damp streets unusually clogged, but it was early still by London's night-time standards.

'Can't you hurry?' he called up to the driver.

'This is London.'

It had got colder. The horse's breath showed, and wisps of steam from its back. To a man who wanted to move quickly, the London streets seemed like a garish part of hell: grinning faces, too-bright colours, hooves and wheels and footsteps, crowds on buses and crowds on the pavements, a crush of people and animals and vehicles slowly going nowhere. He had an image of going on like this for ever, like a dream in which the destination is always lost.

'Ah! She's waiting for you in her ladyship's room.' Fred Oldaston was a former boxer who manned the door at Westerley Street. He actually dragged Denton through the doorway and was pulling his overcoat down over his shoulders as he talked. 'Oh, you ain't dressed—well, no matter. The missus is strict about it, you know—' He gave Denton a little push on the shoulder to set him moving.

He passed through the first public room, where several young women sat about, one or two with men. They smiled; he passed on, turning right into Mrs Castle's reception room, where she lounged on a sofa and drank champagne and received her clientele.

'Oh, God, Denton, you look absolutely déclassé. Go on through the little door there before somebody sees you—go on, go on—!'

She was not yet even moderately drunk but certainly annoyed. The door was at first hard to find, covered with William Morris paper to match the walls. He found the dark-swirled china knob by feeling for it and let himself through. On the other side was a room so different in its simplicity and its calm greens and blues as to have been in another world. Against the far wall, sitting on a dark-green love seat, was Janet Striker.

'What is it?' He went towards her.

She held up a hand to ward him off. 'I'm all right now.'

'Janet, what's happened?'

She looked quite normal, except that she didn't smile. 'He's been in my rooms,' she said. 'You were right.'

'Tell me.' He tried to sit beside her but she wouldn't give him room, and he fetched a chair that was too small for him. 'Janet, what is it?'

'I sent for the police. I've talked to them. They didn't understand, of course. It sounds silly.' She put a hand on his sleeve without looking at him. 'I worked late again—I'm trying to leave things right, clean up the files and old letters and—stuff, you know. I got home—' She laughed unpleasantly. 'My *home*. My two wretched rooms. I opened the door and thought I was in the wrong place. *Everything.* Everything, Denton! Smashed, ripped— he'd poured red paint on things—on my piano, the only thing I cared about—!' A kind of spasm took her chin and neck from the clenching of her jaw. Her eyelids reddened, but no tears came. 'He found the scissors and cut my clothes.' She laughed again, the same harshness. 'I don't own a stitch except what I have on! Everything gone—cut up, red paint poured on it. Clothes I'd haggled over and spent days looking for at the markets, haggled with a pushcart man! You knew they were somebody's cast-offs, didn't you—you didn't think I dressed like this because I wanted to!' She put her face in her hands. He touched her shoulder; she shrugged him off. He bent forward so far his knee almost touched the floor, the little chair tipped on its front legs. 'Janet—Janet, it's all right—'

'It isn't all right with me!'

'Janet—the clothes don't matter; you'll get more clothes—'

'He poured paint on my piano—on the keys!' And now she wept. For a piano. Between her sobs, she said, 'You don't know. I saved—for months to buy that—piano. And it's only an old Clementi, a hundred years old, it's junk you wouldn't give a child to play, but *it's what I can afford*!' She raised her head and sat back, dabbing at her nose with a handkerchief. 'Or could afford. I'll have money soon, and money is happiness, am I right?'

'You know better.'

'Well—poverty is misery, I can tell you that.' She wiped her eyes and sniffed. She looked at him as if she saw him for the first time, as if only now she understood that he was there. She leaned forward and put a hand behind his neck, pulled them together, her face hot and damp against his. 'Well, now you've seen me cry,' she said.

'I didn't think you did.'

'I've been known to.' She kissed his ear. 'I'd like you to take me to bed.'

'Yes—yes—'

She pulled away. 'No. Not here.'

'Come home with me.'

'Not that, either. I shall stay here tonight in Ruth's extra room. I know it seems quixotic, Denton, but I want to stay here. This is my haven—this knocking shop is the closest I have to a home.'

'But you can't go to bed in it with me.'

'We've both been in the beds in this house too often as it is.'

She stood and shook her hair back and walked up and down, looking at herself in a mirror and trying to fix what she saw with her fingers and the handkerchief. She poured herself water from a carafe that stood by the sofa, drank it. She said, 'There's sherry and whisky over there if you want it.' She smiled at him. 'Will that chair hold both of us?'

'It really doesn't even hold me.'

She pulled him over to the sofa. 'Hold me for a bit. Then you must go home.' She looked into his eyes; they kissed; she put her head back. 'I just wanted, as you say, to be with you for a little.' She moved a few inches away. 'Now you should go home.'

'I don't want to.'

'I'm going to take one of Ruth's laudanum pills and slip into the land of dreams for a while. I used to do it rather too much. But not in a long time.' She leaned into the curved back of the sofa, which rose towards the ends in great loops like bows. 'He painted "Astoreth" on the wall. I take it to mean that I'd been paid a visit by his demon.' She exhaled shakily. 'What sort of demon takes an interest in old clothes and a lot of odd bits picked off the rubbish tip? It makes me question the demon's judgement.' She looked shrewdly at him. 'It was meant for you, you know.'

'Partly.'

'And part for me? Yes, perhaps. "See what I can do." Be careful, Denton.'

'Will you be safe here?'

'Between Fred, Ruth, the girls and the clientele, I shall be safer than in the Tower of London. Go home now.'

'Can I come back tomorrow?'

She frowned. 'I'll come to you. When do you stop working? Four? By then I'll have begged or borrowed some clothes. I'll come to you. Four?'

He held her again, kissed her and slipped out of the little door. In her receiving room, Ruth Castle was now surrounded by men, two or three with women of the house. Everybody was in formal dress. There was a smell of cigars and alcohol and perfume. Denton was impressed by the fact that he hadn't heard them from the inner room—nor they he, therefore.

'Denton, you look a fright—I've seen better-dressed navvies. Do go away.' Mrs Castle looked to the sleek, well-dressed men. 'When he's properly turned out, he's quite one of my favourite people.' Her voice was nasal, easily mocking; she dropped the H in 'he', perhaps intentionally. The received wisdom was that Ruth Castle had been a child from one of the rookeries who had been plucked out, bathed and raped by a wealthy man who had kept her for several years before sending her off to a house. From there, she had continued to rise—a 'personage', a marriage (or at least the honorific 'Mrs'), her own house.

She held out a hand, which he kissed, something he'd have done with nobody else. She pulled him close. 'Take care of her,' she murmured. The sour breath of champagne washed over him.

'I mean to.'

'You'd better.' She shoved him off. 'Now take your awful suit away.'

Seeing Oldaston again as he went out, he said, 'You ever know somebody called the Stepney Jew-Boy?'

'Jew-Boy Cohan? Haven't heard that name since Hector was a pup. Yes, I remember him well—mind, I never fought him, too small for me by a couple of stone.'

'He says he was never knocked down.'

'That's a fact. Very tough. But not fast enough. He could take a terrific blow, but he couldn't move his hands quick. Mind, he won fights, quite a deal of them. But lost, too.'

'He's looking for work, if you hear of anything.'

'No! Well, that's the pugilist's life in a nutshell. He addled?'

'No—seems quite sharp.'

'Tell you what I'd do if I was him—go to Mrs Franken. She's a Jewess herself, nothing wrong with that. She might have something in my line of work. She has a couple of houses, you never know.'

Atkins was waiting at home. He'd found Janet Striker's telegram beside Denton's armchair. And he'd read it, of course, so there was no point in pretending nothing had happened, some gain perhaps in telling him.

'I think I'll keep carrying that derringer,' Atkins said.

'You have Rupert.'

'All very well for you to say. You're sitting on an arsenal.'

'Don't shoot yourself.'

'Oh, ha-ha. Thirty years in the British army and I never so much as pinched my thumb in a breech. So your loony's turned dangerous. Well, you said he would. Now what?'

'A good citizen would wait for the police to catch him.'

'Yes, but what are *you* going to do?'

Munro and Markson showed up at three-thirty the next afternoon. The two detectives were sombre, Markson clearly nervous, perhaps blaming himself somehow for the attack on Janet Striker's lodgings. Munro, phlegmatic at best, was apparently calm, but he acknowledged what Markson's jerkings of a leg and facial tics indicated: the police were worried.

'He isn't just some Bohemian would-be writer now. He's a threat,' Munro said. He was sitting in the upholstered piece opposite Denton's armchair; Markson was on an armless side chair that Atkins had fetched from farther up the room. 'What he did was an act of violence.'

'Symbolic violence, anyway,' Denton said. 'Paint looks like blood, but it isn't blood. Cutting up clothes isn't the same as cutting up a woman but gives the sense of it.'

'You're not defending him, I hope.'

'Trying to be accurate.' He was remembering what Janet Striker had said about insanity.

Munro grunted. 'For this copper, he's only one step away from real blood.'

'You're the police. Go catch him.'

Munro pushed his lips out and drew his brows down in an expression that, in a saloon, would have meant that a fight was coming. Markson said, 'We're trying. Mr Denton, we've had men on you all week.'

'They did a particularly fine job of catching him while he watched Mrs Striker leave this house.'

Munro raised a hand to silence Markson before he could complain. Munro twisted in his chair, crossed his legs, looked at Denton sideways. 'How did he find her, do you think?'

'Followed her, I suppose.'

'"Follow that cab"?' Munro snorted. 'What is he, invisible? One of Mr H. G. Wells's inventions, is he?'

Markson twitched. 'One of the watchers happened to be on his tea break.'

Munro groaned. 'Jesus wept.' He wiped his right hand over his face, then leaned his head on that hand, the elbow on the chair back. He looked like an actor playing great pain. 'I apologize, all right, Denton? For the Metropolitan Police, for myself—I apologize. We should have done better. All right?'

'I didn't ask you to.'

'No, but it makes me feel better. It's also a lesson to young Fred here—we're not always perfect.' He leaned forward, elbows on knees. 'Now look. We need to know where we are. How much danger is the woman in? You've got to be frank with me, Denton. Fred says she was here while he was here that day—she was collecting for some charity—'

'The Society for the Improvement of Wayward Women.'

'This is the same woman that got her face slashed last year and you saved her life, am I right? Now—don't get your dander up—is there more to it than her stopping by to pick up a contribution?'

'Why should there be more?'

'Because I'm a suspicious, cynical Canuck who doesn't share the English taste for pussy-footing about. You saved her life last year. One of the watchers reported following you to the Embankment where you met with a lady. Now she happens to be here collecting a contribution, which seems bloody odd, as the Royal Mail worked efficiently the last time I looked.'

Denton looked into Munro's eyes without wavering. 'We're friends.'

'Was she here before? Could Cosgrove have seen her with you before?'

Denton knew what Munro was after, knew that it was foolish to splutter and object. 'Yes.'

Munro looked at Markson, back at Denton. He sat back in his chair, his hands gripping the ends of the velour-covered arms. 'I'm going to have to put a watch on her.'

'Bit late. I don't think she'll like that.'

'Nor would I, but we have to catch the bastard.' He looked at Markson. 'Report?'

This had been arranged, Denton guessed—a kind of briefing to make him feel that at least he was included, even if little progress was being made. Markson said, one knee vibrating as the heel of that foot went up and down, up and down, 'The letters have been posted from eight different places in London, but we've plotted them on the map and we think it's west. He's gone as far afield as Earl's Court in that direction but only east as far as Holborn Viaduct. We think he's walking, not using the steam underground or anything like the electric trams to get far out.'

Munro spoke up. 'Walking would be trying to be like you again, Denton.'

Markson said, 'Taking into account what you said about him being educated, we think maybe well off, then Mayfair or

Kensington or some such.' Nobody said anything. There was no point in saying the obvious. Munro, however, muttered, as another apology, 'We admit, it's thin.'

'I know you're doing what you can.'

'There is something—' Markson looked as if he'd startled himself by speaking. He glanced at Munro for approval. 'Is there anything else he could have stolen? Anything at all? There might be a clue...' His voice drifted off.

'Books?' Munro said. He looked at the wall of books that framed the fireplace. 'You said he started off asking for your books. Any chance he stole them when you didn't answer?'

Denton shook his head. 'I don't keep my own stuff out here. I need the space.'

'In your room?'

'No.'

'You don't have *any* copies of your own books?'

'They're put away someplace. In a box. You think I sit around reading my own books, Munro?'

'Well—' Munro squirmed in the chair. 'I daresay if I'd written a book, I'd have it out where people could see it. Might put it under glass. Hmp. Well—any chance he could have got into the box?'

Denton called Atkins (who was probably listening by the dumb waiter, anyway) and asked him to check the book boxes. While Atkins plodded back downstairs—what passed for a box room was an old pantry off the ground-floor kitchen—Munro tried to put together the sequence of Albert Cosgrove's actions. When he had led the three of them through it all up to the attack on Mrs Striker's rooms, he said, 'So it began three months after you left on this trip you took. Any significance to that, do you think?'

'You mean, he didn't break in right away? Maybe the thing grew on him.'

'So at the first, he really *was* asking for your books.'

'All right, say he was. And?'

'He doesn't get a response, he's a bit shirty. He writes again.'

'The letters that were waiting for me here didn't seem angry. On the contrary, they were soapy and overdone. Worshipful.'

'Until you got home.'

'A bit after.'

'But he's waiting in the house behind by then. He even more or less shows himself at the window—you think that was what he was doing, by the way, exhibiting himself?'

'Like the old men in the park? I don't think it was a sex thing.' He listened to himself. 'Or maybe it was.'

'Well, you were the one talking about symbolism, not me. But anyway, by the time you come home, he knows you've been away. And as we know now, he knows it so well he breaks in here and steals a manuscript of yours and a pen—a bloody pen! But nothing else? That's almost incredible.'

'What would you have had him steal?'

'Something that's truly you. One of your Western hats. Your gun. Your—You've checked your guns, have you? It'd be terrible if he's out there with a gun.'

'The guns were with me. Except two parlour pistols, and they were locked away upstairs and were there when I got home.'

Markson jiggled his knee. 'If I could say, sir—' Markson's face twitched. 'Is it significant that he didn't put his own address in those early letters? Heaven knows there was none on the recent ones.'

'I didn't say he didn't put an address in them,' Denton said. 'I told you I couldn't remember an address.'

'Yes, sir, but suppose there *hadn't* been any address.'

'Oh.' Munro was nodding. 'Then he never really wanted Denton to send the books, you mean.'

'Why write, then?'

Markson said, 'Maybe so he could tell himself you didn't bother to answer, sir.'

Munro looked as if he'd smelled something off. Denton started to make a face, too, then thought about what Markson had said. 'So that he could worship me and resent me at the same time?'

'Fanciful,' Munro growled.

'But it would mean, Sergeant, that he never intended—I mean, if he's capable of "intending" anything—he never intended just to be a well-known author's follower. He was always after something else.'

'It's fanciful, and it doesn't get us any closer to finding him.'

Atkins came up from below then and announced that the boxes were where they belonged, and there was no sign they'd been opened. 'I took Rupert and had him give it all a good sniff. He didn't find anything, either.'

'Rupert is that animal?' The dog was sitting behind Atkins, wagging its massive rear because the stub of tail was planted in the carpet.

'Rupert has the nose of a hound,' Atkins said.

'Rupert has a little bit of every dog that's been down the street this ten years, from the look of him. However, we'll take it as read that Cosgrove didn't steal the books.' Munro grunted. 'Now I think of it, your own copies wouldn't be signed anyway, would they? If he meant anything by asking for signed copies— really wanted them, I mean.' Munro put his hands on his knees. 'It's so much a question of just how mad he is, isn't it? I mean, we know what some criminals—perverts and so on—do with books. What the sex maniac does with pornography, pictures of children—A madman can pull his wire over *anything*.'

'Stewart Caterwol,' Markson said.

Denton didn't know the name. Munro said, 'Chap who stole women's shoes to get off into. He was a drayman, used axle grease from his wagon to get his meat into the shoes—long, pointy toes some of them had. Kept the shoes in a trunk— forty-one pairs, every one full of axle grease and duff. Harmless otherwise. Got five years for petty theft times forty-one plus inde-cency plus moral turpitude. All done, so far as we know, in his own bedroom. Sometimes an Englishman's home isn't his castle, after all.'

The doorbell rang.

Denton went to the window and looked down. A cab was waiting at the kerb. When he turned back, he could hear Janet

Striker's voice as she came up the stairs. Atkins would already have told her that the police were there, he knew.

The effect of her coming into the room was as if some loud sound had jolted both policeman to their feet. They shot up, then stood there staring at her, Markson even with his mouth a bit open. Denton said 'Mrs Striker,' in a voice that seemed to have been hit almost as hard.

She was transformed.

She was wearing a dress in the nominal colours of autumn— 'fillemot', the pale brown of dead leaves, grey-green, dusty yellow—but an autumn that was autumnal only in its muting, the total effect lively and almost summery. The cut was of the moment, perhaps a step in advance of the moment, the skirt above her shoe-tops, the sleeves tight, the fall of the silky fabric almost clinging. Even the usually livid scar seemed to have been muted; he thought that somebody had dusted powder on it. Her hat, which matched the dress, was jaunty, pretty, with a wisp of veiling. Atkins followed behind with her coat and umbrella, both coordinated with the dress. 'I came,' she said, smiling at their reaction, 'to tell Mr Denton something, but as you gentlemen of the police are here, I shall be delighted to tell you, as well. I believe I have found Albert Cosgrove.'

Munro grunted; Markson twitched; Denton ordered tea and put her in his own chair and then retired to the fireplace to look at her. She raised her bit of ecru veil and all but winked at him, then smiled again at the detectives. 'Do sit down, gentlemen.'

'You've *found* him, Mrs Striker?'

'I'm not *sure* I've found him, but I think I have.'

'Where, ma'am?'

'In a bookseller's. That is, *he* isn't in the book shop. He left his name and address at the book shops, quite a long time ago. Half a dozen shops. I've been all over Charing Cross Road and Booksellers' Row. It was an idea of someone else's, told me by Mr Denton. And if it's the right man, his name isn't Albert Cosgrove, of course.' She had a small handbag, which she opened to take out a notebook, from which she took a folded piece of paper.

'Struther Jarrold—an address in Belgravia.' She passed the paper across to Munro, who was sitting again. Munro looked at it and passed it to Markson.

Markson said, 'We would have got to the booksellers on our own. Shortage of personnel.'

Munro shook his head and said to her, 'We looked for you this morning, Mrs Striker. About the invasion of your rooms, most unfortunate—'

'I went rather into seclusion, I'm afraid—hid in the house of an old friend. I was shaken.'

'Anybody would have been.' Munro was studying her, not without admiration. 'You're taking it wonderfully well.'

'I didn't yesterday. I work, Mr Munro, as I guess you know. I have—had—very little in those rooms to lose. Still, it was a shock. Even for a resident of Bethnal Green.' She looked up at Denton and smiled.

It was the first time that Denton had known where she lived: he had guessed it was in a working-class part of London, but not one with a reputation for immigration and hopeless poverty and some of the city's worst slums, the reputation now perhaps somewhat dated. Nonetheless, despite improvement schemes, 'model' housing, and a lot of good intentions, Bethnal Green still had an average income somewhere below fifteen shillings a week. He smiled back at her to show he didn't care.

Munro asked how she had found Struther Jarrold's name at the book shops.

'Oh, I told them I had a set of signed copies of Denton's books, and did they know anybody who'd buy them. They said *they* would, of course, and I said each time that I'd get more money from a collector. That was thought amusing; one of them said I ought to go into the book trade. But most of them looked through their lists of customers with special wants, and five of them came up with this Jarrold. I can give you a list of the shops, if you like.'

Munro looked at Markson, then at Denton. Denton said, 'Well?'

Munro shifted his bulk, looked at Markson. The younger detective said, 'We don't want to, uh, take the wrong step—'

Denton plunged his hands deep into his trouser pockets. 'You've got enough now—the letters, the threat, the attack on me—'

'And woe betide us if we're wrong,' Munro growled. 'If this what's-his-name—Jarrold—is like anybody else in Eaton Square, he'll have a solicitor beside him before we can get our first question out, and if we try to take him up on a charge, he'll walk because we can't prove he attacked you, we can't prove he wrote the letters, and we can't prove he was ever inside the house behind yours.'

'Search his lodging.'

'I don't know how you do it out West, sheriff, but here we have to get a warrant. Nobody on the bench is going to give me a warrant on a suspicion that there might be something in somebody's lodging that had come out of your house. I grant you there's a circumstantial case. I'll take it to the prosecutor, but I know what he'll say: get me the evidence.'

Markson gave Denton a pleading look. 'Fingerprint Branch are at the lady's now.'

'My piano,' she said.

'Yes, ma'am, they'll do the piano, too.'

'No, I mean they must take extra care with the piano.'

The two detectives laughed, then saw too late she wasn't joking. There was some lame fence-mending, some temporizing, and then Janet Striker said, 'Do you mean, then, that you won't be arresting him?'

'Well—not at once, ma'am—' Markson made the mistake of trying to explain the rules of evidence in a tone he'd have used to a child. Things started to get worse, and then Munro dragged Markson to his feet and the two detectives took themselves off.

When the street door had closed on them, Janet Striker gave a horrible laugh, pulled her hatpins out and threw her little hat as far down the room as she could. 'Oh, the majesty of the law!' she shouted.

'They're doing their job.'

'Don't patronize me! Bloody fools! At least they were stunned when they first saw me.'

'I hardly recognized you.'

'It's the dress.' She held out the sides of the skirt. 'I borrowed it from one of Ruth Castle's French girls.'

'You look wonderful.'

She was going to say something angry, then caught herself. 'It isn't you; it's *them*.' She shook herself. 'Damn them.' Walking up and down, she quieted, then laughed, apparently at herself. 'I had to go to Oxford Street for underclothes—oh, dear God, a corset! I haven't worn a corset in ten years! I can't wait to get out of it.'

'Do.' He knew at once it was a mistake; sexual innuendo didn't work on her.

She looked angry. 'I have to see my solicitor and I have to find a removal man and I said I'd have this dress back by six. First things first—appalling thing to say. I know it, I know it. Oh, God! Oh, damn the police! That they should make this fuss over *my* rooms in Bethnal Green, and they wouldn't stir out of New Scotland Yard if my neighbours had had their throats slit!' She began to stride up and down again. 'I live in half of what used to be a weaving loft at the top of a ramshackle house. Now the weaving trade's gone west and the room's been divided, me on one side and three girls in the other. There've been robberies in that house, beatings, drunken abuse, and the only time the police have come is now—you know why? Because of you!' She turned on him. 'It isn't your doing, I know, but if Cosgrove or Jarrold or whoever he is hadn't painted his demon's name on my wall, I'd have rated nobody higher than the local constable. But they connect him with you, and you're well off and you're famous! Don't you see the unfairness of it? The comical, terrible unfairness of it? And then I present them with his name and they won't charge him!' As quickly as it had come, the mood vanished. 'Oh, to hell with it.' She laughed a little nastily. She snatched up the hat and grabbed his hand and started towards the door. 'See me into my cab.'

While he was out getting dinner, a constable came with a message from Munro. Atkins met him with it at the front door: *We have a fingerprint. Keep it to yourself.*

Denton was at New Scotland Yard at eight the next morning. He felt guilty at not working; on the other hand, getting Albert Cosgrove out of his life would certainly make the writing go more easily. He expected to be told that Munro was not yet in; to the contrary, Munro was sitting at his desk in the CID room, the space mostly quiet now as a new shift began. Several men were gathered around a movable blackboard, talking and rubbing chalk from their fingers; a couple of others were at the desks. Munro looked grey, older, somehow handsomer because of his obvious fatigue.

'You have somewhat the look of a Romantic,' Denton said. 'Not one of the ones who died young.'

'Spent the night here. I was at the magistrate's until half one, then back here to get it on paper. No way to get to Peckham that hour of the morning.' He had a mug of tea, waved to somebody to fetch one for Denton. 'Hope you've eaten. The canteen's swill.'

'Have you?'

'Been eating all night—the only way to stay alive—if you can't sleep, eat. Stopped at a coffee stall and got a bag of buns. Horrible sweet things—the stuff of police life.' He rubbed his eyes. 'You want to hear it?'

'Of course I do.'

'We picked Jarrold up last evening. Took his fingerprint. Matched the one on the piano lid. Like he'd dipped his finger in the paint to do it. Took him straight to police court; magistrate was an antique, but he was up on fingerprints—new Bureau has done its work. Got a warrant to search, too.'

'What's Jarrold like?'

'Like a plant that's been kept indoors too long. Pale, not so much fat as he doesn't seem to have any muscles. Bag of jelly sort of thing. Perfectly amiable. Smiled, wanted to talk, but not about the case. Absolutely mum on that. Half an hour after he got here, two legal gents showed up, very high on the tree, one in evening dress, both making I'd guess about ten times what I do.'

'You said that would happen.'

'Yeah, well, what it turns out, Denton, is that Struther Jarrold comes from a very powerful and very rich family. He lives with his mother—that's the Belgravia address—and she's Lady Emmeline Jarrold.'

'Where's Lord Jarrold?'

'There isn't any Lord Jarrold; why would there be a Lord Jarrold?' He sounded irritable.

'You say she's Lady something or other.'

'Lady Emmeline. Because she's the sister of the Duke of Edderton.'

'Who's her husband, then?'

'Dead. He *was* Captain Jarrold.'

'But—'

Munro leaned forward, his huge hands splayed on the desktop. He spoke slowly, as if to a backward child. 'Duke's daughters get called "Lady". They marry commoners, the commoners stay common. Can we take that as read now?' He wiped a hand down his face. 'I'm too tired for this. Find yourself a *Debrett's.*'

'I'll never understand this country.'

'Nor me, and I'm Canadian.' Munro produced a crumpled white paper from a drawer, then took a sugar bun, somewhat the worse for the night, from the paper. He munched. 'Markson's the officer of record, so he laid the charge, but I was there because I thought the legal gentry might make mincemeat of him. Also had somebody from the prosecutor's shindig. In the event, Markson did all right.' He finished the bun and dusted grains of sugar from his fingers. 'However.'

'I thought you might be leading up to that.'

'Feeling of nameless dread? Yeah, I had it all through the arraignment.' He put his forearms on the desk again. 'Here's where we are: things are not ideal, but they're passable. Markson laid a charge of breaking and entering at Mrs Denton's, a charge of wilful destruction of property, and a charge of denial of quiet enjoyment. We laid no charges having to do with you, your house, or the house behind because we don't have hard evidence and it's better to wait until we do.

'My super got the chief super out of the theatre last night to tell him that we'd arrested a relative of the Duke of Edderton. Chief Super's immediate judgement—wise, I think—was that we go only with the things we can prove. Can always build a case on the circumstantials later, hope Jarrold gives us more in examination.

'Jarrold's counsel objected ten times—this is in *police court*!—and pled him not guilty on all counts. Magistrate let him out on bond of ten pounds and his recognizance.'

'Oh, my God.'

'He's got no record, Denton. We cited no crime against persons—the attack on you wasn't in it—and you're talking about a duke's nephew, or whatever the hell he is, and invasion of two rooms in bloody Bethnal Green! The clothes were old and shabby. The damned piano is good only for firewood. It's the sort of thing you call a prank if you're counsel for the defence.'

'He's dangerous, Munro.'

Munro took another bun from the sack. He wet a finger and used it to lift loose grains of sugar, then licked it. 'His lawyers will fight the fingerprint evidence as an untested theory. They said so. They were quite jolly about it—strong suggestion that it would be like a slice off the rare to them. Not quite honest of them—they know it would be the test case for fingerprints, so the police and the prosecutors would throw everything into it. In fact, I suspect they'd rather not go to court over it.' He put his head on one hand. 'However, Crown Prosecutor's office had a message from the Home Secretary this a.m. that he doesn't want to use this as the test case on fingerprints.'

'But that's the strongest evidence you have!'

'His view—and looked at from his place, Denton, he's right—his view is that when we go to court on fingerprint evidence for the first time ever, he wants a sure conviction. To him, that means a full hand of prints and corroborating evidence—that is, good enough that we could convict without the prints. From his viewpoint, it's important to the whole future of the use of fingerprints. I mean, imagine what would happen if we went to court on Jarrold and lost.'

Denton broke off a piece of the sugar bun and chewed it. The currants on the outside had got hard; inside, they were still fairly good, unlike the bun itself. He said, 'Tell me the worst.'

'If he'll plead guilty, we'll reduce the charges to trespassing on the premises of another and disrespect of private property.'

'No imprisonment.'

Munro shook his head. 'Counsel hinted last night that they'll go for such a thing. They're putting it out this morning that Jarrold has been under strain, temporarily unbalanced. Prosecutor thinks they'll be willing to accept some sort of house arrest under medical supervision, meaning in fact that young Struther will tiptoe off to Mummy's castle in Sussex and be very quiet for a while.'

'He's dangerous!'

'And there's something more.' Munro had sat back, now turned sideways in his chair. He was looking at the edge of the desk, not at Denton, picking at a splinter with a fingernail. 'If they go to court, everything about you and Mrs Striker will be splattered over the papers brighter than the paint on her walls. No, let me speak. I don't know what's between the two of you—it isn't my business—but it was plain yesterday there's something. You lit up like a magic lantern when she came into your room.

'These people will be ruthless, Denton. They'll hire detectives by the long ton. They'll find out everything, and then the papers will double that with half-truths and plain lies.'

'I don't give a damn.'

'And everything will come out about *her*. I know who she is, Denton. Do you want to put her through that again? They'll start up the old crap about her killing her husband. They'll say she was insane. You and I know she didn't kill him; he was a rotten bastard who treated her like shit, but that's not the line they'll take. He put her in a mental institution to tame her, but what'll be said is that she was mad and he committed her because she was dangerous. Do you want her to go through that?' Before Denton could answer—the question had been rhetorical, anyway—Munro said, 'They'll put Mrs Striker on the stand and ask her under oath if she's been a prostitute. Their line will be that she still is and she lured Jarrold to her rooms and did something to make him angry—tricked him, mocked him. Do you want that?'

Denton breathed noisily. He said, 'You'll have to ask her.'

'I thought you'd be in touch with her.'

'It isn't like that. She makes her own decisions.'

Munro stared at him, shrugged.

'What's the alternative to a trial?' Denton said.

'Let him plead him guilty to lesser charges. Wait.'

'Until he does something worse?'

Munro picked at the bit of wood. 'And then only if he leaves evidence.'

Denton wasn't present when Struther Jarrold pled guilty to the reduced charges. He saw Jarrold outside the courtroom for an instant, got what he thought was a shy smile of recognition that was also a look of satisfaction. The pasty face was that, he thought, of the man he'd seen on the bench at New Scotland Yard days before.

The actual proceedings happened in chambers, to the disappointment of not only Denton but also a small crowd of journalists. Balked of Jarrold—his legal counsel took him down the judge's private stairs and out a back way—the newspapermen crowded around Denton. He was prepared, however: his tale was that he was there looking over the courts for a new book;

he knew nothing about Jarrold; it was all a mystery to him; why didn't they go after Mr Jarrold?

'Mr Denton, what's your relationship with the Striker woman?'

'What's that?'

'Woman whose rooms were vandalized. What's the connection?'

'No idea what you're driving at.' Where had he learned that expression? Guillam—the former CID man had said that to him. Useful line.

'Isn't the Striker woman the same one whose life you saved a year ago? Shot the eye out of the crazed killer that was holding her?'

'Oh, really?'

'Mr Denton, Mr Denton! There was a crime at your premises—any connection?'

'My premises?'

'Break-in at the house behind. What's the connection with this Janet Striker?'

'I think you've got the wrong end of the stick.'

'Mr Denton, is this Striker woman the same one who was put in an institution by her husband some years ago? Great scandal—hospital for the criminally insane—did she do this to her own premises? Is she at it again?'

He bit his tongue. 'You're asking the wrong man.'

'Mr Denton—Mr Denton—!'

He pushed his way through them. 'I've got work to do—Sorry—Let me pass, please—' He was almost free of them when a florid man his own height blocked his way. When Denton tried to go around, the big man put a hand on his chest. Denton looked down at the hand, up at the man's eyes. He said, 'I'll give you three seconds to take that hand away.' The man flushed, dropped his hand. The others hooted.

Mostly, the newspapers judged that either there was no story to be told, or the story was about powerful people whom they didn't discuss in the public press. *The Times* reported nothing. Another paper buried a short piece headed 'Peer's Relative Pleads' on an inner page. Only the *Daily Mail* attempted to make a story of it, raking up Janet Striker's past and her connection to Denton through the violence of a year before but suggesting no other link. It did quote 'a gentleman close to the said Jarrold's legal counsel' who had said that 'Jarrold was a loyal reader of Mr Denton's well-known works', but he had offered no other explanation for the attack on Janet Striker's rooms than 'the great stress felt by a sensitive nature'. Denton frowned at a single sentence near the end of the piece: 'A source close to New Scotland Yard expressed concern at the possible connection between the American novelist, a guest in this country, and recurring acts of violence.'

Guillam.

'Damn Guillam!' he shouted.

'Sue him. We've strict laws of libel this side of the water, Colonel.'

Denton flung the paper back at Atkins. 'I don't know how you can read that trash.'

'Down here in the lower classes, we don't know any better.'

'Oh, dry up.'

'There's tea made. Want some?'

'Ever occur to you that we were better off in prison, Sergeant?'

'Book going badly?'

'No, it's going like a house afire—when I can get away from these damned distractions. Bring me tea, yes. Upstairs.' He went up and worked until evening. The stack of manuscript had grown thick, that already typed representing at least half of the book in its neat pile on the corner of the desk. He was able now to spend most of the day writing new material, then take the typed part to bed to correct before he went to sleep. Janet Striker had got herself a room in a small private hotel in Bayswater. Her piano, minus the lid—it had gone off to the Yard with its finger-print—had been carted down to Collard and Collard 'successors to Clementi and Company' for repair. If she was dismayed by the newspaper's raking up of her old life, she didn't say so, murmuring only that she would stay away from him for a few days while the newspapermen cooled down, at her legal counsel's advice—she dared do nothing that might threaten the resolution of her lawsuit.

'And I'm to stay away from you, I suppose.'

'I suppose.'

It didn't seem to him a very good reason, but neither did her concern with propriety or with his public self. She was, he thought, making excuses, and not because of the sex itself. Unless she was pretending (and there was always the knowledge that she had been a prostitute, that dissembling might be habit), sex came easily and rather happily to her. It was, rather, that he was a man. She believed men hated women. All men, all women: there seemed to be no exceptions. She had been raped by a man, abused by a man, humiliated by a man, institutionalized by a man. Men had paid her to invade her. Why, then, should she trust him? Why should she run to have him invade her—although he hated that notion of it, that one of them invaded and the other let it be done: surely it was a mutual wanting, the desire to become one? Or was that a man's self-congratulation?

One day, he feared, she would go away. Perhaps she would write him a letter; perhaps she would simply go, and he wouldn't know how to find her. Once she had money, she could go wherever, be whatever she wanted. Her present skittishness, as he thought of it, might be prelude to something more permanent. It wasn't coyness that was keeping her away from him; it was fear—of the maleness she believed hated her femaleness—and perhaps a bleak sense that it was too late for her, or perhaps that he was the wrong one. Or she was the wrong one. Better a life alone than one that rested on a bad bargain—he knew that feeling.

So he shared his bed with the typed page.

The next day, he went to complain to Munro about the 'source close to New Scotland Yard' that had been quoted in the *Daily*

Mail. 'That's Guillam!' he all but shouted at Munro. 'What the hell is he doing messing in the Jarrold business?'

Munro was busy and tired. His expression suggested a stomach ailment. He looked at Denton through splayed fingers and said, 'The Jarrold business *is* Guillam's business. Jarrold's fallen into Guillam's pocket.'

'What the hell is that supposed to mean?'

'It means that Georgie Guillam knows how to work the system. I told you—his new office is a catch-all. He persuaded somebody that house arrests are his.'

'That's because of me! It is because of me, isn't it?'

Munro shrugged. 'I told you he doesn't forget. Yes, maybe he saw your name on it and thought there's something in it for him. Nothing I can do about it. It's out of CID. You want to complain, complain to Georgie.'

'Oh, hell!'

'Yeah.'

He got his friend Hector Hench-Rose—his baronetcy still so new it sparkled—to write him a letter of introduction to Lady Emmeline, Struther Jarrold's mother. Jarrold was said to be under medical supervision in Sussex; the mother, Denton thought, might be amenable to a serious chat about her son.

His first look at her suggested to him that perhaps she would.

She was at least as old as he, probably older, but with the most beautiful posture he had ever seen in a woman; she stood straight, not affecting the buttocks-out curve of the new corsetry. A former 'beauty', she still had magnificent facial bones, a figure as slender as a girl's. Her pale hair, partly silver that blended into its original gold, was piled high on her head. She wore a dress of very pale beige with touches of apricot, her slender arms covered in lace, a jabot of the same cascading down her front to below where a vulgar eye might have imagined her to have a navel. She was holding his friend's letter of introduction.

'I am so pleased we can have this talk,' were her first words. She seemed able to speak almost without moving her lower jaw; her accent was odd and to him unidentifiable, reminiscent of Ruth Castle's when she was well into the champagne. She raised the letter a few inches. 'I am unacquainted with the current baronet but knew his father, I think. Such a gentle man.'

'I wanted to speak to you about your son, ma'am.'

'About Struther, yes, poor dear. Have you come to apologize? Oh, I do hope you have come to apologize.' Her tone was sad, her voice lovely.

'Apologize, ma'am? For what?'

She sat. Her back was wonderfully straight; he doubted that her shoulders had ever touched a chair back. Her sadness seemed to expand to include pity, as if she knew that Denton was the sort who couldn't help himself and therefore might—*might*— be forgiven. 'For seducing my poor boy. For forcing him to this unfortunate incident that the police say took him to East London.'

'Ma'am, it's not I—'

The sadness in her voice grew metallic. The metal, he thought, was steel. 'I know how you have worked to seduce him! I know how you have played upon his sensitive nature! I have seen the copies of your *books*—' she made the word sound like a synonym for excrement—'which you inscribed to him. Oh, sir, though I feel distaste for saying it—*for shame!*'

'I haven't inscribed any books to him, ma'am.'

She sighed. 'You are a practised liar, too, I see.'

'Any books inscribed to your son are forgeries.'

'Do you dare to suggest that my son is *a forger?* You are pathetic as well as untruthful.' The sadness fled; only the steel was left. 'Leave me.'

'He did ask me to inscribe books to him as Albert Cosgrove. Why did he call himself Albert Cosgrove?'

'He did nothing of the sort.' She looked away. 'Although pseudonyms are not unknown among literary artists.'

Denton was still standing; he saw no hope of being asked to sit. 'Your son is mentally unbalanced, Lady Emmeline.'

'How dare you!'

'He's dangerous—what he did in Bethnal Green is one step shy of violence—'

'You go too far, much too far—'

'Against a woman—'

'We shall sue you—there is no escape—' She seemed to have heard what he had said, at last, for she hissed, 'A *woman*! Do you mean the trollop who lured him to her squalid room? I warn you, Mr, Mr—' she made a gesture that rendered Denton's name worthless—'we shall learn everything and we shall sue you and see you broken. Justice will be on our side. I had thought you had some spark of decency, that you had prevailed upon *a baronet* to write a letter so that you might confess your crimes, but you—*you are contemptible.*'

'Lady Emmeline, your son is not sane!'

She somehow managed to sit still straighter. 'You are speaking of the nephew of a duke!' Her bizarre accent made it come out as 'the nivioo of a juke'.

'The dangerous "nivioo of a juke", I think, ma'am.'

She stood. Her nostrils flared ever so slightly—as extreme a sign of passion as she allowed herself, he supposed—and she said, 'Leave my house, you *vulgar* little man!'

He bowed. 'Vulgar I am, ma'am. Little, I ain't.' He headed for the door. There seemed no point in staying.

CHAPTER

14

'His mama implied that you had lured her poor boy to your room. I suppose she thinks you provided the red paint, too.'

Janet Striker made a face. 'And Jarrold-known-as-Cosgrove has been sent off to Mama's country house with two male nurses. Detective Sergeant Munro is keeping me up to date.'

Denton scowled. 'Some house arrest—hard time in a stately home. Couple of medical men to look in weekly, presumably with lunch laid on. Hard on them, too.'

Janet Striker laughed. 'No good being angry.'

'He's getting off as good as scot-free. I'd tan his hide for him.'

They were eating at Pinoli's in Wardour Street. He was in 'informal' evening clothes—short black jacket with silk revers, white waistcoat, white tie—and she was in a new suit of a dark-green wool tailored to an almost masculine cut, the jacket thigh-length like a frock coat, the skirt box-pleated at the front and back to accommodate her long stride. 'I like that dress,' he said.

'It isn't a dress; it's a suit. You look like a successful manufacturer.'

'Good a disguise as any.'

'I thought you enjoyed being an outsider.'

'It's no good if you have to work at it. Working at it is Bohemian, isn't it—the Slade kids in their rags?'

She laughed. 'I'd never take you for a Bohemian.'

A week had gone by. The book's end was in sight, if he could keep up the pace. She'd spent a night at his house; a meeting at her hotel had proved less happy—he'd taken a room overnight, had come to her room. It had seemed 'sordid', in her word. He had had to admit it had been pretty scatty. He said, 'We have to make some better arrangement.'

'We will.' She had a small, ridiculous hat perched on her forehead; it looked like a soldier's pillbox, except that instead of a chinstrap it had a ribbon that went around the back of her head. She said, 'I keep feeling that that thing is falling off into my food.'

'It's perky.'

'"Perky"! Mrs Cohan has an idea for a kind of homburg with a fancy band.'

'*Mrs* Cohan. Wife to the Stepney Jew-Boy?'

'They live in the same house as I did, two floors down. She sews—six days a week, making shirts to sell for three-and-six apiece, for which she gets fourpence each. He has no job, as you know. And they're good people, Denton! She does magnificent embroidery—in Poland, she did wedding dresses and court gowns. She's going to make me more dresses. We're thinking along rather Janey-Morris-y lines.'

Denton looked blank.

'William Morris's bride. The original Pre-Raphaelite woman. *No* corset and her hair unbound. Ruth Castle told me about her when I was a beginner.'

'You'll be a sight on Oxford Street.'

'I shan't wear them on Oxford Street. I'll wear them at home, and this sort of thing—' she pulled at one lapel of her jacket—'when I'm out.'

'Now who's planning to wear a disguise?'

'Well—There'll be a real me and a pretend me, and the real one will live at home—if ever I get a home again. I'm so sick of hotels!'

'I don't know much about women's clothes.'

'Do you know much about women? Yes, of course you do. I think you mean you don't *care* about women's clothes.' She sipped wine.

'I care about you.'

They stumbled along. Cohan finished getting the weeds and brambles out of the back garden. He and Atkins started to plan what they'd plant in the spring. Mrs Striker moved to another hotel. When Denton said to Cohan that he understood he was a priest descended from Aaron, Cohan said, 'I am not beink a very good Jew.' Nonetheless, when Denton told him what Fred Oldaston had said about Mrs Franken and her two whorehouses, Cohan had looked severe and said he didn't need work that much.

Denton continued to write, the end now in sight. One day, Atkins reminded him that he was supposed to go to a party at his publishers—the launching of the book of ghost stories that Lang had told him about. He groaned, said he wouldn't go, but he did go, because Janet Striker told him he should. And because he couldn't be with her that evening.

At six on a blustery afternoon, he went up the creaking stairs that led to Gweneth and Burse and through 'reception', which was simply a part of the corridor that connected the offices. The party was in the room where they packaged the books, swept more or less clean and provided with a table where sherry and several platters of things in jelly stood. He looked around from the doorway, seeking somebody to kill the time with before he could decently leave. He was wearing an old morning coat, which Atkins had said 'would do' because it was still early and he wasn't going on anywhere, but most of the other men—and they were mostly men—were in some form of evening dress.

Standing near the outer wall, where windows looked down into Bell Yard, was Henry James, who was undoubtedly going on to dinner somewhere, to judge by his formal evening clothes and the fact that he was an aggressive diner-out. As Denton looked his way, James raised his eyes, recognized him and nodded. James was tallish, rather heavy, with shrewd, hard eyes; only a few years older than Denton, also American, but he had sat out the American Civil War while Denton had fought it—a divide that was to separate their generation for the rest of their lives. Denton felt towards him the faint resentment the soldier feels for men who haven't served, then a counter-balancing remorse for his own prejudice; James, on the other hand, seemed to feel something the reverse, so the two were always pleasant to each other out of guilt. As writers and as men, they were very different, yet they always gravitated towards each other.

'I read your latest with considerable interest,' James said as soon as Denton was close, 'and, I think, with satisfaction, although that is hardly a word that honours a work, I suppose, when heard by the author, or am I presuming to impose my own sensibilities on someone else's, hardly unheard of in the world of books.' He chuckled. Denton said something vague; he was never good at accepting praise, worse at giving it when it came to other people's books. James was *le maître* to his sycophants, but Denton couldn't pretend to worship at his shrine. James put his fingers and thumb around Denton's arm just above the elbow as if measuring it. He moved in closer and said in a low voice, 'Do they do you pretty well at this publishers?' He looked around the room.

Do him pretty well? Denton said, 'We mostly get along.'

'I'm never entirely confident of my publishers, whoever they be. The matter of royalty is vexing, constantly vexing, offered at a certain level and then haggled over as if the Man of Galilee had driven the money-changers out of the temple and into the publishing office.' He shook Denton's arm a little. 'What do you think of these people who call themselves "agents"? They assure me they can lever better terms from the publishers, their letters sometimes quite impertinent, but then they confess they require some of it for themselves, a situation that I must admit gives me unease, not because I am naive in the ways of business, because I am not, but rather the opposite, for no one can have hovered about books for as long as I without learning that the income to be made from a book is finite and represents a sum that can be divided into only so many pieces without, like the crow in the Aesop's fable—or is it the monkey? how one's memory plays tricks—dividing it into nothingness. I wonder if these would-be "agents" are not simply opportunists who think authors are fools.'

Denton admitted that he had had some letters from would-be agents himself and was tempted.

'Exactly. But one doesn't want to be the first to step into this perhaps inviting pool and find it to be not sweet water but something unsavoury, perhaps in fact corrosive.' James stood with his head slightly bent, still holding Denton's arm, his bright eyes scavenging the room like those of some intelligent bird, a pied crow that, if its tongue were split and it were taught to talk, would say malicious things. It was as if James were always on the lookout for scandal or at least its potential, James's idea of the world of fiction, at least in Denton's view, being very close to gossip. Such an approach was not Denton's, just as James's ambience was not his. As if guessing his thought, James shook his arm again and said, 'Our work is very different, yours and mine, yet both are to be admired. That is rather a conundrum. I have been thinking about it a good deal for a preface. The house of fiction has many windows, has it not?'

'For us to look out of?' Denton laughed. 'I'd have said it was a house that had many doors.'

'Aha, you shift my metaphor. Perhaps a separate entrance for ladies, at least, if not a separate house. No, I was thinking of the way we see and what we see and then what we do with what we see, each from his own window. Tell me now, what do you make of the vulgar concept of "the plot"? People who don't know any better are forever asking me where I get my plots, as if I bought them with my shirts at a guinea a dozen. You don't worry yourself greatly over "the plot", surely?'

Denton tried to think about it. He lacked James's interest in criticism, seldom worked in such terms. 'I suppose I begin with situation,' he said. He thought of the book he was trying to finish, the husband and wife and the ghostly child. 'Or an exchange. Some kind of interaction.'

'Aha! Very good. Interaction. Mmm. And then "the plot" comes along like a child's wooden toy that gets pulled on a string, mechanically bobbing its head and wagging its tail. Yes. I quite agree. Although I begin rather differently; how matters not.' His eyes had continued to dart about, even though his head was down and he and Denton might have seemed to be discussing secrets.

Denton thought about how they must look, then reminded himself that they were the only Americans there. The outsiders. It might have been the title of a Jamesian novel. He said, 'I'd have said that you and I stand on the outside of the windows with our noses pressed against the glass, not that we were looking from the inside out.'

James let go of his arm. His little smile seemed almost apologetic. 'You are made of even harder stuff than I. I fear it's important to me to be safely inside.' He prepared to move off. He pulled down a cuff and touched his white necktie. 'I see Edmund Gosse over there. I must ask him about someone to paint my portrait. My publisher insists upon a portrait frontispiece for a collected works. I was to have been painted by Himple, RA, but he suddenly decamped for places unknown. I suppose this was "artistic" of him, but it leaves me in what Americans of our generation call "a pickle". I have waited for him for months. Really, one should be able to be "artistic" and still maintain some regularity to one's life.' He gave Denton his small smile and a glance from his sharp eyes, up through his brows. 'Thank you for your most helpful comments about our craft.'

Denton was able to get away twenty minutes after that. He had smiled at Lang and avoided Gweneth, the publisher who thought he had cheated them out of the motor car.

Atkins had circled a small article in the military-affairs page of *The Times*. Denton found it open on his morning tray:

END OF AN OFFICER'S TRIAL
'Compassion' Cited in Guilty Verdict

The court-martial proceedings against Lieutenant Aubrey Heseltine, Imperial Yeomanry, ended yesterday with a verdict of guilty to a lesser included charge. The reduction in charge, from Withdrawal in the Face of the Enemy to Failure to Obey a Lawful Order, was the result, a spokesman for the court-martial board said, of consideration for Lieutenant Heseltine's medical condition. He is said to be suffering from a nervous disorder.

The officer was sentenced to loss of three months' pay, loss of emoluments and privileges, and return of his commission to the Crown without compensation. He is not to use the rank or wear the King's uniform again in any circumstances.

Several witnesses spoke to his medical condition and to his good conduct before the incident at Spattenkopje which led to the charge.

'Poor devil,' Denton muttered.

'If he'd been other ranks, they'd have shot him.' Atkins was pouring tea. 'Bloo-ha! Discipline! Make an example of him!' Atkins had turned himself into a fat general of about seventy. 'My hat!'

'I'll go see him.'

'You finish that book, General. There's bills to pay.'

'I can finish the book *and* go see him.' He bit into a piece of toast. 'What's happening?'

'Today, you mean? The usual. Mrs Char coming to do the rooms.'

'Good time for me to be out of the house. Don't let her into my room.'

'Cleanliness is next to godliness.'

'God isn't an author.'

He thought he needed a reason to visit Heseltine—he could hardly show up and say something like *I thought as you'd been found guilty, I'd drop by*—so he put one of the photographic copies of Mary Thomason's drawing into a leather case and carried it along. And it would be an opportunity to try the art dealer, Geddys, again. Or hadn't he promised Munro to leave Mary Thomason to the police? Meaning to Guillam and his little empire. Who had done nothing.

A sleety rain was coming down. He put on a pair of heavy tweed trousers he'd had since his first winter in London, a single-breasted wool coat that matched nothing but its own waistcoat, and another of the high collars that he despised.

'Find me some shirts with soft collars,' he snarled to Atkins. 'Not proper.'

'To hell with "proper". I feel as if I'm wearing a slave collar.'

'Have to get them made special, Colonel—cost you.'

'And worth it.'

He pulled on an unfitted tweed ulster that billowed around his legs, something else he had bought years before. It had the virtue of keeping the rain off, but it was as heavy as the flock of sheep it had come from. Only as wide as his shoulders at the top, it expanded to yards of circumference at the skirts.

'If the wind is blowing, I'll sail away over the rooftops of London,' he said as he went down to the front door. 'I'll send you a postcard from Paris.'

'If you'd had me when you bought that garment, you'd not have bought it.' Atkins handed him a soft tweed hat. 'This hat's really for shooting, mind.'

'Maybe I'll shoot somebody, then.' He didn't, however, take the new revolver, the danger supposedly over now that Jarrold-known-as-Cosgrove was in his luxurious detention.

He wanted to walk, but it was too foul a day—sleet blowing in sheets from the west, wet slush piling up along the edges of pavements; part of a newspaper came pelting down the street, head-high, and he backed out of its path. His elastic-sided boots were soaked by the time he reached Russell Square, and he gave in and waved over a cab.

Albany Court was deserted, its plane trees bare now, the old man who stood nominal watch at the gate huddled in a kiosk. He merely waved Denton through, not willing to suffer a wetting. Heseltine's 'man'—what was his name? Jenkins? Jenks?—opened the door. He was freshly shaven but his skin was blotchy, splashes of red on his nose and cheeks like stains. It was early in the day; he seemed sober. He even seemed to remember Denton.

'Mr Heseltine isn't well, sir.'

'I just thought he might like to look at something.' Denton lifted the leather case a few inches.

'I'll just see.' Jenks—the name was certainly Jenks; he was sure now—made a slow about-face and felt his way across the room. Presumably he was drunk, after all. Denton wondered if it suited Jenks best to have Heseltine 'ill', confined to his room, not out and about where he could check the level of the sherry and ask questions.

'Coming right out, sir. Tea? Or coffee? It's morning. Isn't it?'

'Nothing, thanks. And yes, it's morning.'

Heseltine appeared, again in a long dressing gown, a common wool scarf at his throat instead of collar and tie. They shook hands. Heseltine said, 'You heard, I'm sure.' He seemed quite calm.

'I'm sorry it turned out as it did.'

'It could have been worse.' Heseltine took a cigarette from a box, offered Denton one, then stood with his unlighted. 'There comes a point during the court martial when you say, "What's the worst that can happen?" and you realize that the worst *is* happening. That you're already there, already prepared.' He struck a match. 'My father was heartbroken. For me.'

'I'm sorry.'

'He's a clergyman. Had I told you that? Quiet little village, rather quintessentially English, quite out of date. He believes in goodness. Is a good man himself. He said, "Come home. All will be well."' He lit the cigarette.

'Will all be well?' Denton murmured.

Heseltine tried to laugh; the voice sounded cracked.

'I thought you might like to see this.' Denton opened the clasp on the leather envelope. 'It's a drawing of the young woman who wrote the note you found in your painting.' He looked towards the Wesselons.

'Wherever did you get it?'

'Probably somebody she modelled for did it.' He handed the drawing over. Heseltine looked at it, perhaps more out of politeness than real interest. Denton watched his eyes travel over the drawing, then down to the corners where the two miniatures were. For an instant, something happened to his face—a gathering between the brows, a dipping of the head to look more closely—and then there was an almost visibly conscious recovery that included a glance at Denton. 'Very nice,' he said. He handed the drawing back.

'I thought you'd seen something.'

'Oh, no. The little sketches are hard to see. The head is quite well done.'

'Some of the students at the Slade recognized her, anyway.'

'What's happened to her?'

Denton shook his head. 'I've reported it to the police. Nothing else to be done, I guess.'

'I've been thinking about that young woman. Rather looking for things to think about, you know. I wondered—you'll find this the morbid thought of a disappointed man, I suppose—I wondered if she put the note in the painting so it would be found.'

'And you found it.'

'Not by me. Somebody else. It sounds rather daft now I say it. I thought she might have meant it for the person who was trying to "hurt" her—isn't that what you told me? Put in the back of the painting like that, it could have been for somebody at the shop. Or—I told you somebody else had been going to buy the Wesselons.'

'In an envelope with my name on it?'

'Yes, that's rather the sticking place, isn't it. Well, it was just a thought. Not much of one, as it turns out.'

Heseltine didn't seem really to care. If Mary Thomason had once had some interest for him, even some idea that he might achieve something by helping her, it was gone. They chatted in a desultory way for a few more minutes. Denton said, 'How's Jenks been behaving?'

'Oh, he's atrocious. I shall have to get rid of him.' But he had said that before. He came to the door with Denton and paused, fingers on the knob as if he meant to hold it closed. 'My father wants me to come home.'

'It might be the best thing.'

'It sounds absurd, but I can't face those people.' He put his hand on the doorknob. 'I may go away.'

'Going someplace for a few years might not be the worst idea—Australia, Canada, the States. Put it behind you. Everybody west of the Mississippi is putting something behind him.'

'I've lost my nerve.'

The rain had turned away from sleet but was still coming down. Denton pulled the hat brim lower and took the few steps along Piccadilly to the arcade and moved into its welcome shelter. What Heseltine had said about the note and the painting didn't seem convincing, but it did suggest one or two possibilities. He had promised Janet he would talk to Geddys, anyway—how long was it since he'd tried and been told Geddys was travelling? Turning into Geddys's shop, he saw Geddys standing there looking more than ever the gnome—some bent, malicious creature standing guard over a cave full of valuable, probably stolen things.

'I was in a while ago,' Denton said. 'I came back, but you seem to have been travelling.' Geddys gave no sign of recognition, but Denton thought that in fact he remembered him. 'About a note that was left with a painting. A Wesselons sketch of a lion.' He wondered if Geddys had been away at all.

'Oh, yes?'

'Mary Thomason.'

'Oh, yes, I recollect.'

'Mr Geddys, you told me that you didn't know where Mary Thomason lived.'

'Naturally.'

'Her landlady says you sometimes saw her home.'

'Did she.'

Denton waited for more. Apparently there was to be none. He said, 'I've reported this to the police since I was here. Have they been to talk to you?'

'Of course not.'

'I could make sure that they do.'

Geddys looked up at him, his neck twisted to one side. He said, 'I don't get what you're about. You've no authority to come in here asking questions.'

'Why did you lie to me?'

'That is offensive.'

'Look, Geddys, it's me or the police. They're a good deal more offensive than I am. Why did you lie to me?'

'Please leave my shop.'

'You saw the young woman home a number of times. Why did you want to hide that from me? What was going on?'

'I'll have a constable called if you don't leave.'

'Was there something between you?' Geddys was ready to make a battle of it, but Denton jumped in. 'She wrote me that she was afraid somebody was going to hurt her. She's disappeared. You lied about how well you knew her. What do you think the police will make of it?'

Geddys licked his lips. 'I don't wish to be involved.'

'But you are involved. You involved yourself by lying to me. What was going on between you?'

Geddys turned away and walked the few steps to the front of the shop. He bent to arrange something in the front window. 'Do the police have to come into this?' His voice was a whisper.

'I don't have to call them specially, if that's what you mean.'

Geddys began to examine small objects on a low table. 'She was a very—captivating girl. I became a little—interested in her.' He looked up quickly. 'But nothing happened! I swear it. I'll swear it to the police. Yes, I took her home in a cab several times when the weather was bad. It was a chance to help her. But nothing happened!' He finished moving the things and straightened. 'I'm a coward. Look at me—you think it would be easy to offer yourself to a young woman if you looked like me?' He walked to the shop window again, stood looking out past the paintings and bric-a-brac that were exhibited there. 'That's all there was to it.'

'I doubt it.'

'A man like you wouldn't understand. But I'd never have hurt her, never.'

He was believable, Denton thought. He didn't entirely believe, but he wasn't any longer sure that Geddys was lying, either. An older man, something like infatuation—was some sort of purity possible here? Remembering what Heseltine had suggested, he said, 'Mr Geddys, who else might have looked at the back of the Wesselons?'

'I don't see what that has to do with anything. Because she put the note there? She probably put it there so she wouldn't forget it.'

'But she did forget it.' Or did she? Perhaps Heseltine's theory was not so entirely wrong. 'How many other people worked in the shop when Mary Thomason was here?'

'Only one.'

'Man or woman?'

'A woman.' Geddys put his hands behind his back, stared out at the empty arcade. 'An older woman. She and Mary got along, neither friends nor enemies—you know. But the Wesselons was out here in the shop; Alice had no reason to come out here and handle it.'

'But you did.'

'Well, of course I did! I *owned* it!' He turned his head towards Denton but didn't meet his eyes. 'Please leave. I've nothing more to say.'

'Who was going to buy the painting? Somebody was going to buy it and then didn't want it.'

'The Wesselons? I can't tell you that.'

'I think you'd better.'

'I have a responsibility to my clients.'

'Do you want to tell the police about that?'

Geddys whirled on him, his face reddening, his head tilted on the neck, then strode to the back and came out with a large ledger. He opened it on one hand, turned pages with the other, read until he found what he wanted. 'Francis Wenzli put down a guinea on it. He never came for it. I wrote to remind him that the painting was here, and he sent back my note with a scribble on it to the effect that he was no longer interested.' He slammed the book. 'Rude of him.'

'Who's Francis Wenzli?'

Geddys looked at him as if he were simple. 'The painter.'

'You didn't give him back his deposit?'

'He didn't ask for it.' Geddys shrugged. 'I'd lost the sale, after all.'

Denton went over some of it again, but Geddys wanted him gone. The story didn't change. A couple of hard detectives might get more—Denton thought there might be more to ask about the relationship with Mary Thomason—but he wasn't going to get it today. He could come back another time. Or put Guillam on him, ho-ho.

He had missed lunch. The rain was steady now, the wind slacked off; Piccadilly seemed dispirited—the tops of the buses empty, the horses plodding with their heads down, black umbrellas everywhere. He realized he was hungry. His watch told him it would be the low period at the Café Royal, but he could at least find something to eat there, and he might, too, find somebody who could tell him who Francis Wenzli was. Not Frank Harris: Harris was one of the nighttime habitués. Oddly, he thought of Gwen John, and not without interest. He set off for the Café Royal.

Inside the door of the Domino Room, shaking the rain off his ponderous overcoat, he looked for a familiar face. The room was all but empty, waiters leaning against the backs of chairs, arms folded. A single pair of long legs stuck out from a banquette half-hidden by a gold-and-green pillar—somebody either asleep or telling the world with his posture to go to hell.

It was the latter. Denton saw a big, dark hat, the glitter of a gold earring.

'Hullo, sheriff. What the hell are you doing here at this hour?'

It was Augustus John, Gwen's brother, astonishingly cheeky for a near-boy of twenty-three. Denton slid into the banquette and said, 'I might ask you the same thing. I like your hat.'

'Bought it off an Aussie I saw in the street.'

'I thought you were in Liverpool.'

'I was. I couldn't stand any more of it, so I took a few days off.' John was sitting low on his spine, arms folded, the wide-brimmed hat pulled down over his eyes. His costume—an almost threadbare velvet jacket in olive green, once apparently belonging to a gamekeeper, corduroy trousers much bagged from the rain, thick boots—proclaimed the artist. So did the earring, the almost black beard.

'Liverpool isn't London?' Denton said.

'The Liverpudlians believe that only Greece, Rome and dead people in fancy clothes can be proper subjects for art. They're astonished and censorious that I could think the gypsies in the fields or the workers at the docks could interest me. They display the very best taste of the eighteen-fifties.' He sighed heavily and looked over at Denton, who was beginning a negotiation with a waiter about the choucroute garni. John said, 'My sister said she'd seen you. Gwen was rather taken with you. She likes older men.'

'I'm certainly one of those.'

'She said you were looking for a girl.'

'Not what you think.' Denton passed over the leather envelope that held the drawing and told the waiter he'd have the chicken pie.

John took the drawing out and looked at it. His head came back as if his eyes were too close to it. 'Right piece of shit, isn't it,' he said.

'Gwen said Burlington House.'

'Oh, yes.'

'You don't recognize her? She was in her first year at the Slade.'

'Might. I used to drop into the drawing classes, might have seen her. Dreadful piece of work, this.' He put his head forward and brought the drawing up almost to the brim of his hat. 'The remarques are more interesting.'

'The little drawings in the corners?'

'Not awfully well done, but they're Slade work, which is something.'

'Different hands did the head and the little things?'

'Oh, of course. The girl might have done the remarques, in fact—they look about right for first-year work. But she didn't do the head—that's Academy stuff, somebody immensely pompous and outdated. Bit odd, putting remarques on somebody else's drawing, more so when the drawing's of you. Little mementoes.'

'Of what?'

'Who the hell knows? One's a doorway; means nothing to me. The other—' John laughed. 'Christ on a crust, it's Himple!' He laughed again. 'Sir Erasmus Himple, RA—one of the great old turds of Burlington House. The drawing is his Lazarus. It's obvious. I have a friend who insists that it looks like a man preparing to let out a colossal fart. That look of intense stupidity—the open mouth, the rolling eyes—old Himple said it shows Lazarus at the moment of realizing he's alive again. I suppose one could wake with a fart, eh?'

'"His Lazarus"?'

'Himple put a painting of the raising of Lazarus into the last exhibition. Huge thing—took up most of a wall. He described it as his "chef-d'oeuvre" and made much of the fact that his Lazarus is young and his Jesus is a Jew. And indeed, the Christ has a nose like Shylock in a burlesque, but everybody else in the painting is as English as Boadicea, so it looks as if the Jew of Malta has wandered into a palace garden party. Himple is unmatchable—a genus unto himself.'

Denton was turning over the name—Himple. Somebody else had mentioned Himple. Who was it? He was eating chicken pie, bending to look over John's shoulder at the drawing. 'I thought maybe the man in the drawing was screaming.'

'Well, he could be. One's never quite sure with Himple. You know, on closer inspection, I think that Lazarus looks a bit like the woman in the big drawing? And I wonder if she was perhaps the model for Lazarus's sister, who's shown in the painting as tripping over the ground as if she's weightless, one hand extended like a hostess introducing the dustman to the Prince of Wales.'

'I should have a look at the painting.'

'It's worth the trip, if only for the comic effect.'

'But why would Lazarus look like a woman?'

'The girl in the drawing was a model?'

'Now and then, they say.'

'There you are.'

'For Lazarus *and* the sister?'

'Well, it's like old Himple to want to show a family resemblance. He likes to be authentic, you know—brothers and sisters always look alike, right?' He laughed. 'Like Gwen and me.'

Denton looked more closely at the little drawing. 'And Lazarus is what she'd look like as a man?' He was thinking of the brother who had picked up Mary Thomason's trunk from her lodging house.

John stirred. He found a pencil in a pocket, searched through others until he found a folded piece of cartridge paper, on one side a list of some sort. He smoothed it out on the table and began to draw with quick, sure strokes. To Denton, it was like theatrical magic: one moment, blank paper, the next a face very like Mary Thomason's but male.

'I've cut his hair for him. Or we could have him with a beard, like Lazarus.' He made another sketch just as quickly, and the same young face appeared with a short beard, even the slight scantiness of the youthful hair shown. The economy of line was remarkable, and all at once Denton understood 'the Slade look'. He told John as much, praised his ability.

'I've thought of doing portraits in Trafalgar Square— sixpence a head. I'd make a fortune.'

'Can I keep those?'

John slid the paper over the tablecloth. 'You can tell your grandchildren you own an original Augustus John.' He took the paper back and dashed off a signature, shoved it over again.

'You're not lacking in confidence, anyway.'

John laughed. 'Not on Tuesdays and Thursdays.' He sighed. 'I mean to get very drunk and possibly find myself a woman. That sound like a programme that would interest you?'

'Afraid not.'

'I think Gwen wondered if you were attached to anybody just now.'

'I am, actually.'

'Oh.' John slid down on the banquette again. 'It's just as well. Gwen's really interested only in her art. Everything else is "secondary", as she puts it. I wish I had her concentration. You heard I was married?'

'Mmm.'

'Hard on the concentration. Gwen's quite right, actually. She'll wind up a nun of art. I'll wind up a bigamist. Or a trigamist. I can't live without women. Half a dozen of them, if I could afford them. Oddly, having only one is surely more distracting than two or three—they could entertain each other. Isn't that so?'

Denton had ordered coffee. He sipped. 'I was married once. It was distracting, yes.'

'What happened?'

'She killed herself.'

John seemed to ponder this. He put his eyebrows up, then cocked his head, frowned. He said, 'I came to London to cheer myself up, and I'm not being cheered. It's time to get drunk.' He wandered away.

Denton remembered that he had meant to ask about Wenzli, the man who had put down the deposit on the 'little Wesselons'. He also remembered who had first mentioned Himple—Henry James, at the dismal party at his publishers. Something about Himple's having gone away.

Maybe he had come back.

'Mary Thomason as a young man, with and without beard.' He spread the piece of paper on his desk. Janet Striker, his dressing gown held closed at her throat, bent to look at it. It was Atkins's evening off.

'We should look at the painting,' she said.

He put his hand on her buttock. She flinched.

'I'm taking liberties,' he said.

'Perhaps I'll get used to it.'

'I hope not.' He tried to make it a joke, but it wasn't.

It was the same skittishness. He wondered when she would end it.

The Raising of Lazarus was indeed an enormous painting, the figures life-sized, the landscape so expansive that it was impossible to take in the whole thing at once. A printed note said that the actual site of the Apostle John's account was shown, sketches for it made in the Holy Land by the artist himself. The clothes, mostly cloaks and shifts, were 'archaeologically authentic', but the faces were, as Augustus John had said, as English as Spotted Dick. Despite the seriousness of the subject—a man raised from the dead, after all, a miracle by the Messiah—there was something terrifically lightweight about it.

'Like Handel played on the tin whistle,' she murmured.

He actually knew who Handel was. 'They're all play-acting,' he said.

'Oh, that *is* it, isn't it. He's posed them all. As if it's a studio photograph that went on too long. It is frightful, isn't it.'

He went closer and studied Lazarus. There was no mistaking that face now. With the memory of the drawing and John's sketches in his head, he thought of Lazarus as 'Mary's brother'. He said, 'Himple used her for the sister and her brother for Lazarus.'

'If they really look so much alike, he could have used either to model both.'

A lot of handsome young men filled the crowd that followed Jesus. Denton said, 'Either Jesus or the artist favours the good-looking ones.'

'Mmm, boys. Yes, I suppose. That might cast another light on the brother.'

'What are you saying—Himple liked young men but used Mary as a model? Or her brother? I told you that James said that Himple had "decamped". I wonder if we can find him to ask some questions.'

She turned back before they left the gallery. 'It's so huge. Can you imagine having that on your wall?'

'It would cover a lot of cracked plaster.'

Denton wrote to Erasmus Himple, RA, but had no answer as yet. On her own initiative, Janet Striker went to the Reading Room and brought back what there was in the obvious sources about Francis Wenzli, the artist who had put down a deposit on the Wesselons. Wenzli was apparently a few years younger than Denton, the latest in a line of minor, originally Austrian painters who had emigrated to England to escape Napoleon. The current incarnation, according to an article on 'Our Contemporary Artists' in *Pearson's*, was a society portraitist and landscape painter who specialized in country houses.

'It appears he can put both your wife and your country place on the wall for you,' Denton said to Atkins. 'And you, yourself, if you've a mind.'

'Maybe he gives discounts for quantity, like the insurance men—"Family Rates Our Speciality".'

Denton was getting ready to go out, his work day over. His brain felt blurry. He thought that if he didn't finish the damned novel soon, he was going to take a rest. However, he didn't say this to Atkins; Atkins liked his employer to be busy making money. Denton said, 'How's the moving-picture business?'

'We're doing what they call "casting". Theatrical term. My pal, the one who owns the camera, worked for Dan Leno, *he* calls it casting—like casting about. Trolling for pike, more or less. Thinking of hiring Cohan as a Boer.'

'How's the housemaid?'

Atkins made a rude noise. 'Getting full of herself. Wants her young man to be hired for the soldier. Says she won't kiss anybody else. Her young man looks a bit like a rat and is about the size of a kid just out of skirts. I told her if she didn't shut it I'd hire the parlourmaid from Number 17 instead, who's her worst enemy.' He shook his head. 'Not the walk in the park I thought it'd be. You going out?'

'To talk to that painter, Wenzli. Sent him a note; he, at least, answered.'

'Sounds a bit rum. Pushing for a knighthood, they say.'

'Who says?'

'Gossip in "Society Talk".' This was a column in the new magazine that Frank Harris was editing. Denton suggested it was odd reading for Atkins.

'Learning from my betters.'

Wenzli wasn't Augustus John's sort of artist, certainly. He lived in Melbury Road in Kensington—'the artistic environs of the late President of the Royal Academy, Lord Leighton' as *Pearson's* had it—but kept a studio in St John's Wood that had been 'at one time the artistic demesne of Mr Bourke', which meant nothing to Denton, but once inside it he thought he understood: it was a studio for an artist who wanted to live like a stockbroker.

Wenzli was already there, in fact was waiting for him. He hadn't been working—there was no paint on him, no smock, no paint-loaded palette. He was wearing a grey sack coat and waistcoat, rather too-light fawn trousers, a high collar, had somewhat the air of a dandified military officer in mufti. Bearded, moustached, he gave the sense of having just been let go by the regimental barber, who might be still snapping his cloth out of sight somewhere.

A butler had opened the door, ushered Denton into a building in the style called Queen Anne, and up to a first-floor studio the size of a provincial city's railway station. The ceiling was more than twice his own height away; carpets covered the floor; a fireplace with a Gothick chimney-piece big enough to have parked a cab in took up part of one wall; easy chairs stood here and there; and, on a marble-topped table that could have sat twelve, the tools of the trade were set out, as if to prove that in fact an artist was here somewhere. Near it stood an easel ten feet tall, on it a six-by-four canvas filled mostly by two young girls and a dog. The artist himself stood in front of it as if prepared to defend it.

'I'm Denton.'

'Yes. Yes. You wrote for an appointment.'

Actually, Denton had mailed his card, with 'Re: Mary Thomason' pencilled on the back; Wenzli had sent him a note telling him to see him at his studio, not his home.

'Your house and your studio are at different places.'

'I must be free of distractions.' Wenzli exhaled and relaxed the abdomen he had been holding in, now proved a rather soft-looking man, his belly slack but pouty, well-filled—not a nun for art. Denton said, 'Mary Thomason.'

'That was written on your card, yes.'

'You know the name.'

'Why, yes. She was my model once or twice. She had an interesting ambience.'

'She's disappeared.'

'Ah. Oh.' He seemed unsure whether to be surprised. 'Yes.'

'You knew that she had disappeared?'

'I heard something or other.'

'Where?'

'Why do you ask?'

Denton studied the man's face. There was an expression at the sides of the nose and around the eyes as if he might weep easily. There was also a hint of fear. Denton said, 'What was your relationship with Mary Thomason?'

'There was no "relationship"! What an improper question!' Wenzli tried to straighten his back to assume the military pose again, but he stayed several inches shorter than Denton. 'What are you driving at, sir?'

'Before she disappeared, Mary Thomason wrote me a letter. She said she was afraid of somebody.'

Wenzli flushed. 'I was kindness itself to the girl. When I saw her, which was only—two or three times—'

Denton looked around the studio. 'This is a private spot. Very private.' He turned back to the painter. 'She came here?'

'I *work* here!'

'You put down a deposit on a painting at Geddys's in Burlington Arcade. Where Mary Thomason worked.'

'What can you be getting at?'

'And then let the painting and the deposit go—immediately after she disappeared. Why did you do that, Mr Wenzli?'

Wenzli started to pull in his belly again and gave it up. He managed to look stern, nonetheless. 'I have work to do. You will have to leave.'

'Did Miss Thomason model in the nude?'

'There spake the voice of Mrs Grundy! And of ignorance; few real artists need the nude model. No, she did not. What you imply is libellous.'

'Slanderous, I think.' Denton picked up one of the brushes and spread the bristles with a thumb.

'That's an expensive brush!'

Denton put it down and leaned back against the marble table. 'You didn't ask what I do or what I am, Mr Wenzli, so I assume you know. Did Mary Thomason ever mention my name?'

Wenzli started to say something, hesitated. 'She might have said something. Your articles on travel were very popular just then.' He meant the articles about the motor car adventure, which Denton had turned into the book.

'"The former American lawman".'

'That's the reputation you have, I suppose. I really don't see what this is in aid of.'

'So that if you saw that Mary Thomason had written to me asking for protection, you'd know she was serious.'

'Ah—why—What's the point of all this? You must go, really—!'

Denton went and stood quite close to him. 'Her letter, in an envelope addressed to me, was in the back of the painting you were going to buy. There's no question but that she put it there herself. There's really only one reason for her to have done that that I can see, Mr Wenzli. She wanted you to find it.'

'This is madness.'

'You'd know my name; you'd read that she was afraid somebody was going to hurt her; you'd know she was serious. It was a warning.'

'But I never found it! I never found such a damned thing!'

'Were you going to hurt her, Mr Wenzli?'

'Certainly not!'

'Had things got to a certain point, Mr Wenzli? Despite yourself? Did you kiss her?'

'This is infamous!' Wenzli went to a bell-pull that hung beside the vast chimney-piece; it was heavy enough to have rung changes on cathedral bells.

Denton said, 'The police have been told about her disappearance.' He paused an instant; so did Wenzli. 'I think you'd do better to talk to me than to Detective Sergeant Guillam. He's a right bastard.'

Wenzli looked more than ever as if he might weep, but he was actually tougher than he looked. He said in a testy voice, 'I'll have you thrown out if you won't leave.'

'You and that butler couldn't throw me out between you.' Denton crossed his arms. 'It's the police or me.' He walked down the studio to look at the portrait of the two young girls, then addressed them rather than Wenzli. 'Did you kiss her? Was there more than that—touching—?'

'Get out!'

'You won't get a knighthood by lying to me, Wenzli. Did you touch her or didn't you?'

'There was nothing between us!'

'I think there was. You did kiss her, didn't you. And then there was more—she didn't discourage you—she wouldn't undress for you but she'd do certain things—with her hands, was it, Wenzli? Or her mouth?'

'Stop it, stop it! This is disgusting!'

'You could take me to court. But I don't think you will. I think that those things happened and then—' Denton could see it. He knew how it went. He knew how he had done it himself, once upon a time. 'And then you got a bit rough. And you frightened her.'

Wenzli was red-faced. He had moved away from the bell-pull and had, perhaps unconsciously, taken up a mahlstick, the padded stick that he used to support his painting hand when he was working on fine detail. It wasn't much of a weapon, but it told Denton that he'd touched a spot. And he realized that Wenzli was capable of frightening a woman, even with his softness and his apparent weakness. He was arrogant, and frustration made him angry, a potent combination. Wenzli might well be capable of hurting a small woman. 'You frightened her, Wenzli.'

'I didn't do anything of the kind.'

'So she wrote the note for you to find, but I believe you that you never found it—or you'd have destroyed it. But she disappeared, and you heard that she'd gone—or maybe she just didn't come back, didn't keep an appointment—and then *you* were frightened. You wanted to erase your relationship with her. You never went back to Geddys's. You wrote him you didn't want the painting. You let him keep the deposit.'

Wenzli tapped the mahlstick against his thigh, then threw it towards the marble table; it hit and bounced off and thudded on the carpet.

Denton kept pushing. 'What was so important about the painting?'

'I decided I didn't like it.'

'No, there was more than that. What?' He waited. He said, 'I really don't want to bring the police into it, Wenzli. They won't pursue her disappearance unless I stir it up for them. They're busy men; they have more important cases. She's been gone a long time. But if I lay it all out for them, they'll come to question you. Do you want it in the cheap papers—"Noted Artist Questioned in Girl's Disappearance"?' He waited. 'Does your wife want that?'

'You *shit*!'

'What was the Wesselons to her?'

Wenzli threw himself into one of the armchairs. 'She wanted it. I said I'd buy it for her.'

'A present.'

Wenzli nodded.

'Pretty nice present for somebody who modelled a few times.'

Wenzli waved a hand. He put his forehead on the fingers of the other hand, elbow on the carved chair arm. 'She was a greedy little thing. I gave her money—small amounts. I—I didn't want her to go without.'

'You bribed her, but you never got her.'

Wenzli shook his head without lifting it from his hand. 'She was fascinating. Innocent, but—' He shook his head again.

'Did she blackmail you?'

Wenzli snorted. 'Nothing happened that I could have been blackmailed for! I tell you, it was all innocent! I only wanted to give her things. To please her. Then when she didn't come for an appointment, I thought—perhaps it was better. To stop seeing—employing her. Seen in that light, I thought giving her the painting was a mistake. So I wrote to Geddys.'

'She missed an appointment to model?'

Wenzli nodded.

'But she needed money?'

'She always *wanted* money. She was greedy. But innocent. Like a child.'

'And because she missed one appointment, you knew she was gone?'

Wenzli put his face in his hand. 'She came every Tuesday and Thursday. She missed both days. Then I thought—I waited until the following week.'

'It didn't occur to you that something might have happened to her?'

Wenzli's head moved back and forth on his hand. He said, in almost a groan, 'I was *glad* she was gone—don't you understand?'

Denton waited. There was nothing more. He found that he believed Wenzli. The man looked abject, worn out. By his admission, or by the infatuation that lay behind it? It was a new slant on Mary Thomason—an innocence that had the power to make a man like Wenzli risk a fall. The same innocence that had apparently infatuated Geddys.

Denton said that he would keep what had been said to himself, and he went out, Wenzli still sitting with his head on his hand, looking at nothing.

'But it doesn't hang together, Denton. Why did she run off if she wanted the painting so?'

'Something more important happened.'

'I can see her putting the letter in the back of the painting as a warning to him. But that would mean she really expected him to pick the painting up, pay for it and then handle it, or his man handles it, and the letter is found. And then he turns the painting over to her.'

'Out of guilt, if nothing else. She didn't mean to end it with the letter, I think. Just to warn him. Then he gives her the painting, and he's warned, and he'll behave. There may have been more to it—maybe she was going to deliver the painting to him, make sure he found the letter. But the point is, I don't think Wenzli was responsible for her disappearance. I believe him.'

'The type who'd hit a woman but not kill her?'

They were in her favourite Aerated Bread Company shop in Aldgate. She was saying goodbye to her former job; she'd taken the two women who had worked for her to tea and was going on to a dinner at a hotel with the well-to-do men and women who funded the Society.

'Are they giving you a testimonial?' he said.

'If the worst thing people do, Denton, is mean well, I shan't be too unhappy. What I've done for the last ten years didn't accomplish much, but the Society at least tries. Better to try than not.'

He shrugged. 'Anyway, Wenzli looks like a dead end. He was really frightened, maybe of himself. Like a man who finds he likes drink—suddenly understands he's got it in him to destroy himself.'

'He didn't call it love? Most men would.'

'Once she was gone and he'd had a few days to think it over, he knew he was well out of it. I must have come like the ghost at the banquet. He'll be shaking in his boots for weeks.'

'But it rounds off Mary Thomason. You know now why she wrote the letter, and you've done what you could.'

'I'd still like to talk to Himple, RA. So far as we know, Mary Thomason is still missing, and Himple knew her.'

'I still don't entirely trust Wenzli.'

He shook his head. 'I believed him. Let's see what Himple, RA, has to say. I haven't heard from him—maybe RAs don't answer letters from mere authors—so let's see what happens if I simply call on him.'

CHAPTER

16

Erasmus Himple, RA, lived in Chelsea, not particularly at that moment an artist's neighbourhood—but then, as Augustus John might have said, Himple wasn't particularly an artist. Denton liked Chelsea without wanting to live there, liked to walk its small streets and its embankment, although the place was, he was told, very different from the village of 'little houses surrounded with roses' that Stendhal and others had found. One of the art magazines reported that Himple had said that 'he liked to live where my great namesake, Erasmus, visited, and where great painters have painted'—presumably Holbein and Turner, if 'great' was to be taken literally, perhaps less so Rossetti and Whistler. At any rate, it was to Chelsea that Himple had come, leaving Melbury Road and the farther reaches of Kensington to other RAs.

The house was a fairly small one around the corner from All Saints Church. Denton approached it along the Embankment, pausing to look at the river—he still had thoughts of rowing on it, never seemed to turn them to reality—and the suspension bridge. He tried to picture it without the Embankment, a muddy tidal shore, here and there some steps to the water, but the idea of a distinct village where now this accessible part of London stood wouldn't come clear. His mind was fuzzed by his book, anyway, now nearly done. There was a familiar sense of the sprint to the finish, already an anticipation of the mental slump after.

He had no eagerness to see Erasmus Himple. It was late on a sombre, cold day, although he was cheered by a flight of duck that came winging down the river to land splashily almost in front of him. The sky was iron overhead, the sun a slightly brassy brightness far down to the west; the bare plane trees rose against it in hard, black silhouette. The air smelled of the river and of soot; his breath steamed in it before drifting and dissipating.

'Mr Denton to see Mr Himple, if he may,' he said, handing in his card. He had expected, after the experience with Wenzli, some sort of potted grandeur, the same air of arty *nouveau riche*-ness, but the house was little more than a double cottage, the middle-aged woman at the door a housekeeper rather than a butler. She had an air of austerity, could have been housekeeper to some Irish priest, dedicated more to preservation of his celibacy than even her own; she wore black, some sort of white headgear like a mob cap, but in lace. She had bristling, hairy eyebrows and a nose almost as formidable as Denton's own, the nostrils more hirsute than his.

Without looking at the card, she said, 'Mr Himple is away.'

'Oh.' That didn't surprise him, after what James had said. It did trouble him that Himple had been away so long. 'Will he be back soon?'

Now she used a pair of steel-rimmed spectacles that hung on a ribbon to read his card. 'Is this about having your picture painted, Mr Denton?' She had a deep voice, almost mannish.

'I wrote a letter. There's a young woman who seems to have disappeared. I think she was a model for Mr Himple—the painting of Lazarus.' He stood uncertainly, found he was speaking in jerks. 'I've reported it to the police. I just learned about Mr Himple. Her modelling for him. I thought—' He didn't say what he thought.

'Oh, yes.' She looked him up and down. It was as well that Atkins had insisted he look like a gentleman that day. 'Come in, please.' No hospitality was implied by the tone.

She led him to the back of the house down a central hall, paintings on the walls, not Himple's own, he thought (they seemed to him 'older', whatever that meant), and stood by an open door with her left arm extended as if to say, 'If you must be here, go in this room.' Inside was what he took to be her own sitting room, as austere as she, black-and-white engravings on the walls instead of paintings, an open Bible on a shawl-draped table.

She didn't ask him to take off his overcoat. She told him she was Mrs Evans. When she sat, so did he; the chair was merciless. He told her the well-worn tale of Mary Thomason, abbreviated, trying to keep his voice from falling into the sing-song of a guide detailing some third-rate wonder for the thousandth time. He produced one of the copies of the Mary Thomason drawing. 'I believe that Mr Himple did this drawing. Do you recognize it?'

She had as sharp an eye as Augustus John's. 'The little one in the corner looks like his Lazarus.'

'Yes.' He waited. 'Do you know the woman's face?'

'Mr Himple's studio is over the road.'

It took him an instant to guess what that meant. 'You don't see his models?'

'I hardly pry into my employer's business.'

'I didn't mean to suggest that. You might have seen her, I meant.'

She handed the drawing back. Denton waited; nothing came. He said, 'When will Mr Himple be back?'

'Mr Himple has gone abroad.'

'Ah. For how long?'

'I'm sure I don't know. He made arrangements that would allow him to make an extended journey. You would do best to write to him, perhaps. Or not.'

'I did. May I ask when he left?'

'Some time ago.'

'When?'

She enjoyed being a dog in the manger of information. No amount of niceness was going to get it out of her. Denton bore down, gave as good as he got, showed in a changed voice that he could be just as stern as she. Reluctantly, she admitted that Himple had gone some time ago, then that he had gone in August, then that he had left on 9 August.

One day after Mary Thomason had written to ask for help. Denton felt himself coming out of his end-of-book daze. 'Did he go alone?'

She got her back up at that: what did he mean? What was he suggesting? She would have to ask him to leave if he was going to make insinuations.

Denton produced the drawing again. She said, 'He would hardly travel with a young lady!'

'Did he travel with anybody at all?'

'His man, of course.' She glanced down at the drawing, looked out of a window, said in a different voice, one for the first time suggesting—was it disapproval? Or some personal hurt? 'A man. A servant, I mean.'

Denton had to figure this through—his man but apparently not his man, *a* man—and he said, 'Not his regular man?'

Again, she didn't look at him, spoke in the same aggrieved voice. 'He wanted someone who could speak French.'

'His regular man didn't speak French?'

'Brown does not speak French.'

'Brown is his regular man? Can I speak with Brown?'

'Brown lives in Strand-on-the Green. He comes in once a week to tend to the studio and do the pictures.' Denton had no idea what this meant; it didn't matter. She said, 'Mr Himple made an arrangement with Brown for his absence—until he returns.' She looked again at the drawing. Her expression was even more severe.

'You didn't approve of the man he took with him.'

'It's hardly my business to approve of my employer's judgement.'

'I thought perhaps you didn't like the new man.'

'I hardly knew him.' She looked yet again at the drawing.

'You recognize the drawing, don't you.'

She handed it back. The edge of the paper vibrated; her hand was trembling. Looking at her again, Denton felt a sudden sympathy, had a glimpse into her life and its isolation, probably its loneliness. He said, 'Did the new man look like the woman's face in the drawing?'

She sat very straight. 'I believe he resembles the face in the corner, at least.'

'Lazarus.'

She was silent. Her head may have trembled; maybe he was wrong. He said, 'Have you seen the painting?'

'Mr Himple kindly invited me to the studio to see it before it went to the Academy.'

'Do you think the "new man" who went abroad with him was the model for Lazarus?'

'I—thought that might be so when I saw the painting. It was not my business.' She looked at him. 'Nor yours, sir.'

'I think the man who modelled Lazarus may be the brother of the missing girl. He may know where she is. Mrs Evans, this is quite important. I want to get in touch with the young man.'

'You may write a letter, I'm sure.'

'Where are they?'

She licked her thin, dark lips. 'Brown—Mr Himple's regular valet—is in touch with him. If I have anything to report about the house, I do it through Brown.' She smoothed her dress; her fingers plucked at a square inch of fabric as if she saw something on it. 'I had an address for him at the beginning, but it was only a poste restante. They're long gone from there, so Brown says.' Through tone alone, she made it clear that a housekeeper should not have to communicate with her employer through a valet.

'Where?'

'I've told you, I don't know!' As if she regretted her sharpness, she said, 'They spent the first month painting in France, a village, Hinon. In Normandy. They were supposed to spend the summer there, but he changed his mind. Quite an unspoiled spot, Mr Himple said. That's why he wanted a French speaker. But he moved on.' Her expression changed, suggested malicious pleasure. 'Perhaps it was too unspoiled.'

'The "new man", too?'

'I assume so. Although—' The expression, malicious, almost a smile, touched her mouth. 'Brown said Mr Himple has discharged him.'

'Why?'

'I have no idea.'

'When?'

'I don't remember. The end of summer, perhaps.'

'Then writing to him care of Mr Himple wouldn't reach him.'

'No, I suppose it wouldn't.'

Denton was angry with her, made himself see her side of it. She had tried to fob him off at first with the idea of writing to the 'new man'. She had wanted to get rid of him—Mary Thomason was nothing to her; why should she bother helping him? She wanted him to go, to leave her to her isolation and her loneliness. 'But you're sure you haven't seen the young woman in the drawing.'

'Quite sure, of course.'

'But Mr Himple drew her.'

'I don't know that he did. Perhaps he did.' She was looking towards the door, towards a black stone clock on the mantel.

'Was the "new man" English?'

'Certainly he was.'

'You heard him talk, then.'

She compressed her lips. 'Once or twice.'

'What did he sound like—educated? Rough?'

'He sounded like his class.'

'But he spoke French.'

'So Mr Himple said. I wouldn't have known if he had. I don't bother myself with foreign things.'

She didn't know the new man's name—he'd have to ask Brown. He asked if he could see the studio and was told he'd have to apply to Brown. She was eager for him to go now; she had said too much, he thought, not because she had anything to hide but because information was all she did have. Perhaps she got pleasure from treating as secrets things that were merely ordinary. He got Brown's address from her and went away, glad to get into the gathering dusk and the cold.

The ducks were gone. The sun was gone, too, the dwindling light throwing everything into shades of lavender and dark grey-blue, the last light on the water like much-rubbed metal. On the Albert Bridge, the traffic rumbled and growled. A steam launch came down the river, its lights like tantalizing hints of certainty in the gloom.

Next day, he visited Brown in a tidy little house on the river almost as far as Kew. The valet was not yet forty, heavy-set, unintelligent. Yes, Mr Himple sent him regular letters. Yes, Himple and the 'new man' had stayed at Hinon for a month; yes, they had left there early and gone on to Paris and then 'the South'; yes, Mr Himple had written that he had discharged the new man and was taking a villa with its own staff. No, he wasn't sure of the villa's location; he had been told only a poste restante address. But Mr Himple had moved again, heading for Italy incognito because of the crowds of English tourists, he said. He planned to winter in Florence, where he had a large acquaintance. He had sent back four paintings—'What artists call sketches in oil, sir.' Mr Himple was 'renewing his style'. It sounded like something Brown was quoting from one of Himple's letters.

When would Himple be back? Brown didn't know, didn't know, sir, it was all a little puzzling—but Mr Himple was an artist, after all.

And the new man?

Gone. (Brown seemed relieved.) Never meant to be a permanent addition to the household, after all. (Brown hid his satisfaction at this pretty well.) His name was Arthur Crum. Yes, he was young. Thin, sir. Yes, the face in the drawing without a beard could be his. Yes, he believed the man Crum had modelled Lazarus. Brown knew nothing of a sister, however, either of the new man or of Lazarus. He was seldom at the studio when Mr Himple was painting, seldom saw the models. No, he was deeply sorry, but it wasn't possible to see the studio in Mr Himple's absence. Art was sacrosanct.

'What did you think of the new man—Crum?'

'It isn't my place to think anything of him.' Brown's stolid, fleshy face closed up. 'I have a very good position with Mr Himple, sir. My wages continue while he's away. I don't want to give any cause for Mr Himple to—think less of me.'

'But this Crum, you said, has been discharged. Your opinion of him won't matter now. You do have an opinion of him, I think.'

'Yes, sir.' Brown shifted uneasily. He cleared his throat, then burst out: 'An upstart. He was an upstart, sir. He didn't know his craft, between you and me, sir.' Brown became almost animated. 'I was a footman for nine years before I was allowed to even lay out my employer's clothes. This Crum hadn't done any of that.' Brown was sitting in a small armchair. He stared at his large hands, then abruptly broke out again: 'He couldn't even speak good English, sir! He was a—a— He was of a very low sort, sir. Mr Nobody from Nowhere.'

'Why did Mr Himple hire him, then?'

'I'm sure I couldn't say, sir.'

'Was there something personal between them?'

Brown simply looked at him. His worry seemed to increase: to say anything on this score was to endanger his place, he meant.

Denton said, 'Do you know how Crum and Mr Himple got acquainted?'

'Crum was a model, sir. As I say, he modelled Lazarus. I believe that's how he came to Mr Himple's attention.'

'Did he know anything about painting? Was he an artist himself?'

'I think he knew the studio, sir—by that I mean, he could care for the brushes, and he knew how to make the varnishes and grind the colours. The rude work of the studio.' Brown sniffed. 'Hardly an artist. No idea of art, I suspect, although I'd never have engaged him in conversation about such a subject.' Again, he seemed to have done talking and then abruptly realized he had more to say. 'He was beneath me, sir! I wanted nothing to do with him. Mr Himple realized that, I think. If it hadn't been for speaking French, there'd have been no thought of employing him, I'm sure. Mr Himple made that very clear to me when he continued my wages in his absence and put me in charge of the studio. Crum was merely temporary.'

'Did Crum have some sort of hold over Mr Himple?'

Brown's eyebrows drew together; a look of pain, almost of illness, took over his face. 'I'm sure I wouldn't know about that, sir.'

'It has a stink to it, Munro.'

'Not my manor. It's Guillam's business, missing persons.'

'Guillam won't give me the time of day, and you know it. Don't you think it's peculiar?'

'Peculiarity isn't a crime.'

'An artist just happens to draw a picture of a girl who's missing. A man who looks like her, probably her brother, models for the same artist, then goes off to the Continent as his valet right after she writes me a letter and disappears. The artist and the man travel together, then the artist reports he's fired the man. So the girl's missing and now the brother's missing.'

'What makes you think he's missing? What you mean is, you can't find him. Not the same thing.'

'I asked at the Slade about Arthur Crum. Asked a couple of the sister's friends. Had somebody look in the Kelly's. No Arthur Crum.'

'What're you suggesting—an RA took him to the Continent and did him in? Save it for a novel.'

'Munro, you're as hard to move as an elephant.'

'And a good deal busier. Want a word of advice?'

'No.'

'We got enough crimes without you inventing them. Leave it.'

'I can't leave it. I thought I had; it came back.'

Munro looked up from his paperwork. 'Where'd you get a picture of her?'

'It turned up.'

'Convenient.' He went back to scribbling on a piece of typescript. 'You hear that the docs sent in a report on your man Jarrold?'

'"My man Jarrold"—my God!'

'Guillam's office filed it with the magistrate—"given to harmless childish fantasies but improving". Docs recommend more of whatever they're doing and a continuance of the charges. Guillam's recommending to Mrs Striker that she agree.' He raised his head. 'She hasn't told you?'

'I haven't seen her in a bit.'

'Mm. Perhaps you should. Better than mucking about with missing persons.' He started to lower his head to his paperwork again but lifted it and said, 'Anyway, they've pulled the watchers off you because of the report on Jarrold. You're on your own.'

When he saw her two days later, he said, 'You didn't tell me you'd heard about Jarrold.'

'I haven't seen you.'

'You could have sent one of your telegrams.'

'I didn't think it was important.'

'It's important to me. Jarrold's hoodwinked them. If they think what's behind that moon face of his is a "harmless childish fantasy", they should be disbarred or defrocked or whatever it is you do with medical men.'

'Their report is quite positive. He's "calm". They're giving him chloral at night and he's sleeping. He's given up wandering about in the dark, sleeps the night through. The Lady Astoreth has dropped out of his life.'

'He's pulling the wool over their eyes.'

'Maybe the Lady Astoreth has run off with Arthur Crum.'

'If Arthur Crum actually exists somewhere.'

'Not to mention the Lady Astoreth.' They were in his sitting room. Outside, it was crisp and cold; thin winter sunlight showed the sooty patterns on his windowpanes. She was wearing another suit, this one in a heavy rust-red wool; she had taken off the jacket to reveal a plain white blouse with a mannish necktie. She said, 'Maybe Munro's right about both Mary Thomason and Arthur Crum. They're both much ado about nothing.'

'I think the Thomason business is nothing, then I swing the other way and am certain something's really happened. The coincidences—the drawing, Himple, Crum going off with him—' He struck the velvet arm of his chair and dust motes jumped into the room. 'The little drawings, the remarques—if they mean something, if they're some sort of code—Augustus John and the housekeeper both recognized the one of Lazarus, so that one's clear enough. If she drew it, she was referring to the man who drew her picture, to Himple. But the other one—'

'You said nobody recognizes the other one.'

'It's a doorway, just a doorway.' He put his legs out. He touched her foot with one of his, frowned at her small boot. 'Heseltine looked funny when he saw it, but he said he didn't recognize it. No, he didn't say that—he just said something about—what? It was too small to see, or something. But he did look funny.'

'Ask him again.'

'I hate to bother him. He's in a bad state.'

'So are you.'

He looked at her with the same frown. He meant that he didn't think his own frustration was anything like Heseltine's despair. She reddened.

'Anyway, I don't like the docs' report on Jarrold. And the police have pulled off their watchers because of it. Damn them.'

Next afternoon, he walked down to Albany Court when he was done working. He had had the satisfaction of writing 'end' below a final paragraph, then underlining it. He had got the whole book out of his head and on the page, now had only to wait for the typewriter to do the final sheets, then take them to bed, revise, edit, get them down to the publishers. The great anticlimax.

Heseltine opened his own door. He answered a question about Jenks with only a shake of his head. Heseltine hadn't shaved; he was still in a dressing gown, again with an old woollen scarf around his neck. The place smelled of benzoin, as if he really had been ill. When they had talked banalities for a few minutes, Denton let a silence fall and then he said, 'Do you remember the drawing I showed you?'

'Drawing?'

'The young woman.'

'Oh, of course.'

'There were little drawings in the corners.'

'I don't recall.'

'I thought you recognized one of them.' Heseltine didn't react. Denton pulled out a photographic copy and held it towards him. Heseltine hesitated and then took it.

'The lower left one.'

Heseltine looked at it, but he spoke before he looked. 'Afraid it doesn't mean a thing to me.'

'The light's poor. I'd be grateful if you'd look at it in better light.' Denton handed him a folding magnifier he'd brought on purpose.

Heseltine took it to a window. The Wesselons hung on the wall next to him; his shoulder almost brushed it as he leaned against the window frame. The light was colourless but bright. Denton got up and stood at his shoulder. 'Recognize it?'

'No—no—' The corner of the paper quivered.

Denton said, 'It's important. It means something. You wanted to help me find this young woman, remember?'

Heseltine turned around him into the room and went back to where he had been sitting, a rather grubby love seat; he leaned over and put the drawing on the cushion of Denton's chair, then dropped his head on the fingers of one hand and looked at the raddled carpet. He said, 'I don't know what I'm going to do.'

'You were talking about going away.'

Heseltine rubbed his forehead with his fingers as he leaned on them. 'The little drawing is of a doorway in Mayfair. It's a place called the Mayflower Baths.' His eyes were shut. He kept rubbing. 'I was taken there when I was a schoolboy. I didn't know—A friend of my father's took me. It was only the once, I swear. I'm not—' He stopped rubbing, then put his thumb and first finger on his eyes and seemed to push. 'It's *that* kind of place, do you understand?'

'You mean—women, or men?'

'Men, of course, dear God—women!' He threw himself back, his eyes still closed. 'I was deeply ashamed. I'm still ashamed. And the man who took me was a friend of my father's, I trusted him, but looking back I realize he'd said things earlier, made insinuations.'

'You were a boy.'

'I was seventeen. I knew enough. At school—there's always a certain amount of that sort of thing. I won't claim I was innocent.' He sat up. 'But it was only the one time!'

'You're sure that's what the picture shows.'

Heseltine cackled. 'It's unmistakable. I used to pass that doorway before the war, going to a house where I often looked in after dinner. I could never see it without flinching.' He swallowed. 'I learned to look away.' He laughed.

Denton stayed to talk about other things, but he knew when he left that he'd made Heseltine's day worse, not better.

He wanted to talk to somebody about it, but Janet was off with her lawyer; Atkins's was the wrong ear. What did it mean that Mary Thomason had drawn the doorway of a male rendezvous on her portrait? Did she know something about Erasmus Himple and thus was making a threat? Had she learned something from her brother, who then went off to the Continent with Himple? Did this make Himple the one she feared was going to hurt her?

He went in the Regent Street entrance of the Café Royal and then into the Domino Room. He was hoping for Frank Harris, but it was far too early. No Augustus John, either; he would be back in Liverpool by now. He sat, still wearing his hat and overcoat, and drank a milky coffee and tried to think it through. It was the same squirrel cage—round and round, too much suggestion and not enough fact.

A little after six, a disreputable figure shambled across his view of the room.

'Crosland!'

Crosland was pushing fifty but looked older, untidy grey hair surrounding a pouched and lined face. He wore an enormous unfitted ulster that, like a magician's cloak, had pockets both inside and out. Papers stuck out of them. His hat had once been a silk topper. His waistcoat, unmatched to anything else he wore, carried old egg yolk down it like candle drippings. Crosland was nominally a hack journalist, really a polemicist and an information peddler; he prided himself on being able to cobble up a fire-breathing pamphlet on both sides of any subject.

'Got a minute?'

'Buy me a drink?'

Denton signalled for a waiter. Crosland, never absolutely drunk, was usually on the way; beery breath blasted from him—always a sign that he was on his uppers, his preferred drink brandy—and, under and around it, an odour of wet wool and sour milk.

'I need some information.'

'Cost you.'

Denton dropped a shilling on the table. 'The Mayflower Baths.'

'Ha! Cost you more than that.'

Denton fished out another shilling.

'Make it half a crown. Pricey part of town.' When the other sixpence had gone on the pile, Crosland removed his hat and rubbed his dirty hair with his left hand, then put the hat on the table. A glass of brandy had appeared by then; he sipped. Denton's own glass was empty; Crosland indicated the money and said, 'Buy you a drink?'

'I'm fine.'

'Well, then. The Mayflower Baths. Ah, well. Discreet spot for gents of a certain taste to find young 'uns, if you follow me. Mm? Used to be any evening after seven—very different during the day, ladies' Turkish bath and so on—but at night, this other drama. Oscar was known to drop in. Had a taste for some of the rougher ones.' He drank again. 'Gone now, if you'd been thinking of stopping by.'

'Gone?' Denton had a vision of some sort of demolition, London nowadays gobbling up older buildings as if they were chunks of candy.

'Closed. Coppers raided it. After Oscar's trial, the Baths put out the word that it had gone out of the man-and-boy business entirely. I was told that as gospel truth. Maybe it was, for a bit. However, they started up again, Tuesday and Saturday evenings. Did regular business other days, other times. Perfectly respectable. But Tuesday and Saturday after seven, if they knew you, the old times were back. Never there myself, but my understanding is it was a bit like Smithfield Market. Very little love lost, if you follow me.'

His glass was empty. Denton ordered another, but Crosland insisted on paying for his own this time. 'Sure you won't have something yourself? Always like to be hospitable. Failing of mine. Anyway. The police raided it last summer, probably to make an example. Some very well-placed people got snagged in the net. It never made the papers, except for "Closing of Mayfair Landmark" sort of pieces, kind of thing would let would-be patrons know that the cat was out of the bag. I wrote something m'self, "Memories of the Mayflower Baths", that was as innocent as a maiden's dream but capitalized on the moment—editors looking for stuff that would titillate. A dozen boys went up on charges, couple of minor gents—public indecency, that sort of thing, nothing huge—and the point was made. Owner doing time for endangering public morals. It's going to reopen, I'm told, as a therapeutic spa for ladies. New name, of course.'

'You know the names of the people arrested?'

'Arrested, yes. Detained, no. The tale is the coppers swept up about thirty people but let most of them go at the door of the magistrates' court. Some rather soiled drawers that night, they say. Names we'd recognize if we heard them.'

'Himple? Crum?'

Crosland shook his head. 'Himple the artist? Always rumours about him. You know anything I can use?'

Denton shook his head. 'When exactly was the raid?'

Crosland raised a finger. He began to spread the coat's big pockets with both hands, peering down into the messes of papers; at last, he drew out a small black notebook. He leafed through it. The pages looked like damp leather, thick and soft with use. 'August the seventh.'

'That was the day of the raid?'

'Night. Coppers went in the door at nine-forty-five, August the seventh.'

Denton put out another shilling. 'Worth every penny.'

A day before Mary Thomason had written her letter. Two days before Erasmus Himple had left for the Continent.

When he got home, there was a note from Janet Striker: 'I am going away for a little. Ruth Castle will know how to reach me.' He flushed and swore, then saw himself, a large man about to have an infantile tantrum. *She has the right to do what she wants.* It was difficult to tell himself that and mean it, yet he had to: sometimes when he looked at her, he saw a look of something like absence, and he knew she was away in one of the dark places to which he would never be admitted. He had them, too, those sinks into which the inevitable sorrows of being alive were poured and, for the most part, covered over. But it hurt that she had gone to get away from him, for that was what he was sure she had done.

And damn Ruth Castle, of whom he was thoroughly sick and whom he didn't want to see. Not now, anyway. Maybe it was not having a book to write, something to concentrate on. Maybe in a few days. Maybe Janet would come back quickly. Maybe—

He crushed the paper in his fist.

'Do you speak French?'

Heseltine's reactions were a semiquaver slow, as if he were thinking about something else. 'A bit.'

'I want to go to France for a few days. I need a translator.'

Again, the delayed response, and then a flicker of what might have been suspicion, some recollection perhaps of the discussion of the Mayflower Baths: what was Denton proposing? Heseltine's cheekbones got some colour. Denton said, 'It's about the girl who sent me the note. You said you wanted to try to help her.'

'In France?'

'Her brother.' He told him quickly about Erasmus Himple. 'I don't understand.'

'I don't either. Something happened in Normandy. They were supposed to stay the summer, but after a month they packed up and went to the South of France. Then Himple fired him. Something started in Normandy, I think. Maybe a lovers' quarrel.' He kept his eyes on Heseltine's. The younger man's cheeks got bright spots high on the cheekbones. 'It might do you good to get away. Get a new perspective on things.'

'I wouldn't dare take Jenks.'

'Neither of us needs to take anybody. We can be there in a day, back in another couple. It isn't as if we'd be staying at the Ritz.'

'My French is terribly rusty.'

'Rust is better than no metal at all. I'd just get the spike and shout at them.'

Denton insisted that they could start the next day; he didn't say that the post-partum depression of having finished the book now gripped him. Heseltine at first demurred, then became almost manic, swinging from torpor to excitement. Now he was sure he could be ready in an hour. They could take the night boat. Anything was possible.

Denton bought two tickets on the morning train and the Le Havre boat. Atkins made a face when he told him but didn't ask to go. In fact, he made it clear he wouldn't go on a bet. 'Had enough travel, thank-you-very-much. Roast beef of olde England's plenty good enough for me.'

'You mean you have other plans. How's the moving picture?'

'As it happens, we're scheduled to do the Battle of Ladysmith day after tomorrow, but that's nothing to do with me and France.'

'How's the housemaid?'

'An insufferable little monosyllable, is how she is. My pal with the picture machine has decided he's sweet on her. Disgusting.' He was picking up Denton's supper tray to take it back to the Lamb. 'I can get you somebody from an agency if you have to have an attendant on this jaunt.'

'Much as I hate to hurt your feelings, I don't need anybody.'

'Hard to believe.'

'I lived most of my life without somebody to pick up after me.'

'That was then, General. Times change.' Atkins cocked a cynical eye at him. 'You going to a respectable hotel?'

'There are no hotels. There's some sort of village inn.'

'Oh, well. Wear the old brown tweed. Frenchies won't know any different.'

Denton didn't dare let Atkins pack for him after that exchange. He got a somewhat chipped and scuffed pigskin valise out of a wardrobe and put a couple of shirts and collars and a set of woollen combinations in it—it was now almost December— and threw in extra stockings and then stood looking around the room, thinking about what else to pack. A flannel nightshirt, of course. What else would he need?

He decided that the answer was court plasters—he anticipated a lot of walking—and he found one in his desk, then remembered that he owned somewhere a small leather case of plasters, the perfect thing because it came with scissors. Where was it?

At the bottom left of the desk was a drawer he never used except as a place to throw things he wouldn't want again but couldn't quite throw away. He grasped the brass handle and pulled hard, because the drawer was always slow to open. To his surprise, it shot back towards him. He bent over it, seeing a lot of useless stuff, through which he tunnelled. Towards the bottom was a small basket in which he found the court-plaster case. Below the basket was only—or should have been only—a pistol almost as ancient as his Navy Colt, a Galland .450 with a curious contraption under the barrel that allowed barrel and cylinder to be moved forward for loading. The pistol was huge and heavy; he had got it for a few shillings from a pal of Atkins's who had been 'caught short' for money. For a while, he had used the gun as a paperweight; then he had thrown it into the drawer.

Where it now most certainly was not. He understood why the drawer had opened so easily now—no mass of iron to weight it on the rails.

He searched the drawer again, then the entire desk.

'Jarrold,' he said aloud. Munro had asked him if Jarrold could have stolen any of his guns and he'd said no. He'd entirely forgotten the awkward old weapon.

'Dammit!'

He wrote a note to Munro and left it with Atkins to be posted first thing in the morning. When he told Atkins about the missing pistol, he said only, 'Crikey.'

CHAPTER

17

The village inn at Hinon turned out to be less an inn than what Denton's English friends called a dosshouse. Downstairs was a café; above it were several rooms where, he learned later, the proprietor stowed the village drunks to sleep it off. This happened on Saturday nights, however, and in the middle of the week the rooms went unused—unheated, grubby, bare. The room they were shown—'the best room'—had a nominally double bed in painted and chipped iron, its mattress deeply furrowed in the middle. The bedspread had been darned in half a dozen places, then given up, the most recent tears left unrepaired. Except for a candle and a tin-topped washstand, that was it. The *cour* was down a corridor and then down a flight of unpainted, much-worn stairs, through a door and across a yard that was decorated with piles of horse dung. There were a long metal urinal and a single stall, its walls and floor soapstone, a hole to squat over.

'It could be worse,' Heseltine muttered. 'The family *live* here and use the same facilities all the time.'

'Hell of a place to get drunk in,' Denton said. Nonetheless, he felt rather sprightly, action brightening his gloom over Janet Striker.

'*Monsieur le propriétaire* says that he puts them in the rooms when they can't stand up any more, but they come down to use the *cour* and end up sleeping in the manure.'

'Kind of makes you understand why they move to the city. You going to be able to put up with this?'

Heseltine snorted. His colour was better, his eye livelier. 'I've seen lots worse in the army.'

Denton told him to insist on two rooms, but it turned out they couldn't have two. Only the one was made up (as what? Denton wondered) and *madame* didn't like to climb the stairs to do another. Denton demanded at least more blankets and did manage to get those—he had to carry them up himself—and arranged them on the floor so that Heseltine could have the bed. 'I don't want to keep rolling to the middle and finding you're already there,' he said. Heseltine seemed relieved, but in the midnight darkness he swore and lit the candle and lay down on the floor himself. The bed was full of bugs.

'That was rather desperate,' Heseltine said next morning. They had been up at daylight, walking the village streets until they could be off. 'I'm all over bites.'

'The floor was no better?'

'They came with me in the blanket. I thought some might make their way over to you.'

'Not so many. For a man who was eaten alive, you seem pretty cheerful.'

Heseltine blushed. 'It's good to get away, even to bedbugs.' Still reticent despite a day and a night together, Heseltine perhaps regretted his earlier confidences.

They had hard rolls and little coils of butter and milky coffee in the café. Men from the village came in and stared at them.

'We seem to be good for business.'

'They're not buying anything. *Monsieur* keeps shooing them out.'

The villagers were an unappetizing lot. Stout, red-faced, they were mostly agricultural labourers or small farmers whose hands proclaimed their work. Denton wondered if they had ever been more than ten miles from the village. Half of them affected expressions of great slyness, the rest of great stupidity. 'I've seen better-looking people in the steerage of an immigrants' ship,' he said.

'The immigrants are the ones who are bright enough to leave.'

They rented a rickety one-horse carriage to make the search for the place where Himple and Crum had stayed. Heseltine had asked the proprietor of the café, but he had said he knew nothing about any 'English milord'. Heseltine said he thought the man was put out because Himple hadn't stayed with him.

'He must have seen one of the rooms.'

The horse was a surprisingly good one, with a trot that spun them over the unpaved roads, puddles from recent rain splashing up from the wheels. At each farm, each crossroads, wherever they saw people, Heseltine asked after *un milord anglais qui peint,* and now and then they got a waving arm and gabbled instructions that, Denton found, Heseltine only partly understood. He learned, himself, to recognize the phrase *le milord qui peint,* which he heard as 'le meelor key pent', until he could repeat it himself. He tried it on a woman who was standing at a wattle fence to watch them go by; her answer was voluble and entirely incomprehensible.

'I'll let you ask the questions,' Denton said.

'It's always the way—you put the question together in your head, and then the answer absolutely goes by you like an inside-out umbrella in a gale. I don't pretend to understand everything they say.' Heseltine was driving, the reins held expertly through his fingers. He flicked them on the horse's back. 'Anyway, the local accent is ferocious.'

'You're doing fine.'

The day was cold but dry. Pale sunlight warmed their backs; clouds like streaks of whitewash lay against a soft blue sky, and the rows of poplars, like slow, uncertain dancers, waved their tops in the wind. Heseltine said that many painters came there. Denton asked him why.

'It's very picturesque.'

'What does that mean?'

'Oh, you know—lots of old churches and things, peasants in quaint costumes—that sort of stuff.'

Denton didn't think the peasants were quaint. The men wore short jackets like the one he'd seen at the party with Gwen John; the women wore lace caps and, some of them, enormous white collars. Were they quaint? And why was 'quaint' paintable? 'I'd think a painter would want to paint what's usual. The real world.'

'This is a real world, isn't it?'

'Real bedbugs and real peasants. But they don't paint the bedbugs, and they make the peasants look a hell of a lot less like apes than they do in real life. I don't get it.'

'The light is said to be awfully good,' Heseltine murmured. 'And the skies.' It was like him, Denton was learning, to talk about what 'was said' rather than what he thought. The more time they spent together, the more Heseltine spent on the surface of any subject.

'I don't get travelling all this way for it.'

Heseltine laughed. 'A French painter went to London to paint.'

'I could see painting London. London's the real thing. But this—'

'The coast is thought quite dramatic.' Heseltine seemed to feel he had to defend the place they'd come to. 'These people are the ones the French sent off to settle Canada, you know. Some of them are the heroes of your Longfellow's poem *Evangeline*.'

Denton knew very well who Longfellow was, and he had some idea of what *Evangeline* was about. He said, 'That wasn't Canada.'

'No, your state of Louisiana. We British shipped them there after we won some war or other.'

Denton thought of the Louisiana boys in the prison camp at the end of the Civil War. Dressed in rags, mush-mouthed, they had seemed to him loutish and alien, but religious and passionate with a brutal anger that was still dangerous in their defeat—what a sergeant had called 'good haters'—and they had spoken in accents he couldn't understand. He tried to see them in the peasants they passed but wondered if what was common to them was their insularity and suspicion and not their Frenchness. 'I don't think Louisiana did much to improve them.'

They found the farm late in the afternoon, when it was colder and the sun was without warmth. A great flock of crows came out of a field and flew over them, swinging like a wheel as if to have a better look at them before dropping into a clump of oaks. The mostly flat landscape, marked by hedgerows and ditches and two rows of poplars along the road, looked angular and inhospitable, a distant, square-topped steeple the only interruption of the austerity of line. To their right, away from the coast, the land sloped gradually upwards; at the top, a distant house and a vast barn were silhouetted. The air smelled of the sea.

To their left, farm buildings—a stone house, stables and two stone barns—enclosed a courtyard, its harsh urine-and-manure smell meeting them before they reached it. The farmer, if there was one, was away; the woman who came to the house door was heavy, suspicious. She wore the wide white collar and lace cap, and Denton thought she looked about as quaint as a London cab driver. Heseltine yammered at her—le meelor key pent came into it a lot—and she stayed back in the shadow of her doorway as if she were trying to hide. She had a habit of looking away out of the corners of her eyes. Her mouth was set, unhappy. He supposed her favourite word was *non*.

'She says that there was a milord who painted near here, but I'm having the devil's own time getting details out of her.'

'Ask her if there were two men.'

More gabbling, then, 'She wants to know who we are.'

'Tell her we're both meelors and we're looking for our pal the meelor key pent.' More talk, and Heseltine said, 'I told her the young one is your son.'

'Oh, good grief.'

'I had to tell her something. She thinks we're from the customs. There's a lot of smuggling here.'

Denton looked around at the drab landscape. 'Tell her my son has run away from home and I'm trying to find him because his mother's heartbroken.'

Heseltine spoke in French; the woman answered. He said in English, 'This is not a sentimental woman.'

'She doesn't care about the grieving mother?'

'She's worried about her cows.'

'Give her some money.'

They had been standing there for several minutes. Denton shivered despite his ulster. The wind had risen, bringing an edge to the cold. The wrangle went on and on until a big, red-faced man drove a herd of milk cows past them and through a gate into the farmyard. Denton got a glimpse of hoof-pounded mire; he had a memory of the Chicago stockyards. When the man came back, he pushed the woman into the house and pulled the door closed and said something in French so aggressively that Denton knew he had asked what they wanted.

Suddenly, both the questions and the answers became short. Le meelor key pent had been there, not here—a big arm, with a hand like a slab of beef, gestured behind them at the distant house and barn. Yes, with another man. Yes, yes, they were gone. What was it worth to them to see where they had lived? It was clear even without translation that he didn't care who they were so long as they paid.

'Tell him yes, we'll pay to see where they stayed. Tell him we'll pay for a place to stay tonight, too—clean, no bugs.'

Something in that caused an explosion of red-faced resentment. Heseltine said, 'It was suggesting they aren't clean. He says they're as clean as the angels.'

'Tell him about last night.'

Heseltine spoke, then pulled up a sleeve and showed his bites. The farmer was thrown into loud laughter, displaying dreadful teeth, and was suddenly as good-natured as he had been surly. He clapped Heseltine on the shoulder. It was so comical to him that he had to go inside and tell his wife.

'He says he'll put the horse in the barn and do something or other with the buggy; I couldn't follow it. He wants a hideous amount for us to spend the night—I could stay at Brown's in London for what he wants to charge us, but—' He looked around at the dour scene, now falling into darkness.

'Beggars can't be choosers.'

'We're hardly beggars.'

But they were each given a room with a tiled floor and a bed piled high with feather-filled quilts. Overhead were hand-adzed oak beams. A water pitcher, a basin, a chamber pot, a candle. A painted armoire that could have been one year or five hundred years old and held somebody else's clothes, both male and female—had he taken away some couple's bed? No other light, no heat.

And then the food.

The ill-tempered housewife was apparently used to feeding a dozen ravenous people; two more made no difference. They sat down at a huge table with the red-faced farmer at one end and an empty chair at the other—the woman never sat until they were almost done—and three younger men and two women between them on benches on each side. Heseltine sat at the end of one bench, Denton opposite him. Three younger women, really girls, helped the unhappy wife serve a meal that, if not quaint, was authentic and enormous and superb: a dish made with freshly killed chickens and beans and pork; another of what he took to be wild rabbit in a dark gravy; part of a pike that must have weighed a dozen pounds when it was caught; home-made sweet butter, home-made pot cheese; a dark, pudding-like thing he decided was made from congealed blood; haricots and endive and potatoes the size of cricket balls; three rough breads that had been baked that afternoon and, an oddly Germanic touch, a sweetened bread with gooseberry jam. They began with a soup that might have made a meal in itself, thick with dried peas, rich with carrots and onions and flavoured with rosemary. After the soup, the other dishes began to appear, Denton thinking each one would be the last. Glasses of both beer and wine were put in front of him.

At one point, Heseltine met his eyes and widened his own, smiling, shaking his head. Heseltine was keeping up what seemed to be a pretty good flow of conversation in French. A couple of the younger women looked rather flushed when they talked to him; so did he.

The women, Denton thought, were daughters or daughters-in-law; the men were sons, or husbands of the women. They were not a cheerful lot, certainly not talkative: farm work was hard, they seemed to say, and food was fuel. But what fuel! They stoked it in and reached for more; the women, although diffident, ate their share.

Why, he thought, *did Himple and Crum ever leave?*

After the older woman had sat and eaten quickly, when the men were done and were leaning back, when desultory talk had started, the women cleared off the dishes and the meats and brought a bowl of apples and a kind of cake made of apple slices and tasting of yeast, then three kinds of cheese. Denton had loosened his waistcoat; now he made a face at Heseltine. A bottle appeared. Heseltine said it was apple brandy, the local speciality.

The sons and the women drifted away. The farmer sat on, insisting that they sit with him. His face got redder. So did Heseltine's. So did Denton's, he supposed. Denton found himself talking about farming, the talk curving down the table to pass through Heseltine, then back, but Denton and the farmer looked at each other and it was as if they were speaking the same language. Then they were drinking the apple brandy, and the farmer, standing now, flaming-faced, shouted, 'Ah-ee spik anglaish! Sheet! God-dam! Ha-ha-ha! Sheet! God-dam you! Ha-ha-ha!'

And then Denton was in the big bed, under the warm feathered quilts, the rough sheets cold, then warming to his cold skin, the wind outside rattling the glass in the windows but unable to touch the comfort within.

CHAPTER

18

He had no hangover next morning. It was remarkable. He was no stranger to hangovers and he was sure he deserved one, but when he had splashed icy water on his face and swabbed out his crotch and his armpits, then pulled on his wool all-in-ones, he stood by the window and realized that he felt wonderful. The day was going to be dark, he could see; it would rain. Still, he felt content—at peace, even. A knock at his door produced one of the youngest girls with a pitcher of hot water. He shaved, washed himself again, dressed and went down to the central room where they had eaten. The farmer was there already. He got up from the table and came to Denton, muttered a question, then peered closely into an eye, clapped Denton on the shoulder and laughed. Later, Heseltine explained that the man believed that apple brandy never left a hangover; he would have been disappointed if Denton had had one.

People came and went. Children's voices sounded somewhere, the kitchen or some room beyond it. There was no repeat of last night's feast; rather, men took bread, one a piece of cheese as well, and went out. Heseltine explained that they would come back to eat when the milking and the morning chores were done. Denton understood that routine.

He was given hot milk and a small cup of coffee. The bread was pushed towards him, a hand waved at a bowl of eggs in the shell, presumably boiled, the platter of cheeses. He thought, *I could live here.* He thought, *This is the way we should live,* and then was ashamed of himself, remembering the brutal labour of farming and the price you paid for such plenty. And you didn't earn it alone: you needed those sons and daughters.

They walked out into a blustery morning with flecks of moisture flying in the air to strike their faces like sea spray. Frost glittered on the stones. The farmer insisted on showing them his castle: the house, huge, one end of it unused and derelict; the yard, ankle deep in dung and the mud made by cow urine. Chickens strode across the mire, several climbing the head-high dungheap in one corner. Along each side of the house's back door, heavy boots were ranged under the eave, the same foul mud caked on them. The wife didn't allow anybody to track dirt inside: the men and women, Denton remembered, had worn home-made, heavy slippers in the house. The women wore pattens outdoors but left them inside the door.

On the left side of the yard stood stone stables with five huge Percherons in them, a warm place that smelled like brewer's mash and urine; along the entire back ran the barn, Norman (or so Heseltine said), slashes like arrow slits high in its stone walls, raftering like a church. The farmer smiled at it all, smug with the pride of possession.

The Bohemian Girl

They walked up a cow track to the house where Himple and Crum had stayed. It was a quarter of a mile off, no road to it; on their right, a field of beets lay grey-green, the topmost leaves glinting with frost, the wind gusting through them and changing the colours like water. As they walked, Denton asked questions and Heseltine translated the answers that came back: the milord and the servant came here in the summer; the oak leaves were big; we were cutting hay the second time. They took the house for the summer but they didn't stay, they were city folk. The milord painted pictures; we'd see him and his easel up here on the horizon. You can see the coast from up there. We supplied them with milk—one of my daughters carried a pail up every morning—and cheese and gammon and vegetables. Sometimes one of my daughters would cook, not always; they asked each time. I made sure they paid her well.

In the beginning, the servant went into Caen and came back with a buggy-load of artificial food. (Denton took this to mean canned goods.) They left some behind; we had to use a chisel to open them; it wasn't worth it; we sold them back to somebody in Caen.

They kept to themselves. The servant spoke good French, better French than I do, but he didn't have much to say. The milord smiled when he saw us. He knew a few words. We weren't their kind of people. Sometimes we didn't see them for days.

When they left, they gave me five days' notice. I made them pay another month, because of my losses. They left early one morning in a buggy. *Both of them?* You think one of them stayed to help on the farm?

Denton was thinking of Mary Thomason. 'Ask him if there was ever a young woman with them.' He got his answer without translation: the farmer laughed the haw-haw roar of *double entendre,* meaning, Denton guessed, that they weren't that sort of men.

Denton had given Heseltine one of the photographic copies of the drawings that Augustus John had done. Yes, that was the servant, only he had no beard when he got here. He grew it while he was here. Not much of a beard. He wasn't much of a man, really. A day on the farm would have killed him.

I don't know what they did except paint pictures. I know when I'm not wanted. They stayed to themselves. They paid their money; that was what mattered to me.

The three of them reached the house, and Denton stopped asking questions.

The house was stone, certainly old, much smaller than the farmer's. One chimney had fallen in. It had a stone privy and a lower stone building, perhaps a smokehouse, whose roof had collapsed. Inside, it was dead and cold. If Himple and Crum had left any traces, the farm women had erased them: there were signs of vigorous cleaning in the sparkling windows, the swept hearth. The kitchen had no sort of modern stove, but a series of shelves, almost terraces, took up much of a vast fireplace, with places to shovel in coals and cook over them on iron plates. It would have been a brutal place for one person to have to cook, he thought—perhaps a factor in their leaving.

Behind the house, a low hill sloped up to the clean horizon, the oak copse off to its right. At the top of the slope was a building that looked like a cathedral without a steeple—the stone barn. The farmer pointed at it. 'When it rained, the milord painted up there.'

Denton insisted on seeing it. They trudged up the slope into the wind. The thin spray was threatening to turn to snow. The barn loomed over them until, when they were right under its walls, it wrapped them in its shadow and seemed to freeze them. Doorless, it had an earth ramp up to the opening for wagons.

The inside was vast. Pigeons flew in the rafters, the sound restless and irritating. Smaller birds, swallows and sparrows, flew in and out of the vertical slits that were meant to aerate the hay the barn had once held. It must have been, Denton thought, a horrible place to paint in, maybe another reason they had left. The light was bad except near the door; it was cold; the pounded dirt floor made the place smell like a grave.

Denton walked around the inside, taking stock of the farming implements left there to decay, most of them broken, antiquated, speaking of some misplaced sense of thrift—a culture where nothing was ever thrown away. One corner of the building was taken up by four horse stalls whose plank floors had fallen in, the oak boards now porous and spongy, although once they had held the weight of animals as huge as those down at the farm. He walked along the edges of the stalls, bending to look under the boards where he could, seeing nothing. Along the outside of the stalls, ancient straw still lay in a damp pile, the fibres broken short, the pale amber long since turned to brown and black as it had moulded and declined towards earth. Partway along, where the pile ended and the dirt floor began, he scraped his toe over the earth, pushed some of the straw back. It was compacted into clumps almost like horse dung. He moved more of it with his foot and exposed uneven earth.

'Take him outside and keep him busy for a bit, could you?' he said to Heseltine.

Heseltine looked uneasy. He didn't like to lie and didn't invent very well. After several seconds, he said, 'I'll ask him to point out what things the milord painted.'

Alone, Denton went back to the decayed hay. He moved more of it with the side of his boot and then went to an untidy heap of broken tools and rattled around in it until he found a wooden hay fork with one broken tine. He began to move the hay with it; the easy swaying motion coming back to him as he moved along, pitching it deeper up the pile. When he was done, he had cleared an area about ten feet by six. He got down on his hands and brushed wisps of hay out of his way, studying the dirt and even, close to the wooden wall of the old stalls, bending close to sniff it. Satisfied, he took the fork and pitched the hay down again until it lay as it had before.

They walked back down to the farm compound and shook the farmer's hand and paid him. He gave them the sly grin that meant he thought they were idiots, city pigeons ripe for the plucking. When they came down from their rooms, nonetheless, their buggy was outside, the horse in the shafts, its coat brushed and sleek. One of the younger women gave them a sack, rather heavy. Heseltine peeped in, said it was bread and cheese and apples and a bottle of wine. 'It's like the hotelier who gives one a free drink when one's paid several pounds too much.'

'Don't look a gift horse in the mouth.'

When they were rocking up the road behind the horse's trot, true snow blowing in from Denton's side, Heseltine said, 'What did you find in that barn?'

'I'm not sure.'

'Are we pushing on to Paris?'

Denton was driving, enjoying the feel of the reins between his fingers, the almost electric connection with the horse. 'Not this trip, I think.'

'Then you did find something in the barn.'

'I'm not sure.'

The truth of it was, he wanted to think. He was sure the earth had been disturbed along the stable wall where the hay had lain. If it had been, if it wasn't simply some effect of the hay's lying on it, was it something the farmer had done? Or something the two visitors had done? He couldn't imagine what, except the obvious. Bending over the apparently loose dirt, smelling its mouldy odour, he had had a sudden sense of disorientation; some of it was the evening spent with people whose language he didn't know, a severe reminder of his foreignness. He had told Janet Striker he was an outsider, but he had not meant that he was an alien being; there, bending over small clods of dirt, he had quite simply thought he was meddling in a different world.

At any rate, to dig there himself was impossible. The English police couldn't do it, either, he thought; they were as foreign as he, would be even more precise about not stepping on somebody else's toes. It would be a job for the French themselves, but to bring them to it would be an extraordinary task.

Not enough evidence. There had never been enough evidence.

He was having the rare experience of believing that he might best let sleeping dogs lie. And he wanted to go home, to be an outsider in a place he understood. And to see Janet Striker, who might have ended her absence already.

The next morning at Waterloo, they made their way through the station and hesitated outside by the cab rank. It was a small awkwardness: two men who didn't know each other very well yet had shared several days together, neither easy with any show of sentiment.

'I can drop you,' Denton said.

'Oh—no, thanks. I'd rather—I have an errand or two to run.'

'Well, then.' Denton held out his hand. 'Thanks for helping me out.'

'Oh, not at all. It's I who should—I feel so much better. I mean to say, getting away rather clarified things.'

'Good.'

'I truly enjoyed it.'

'Some memorable food, anyway.'

'No, no, all of it—the sense that—Life goes on. There are other lives, very different lives to mine, and they're utterly indifferent to me and my—history. I'm truly grateful.'

Heseltine shook his hand again. Denton motioned for a cab and the front one in the rank trotted forward the few steps to him.

Heseltine said, 'A friend, an acquaintance really, said he thought I could find something managing a plantation in Jamaica. He has relatives there. I value your opinion—what d'you think?'

Denton's flash of thought told him that 'managing a plantation' in Jamaica was probably as much like being the overseer of the slaves in the old American South as you could hope to find, but he knew he shouldn't say that, and he muttered something about the climate.

'Yes, well, it's hot.'

American slaves had once been threatened with being 'sold to the Indies'. It had been meant as a death threat, not from heat but from disease. He said, 'I think you can do better.'

Heseltine blushed and shook his head. Denton got into his cab and waved as it clip-clopped away.

The snow that had been falling on Normandy had already disappeared from London; new weather had blown in from the west while he had slept on the overnight Channel steamer. The sky was bright blue, splotched with white clouds that looked like some sort of meringue that had been twisted into rounds and curls; when they passed across the sun, the streets were suddenly bereft, almost grim, but in the returning sunlight colour shone and he felt cheered. When they got to Russell Square, he felt his tension rising and knew it was worry about *her*: would she be back? Or would there be some final letter from her, *I have decided to move away*? When they turned into Guilford Street, he was angry that she could have this effect on him; when they turned into Lamb's Conduit Street, he had thrown himself back and was rubbing his lips with a hand, hopeful, anxious, eager to forgive. But forgive what?

'You look a sight,' Atkins said when he opened the door. 'Been sleeping in that suit, have you?'

'I'm not in the mood.'

'No offence intended, General, only trying to lighten the prodigal's return. Sincere apologies, truly—'

They were going up the stairs, Denton's Gladstone bag bumping against Atkins's calves and then the treads with the sound of a small boat bumping a dock. At the top, Denton ripped off his hat and overcoat and went straight to the table where the mail lay. He went through it quickly, waiting for Atkins to say something like *Nothing from her, don't get your hopes up,* but Atkins, once cautioned, was wise. He simply gathered up the coat and hat and the valise and carried them up the stairs.

There were bills, there were notices, there were invitations, but there was nothing from Janet Striker.

Damn her.

He took a much-needed bath and announced that he was going to New Scotland Yard. Atkins looked innocent but said, 'Something you found in France?'

'I don't know. That's why I want to talk to Munro.' He knew that Atkins wanted to be told about it, but this morning, for once, he didn't want to talk to Atkins. He was hurt; he was angry; he wanted more action. He thought, *I should have dug up the damned barn while I had the chance.* Of course, he hadn't had the chance—the farmer, cautious and fearful of novelty, would have stopped him—but he didn't admit that to himself.

'Get you a cab, then?' Atkins said.

'I'll walk.'

'Going to rain this p.m.'

Atkins provided an umbrella, and Denton, looking entirely proper in an old but beautifully cut frock coat, one of the hated high collars and a necktie the colour of strong Burgundy, took it without a word. He even wore a mostly waterproof bowler.

The sense of being imposed on, of being ill-treated, stayed with him. She should have written. She should at least have done that much. She was playing some game. He turned right at the end of Lamb's Conduit Street and, instead of heading for New Scotland Yard as he'd said, walked straight on towards Westerley Street and Mrs Castle's. He cursed his own inconstancy.

He turned back twice, once lingered by a shop window, feeling irrationally that he was being followed, but there was nobody. What was the matter with him? It was the sense of ill-treatment, he thought.

Fred Oldaston was not on the door at Westerley Street. It was not yet noon; the door was opened by a middle-aged maid in a perfectly proper black dress and white apron. 'I'm so sorry, sir, we're not receiving,' she said.

'I need to see Mrs Castle.'

'She's not receiving callers yet, sir. If you'll come back—'

He produced a card and insisted she take it in. Something about him impressed her—frightened her, more likely—and she held the door for him, then left him in the little entry where Fred usually sized up the clientele. She wasn't gone long, gave no sign that anything unusual was happening; she took his umbrella, thrust it into a gold and blue ceramic cylinder, said only, 'This way, please,' and led him through the public rooms and into the one with the William Morris paper where Ruth Castle usually received the male world, and then through it and into the cool blue-and-green sitting room where he had met Janet Striker after her rooms had been invaded.

'Please wait, sir.'

Waiting was the last thing he wanted to do. He wished now he had gone straight to Munro's. At least Munro would have given him an argument, stirred him up. If Munro was no help once he did get to New Scotland Yard, he decided, he'd go right back to Normandy and do what he should have done yesterday, dig up the damned barn and the hell with it. Buy off the farmer. He'd need Heseltine again. Catch the evening train out of Waterloo, be in Le Havre at—

'Do take off your coat, Denton, you'll catch your death when you go out.'

'Where is she?'

Ruth Castle had touched her cheeks and lips with red, but she looked worn at this time of the morning; he thought the veins in her cheeks were starting to show, and serve her right. But her figure was still good, evident in the floor-length wrapper she wore, a blue-grey shot silk with an elaborate ruffle up the front and around the back of the neck. She stared at him and then opened her eyes wide and sat down on the love seat and extended her arms up the curves on either side. 'I do want you to be civil, Denton.'

'Where is she?' He was still sick of Ruth Castle.

'Well, she isn't here, if that's what you mean. Nor is she in London, so you can't rush off and bedevil her when she wants to be by herself. Give her some breathing room, Denton.'

'She hasn't even written to me!'

'Why should she? What is it you expect—comments on the weather, the news of what other ladies are wearing? Billy-doos?'

'Don't mock me.'

'Hard not to, my dear. Men in love are so mockable. Where have *you* been, one might ask.'

'France. Business.'

'Paris—that business?' She laughed.

'Ruth, look—' He put his hat on a table and ran his hands through his hair. 'I'm sorry if I was rude. Yes, I suppose I'm a man in love. I don't know what she wants from me. She's avoiding me, isn't she?'

'She's afraid of you.'

'I'd never hurt her!'

'That's not what she's afraid of. The world is full of women, my dear, and you picked one of the tetchiest. Well, that's you—if you'd picked somebody else, you wouldn't be yourself. So you must take the consequences.' She lit a cigarette and stared at him, drawing in the smoke.

'Meaning that I leap through whatever hoops she holds up for me.' His impatience with Ruth Castle had attached itself to Janet, too.

'That's your way of looking at it, not hers.' She exhaled the smoke and put her head back while it dissipated in the room. 'Denton, she isn't *doing* anything to you. She's trying to do something *for* herself. She doesn't believe there's such a thing as love. She doesn't trust men. She doesn't believe she deserves anything, good or bad. She'd make a fine nun if only she'd knuckle under to the idea of a God who's a very demanding old man.'

'She's told you everything?'

'Janet doesn't tell anybody "everything". Until you came along, she was going to win her lawsuit and take her money and go away somewhere that nobody knew her, and she was going to be self-sufficient. No men, no women, no fears, no hopes. Now you've spoilt all that.'

'I don't think I've spoiled anything. God knows I didn't mean to.'

'Hell is paved with good intentions. Let her be, Denton. She'll come back.'

'How do you know?'

'She always does what she says. She'll come back. You may not like what she tells you when she comes back, but she'll tell you to your face and she'll be honest.'

'You know what she's going to say, then.'

'I know nothing. But I know *her*. You must wait, and then you must listen, and then you must either try not to make a fool of yourself in your delight, or you must live with a loss.' She put the cigarette out in a small China tray. 'Now I want you to go. I have to dress, and I've the accountant coming. Be a man, Denton.'

He made a hollow laughing sound in his throat. 'That's what a woman who was throwing me over said to me once.'

'Well, it's good advice. Go away. Don't forget your hat. You look quite nice, by the way.'

She rang a bell and the middle-aged maid appeared and led him back through the house. In one of the rooms, a young woman in a sleazy wrapper looked at him with a kind of horror and hurried away. The maid handed him his umbrella and opened the door.

He gave her a coin. She bent her knees an inch or two, a symbolic curtsey. Perhaps the coin was too small.

The clouds that had looked like meringues when he had come out of Waterloo station had darkened and congealed and now lay over London in layers, with darker streaks lower down that slanted on a diagonal towards the docks. Ahead of him in the gaps between the houses and the leafless trees, a sliver of blue still showed, closing as he watched it and becoming a pale grey with tendrils of darker colour hanging over it like vines.

He was angry, but in a sullen way now, angry with her and with himself. He wanted activity, action. He tried to rehearse what he would say to Munro—the journey, the farm, the barn, the hay—

He heard sound behind him, its meaning unclear—breathing? Scuffing feet? Then he was hit a stunning blow in his right lower back, and sound exploded around him. The sound hammered again and he felt an agony in his right shoulder, and he was falling forward. His face hit the pavement. His right arm had been useless to stop the fall; the left one was caught under him. He tried to speak, raising his head, rolling to his left side in a slow, seemingly drunken turn.

He couldn't hear. He knew his mouth was open; was he making sound? He tried to raise his right arm to protect himself.

Ten feet away, Struther Jarrold was holding a revolver in both hands. Black-powder smoke drifted between them. On his face was a look of ecstatic glee. His mouth was open and moving, but Denton heard nothing. He knew that Jarrold was going to put another bullet in him and finish him, and then a big man in a checked overcoat put his arms around Jarrold from behind and lifted him off his feet. Denton's head struck the pavement again.

CHAPTER

19

They came at night, night after night, and led him out over the prairie. They had horses and they made him ride one, a raw-boned old stallion with gaunt ribs. The beast had a terrible canter and it was torture for his back, but they rode on and on and then every night it was the same: the empty town, the doors blowing in the wind. Alone. He had been in a hotel but he was out in the town looking for something and then he couldn't find the hotel where Janet was waiting for him, only the dark streets and the deserted railroad station, the iron tracks gone and the sleepers decayed among the cinders, the pain of the brutal ride always with him. People came and went but were not people, only shadows, shapes. He thought he would have to kill them or they would kill him.

He found a store with the shelves still stocked but everything dusty and gritty, no light, feeling his way, looking for a gun. Somebody was going to kill him. He could feel his heart seize up and almost stop. The shelves were full of boxes. He'd take down boxes and go through them and find women's hats, coffee pots, dolls, and some stuffed with bloody rags, and he'd put them all back and put the boxes back on the shelves and he'd take down more boxes and they'd be the same ones, women's hats, dolls, blood-soaked rags, and he'd put them back and go to a different part of the store, different shelves, and he'd take them down and they'd be the same ones, women's hats, rags brown with dried blood. His back was breaking from bending over. There was a gun there, he'd left a gun there, bought it one day and said he'd come back for it and now the store was closed and he had to find it. He found ammunition and set it aside and then he went through more boxes and he couldn't find the ammunition. There were more boxes, a huge pile of boxes; he had to stand on boxes to reach the boxes he wanted; he needed a knife to open them but there was no knife—

They came for him and gave him a hideous, raw-boned stallion to ride and they galloped over the prairie, the ride painful; he couldn't keep his seat in the saddle, bouncing like a beginner, feeling his back almost break, blisters forming down his thighs. He had trouble walking because of the blisters. The town was dark, empty, dead. They were coming for him and he had to get a gun, but he'd left it in the hotel and he couldn't find the hotel, they kept lying to him about where it was, an evil-faced child laughing while she lied to him. In the store, he began to pull boxes from the shelves in the dark, looking for a gun; the boxes piled up, box after box of women's hats. Then they were coming for him. Most of them came to watch; only the one came to kill him. The figure came into the store carrying a shotgun, saw Denton and came very close and in the dark Denton could hear and he could smell the approach, the figure in a long duster with the collar turned up and hat low over the eyes, tobacco breath and horse and something foul, as if somebody had soiled his trousers. Denton turned and the boxes were in the way; he ran over them, jumped them, climbed them, and the figure shot him in the back, the pain intense, heart-stopping. He put a hand to his back and felt blood, a hole his hand went into, meat. The figure shot him again.

When they gave him the horse, he said he couldn't ride because he'd been shot but they made him get into the saddle and they tied him on. The horse was ugly, emaciated, huge. He bounced in the saddle; his back was on fire. At the hotel he asked for a doctor and they said down the street, but down the street it was dark, everything closed; there was no doctor. He couldn't find the hotel where Janet was waiting for him. He went into a store whose door was hanging open, banging in the wind like gunshots. He thought he might find a gun in there. They watched him, laughed at him. They bent over him and stared into his eyes and an evil-faced child laughed. He began to take down boxes, women's hats, smelly rags all bloody, the warehouse was full of boxes, all the same, and he opened each one the same, took out the hat, put it back, checked it off on the paper and closed the box and took down the next. Over and over. Over and over. Over and over—

When it was light men came and looked at him and spoke in some language he didn't understand and shook their heads and went away.

They said when he'd finished the boxes he could have a bath but he had to finish the boxes. When he made mistakes they laughed at him. Over and over. Over and over.

He spoke to one of them. She put her hand on him. She was praying. He didn't like her laughing at him. They made shadows on the ceiling. If he could recognize the shadows, they said, he could have a bath. They kept projecting shadows on the ceiling. Over and over. He made mistakes and had to do it all again. Over and over. Over and over.

The figure with the shotgun said he'd never do it right and shot him in the back. They took a pair of blacksmith's pliers and reached down into the hole the buckshot had made and twisted his bones. He screamed. An evil-faced child laughed. He was dying. They said he was dying. They reached into the wound again. Over and over. Over—

'Can you hear me?'

'How are we this morning?'

'If you can hear me, blink your eyes.'

They gave him a half-dead old horse with a blind eye to ride and said he could escape on that, but he couldn't, he couldn't find the way out of town; they kept changing the streets, a street he had just been on suddenly having a dead end. If there was a doctor's office there, he couldn't find it. The horse was labouring and it stumbled, the wrench it gave his back like fire. He got down off the horse, almost falling; he couldn't lift his leg over the pommel. Finally, he fell off. The horse staggered. It was dying. He led it by the reins, but it wouldn't go and he left it there, pitying it but unable to help it. The town was empty and dead. Everybody had gone on west, they said. They'd taken up the tracks behind the last train. He sat in the empty saloon and waited for them to come. If he could find his office, he had a gun there. Over and over.

'Mr Denton? Can you hear me, sir?'

He tried to speak, but his mouth was dry as sand. A huge shadow was cast on the ceiling by the man bending over him. He knew the man, he was sure. He had an accent. A beard. A kindly eye. He tried to say the name: Bernat.

'Try to drink a little. Your mouth is dry. I keep telling them to give you water but they don't. Here—drink—drink—'

He felt the coolness in his mouth; then he choked. He tried to cough, tried to sit up. Pain grabbed his back across the kidneys like a huge hand.

Where was the hotel? The streets were dangerous and dark. He was afraid. They would hunt him down and kill him. If he could get to

the hotel, he could hide. Janet would hide him. Or Mrs Castle. Or Jack Pendry. Pendry would give him a gun. If only—

She cast a shadow on the ceiling, but it was very pale because the room was full of light. Her eyes were huge. Her hair was different.

'Janet.'

'My God.'

He felt her hand on his forehead, then the back of her fingers against his cheek. He tried to sit up, and pain pushed him back like a big hand. He made a sound, half scream, an animal.

'Don't try to move. You can't move; you're strapped down.'

The room was bright. The air smelled of carbolic. Something smelled fetid. He guessed it was himself. He said, 'Don't let them get me. They'll try it again.'

He heard her say, 'I know,' and he passed into blackness, not understanding what it was she knew.

He slept. The dreams came back, but they were wispy, as if they'd lost their power. He had to repeat some of the old tasks, but he kept waking out of them and then going back to them or other tasks like them. When he woke again, the light was different and Dr Bernat was there. Bernat made him drink from a tube.

'Something is lying on my leg.'

'No.'

'Right leg.'

'You were shot.'

Did he remember that? The feeling of fear clutched him; his heart tried to stop beating. Shotgunned in the back—the hole, wet, meaty—

He had made the animal noise again, and Bernat was clucking at him, wiping his forehead and telling him not to agitate himself.

'What's the matter with my leg?'

'A piece of bullet went close to the spine. It is all well now. We took it out. You will be all fine. Sleep, my friend.'

They woke him now to put the bedpan under him and to change the metal tube that went up inside his penis. He could roll his head and see other tubes, red India rubber, dropping away from him on both sides of the bed. They were draining the wounds, Bernat said.

She came back. She smiled down at him. He said, 'I don't want you to see me like this.'

She said, 'My dear, I've been seeing you like this for weeks.' Weeks?

When she was gone, he told them he didn't want any visitors. No, she was not to visit him any more. No, he wouldn't see the police. Keep them all away.

'What's that music? I hear music!'

'It's almost Christmas. You must sleep, Mr Denton.'

They woke him for morphine injections. He tried to stop them, but Bernat said he would be in too much pain. He remembered the men from the war who had come to like the morphine more than their wives or their children. He said he wanted to do without it, but he couldn't.

They moved him again, this time to a nursing home. Bernat explained what had happened to him: he had two entry wounds and no exit wounds, the big, soft-lead bullets staying inside his body. One had gone in below his shoulder blade and nicked his lung, ending against a rib. The other had entered between his kidney and his spine and had broken into three pieces. The shoulder injury had gone septic, then the lower one, and they had been almost four weeks draining the wounds, waiting for him to conquer the sepsis, thinking for a while they would lose him.

'You are a very tough cut of beef, Mr Denton.'

'Not as tough as two .45-calibre bullets.'

'We had to collapse your lung, but it reinflated when the sepsis ended. You have a small incision in your chest; the surgeon took the ball out that way and put the tubing in. The other injuries are healing.'

'My leg?'

'One step at a time.'

'Have I lost the use of my leg?'

'You talk nonsense. Your nerves are bruised, yes. There is wounding, yes. But you are tough. Also strong. You will walk.'

'I'm as weak as water.'

'Temporary only. Five weeks in a hospital bed, the great Ajax would be being weak. Soon, you get out of bed, you get stronger.'

'When?'

'Soon. Also, I want you to see Mrs Striker.'

'No.'

'You are being very cruel to her. You think you protect her but you make her life unhappy. I want you to see her.'

Denton cowered under his bedclothes. 'I don't want her to know me like this.'

'That is vanity. It is wrong to put vanity ahead of the people who love us.'

He told them to let her visit. They said she was coming every day as it was and sitting outside his room. Now she sat by him, either reading silently or reading to him.

'So you remember it was Struther Jarrold now?' she said.

'I'd been at Ruth Castle's, looking for you. Then—all I remember are the dreams. Nightmares of doing the same things, over and over. And riding, a horse that made my back hurt—'

'They moved you once, from one hospital to another. The ambulance was very rough.'

'You were there by then?'

'I told you I'd come back.'

'Ruth Castle said you would. I don't remember anything after I went down her steps.'

He tried to recall the shooting, but he couldn't bring it back. He started to tell her about going to France with Heseltine.

'Don't concern yourself with it.'

'It matters to me. Anyway, I was going to see Munro. Munro needs to be told what we found.'

'Not yet. You're not to be "agitated"—Bernat's orders.'

'Janet, good God—'

'Shut up.'

He sighed. 'I feel ashamed.'

'Because somebody shot you in the back? You could hardly have prevented it.'

'I should have. I should have seen it coming.'

'How?'

'I need to talk to Munro.'

'Not yet.' She opened her magazine. 'Soon.'

'You sound like Bernat. "Soon."'

Next day, they got him out of bed. Two nursing sisters and the doctor helped him to try to stand; he swayed for a few seconds, and they put him back down.

'You must make an effort, Mr Denton. Doctor's orders.'

'Go away, sister.'

'Get up.'

'Leave me alone.'

'Mr Denton, get up! Oh, why are you so stubborn?'

'Because I can't move my leg! Because I'm a cripple, you stupid bitch!'

CHAPTER

20

The surgeon who had removed the piece of bullet from near his spine was named Gallichan, a black-bearded, handsome man in his forties with the sort of good belly that announced success and appetite. Presumably Irish, he was in fact as English as the new king, whom he slightly resembled. He wore fawn trousers, a broadcloth morning coat in blue-black, a waistcoat that was daring in that it didn't match and was silk, not wool—in fact an anachronism, pale grey with embroidered floral designs.

'I'm told you had trouble standing,' he said genially.

'I'd have collapsed if they hadn't held me up.'

'Of course you would.' Gallichan smiled as if this was the best news in the world. 'Let's have a look at this leg of yours.' The sister pulled back the sheet. Denton didn't want to look at it, forced himself to: the leg looked pasty-white, inert, like something made from dough. Gallichan said 'Mmm-hmmm' several times, very low, and hummed something unidentifiable. 'Does that hurt?'

'What?'

'Mmm.' He pushed the leg this way and that. 'Raise your foot, please.'

'I can't.'

'Raise your knee.'

He couldn't do that, either.

Gallichan took a tool from his bag and drew it up the sole of Denton's foot. Denton felt something like the weakest of electric currents.

'Feel that?'

'A little.'

'Aha!'

Gallichan sent the sister away and then moved the sheet aside to reveal Denton's groin. 'Feel that?'

'Yes.'

'What did I do?'

'You felt my, you know—parts.'

'We say testicles; I'd understand "nuts" or "balls", too, if Latin bothers you. Feel that? And that? Mmm-hmm.' He pulled the sheet back and arranged it over the leg.

'Well? I want to know the worst.'

Gallichan pulled a white metal chair away from a wall and placed it near the foot of the bed. He sat, crossed his legs and leaned back with one arm over the back of the chair. He looked like a man about to light up a cigar, perhaps order a small brandy. He hooked his left thumb into the armhole of his waistcoat. 'I was called in again because I am what is called a nerve specialist. Some think me a nervy specialist.' He laughed. Denton didn't. 'I did the surgery to remove the bit of lead that had given up the ghost near your spine. It's a tricky place. Rather like Piccadilly Circus—traffic coming in from all directions and rushing about and going out all over the shop.' He looked into his satchel, found a piece of paper and a patent fountain pen and put the paper down on the bedsheet. After a moment, he cleared the tray on the bedside table of its water pitcher and glass and put the paper on it and began to draw. 'The lower vertebrae look like something with wings, in profile—not important; I'm not Michelangelo—at any rate, there are holes along the side through which blood vessels and the nerves pass. Your bit of bullet lodged like so—close to the nerves and vessels but not *in* them, do you see? If it had gone into them, we'd have had the devil of a time, but as it was, we were able to get in and out—seventeen minutes, quickly done—and not have to do any cutting in nerve tissue. So the problem is bruising, not cutting. You follow me?'

Denton nodded. The drawing nauseated him.

'Bruising, not cutting. Tissue is elastic, you see. The piece of bullet struck, as it were, a net of India rubber, which absorbed its velocity by stretching and yielding to it, then returning to its shape. But the yielding bruised the nearby tissues, eh? The nerves and vessels coming out on the right side of the vertebrae.' He blacked in the nerves and vessels on the drawing. He looked at Denton for a response and, getting none, put the pen down and sat back again and resumed his old position. 'The nerves there go to the right leg and to areas of the groin.'

'Get to it. Is it permanent?'

Gallichan frowned, the kind of man who despite his jollity was vain and didn't like to be denied his accustomed veneration. 'I don't give snap judgements.'

'How bad is it?'

'You can't stand; you can't move the leg. You have feeling in the sole of the foot, the testes and the glans penis. With time, I think, the leg can be made to function.'

'*Function?*'

'I believe it will bear weight again. Some degree of movement, we might hope.'

Denton stared at him.

The doctor said, 'You're a good healer. I expect good results, if you work at it.'

'Will I walk?'

'I don't predict the future, Mr Denton. I don't plant false hopes. I think—*think*—you will recover some use of the leg, but I can't promise it. And the rest, as well.'

'What *rest*?'

'Mmm, well—The, mmm, rectum and the anal sphincter could be implicated—nerves run close to the path of the bullet—and they are so far somewhat affected, are they not? We shall see about them. The penis, the, mmm, let us say the *mechanism*, although it's far from a machine; it's most wonderfully organic—but that system that causes the tumescence of the organ is perhaps implicated. You see, there are muscles that are meant to shut down the flow of blood—' He had picked up his pen and bent over the paper again.

'You're saying I'm impotent.'

'We don't know yet. Time will tell.'

'My God, what else are you keeping from me? Tell me!' He had forced himself up on his elbows; his upper arms shuddered from the effort.

The doctor flinched back and turned the movement into one of standing, as if he had meant to do that instead of recoiling. 'You mustn't excite yourself.'

Denton fell back. 'You bastard.'

'My dear sir—'

'Don't dear sir me, you sonofabitch. Tell me the worst!'

Gallichan took hold of the lapels of his coat with both hands. He drew himself up, then settled himself, shot his chin out and pulled it back. 'I have told you the worst,' he said.

'I don't believe you.'

'You are in a disturbed mental state, sir. It has been a constant worry to us. Are you aware that twice you fought with the sisters—that male attendants had to be called? You pulled out your tubing! This was early on, I grant you; you were feverish. But you are a violent man, Mr Denton, and you do violent things and make violent statements. Now, I am telling you—your mental condition is abnormal and you are not seeing things clearly. I have told you the truth and you should believe me!'

'Go away.'

'I am here to help you. I will not go away.'

'Go to hell.'

Gallichan looked at him. His face showed disgust. He cleared it almost feature by feature, settling it into the somewhat cautious physician's face—a kind of cheerful blandness, ready at any moment to be sombre—that he usually wore. He sat again in the metal chair, put his right ankle on his left knee, and hooked his thumbs again into the armholes of his waistcoat. 'My work on the nerves has led me to an interest in the mind.'

Denton, consumed with his helplessness, said nothing.

'The mind drives the body. The healthy mind enables the healthy body. I want you to begin a course of exercises to repair your leg. I quite understand that what I told you about your bowels and your erectile tissue has disturbed you, but those things will, I hope, take care of themselves. It's the leg I want to work on.'

Denton was looking at the ceiling. 'So if I fill my pants or can't get it up, it isn't your province. Thank you.'

'You're trying to drive me away by being deliberately offensive, but you won't. I'm the one who can make you better. Whether I can make you the man you were is up to you. Oh, yes, to you—you have to do the real work. I'm just a jolly fat man who studied medicine. You're the one living in that body. As for damage other than the leg, yes, I've suggested indignity and horror to you. They may lie in your future. I don't want them to be your future; I want you to be the man you were before you were shot. But you won't be if you shout vulgarities at me and try to send me away. If your mind won't help me to cure your body, Mr Denton, you will lie in that bed until you rot.'

Denton raised his head. 'That's a hell of a thing to say.'

'I meant it to be. Get hold of yourself, man. I'm not your problem.'

Denton's head dropped back. 'What am I supposed to do?'

'First, I want you to apologize to sister. You hurt and upset her.'

'She was trying to force me to do things.'

'On Bernat's orders and with your good health in mind. I want you to apologize to her and then I want you to do as she asks.'

'To hell with both of you.'

'Mr Denton, I want you out of that bed. For one thing, you've bedsores on your buttocks. You don't feel them because you're full of morphine, but they're getting worse and they're going to go septic. Then I want you on your feet and getting about so you can get out of this nursing home and into familiar surroundings. It isn't good for you here. Your mental state is made worse by isolation—if you don't see it, I do. Now, will you apologize to sister?'

'Why not?'

'Then you'll begin a course of exercises. I also want somebody from your household to learn them so you can do them when you leave here.'

The doctor tapped a finger on his lower lip. His eyes narrowed. 'Will you talk with me—frankly, honestly—another time?'

'About what?'

'I shall tell you then. About your mind.'

'My mind is my business.'

'Yes, I'm sure you think so. Will you talk with me?'

Denton said nothing for several seconds. 'I can't keep you from coming.'

'Good. I want you to start having visitors, as well. Seeing people will be good for you.'

'I don't want to see anybody.'

Gallichan sighed. 'Mmmm.' He stood, lifted his satchel to the bed next to Denton's leg, and put his pen and the paper into it. He replaced the tray and the pitcher and glass. He said, 'I've told you the worst. This is the bottom—the abyss of illness. Now we climb out.' He snapped the satchel with a click. 'Do apologize to sister.'

'I had dreams. They're gone now.'

Dr Gallichan nodded. 'Fever and morphine. They'll do that. What do you remember?'

'Nothing.' He frowned.

'You were violent, as I told you. You pulled out your catheter. You also shouted in your sleep, enough that you disturbed other patients on the ward.'

'What about?'

Gallichan hesitated. 'I think you were afraid of someone.'

'There was somebody— With a shotgun. He shot me in the back. I died.' He said it with wonder.

'In the dreams, you mean.' When Denton said nothing, the doctor went on. 'You *were* shot in the back, after all. Was it the same man?'

Denton shook his head. 'I don't remember being shot. It's—I'm not sure it was a man—' He croaked out a laugh. 'It's like a dream.'

'Well, the dreams. You were under a long time. What else?'

'I don't—I did the same things. That's what I remember, the sense of doing things again and again. Over and over.'

'Being shot?'

'Ye-e-e-s, but—Boxes.'

'Boxes.'

'Yes, boxes. That's all I remember.'

'I was always looking for something in the boxes. It was horrible, but there was nothing horrible about it. It was just—the boxes. Over and over. And the person—thing—with the shotgun. Not Struther Jarrold.'

'Who's that?'

'The man who shot—' He raised himself on his elbows. 'I remember! I think. Not in the dream, in—life. Struther Jarrold with a revolver, standing over me. Laughing.' He put his head back. 'He seemed so—pleased.'

'You're sure this wasn't in the dream?'

'I'm not sure of anything. Maybe you're a dream, doctor.'

'More a nightmare, I expect. How's that leg?'

'White. Dead.'

'I was told you went down the corridor yesterday.'

'Carried by two sisters.'

'Mmmm.' Gallichan pinched his upper lips with thumb and forefinger. 'You use guns yourself, do you?'

'Yes.'

'Carry one?'

'Usually.'

'You've shot someone?'

'I was in a war. Then there was the time they write all their crap about. The dime-novel hero. Three minutes that made me famous. Or infamous.'

'You killed someone?'

'Four men. They were going to rob people; I was a peace officer.'

'You shot them?'

'I did.'

'In the back?'

'Of course not.'

'With what sort of weapon?'

'A shotgun.' Denton lay still. 'Oh, I see what you're getting at. No, I think you're wrong.'

Somebody named Jack Pendry had shot the town marshal in the back with a shotgun. They gave Denton ten dollars a month and a free room in the hotel for being the new marshal. After a couple of months, when he was making his early-morning rounds of the town, nobody up yet, the town dead, he found a man with a rifle on the roof of the building opposite his office. He brought the man down and tossed him into the one-cell jail. The man told him he'd been

supposed to shoot him because Jack Pendry was coming on the train with a gang to rob the bank and tear up the town.

He'd got a ten-gauge goose gun from the rack and gone to the blacksmith's and cut the barrels down to eighteen inches and filled his pockets with buck-and-ball loads. Then he'd waited in the shadows where he could see the railroad station. The town stood a dozen feet above it on a little bluff. A stairway ran from the wooden sidewalk by the station up to the town.

When the morning train came in, eight people got off. One of them was one of the biggest men he'd ever seen. That was Jack Pendry. Six of them gathered around him, and he sent one of them up the pole to cut the telegraph line. The others began to check guns that they had in their pockets and their waistbands and in holsters on extra belts that they took out of their carpet bags. A man and a woman hurried up the stairs and Denton let them go.

Then Denton stepped out and said, 'Anybody else who isn't with Jack Pendry, get out of the way. There's going to be some killing.'

Pendry and his men dropped their carpet bags and scrabbled for their guns. Denton took out Pendry with one barrel of the shotgun and a man near him with the other. They were shooting back with black-powder pistols. He knelt and reloaded. The remaining four split two and two, two to come up the little dusty cliff at him, two to go up the stairs. He cut down the two who were coming up at him, and the other two just kept going and hid in a barn at the edge of town, and he talked them out later without firing another shot. The man who'd gone up the telegraph pole was still up there. Denton made him throw his pistol and then climb down.

The town raised his pay to twelve dollars a month and gave him a two per cent cut from the saloon and whorehouse across from the hotel. A few months later, he drifted on to Colorado.

They allowed him to start reading the mail that had piled up at home. Atkins sorted it, he was told; Janet Striker vetted it more carefully. Nothing was to worry him.

Twice a day, a sister with a chubby, red-cheeked face raised his right foot until the leg was bent and then pushed it up until the thigh almost touched his midriff. He was supposed to push against her. When the leg was all the way up, he was supposed to push it all the way back down.

'The mind drives the body,' Gallichan said. 'We want the brain to tell the nerves to move the leg. You must *think* the leg to move.'

'William James would say it's the other way around—the leg moves and the brain thinks about moving.'

'Mr William James is not here.'

She pushed, and he thought about pushing, and so far as he could see, nothing happened.

One day, however, he could move his toes.

'Tell me about the boxes.'

'They were boxes. Just—Some of them were hatboxes.'

'Were there hats?'

They had raised his torso on pillows. A window stood next to his bed, a good placement to light the room and the bed but bad for looking out; he would have had to lean far to the left, and they wouldn't let him lean yet. By looking out of the corners of his eyes and rolling his head, he could see the glass and the mullions. A sprinkling of snowflakes lay on them. 'Is it Christmas?'

'It's the sixteenth of January. Were there hats?'

'Women's hats. Over and over. Why?' He didn't tell him about the bloody rags; he didn't know why.

'Do you read German?'

'Good God, no.'

'There's a new book, *Die Traumdeutung*—Dream...mmm... Inquiry, no, Analysis. It implies that dreams have meanings.'

'What's the good of meanings if we forget them as soon as we wake up?'

'Well, you didn't, obviously.'

'You said yourself they're the product of fever and morphine.'

'But not necessarily invalid for that.'

'So I was talking to myself?'

'Mmmmm—no, I prefer to think of it—this is all speculation—as working.'

'It certainly seemed like work. What I remember.'

'Working something through.'

'Counting women's hats? What's that got to do with me?'

'Were you counting them? That's new.'

'I was—God, I don't know. No. Yes. There was some sort of list. It was just something I had to do over and over. There was no end to it.' He gave a graveside chuckle. 'There's a cliché—"wearing two hats". When you do two things at once.'

'Why was there no end to it?'

'Oh, good Judas Priest, how would I know? It was a *dream.*'

'For four weeks. What in your usual life do you do over and over again?'

He thought, *Try to hold on to Janet Striker,* but he wouldn't say so. He wouldn't violate her that way, display her for this man. He partly liked Gallichan now, let himself be interested by Gallichan's interest in him, but she was out of it. He said, 'For a long time, I—well, call it going around and around—over my wife after she died. But I thought that was over.' He told him about the dream he'd had after his first night with Janet Striker, although he didn't include her—the dream about the running horses and the bleached and beautiful horse bones.

'You astonish me, Denton—you've believed in the potency of dreams all along.'

'Dreams are like jokes. I do believe that. This one—"Stop beating a dead horse."'

'Why a horse?'

'It's a saying.' He chewed his lip. 'I gave her a horse. After we were married. A little mare, because she thought she wanted to ride, but it got to be more like a dog. She fed it sugar and petted it and it followed her around. After she died, I sold everything. All I had was debts. I sold her horse. It was too small for me; I couldn't keep it. It started following me—I sold it to a dealer at auction. A lot of his horses wound up in the mines. There was a horse in my dreams.' He was weeping.

He had a pair of crutches, and he could make his way down the corridor, dragging the dead leg with him, a sister at his side to keep him from falling. He'd lost thirty pounds. When he looked down at his body, he was aware of how vain he'd been about it, hard and muscled despite his age. Now the skin sagged around his knees and his belly, and his muscles were slack and his ribs showed. He thought of the horse in his dreams.

'It was old. Terrible-looking beast. Horrible gait.'

'What had it to do with the boxes?'

'Nothing. It simply got me to where the boxes were. And the—figure—with the shotgun. And the girl who laughed at me.' He'd remembered her a few days before. 'There's an American saying—"to get taken for a ride". To get fooled. The horse took me for a ride, I suppose.'

'Was the girl your wife?'

'No, good God.' Denton could almost laugh at the absurdity of that. 'She was more like Mary Thomason. But she wasn't Mary Thomason; she was—' He told Gallichan about Mary Thomason and her brother and the drawing. When he was done, he said, 'When Struther Jarrold shot me he shouted, "I did it, I did it!" He was pointing the revolver at me and looking deliriously happy and he said, "I did it, Astoreth." Maybe the girl was this mad creation of his, Astoreth.' He tried to pull himself up. 'I need to talk to a detective named Munro at New Scotland Yard.'

'When Jarrold shot you with your own gun, you mean.'

'It wasn't my own gun; I'd never shot it. It was just a gun I'd paid a couple of shillings for and kept in a drawer.' He looked at

Gallichan. 'All right, it was my gun, in the legal sense. What are you trying to make of it?'

'I'm only wondering what you make of it.'

'I want to talk to Detective Munro.'

Gallichan got up and looked out of the window and made a face at what he saw of the day. He struggled into an overcoat and picked up his hat. 'I don't want you to become agitated.'

One day, he was able to make the muscles in his right thigh twitch. He found that he could make them twitch in a kind of order, going clockwise around the leg. He could move the toes and he could tilt the foot back about an inch when he was lying down. Then one morning he woke up with a partial erection. It was February. He announced to the doctor that he was feeling better. It was time to move things along. 'I want to talk to Detective Munro!'

'I've sent him a message.'

'And I want to see Heseltine.' In fact, he was hurt that Heseltine hadn't tried to see him. 'Have you been in touch with Heseltine?'

The doctor hesitated. 'I'll have a talk with Mrs Striker.'

When Janet Striker came next day, she told him that Heseltine was dead. 'He killed himself a day or two after you were shot. I'm sorry, Denton.'

'All this time—!'

'The doctors didn't want you to be upset. You weren't rational that first month. Then I thought, what difference does it make now, and I did what they asked and kept quiet about it.'

'But—' The trip with Heseltine to Normandy was recent to him, the most recent thing he remembered except for being shot. His feeling was that he had seen Heseltine only a day or two ago, and suddenly the man was dead. Had been dead for months. '*Suicide?*'

'Talk to Munro about it. I don't know what happened.'

After she had gone, he lay in the bed and stared at the ceiling. Mary Thomason, the brother, Himple—all of that paradoxically seemed to him from some long-ago time. But Heseltine? He remembered the young man's pleasure in the French countryside, his good humour about the bedbugs. His look of vitality when they had separated at Waterloo.

'Heseltine wouldn't kill himself,' he said aloud.

Apparently she agreed. The next time she came, she confessed that she, Atkins and Cohan had been taking turns sitting at his door since he had been moved to the nursing home, and she'd warned the staff against letting anyone else in. 'I thought somebody might try again.'

'Why?'

'You and Heseltine—I was afraid it wasn't coincidence.'

'What about yourself? You were in all that with me.'

'I've changed hotels several times.'

He laughed. 'You should talk to Dr Gallichan. You're as crazy as I am.'

He wrote a letter to Heseltine's father. The handwriting didn't look like his own. He apologized for its being so late and explained that he'd been ill. He said that Heseltine had been a fine man. A few days later, the father wrote to thank him and to say that Heseltine had spoken of him and seemed to take strength from knowing him; was there anything of his son's that Denton would like to have as a memento? Denton wrote back and said that he'd like to buy the little Dutch painting of the lion that had hung on his son's wall. The father replied that no such painting had been found among his son's effects. Would Denton like something else?

CHAPTER

21

Munro and Sergeant Markson came and were solicitous and gentle, but he knew that Munro thought he was behaving badly. Munro, at least, should have been allowed to see him.

'I've said I'm sorry. At first they wouldn't let me see you, and then I didn't want to see you. Why didn't you insist? You're the coppers.'

'Well, no harm done, I suppose.'

'I still feel like hell.'

'Two .45s, I'm not surprised.' Munro sat in the metal chair, Markson in a Thonet that had been dragged in from the corridor. Outside his door, sounds that Denton had become used to—the clink of glass and metal, the clack of feet, voices—were distorted and funnelled by the tile-walled corridor. Every day now, he was pushed up and down this corridor in a wheelchair, then made to try to walk on his new crutches.

Markson cleared his throat. 'We'd like to ask you a few questions, if we might, sir.'

Munro grunted. 'Just get on with it, Fred, he knows where we stand.' He frowned at Denton. 'And we know where he stands.'

Denton frowned back. He felt as if he were going to jump out of himself somehow. He didn't sleep at night now without chemicals, and the days were like this.

'Well, sir—' Markson cleared his throat again. 'We'd like to ask you a few questions about the shooting.'

'All right.'

'What do you remember, sir?'

'I don't remember actually being shot. I have a kind of picture of looking up and seeing Jarrold. He looked beside himself with joy.'

'He had a gun, sir?'

'Of course he did. That old Galland.'

'You recognized it, sir?'

'You couldn't mistake that contraption under the barrel.'

'Could you swear it was your gun, sir?'

'Well, of course it was—It looked like my gun, all right?'

'But you can't swear—'

'It didn't have my name on it, if that's what you mean.'

'Something like that, yes, sir.'

Munro leaned forward. Like everybody else who came, he had put his hat on the bed next to Denton's dead leg. 'Do you remember anything that Jarrold said?'

'He said, "I did it, I did it, Astoreth."'

'You're sure of that.'

'I am now. I wasn't at first. He sounded like a kid who'd caught his first trout. I can't tell you how—*pleased*—he looked. What's happened to him?'

Munro shifted his bulk, glanced at Markson, said, 'He's in a prison for the criminally insane.'

'There's been a trial?'

'Not yet. Maybe never. Prosecutor wanted to hear what you'd have to say, and then he may not go to trial. Charge of attempted murder was laid, of course, but in fact Jarrold's been committed on the earlier business with Mrs Striker's rooms, and violation of the terms of house arrest. Either road, he isn't coming out again.'

Denton, sitting up on a pile of pillows, his emaciated chest partly revealed by an unbuttoned nightshirt, stared at Munro. His interest in Jarrold now was rather theoretical, not at all a desire for justice or revenge. 'Before he shot me, you told Janet Striker he was getting better.'

'*I* didn't; his bleeding doctors did. Any doctor who pretends to know what's going on in another man's mind is a bleeding quack. They had him on chloral, so he breaks out and when we arrest him he's been drinking, and now the doctors tell us the combination of chloral and alcohol's the sure way to lunacy. Well, they're right.'

Denton stared at him some more. Not fully aware of his own state, his own motives, Denton sensed he was coming out of the anger and melancholy of the past weeks. He knew that he wanted to show himself to Munro—the gaunt face, the apparently haunted eyes—because he knew that his body was an accusation. Finally, when he could see that Munro was embarrassed and annoyed, he said, 'Tell me what happened to Heseltine.'

'Oh, that poor sod.'

'Yes, that poor sod.'

'Wasn't our case; Division handled it. Still, Fred followed it once he found you'd had some connection with him.'

'How did you find that?'

'His man. Said Heseltine had been travelling with you.'

Markson was going through a notebook, licking a finger every two or three pages to turn them. 'Man named Jenks,' he said when he found the page.

'I know Jenks.'

'He found the body. Coroner's jury ruled suicide, that was it.' Markson looked up. 'He was despondent.'

'Like hell he was.'

Both detectives jerked; Munro looked offended. Markson said, 'Division reported the man Jenks said his employer had been despondent. Just got chucked out of the army. Confirmed by interview with the victim's father conducted by—mmm, local constabulary in—'

'Jenks is a drunkard.'

'Well, still—'

'Heseltine wasn't despondent!'

'Leave it, Denton. It's history now.'

'He wasn't despondent! I'd just spent three days with him. He was talking about going to Jamaica to take a job. When I left him at Waterloo, he was *happy*.'

Munro picked up his hat and leaned his forearms on his knees. 'Leave it.'

'How did he kill himself?'

Munro looked at Markson. The young detective looked at his notes, clearly marking time, and then said, 'Slashed his wrists with his razor.'

'It's done,' Munro said. He stood. 'The coroner's jury got the evidence, Denton; there was no doubt in anybody's mind. He got in the bath with his razor and did it. I'm sorry, especially as you have to hear it in your condition, but it's what happened.'

Denton tried to picture Heseltine's cutting his veins with a razor. Lying in his own blood? He said, 'Dressed or naked?'

'Unh—I don't have that, sir.'

'With the water running? A man like Heseltine doesn't make messes. He'd have known he'd be found by Jenks, who was incompetent; he'd have done everything to avoid leaving a mess. Find out.'

Munro shook his head. 'It's over. Don't tell us how to do our job.' He fanned a fly away with his hat. 'Your job is to get well. It hurts me to look at you. I mean it— I want you to focus on getting your old self back; forget all this business. The young man who killed himself—' He shrugged. 'These things happen.'

Denton held his eyes and then, feeling the pain in his back, the discomfort of the sheet under his buttocks, used both hands to shift the position of his right leg. He said, 'Sit down, Munro.'

'Got a job to do.'

'Not yet. I want to talk to you.'

Munro looked at Markson as if to ask if Markson should stay, too; Denton nodded. Munro lowered his backside into the chair as if he feared sitting on something. He made a demonstration of taking out his watch and looking at it.

Denton said, 'I don't remember everything that happened when I was shot. More of it comes back to me, but I'm still blank where the shooting itself is concerned. Also just before that. I think I was coming to see you—'

'You'd been at Mrs Castle's.'

Denton raised his head. 'How do you know that?'

'Somebody grabbed Jarrold before he could put another bullet into you. Happened to be a private detective.' Munro glanced at Markson, who seemed engrossed in his notebook, slowly turning the pages from back to front. 'He was following you.'

Denton frowned, bewildered. 'I'd just got back from France.'

Munro laid his hat on the bed again. His hair was pressed against his scalp where the hat had rested; he stroked the sides with his palms. 'This is an embarrassment for the Metropolitan Police, Denton. I was going to tell you in good time. It's, mmm, not something we're proud of.'

'I remember now—I thought somebody was following me. I think I'd thought so before, but there was never anybody.'

'Lady Emmeline—Jarrold's mother—was having you followed. She sent copies of their reports to Georgie Guillam.'

Denton's brain seemed slow. He had to remind himself who Guillam was. When he remembered, he was enraged. 'Why?'

'I told you that Georgie'd pulled Jarrold over into his baili-wick. I thought it was just to make the connection—get himself some credit with the upper crust. Maybe that was all there was, to start with. He told the super he'd gone to Lady Emmeline's house and offered her his help. Because Jarrold was now his responsibility. That could have been just Georgie's sucking up. But getting the private detectives' reports from her—He wanted to get something on you. So did Lady Emmeline. She really hates you, you know—a lot worse than Georgie. So they scratched each other's back.'

Denton felt out of breath. 'That's how Jarrold knew where I'd be when he decided to shoot me.'

'His mother wrote to him at least once a day. Sent him telegrams—one the night before you came back from France.' Munro rubbed his forehead and blew out his cheeks. 'One of the detectives had tailed you to the Channel ferry and told Guillam. Guillam cabled the French demanding they tell him when you started back. When he heard from them—' Munro shook his head. 'He did what no copper should ever do. He notified Lady Emmeline. After, he said he did it just so's her detectives could pick you up again. But she telegraphed Jarrold, so what Guillam did meant that Jarrold could find you, too. Jarrold's mother—and therefore Jarrold—knew where you'd be twelve hours before your boat landed that morning. The dicks picked you up again at Waterloo.'

'And so did Jarrold.'

'That's my reading of it.'

'But—' Denton was thinking of the logistics of getting from Lady Emmeline's Sussex house to London, then to Waterloo. Twelve hours would be plenty of time. Still—'But why?'

'Why Georgie, or why Jarrold?'

'Jarrold.'

'Loony.'

'Not good enough, Munro. He's insane, but he's sane enough to get from Sussex to Waterloo, avoid the detective following me and wait for the opportunity to shoot me.'

'Well, he knew about the detective, so avoiding him wouldn't take a genius. Anyway, the detectives didn't know him. The rest—' Munro shook his massive head. 'He's a loony.'

'With all respect, sir—' Markson had put his notebook away. 'It's true it's never been established *why* he shot Mr Denton.'

Munro waved the comment away. 'He shot him because he was a loony that had been pestering Denton for a long time. He couldn't get what he wanted from him, so he took his revenge.'

Denton had put his head back. He wasn't listening to them. He looked at the ceiling and tried to remember what had happened. The shooting was a gap, but the rest was there: Mrs Castle, his returning home, the parting from Heseltine at Waterloo. Before that, the night crossing, the journey down from Caen. The farm. The barn. The hay. He said, 'Heseltine and I go to France. We come back. Jarrold is waiting for me in London. He shoots me.' He sat up. 'How soon after I was shot did Heseltine die?'

Munro groaned. 'Oh, Judas—'

Markson got the notebook out again, wet his finger, went through the pages. 'Um—hmm.' He went to another part of the notebook, licked a finger. 'Mmm. Looks like the Heseltine suicide was the next morning.'

Denton pushed himself up and leaned his weight on his right arm. He pushed his face out as close to Munro's as he could get it. 'Two men travel together and come home and within twenty-four hours one's shot and one's dead! What does that tell you, Munro?'

'Aw, God, Denton—Don't do this to me, man.'

'It's just coincidence?'

'Look— Give us some credit for brains, will you? Heseltine was in a bad way. He went away with you because you'd befriended him; isn't that the way it was? His dad said something like that. He comes back to London, the next morning he reads in the paper you've been shot and are near death. It's the last straw. Don't you *get* it?'

Denton did get it. He wavered: he hadn't seen it that way. It could have happened like that. Maybe Heseltine's cheerfulness had been the rise before an inevitable drop, the shooting the immediate cause. And yet—'Why did Jarrold shoot me *that day*?'

'Because it's the day he slipped his nurses and headed for London. D'you think we didn't interview them? His mother had two male nurses watching him, or so she said; well, what they were was two local ploughboys that could have been diddled by a ten-year-old. Turns out they let Sonny roam the grounds while they had their tea in the kitchen every day and played peeky-boo with the housemaids. He could have slipped them any time he wanted.'

'Then why that day?'

Munro pounded the arm of the chair. 'Because he's a bleeding loony!'

Denton lay back again. He felt exhausted, jangled; his blood seemed to be pounding in his head. 'Why did we go to France?'

'How the hell should I know?'

'Then why didn't you ask me?'

'Because you were unconscious! Because you wouldn't see us! Because it doesn't matter! I suppose you went to give Heseltine a change of air. You'd taken him under your wing, hadn't you? Who the hell cares?'

Denton closed his eyes. He was almost panting. 'There's a barn in Normandy. I think there's a body buried in it.'

'Oh, Jesus—!' Munro clapped his hat on his head and stood up. 'Let's get out of here.' He turned on Denton. 'Look, I'm sorry you're feeling poorly, but I've got a long ton of work to do. This is all old stuff, closed, finished. You get yourself better, that's your job. Don't complicate mine, will you?'

Denton kept his eyes closed. 'Why would two men who found where they think a body is buried in France be dead or near-dead as soon as they get back?'

Munro started to say something. He looked at Markson. 'You're blowing bubbles. Denton, think about it—Jarrold tried to shoot you. The dick wrapped him up and put him on the ground and that was the end of him—he went right to the station and the lock-up, and he hasn't seen the light of day since. Yes, Jarrold tried to kill you on the day you got back from France. But there's no way he could have had a hand in this other fella's suicide the next day—and no reason! Now get yourself better, and we'll have a brew-up together and chew it over someplace friendly, all right?' He jerked his head at Markson.

When the two detectives reached the door, Denton said, eyes still closed, 'Munro? What's happened to Guillam?'

'He was busted down to detective and sent to East Ham—the whole way across London from where he lives. Satisfied?'

'Wasn't Guillam partly responsible for attempted murder?'

Munro sighed. 'Georgie's got friends, Denton.' He and Markson went out, and the door closed.

Gallichan came that afternoon and made himself comfortable so that he could explore more of Denton's dreams. Denton was tired of it. He said, 'I read once about a doctor who found a man who'd been shot in the stomach. The man healed with a hole the doctor could look through. He learned all sorts of things about the stomach. It made him famous. I think you're using these dreams as a hole to look into my mind.'

'I resent the very idea that I'm doing this for some egoistical purpose of my own.'

'It's my mind. I don't like you looking into it. And dreams aren't much of a window.'

'Well, they're not meaningless, either. The German, what's-his-name, says that's the point—dreams aren't some sort of accident caused by eating too much toasted cheese. They have profound meaning. It is our task to find that out.'

Denton was still smarting from Munro's visit. To a degree, he had found Gallichan's interest flattering, the exploration itself interesting, but it had run its course and his mood was bad. 'Get out of my stomach,' he said.

'But we're making progress! We have identified feeling—fear, guilt—and persons: your dead wife, the laughing child, the man with the shotgun.'

'I never said I felt guilt, doctor. Sorrow, yes—the two aren't the same thing. And I didn't say the person with the shotgun was a man.'

'Well, it wasn't a woman, surely. Forgive me, but I think you are deliberately avoiding the obvious conclusion—that the man with the shotgun is yourself.' He seemed very pleased with that.

Denton simply looked at him. Then he burst out laughing—real laughter. When he was done, he said, 'I think you need to read another book. My dreams aren't well-made plays, doctor. They're a mess. I don't know about your dreams, but mine are a train wreck—bodies on the track, wreckage everywhere, people staggering around with blood running down their faces. If mine have meaning, it's for the feelings I have, not some neat tale that's like *King Lear* reduced to a bedtime story.' Before Gallichan could object, Denton raised a hand and said, 'Enough. Get me out of here.'

The portly doctor shook his head. 'Even your imagery is full of violence. You are a violent man, Mr Denton.'

'I don't need you to tell me that.'

Gallichan stood, not entirely willingly. 'We could go so much deeper,' he said.

'Let's not.'

The doctor shrugged. 'What a pity.'

'I want to go home.'

Next day, Munro came back. He was apologetic. Between the two men was a mostly unacknowledged respect, even friendship; if it was made difficult by Denton's putting his oversized nose into police business, Munro still didn't want the relationship to end. He said he was sorry about yesterday; he said he had been to some extent carrying on for Markson's benefit. 'I don't like for a youngster to think we let the public make up our minds for us.'

'Are you going to do anything about France?'

Munro sighed. 'I've been thinking about it.' He lowered his bulk into the metal chair and put his bowler on the bed. It was raining out, and water dripped from it on the sheet. 'Tell it to me—all of it.'

Denton tried. Munro groaned when he went all the way back to Mary Thomason, but there was no other way to tell it—the Wesselons, the note to Denton, the remarques on the drawing, the Mayflower Baths. The only thing Denton skimmed over was the trunk, because of Janet; Munro saw the omission, frowned, said, 'About this drawing—'

'Don't interrupt.'

'Where'd you get the drawing?'

'What the hell does it matter? I got it and I know it was hers!'

Munro gave him a long look. 'So you're hiding something. Better to tell me, you know.'

'No.'

Munro shrugged. 'You'll have to, if I really ask.'

Denton groaned with disgust and finished his story.

'Are you telling me that you believe the missing woman and the servant who went to France are connected?'

'If she did the little drawings of Lazarus and the Mayflower Baths, that's all the connection that's needed.'

'And now you think the brother or Crum, or whoever he is, is missing?'

'He disappeared from the scene.'

'In France?'

'Yes.'

'So you have a man who may or may not exist, who did or did not disappear at some later time, but there's a body buried in a barn in Normandy, and it may be his.' Munro shook his head.

'I don't have all of it, Munro. But something happened there. And Crum's disappearance *later* is a matter of one letter Himple wrote to his valet—Crum could have been dead for weeks. Who would know?' When he saw Munro's pained expression, he said, 'If something happened to the brother in France, then maybe something happened earlier to the girl, as well. Ask the French to dig in the barn!'

'You mean, I should do exactly what Georgie Guillam got sent to Siberia for—use the Metropolitan Police to forward a scheme of a private party.' He picked up his hat and looked into it as if something that made him unhappy lived in there. 'It just doesn't hang together. It's all speculation. Look—bring me somebody who knows this man Crum and misses him. Bring me a mother, the sister, a wife, a lover—anybody who's close to him and knows he's gone. You're talking about a man you've never seen, and you want me to act as if he's missing. Denton, he's something you've created out of whole cloth!'

'The valet knew him. The housekeeper knew him.'

'Have they reported him missing?'

'All right. I'm going home tomorrow. I'll handle it myself.'

'Don't do it! Now, I'm warning you—!'

'What are you going to do, break my other leg?'

Munro, standing now, looked down at him. He shook his head. 'You get well. You look like death warmed over. Stop tormenting yourself with this business and get better.' At the door, he said, 'I think you're on to about half of something. Keep it under your hat until you get the other half.'

Janet Striker came later the same day. She shook an expensive-looking waterproof cape and leaned a new umbrella in the corner. She looked almost pretty. She had come into her money. Rain was driving against the window, which shook from the power of the wind; distant lightning appeared only as a glow on the glass, as if a dim lamp had been turned on and off.

'I'm going home tomorrow,' he said.

'The doctor wants to keep you here.'

'No point. I can make my way about now. I think I'm ready for a walking stick, get me off those damned crutches. Gallichan just wants to keep on playing with my dreams.' He told her about Munro's return visit, his refusal to get in touch with the French police. 'If I could handle a shovel, I'd do it myself!'

'I'll do it.' She lifted her chin. Her skin was pink from the storm she'd come through; she'd put on a few pounds since she'd got her money, too, looked healthier and happier. 'I'll take the Cohans—he can dig, she can make me look respectable. What a good idea.'

'Cohan can't go near dead bodies—it comes with being *kohanim*.'

'No matter. I'll do the digging myself. Or I'll find myself a labourer.'

'You don't speak French.'

'Of course I do. It's one of those things my mother thought would make me more saleable.' Her mother had died, she told him, while Denton had been unconscious; the death made Janet neither more nor less outspoken about her. She stood. 'There's just time to pack and be off first thing.'

'You just got here.'

'And I'm leaving. I'll confess it now; I hate places like this. I'm so glad you're coming home.' She pulled the cape over her shoulders. 'Let's move this matter forward, is what I say.'

'You want to get away from me again.'

'I don't.'

'The doctor told me I'm a violent man.'

'And so you are, but I suspect he doesn't have the slightest notion what that means.' She gave him a quick kiss. 'I'll be back by the weekend. To stay. In London, I mean.'

'I'll want Cohan, as soon as I can have him,' he said. She raised her eyebrows. 'Once I'm home, I think they'll try to kill me again.'

'*They.*' She held the cape open as if she might take it off again. 'Jarrold's in a prison for the insane.'

'Jarrold was just the means. There's somebody else. I thought they might try to get at me here.'

'They—not he?'

'I don't know—I don't know.' He couldn't keep his face from showing his fear of losing her. 'You'll really come back?'

She kissed him again. 'Really.'

CHAPTER 22

Denton thought that leaving the nursing home was the final humiliation—a litter carried by two men older than he, with two more to raise him shoulder-high and push him into the horse-drawn ambulance like a loaf of bread going into an oven—but going up his own stairs in his own house was even worse: humiliation turned into farce. Atkins had picked up three day-labourers who put Denton into an armchair at the bottom of the stairs, and then, each man taking a leg, carried him with the chair tipped back so far he thought he might do a backwards somersault out of it. They rested at the landing with a lot of heavy breathing and exclamations and then picked him up and carried him the last seven stairs, depositing him in his own sitting room after almost taking his head off on the door jamb.

'Well,' Atkins said when he'd paid them off, 'home again, home again, jiggety-jog.'

'If I'd known you were going to do that, I'd have stayed in the nursing home.'

'Listen, General, they wanted to carry you up on the litter. I've seen men dropped, seen the whole shebang go down a flight of steps. I thought the armchair was a stroke of genius.'

'Help me up.' Denton struggled; the bad leg was no help, and Atkins was not particularly strong. 'It's a good thing I'm skin and bones,' he said when he was standing.

Atkins produced a walking stick. 'You're still about three stone too much for me. You're bivouacked down here for the duration.' He jerked his head towards the unused room next to the sitting room. 'Never make it up and down those stairs day after day. Didn't want to maroon you up there.'

'Oh, hell—I hate that room.'

'Yes, well, we do the best we can with what's on offer at this hotel. Can you walk on that stick?'

Denton had tried a stick in the nursing home. He had taken a few steps, the right leg dragging behind, most of his weight hung from his shoulders and supported on his right hand. 'Like running the mile race,' he said.

'We'll have you fit in no time. Mrs O'Cohen has left a pot of soup you're to eat six or eight times a day—very forceful woman.' Denton, out of the habit of Atkins's humour, needed two seconds to realize that O'Cohen was a play on the supposed Irishness of Cohan.

'What's she got to do with it?'

'Oh, ah, she's close to Mrs Striker, isn't she? I'm going to get this armchair out of the way; you walk up and down for a while.'

'I want to rest.'

'Up and down, up and down, General. You've had plenty of rest, if you ask me.'

Denton struggled down the long room, turned at the window and struggled back. He had to pause at the alcove to lean against the cold porcelain stove that stood there, relic of an earlier tenant. Then he went up the room, past his armchair and the fireplace, to the window that looked out on the street. The pavements were wet, the gas lamps on; uneven wiggles of light reflected where the rain, now ended, had collected.

'Let's do it once more for old times' sake, then I'll bring up the tea.'

'I'm worn out, Atkins.'

'That's why you've got to work. Let's march.'

He laboured down the room again. This time he stopped at the window over the back garden, too exhausted in the right arm and shoulders to go on. The bullet wounds ached. 'There are lights in the house behind,' he said.

'Oh, right. But no Albert Cosgrove.'

'What's going on?'

'Workmen. Somebody bought it.'

'Turn your back on the world, it goes right on without you.' He swung around and dragged the leg to the alcove. 'I'm done in. Help me to bed now.'

'I thought I'd serve tea out here.' Atkins's voice became almost kind. 'Look, General, you need to get back to normal. You don't want to start living in a bed.'

Denton looked into his face, then put his left hand on a shoulder. 'Help me along, then.'

He didn't know how to sit down into a soft, deep chair. Now he found that if he put the right leg out in front of him and bent the left leg, he could fall backwards and land more or less in a sitting position; the left leg trembled from the effort. He said, 'Do you know how embarrassing this is?'

'We'll practise that,' Atkins said. 'I'll get the tea.'

He had made an effort. There were three kinds of biscuits, toast, anchovy paste, clotted cream, and a tureen of soup from which he lifted the lid. Steam rose and a remarkable odour drifted Denton's way. 'It doesn't smell like the nursing home, at least,' Denton said. He wasn't sure what it smelled like.

'Mrs O'Cohen's speciality. Chicken and a lot of other stuff. She cooks "kosher", if you know what that is. I don't, so don't ask.' He ladled out a bowl. 'Good for what ails you.'

'They've been feeding me a lot of Bovril.'

'Rare beef is what you need. Increase the blood. I've got a bit downstairs in the ice-cave would delight a cannibal. Thought I'd grill it on some coals.'

'It'll taste.'

'Wood coals, General. Not a green recruit, you know.'

Denton ate the soup, then the toast and anchovy paste, then some of the biscuits. The soup, with enough salt, was edible but peculiar. The sharp saltiness of the anchovies was welcome after the stodge they'd fed him at the nursing home. When he was done, he tried to stand. 'I can't even get out of my own chair!'

'Don't mind my saying so, but you ain't trying.'

Denton gave him a look of hatred. 'I can't bend this damned leg. What's your brilliant idea?'

'Stick it out in front of you and get up on the other one.'

The left leg was weak and his bullet wounds screamed, but he did it, the left thigh now vibrating like a plucked string. He stood looking down at Atkins. 'You've appointed yourself my domestic scold?'

'That's the plan.'

Denton hobbled partway down the room and turned to the left and then left again into the room they never used. Most of the blind wall that was shared with the next house was books; on the street side was a single tall window; to his left as he stood in the doorway was a wall with a fireplace, coal burning in the grate. Opposite it, a divan he'd never seen before had been made up as a bed. 'I'd prefer my own room.'

'When you can go up and down.'

A big stack of mail stood on a table. Atkins said, 'Lots of bills and invitations. Give you something to do.'

Denton felt too tired to respond. He'd given up the morphine, had refused chloral hydrate or laudanum. He was wondering, as he settled in the bed, if he should ask Atkins for some of the headache powders, and while he was wondering he fell asleep.

It was a struggle during the night to get from his rooms to the toilet that was tucked behind the alcove and across the side corridor. Atkins heard him and ran upstairs, trailing an unbelted robe behind him, Rupert plodding and breathing heavily behind that. The nursing home had had bedpans, not lavatories. Life was suddenly more complicated, more frustrating. Still, he fell again into deep sleep as soon as he was back in the bed.

The next two days were elaborations on struggle and frustration. The simple had become complex, the difficult impossible. He complained that he was getting his exercise simply by living, but Atkins chivvied him into limping up and down the long room, back and forth, then doing the leg exercises. After the first set, Atkins holding Denton's feet and pushing the legs for Denton to push back, Atkins said, 'You're using that leg, you know.'

'I'm not.'

'You are. I can feel it. You ought to try putting more weight on it when you walk.'

'Hurts like hell.'

'Not the end of the world, I daresay.'

The meals continued to be enormous, the chicken soup a major part through the first breakfast; by then, Denton had had enough of it and ordered that he wasn't to be faced with it any more. The second morning, there were kidneys and bacon and eggs and buttery rolls, and Denton complained about too much food.

'Got to fatten you up, Colonel. Prodigal son come home, and so on. Fatted calf time.'

Denton read his mail and tried not to wonder what Janet Striker was finding in Normandy. All sorts of people had written to him about the shooting—his editor, Lang, nervously, Henry James a bit pompously but in fact rather touchingly. Denton was still at the stage of feeling a stranger in his own house, still catching up with the world that had passed him by. The good wishes of people he hadn't seen for several months now seemed insubstantial.

At tea, to make conversation, he said to Atkins, 'What's happened with your moving picture?'

'Oh, rather a tale, that. Interesting, amusing, and a delight to both adults and children.'

'Good. Amuse and delight me.'

Atkins was eating bits of Denton's toast and sipping tea from an oversized cup. He smiled. 'Bit of a long story.'

'I have lots of time.'

'Well, then—Well, you disappeared from the scene when we was making pictures up in Victoria Park. I'd learned from earlier adventures and got us a permit to shoot blanks in the muskets. Gave us permission to "perform patriotic manoeuvres with rendered-safe firearms", for which we had to pay for a policeman to watch over us. Also had to provide him with lunch, the which he thought should be a banquet. Anyway, we got through that all right, and then we finished with the pictures of the soldier's return down at your front door again.'

'Why didn't you make that and the farewell at the same time? More efficient!'

'What, and have to cut up the film and paste it back together? Not likely, General! No, we did it all in the order it would play, see? Then we have the film what they call "processed", meaning the pictures come out, and then we bang it back in the camera and project it on a sheet. Did I mention that the camera was also the projecting machine? Well, it was.

'We rented a former scraps and findings shop just off the Whitechapel Road and had a couple of signs made, "The Boer War—Fascination in Moving Pictures! Villainous Boer and Courageous British Hero! Patriotism Personified!" And so on. Even brought in benches from a Methodist mission that went bust over the way—unheard of, sitting down for a moving picture. Great sensation.

'So we were prepared to open on a Friday—"open" is what they say in the theatre world, I suppose from the curtains, which we didn't have—and I was standing outside, ready to take the money of the gathering horde, when up come three fellas with very serious expressions, one of which turns out to be a legal type who slaps a paper into my hand and says, "You're out of business." Then the other two chaps go in and seize the picture machine and carry it out under the watchful eye of two constables they've brought for the purpose.

'Well, you can imagine the weeping and wailing and gnashing of teeth. The housemaid had invited her entire family, which was as rum a lot of human beings as you'd never hope to meet, and my chum was tearing his hair out in handfuls and saying we was ruined. I, however, read the piece of paper and found we were being injuncted against by the courts for violating the patent of some American who claimed that our machine was a fiddle copied from his.

'And so it was. What my chum and partner hadn't found out when he bought the machine was that the Pole that made it had nicked the idea. But I said to myself, Not so fast, let's not throw out the baby with the bathwater, where does it say they can seize our moving picture along with the machine? So I went to the chap that had sold me the insurance—you remember, you'd advised me to get insurance—and they sent a young fellow that was a clerk in a law office. But, by the time we got it to court, the Yanks had already shipped the machine to the States and had destroyed the film—burned our moving picture all to ashes.

'The long and the longer of it was that the Yanks settled out of court for illegal destruction of a creative property not their own; my chum ran off with the housemaid; and I made back my expenses, plus three pounds, seven shillings punitive damages, in loo of one per cent of the net profit of the American company on all future moving pictures. A bird in the hand, says I.'

'I think you did handsomely.'

'One per cent of future profits is one per cent of nothing.'

'You never know.'

'I should of took the long view, you're thinking.'

'Not at all.'

'Moving-picture business is too risky. The Yanks wanted to hire me—said I had get-up.' Atkins laughed. 'The day I leave your employ, General, it'll be for a good deal more than running about Victoria Park with a musket.' He nibbled another piece of toast. 'Now I've got my eye on the truss. You have any idea how many trusses are sold in this country every year? Met a chap who's invented a pneumatic truss. Latest thing. What do you think?'

'Did you ever see your moving picture?'

Atkins chewed, thought, shrugged. 'I saw it made.'

Later that evening, a telegram came from Janet Striker:

> YOU WERE CORRECT. FRENCH POLICE
> INFORMED. HOME SATURDAY.

'They *were* bones, Denton. Bones and some leathery-looking stuff I suppose was skin. I'm afraid I felt a bit faint.'

'You're sure they were human.'

'I wanted to believe they weren't! I'd got a very nice young man named Emile to dig. I told him we were looking for buried money. It gave him something to look forward to. When he found the first bone, he said it was a cow. It seemed to me too slender to be a cow, so I had him dig farther along, where the feet might be. Well.' She gave him a partial smile. 'It was a very human foot, with a lot of the skin still intact.'

'What did you tell the farmer?'

'I'd given him twenty-five francs; for that, I didn't think I had to tell him anything. My story was that I wanted to paint where my friend the milord had painted. I set myself up at the door of the barn with a chair and a watercolour block and my paints and tried to look artistic while Emile did the digging.'

'You paint, too?'

'I can do anything that my mother thought would make me more saleable—insipid watercolours, insipid piano music, insipid talk—but nothing remotely useful. I learned accounting on a course at the People's Palace, but in order to take it I had first to do a course in arithmetic. It was humiliating!'

'And the police, the French police?'

'Very suspicious—of me. I finally told them to wire Munro at New Scotland Yard and he'd explain everything. Of course he didn't. But I looked respectable—meaning I looked as if I had money—and so they didn't toss me into the lock-up. They did want to know why we were digging in a barn, and I told him them the truth, which of course they thought was a fantastical improvisation. Emile confused things by saying we were digging for treasure. However, the main point was that we'd found human remains, and after the second day they let me come home.'

'Do you think it was Arthur Crum?'

'How would I know? I was so sickened by what I saw—I've seen a lot in the East End, Denton; I'm not easily made queasy—but the thought that those scraps of white leather and long bones were human—!'

'*White* leather?'

'Yes, the skin, what was left of it, looked white.'

'I'd have thought it would be brown.'

'Don't quibble.'

She had returned late in the morning, had come straight to his house. She looked remarkable—a travelling costume in a green so dark it was almost black, her hair done in a new way, a mannish hat like a homburg, a single peacock's sword slanting down from it. She could wear clothes with a masculine cut—often a lesbian uniform—without seeming to make any proclamation about herself: she *was* herself, the scar down her face worn now without apology or even powder.

'You're magnificent,' he said.

'You mustn't say things like that.' She had reddened. 'Come, Atkins says you must exercise—walk up and down the room with me.'

'Atkins is trying to kill me—he brought two dumb-bells down from the attic this morning and told me to start lifting them.' He groaned as he got out of his chair. 'Only ten pounds each, and I had trouble getting them off the floor. God, when will this be over!'

They walked the length of the room and back, then up it again to the window over the garden, where he stopped, then leaned against the window frame and looked out. 'Somebody's bought the house behind,' he said.

'Good for Atkins! He didn't tell you.'

'What didn't he tell me?'

She smiled. '*I* bought it.'

She was a few inches shorter than he; he looked down into her eyes. It dawned on him what she meant: she had found a way to live, if not with him, then near him. He pulled her to himself clumsily, off-balance; he kissed her. She tipped her head back and said, 'What did you think I'd gone away for, Denton? I had to decide about you. And I decided.' She kissed him again. 'There's to be a door knocked in the garden wall. For those who want to visit.' When he bent to kiss her again, she said, 'And there's to be a lock on my side of the door. For those who don't want a visit.'

He said, 'I wish we could go to bed.'

'Who says we can't?'

'I'm so—so—'

'Like hell.' She led him back down the room to the short corridor that led to his ad hoc bedroom, then into it, where she took his stick and pushed him gently down. He lay on his elbows, watching her as she undressed—that always-renewed wonder. Naked, she came to the foot of the bed, then climbed him like a horizontal ladder and took him to a place he had feared he would never see again.

Munro came on the Monday about the middle of the day. Denton had been working with the ten-pound dumb-bells on his sitting-room floor, gasping and groaning as if they weighed a hundred; by the time Munro had been shown up, he was knotting a cord around a dressing gown.

'By God, it's good to see you standing.' Munro seemed truly glad to see him; he even shook Denton's hand.

'I've a long row to hoe yet.'

Munro bent and picked up one of the dumb-bells. 'About six stone's worth, I'd say. Well, Rome wasn't built in a day.' Munro sat heavily. 'You've heard from Mrs Striker, I suppose?'

'She's here, in fact. She's staying upstairs.' Denton smiled. 'Where I can't go. Can't do stairs yet.'

Munro didn't say *But she can*; probably he didn't care. What he did say was, 'She's stirred up a hornet's nest at the Yard.'

'You should be grateful.' Denton, for his part, didn't say *You wouldn't do it yourself.*

'A detective arrived from Paris this morning—last night, actually. Was practically waiting on the doorstep this morning. He's very keen.'

'What have they found?'

'Well, you don't think he's going to tell me right off, do you?' Munro laughed. He seemed in good spirits. 'Lot of horse-trading to be done. Whose case, and so on. Matter of jurisdiction. He jabbered something about the Quai d'Orsay, which I found later means their foreign office. Bloody French haven't forgotten Waterloo, I think. Anyway, he seems to be a good copper, and very keen when it comes to murder.'

'You're sure it's murder.'

'Bodies buried under straw piles are usually murder, Denton.'

'The owner of the farm in any trouble?'

Munro grunted. 'When a body's found, you don't want to be the owner of the plot where it's buried. I'm sure they showed him a fairly bad time. No arrest made, however. There's a major problem—they don't know yet how long the body's been there.' He got up and took off his overcoat, threw it over the back of his chair and sat down again, shaking his head when Denton made a move for the bell-pull. 'The body was buried in lye.'

Denton slowly sat back, letting his head roll until it was supported by the chair. 'That's why the skin is white.'

'What's left of it. Lot of lye used—French police think as much as a hundred pounds. Not enough to dissolve the bones, but it's apparently done some major damage. Plus there's a complication.'

Denton raised himself upright.

'There's no head.'

'Oh, dammit.'

'They've sent everything off to Paris to a *professeur* who's some sort of expert in old bones. He's going to tell them—maybe—how long they've been in the ground and what sort of creature it was: male, female; old, young.' Munro leaned forward with his hands on his knees. 'Look, Denton, we're not in it yet—CID have no official interest. They came to me because Mrs Striker gave them my name. We're in it if the body turns out to be English.' His eyes opened slightly; his brow went up. 'I think you'd better tell me everything.'

'I tried to already.'

'I know. I was right not to listen then. Now I'm right to demand you tell me. Everything.'

Atkins came in with a tray, put it down on the folding table, opened the dumb-waiter doors, and turned left and went upstairs. Half a minute later, he came down again and vanished into his own lower regions.

'He telling her I'm here?' Munro said.

'I suspect he's asking her to join us for whatever's on that tray.'

'Hmp.' Munro looked down at the tray, which held mostly crockery. 'Not very nourishing.' He looked at Denton again. 'I daresay it's better that she be here, anyway.' He filled the time until she appeared with chatter. He talked about the coronation, now a few months off. There was great concern about anarchists. Police were going to be brought into London from the rest of England. He was sure the London criminals were already booking accommodation in other cities for the easy pickings. 'Curious thing when you think about it, a coronation,' he said.

'I don't think about it much.'

'Well, it's what your people had a rebellion about.'

'Revolution. Rebellion is when you lose.'

'Ah. Did you win? I thought it was the French who won.' Munro looked sly and laughed. At that point Atkins and Mrs Striker almost collided at the foot of the stairs; she pulled back and insisted that Atkins, carrying another tray, go ahead.

The Bohemian Girl

'Very sorry, madam, very sorry,' Atkins said as he put the tray down on another table.

'No harm done,' she said. 'Hallo, Sergeant. Are you angry with me?'

'For putting the French on me? I'm not delighted.'

'I thought they should have the best the Yard had to offer.' She was bending over a teapot, looking into its steam as if she could read her future there.

'Oh, ha-ha. Well, it might well have come my way, anyway.'

She was wearing an unfussy blouse and the green wool skirt with the box pleats, part of one of her suits; her hair was piled high, a comb with brilliants in it—diamond chips?—at the back. While she passed filled cups to Atkins to hand around, Munro told her what he'd already told Denton. He skipped the part about the missing head. When Atkins was gone, Munro said, 'He hears everything down that dumb-waiter shaft, am I right?'

Denton said in a dry voice, 'I don't try to keep much from him, if that's what you mean.'

Janet Striker sat on a side chair, crossed her legs and set her cup and saucer on them, keeping the saucer in the fingers of one hand. She said, 'You'll want to know everything.'

'Indeed I will.' He glanced at Denton. 'I asked him to tell me "everything" a bit ago, and he didn't.'

She looked at Denton and winked. It was an astonishing performance for that usually grave face. He smiled despite himself and began to tell it all to Munro again. This time, Munro made notes. There was a lot of fluster over where to put things while he dragged out a notebook and pencil from his heavy tweed jacket. Janet Striker occasionally put a few words in; Munro looked at her each time with a shrewd expression, as if to say, *Oho, you're in it as deep as he is.* When they were done, Munro said, 'All right, now I'm going to find out what you wouldn't tell me before. This picture you've got of the girl. Where'd you get it?'

Denton looked at Janet. She said, utterly cool, 'It was in the girl's trunk.'

Munro sighed. 'You've got her trunk.'

'Not at all. It's in the "to be called for" office at Biggleswade.'

'But you've been into it!' He glared at Denton. 'Come on, come on—it's all going to come out!'

'You know, Munro, for a man who's being given a case on a plate, you're being a pill.'

'Case on a plate, my hat! Bunch of speculations and random shots, is what it looks like.'

'Be grateful for what you get and stop pressing us for how we got something.'

'If we go to court, it's all got to come out!'

'Let's deal with that when you go to court, then. Look—' Denton put his cup down. He wiggled himself forward in the soft chair, lifting his bad leg with both hands to raise it. 'I'll take responsibility for getting the drawing. Let's say I was into the trunk—all right. Leave it at that for now.'

'If you were into the trunk, it and everything in it are tainted. You could have planted anything—that's what counsel would say.'

'Damn counsel! You're concerned with what to tell a French cop about how Arthur Crum's body got in a hole in Normandy.'

'Or whoever's in there,' Janet Striker murmured. 'For all we know right now, it could be one of the knights from the Bayeux tapestry.' She smiled. 'I read about it in a Baedeker on the Channel crossing.'

Munro made a rather humourless clucking sound. 'Well, we're going to have the devil's own time making any kind of identification at all as things stand. But one thing at a time—sufficient unto the day, and so on. All right, I'll go easy on the trunk for now but I want a list of everything that was in it—everything!' He glared at Denton, then Janet Striker. 'And mind—the day of reckoning is coming!' He shook his pencil at Denton.

'You should have been a preacher. "My god is a jealous god."'

'The god of New Scotland Yard *is* a jealous god! We also grind very slowly, like all gods.'

'And exceeding small.'

'That, too.' Munro looked at his notebook. 'Well, I don't see the chain—Mary Thomason goes missing; her brother collects the trunk—but where's the link to Arthur Crum? A drawing done by somebody who never saw him, based on the drawing of Mary? That's pure fantasy. This painting of Lazarus?' He made a sound with his lips that sounded like 'peuh'. 'You don't know how many human faces look alike until you undertake police work. Did you show this supposed drawing of the brother to Mary's landlady? What's her name, Mrs—Durnquess? She's the only one I find in this tangle who actually *saw* him.'

'The Irish maid,' Janet Striker said.

'Oh, right.' Munro made a note. 'Have to interview both of them, and I want a copy of these drawings you've built such a sandcastle on. All right—then the Mayflower Baths. I know all about the Mayflower Baths. Lots of jokes about it at the Yard—pardon me, ma'am. I'll ask around about this man Himple. Also, some of the lads who were picked up at the baths are still in prison; they should be shown the drawing of the "brother".' He made another note. 'Then there's the letters home from this fellow Himple. To—a valet—'

'Brown.'

'Yes—can't read my own writing. Brown.' He leaned hard on the pencil. 'Brown seems to be the one who knows where they were when. Or supposed to be, anyway. And where and when the temporary valet, this Crum, is supposed to have been discharged.'

'Brown has all that.'

'Yes, I *said* we need to talk to Brown. Give me an address. Good. If the bones turn out to be who you think, then we'll wire the places where they stayed, and so on—maybe let the French police do that, actually—depends, depends. Hmm.' He pinched his lower lip between his fingers and studied his notebook. 'French are digging up the dust pit at the farm to see if they can find the sack the lye came in. Also going to canvass the shops in the nearby town—what is it? Can? Cane—?'

'Caen,' she said.

'That's it. You sound just like the Frenchman. Plus they'll be looking for the, mm, other missing things—'

Janet Striker looked at Denton. He said, 'There's no head with the bones.'

'Oh, dear God. And I was so grateful we hadn't found that first—I didn't want to see a face that had been—' She shook her head quickly. 'Ridiculous to make more of the face than anything else.'

Munro closed his notebook and began to cram it back into some maw within his suit. 'I don't see that we can do anything until we have an identification. Metropolitan Police can't involve themselves until there's suspicion of a crime. A body found in France isn't suspicion of a crime.' He pulled the notebook out again and waved it at Denton. 'And this doesn't hold together well enough to be a crime!'

'And if the French police say in the end that they're unidentifiable remains?'

Munro stood. 'They'll have saved me a lot of grief.'

'What do you know about women's time of the month?' Janet Striker said.

Denton felt his face flush; he thought she would say next something about not being able to go to bed with him. He started to say, 'I was married,' to mean that he knew what a woman's time of the month was, but didn't get it out because she said, 'I've been thinking about Mary Thomason.'

It made no sense to him. 'What's that got to do with—what you asked me?'

He thought she was smiling, but the light was low and he couldn't tell. She said, 'You're embarrassed. So am I. It's this ridiculous code we have to live by to be "respectable". We can go to bed and know each other well enough to talk about death and madness, but not menstruation.' Her hand touched his. 'I've been making the list of things in her trunk for Munro. Racking my brain to make sure I got everything. I think I remember what was in her trunk, but—What *wasn't* in Mary Thomason's trunk?' she said.

A bit gruffly, he said, 'I suppose you've given me the clue.'

'Women bleed every month. Unless they're ignorant and nearly savage and destitute, they use something to catch the blood. Don't be embarrassed, Denton; this is simple fact. Poor women—that's most of the women in the world—use rags. Men make jokes about them, don't they—"She's got the rag on," to explain anything odd a woman does. Even the black slaves in America used something, would be my guess, at least if they could get them or hoard them. Moss, grass—something. Poor women in London keep old clothes, old bedclothes, anything they can get their hands on; they fold the rags into a sort of pad and pin them to their underskirts, or they fashion themselves a sort of belt and pin them to that.'

'Why are you telling me all this?'

'Wealthy women use pads they buy at places like Harrods. While they're shopping for the highest-quality shirts Mrs Cohan runs up in the attic, I suppose. The pads are disposable, so the well-off can pretend none of it's happening. The poor wash the blood out of the rags and use them again and again, and the rags show the brown stains of the blood.'

'All right, yes—I remember all that.' He was thinking of his dreams.

'The rags are *valuable*, Denton. Not for money but for convenience, for necessity—when the bleeding starts, you must have them. Else you find blood staining through your petticoat to your skirt, and if you wear light colours, it's hideously embarrassing.' She struck his arm lightly with her hand. 'What wasn't in Mary Thomason's trunk?'

'Rags,' he said weakly.

'Or pins or any kind of belt. Not a scrap of cloth with a stain. Nor any stains in her drawers.'

'She wasn't, mm, at that time of the month.'

'On the contrary, the only reason—one of the only reasons— that we didn't find any could be that she was wearing them, or wearing some and carrying the rest. But surely she'd have had more in reserve. You want never to run out.' She hesitated, as if what she would say next might annoy him. 'I went back to Fitzroy Street yesterday and talked to Hannah—the maid at the place where Mary Thomason lived.'

'The plump Mrs Durnquess's.'

'I asked Hannah where the female tenants washed out their rags. She knew exactly what I meant. There's a sink for it in the basement; they dry them on a line down there.' She met his eyes—no trace of embarrassment. 'I asked her if Mary Thomason ever went down there. She said she couldn't recall ever seeing her. She hadn't thought about it, but now she thought about it and she said, "Ain't that remarkable, ma'am."' She tapped his hand. 'What *did* we find in her trunk?'

He'd have been a dunce not to know where she was going. 'The depilatory, but—'

'We at least have to ask ourselves, Denton, who doesn't menstruate and would need a depilatory?'

'You make it sound like a riddle for a parlour game.' He frowned at her, looked away.

'I want one of those cream-filled dessert things,' she said. They were still eating in his sitting room, although Munro was long gone; a small plate of pastries sat on a tiered table nearby. 'Anyway, it's a possibility, isn't it—that Mary Thomason isn't a woman?'

'Anything's possible, but—I've heard of women masquerading as men—even as soldiers—'

'Joan of Arc.'

'Yes, well—But why would a man masquerade as a woman?'

'Perhaps he prefers to be a woman. Perhaps he wants to be a woman. Or perhaps it's simply a wonderful disguise.'

'Even if he has sex with men—the baths, Himple—that doesn't mean he wants to be a woman.'

'Not *that* crazy, mmm? What sane man would be a woman if he had a choice?'

'He'd have had to wear a wig. Where's the wig?'

'She'd have worn the wig when she left Fitzroy Street. Then got rid of it when she became a man.'

'But—' Atkins, who had appeared in response to a jingling bell, followed her pointing finger to a fat eclair. Denton asked for coffee and said when Atkins was gone, 'What would make such a thing worth it?'

She shook her head. She ate, then pulled the fork between her teeth to scrape the chocolate off. 'Living another life.'

'Something to hide.' He shook his head. 'I don't see it.'

'She wrote to you that somebody might be about to hurt her. Might that mean she was afraid she was about to be found out?'

'Well, I've told you, I don't think that letter was really for me. It was to scare Wenzli, wasn't it? And why would somebody hurt her?'

'Well, if she was really a man—If Mary Thomason had a man—a man who wasn't *so,* who wasn't a puff, a man like Wenzli or Geddys—interested in her, then being found out could mean— outrage? Disgust? If they were, you know, physically involved—'

'A man with a man? Oh, I see what you mean—the other man thinks he's a girl—there could be a certain amount of play—like Wenzli—'

'Kissing and so on, even well beyond that—'

'But surely, the man would find out when he—'

'Mmmm.' She scraped chocolate and cream off her plate, licked the fork with a voluptuous extension of her tongue. 'Mmmm.' She put the fork down. 'Perhaps that was the point Mary and Wenzli had almost reached.'

He shook his head. He watched her eat the eclair. 'This is a long tale to have built on some missing rags.' He accepted coffee from Atkins. 'It would be so complicated!'

'To the contrary, it's simplicity itself. A double life isn't necessarily like something in a Pavilion farce—going in and out of doors in different identities. It's mostly a matter of keeping your lies straight—like being married and having an affair. You'd want your wits about you, is all.'

'Not with separate identities—names, clothes, places to live—'

'It wouldn't have been that way. Mary was the identity; her way of life was the principal way. But sometimes he—*he*—was somebody else. Perhaps only occasionally.'

'To do what?'

'Something difficult, don't you think?' She smiled, but only a little. 'Like making a middle-aged man fall in love with you?'

He shook his head again. 'Let's not tell Munro yet.'

'Let's not.'

Ten days later, Munro told him that the French expert had said that the bones were human and almost certainly male. He speculated that they belonged to a man in middle age but couldn't be certain. However, one tibia had an old fracture.

'We checked with Himple's medical man. He'd broken a leg as a boy, falling off a wagon. The French are having local police ask after Himple and Crum at every place he posted letters from.'

Munro again demanded a copy of the drawings that Augustus John had made. A few days later, he sent a note to say that Mrs Durnquess had told Markson that John's drawing was very like the young man who had come to get the trunk; the maid had agreed. Meanwhile, the CID, now accepting the probability of a crime, had found Himple's bank and asked what arrangements he'd made for money while he travelled. He had carried a letter of credit, was the answer, and had used it in three places, for a total of more than three hundred pounds. The CID had also interviewed several of the young men who had been picked up in the raid on the Mayflower Baths. Two of them recognized the John drawing as somebody they called 'Eddie'. He'd been at the baths off and on, but they hadn't seen him, they thought, in a year. Several more of them recognized a photograph of Himple; he was 'a regular'.

Munro had more copies of the drawing made and sent to France. After another week, the word came back that two people at the banks where the letter of credit had been used thought that

John's drawing was like the man who had cashed a letter of credit as Erasmus Himple, RA.

'So he's a forger as well as a murderer. Dear God.' Denton was still shocked. 'I was so sure he would turn out to be the victim!'

'Why?' she said.

'Because—I'm still looking for Mary Thomason.'

'Well, it isn't a she, at least.'

'No, of course not.'

The valet and the housekeeper, Mrs Evans, said that of course the John drawing wasn't Himple; it was the young man known as Arthur Crum.

After another week, Munro said, 'He's skipped. Absolutely skipped. The trail's cold—the last time he was seen was six months ago in Nice. He's beaten us.'

CHAPTER

23

By then, they were into April. Denton wanted to be out, walking in the city. Flowers were blooming; birds were arriving in flocks; some of the days were warm, almost summery. Janet Striker was waiting to move into her own house, with the Cohans to take care of her; she was living partly in his old bedroom, partly in a hotel. He was now sure that her concern for appearances was some irrational personal quirk: she had explained that it was all right for her to sleep on the floor above him so long as he couldn't climb the stairs.

A doorway was being cut through the garden wall. He didn't know what she made of the people who could look into the garden from the nearby houses. Perhaps she meant to wear a disguise when she used the new door.

Missing her, wanting to be out and about, he was restless. He was gaining his weight back, but his strength was coming more slowly. One night when she was staying at her hotel and he was lying awake—the nursing-home insomnia had returned—he got out of bed and limped on his stick to the foot of the stairs. He looked up them. They seemed endless.

'The hell with it.' He put his left foot on the first stair, grasped the banister in his left hand and pulled the right leg up. It was all right. He went another step, then another. He had to balance on the bad leg and the stick while he moved the good leg, but he was getting used to that; his shoulders were stronger. He went up another step. His breathing was heavy. And so he went up to the landing, made the turn, and pushed and pulled his way up to his bedroom.

He limped about, lit the gas, sat in his desk chair and let his pulse and his breathing recover. There was some scent of her in the room. His desk surprised him with its neatness; she must have straightened it, had probably been working at it on something of her own.

When he had explored the room—it had been more than three months since he had seen it—he went out to the corridor and looked at the closed door to the attic. He had the notion that if he could use his rowing machine, he could build the strength of his leg faster. The rowing machine, a huge contraption of cast iron that Atkins had rightly said was never coming down once it had been got up there, was in the attic.

'Nothing ventured, nothing gained.'

He opened the door, lit the gas at the bottom of the stairs. When he put his left foot on the first step, he thought that he was probably doing something stupid, but he didn't change his mind. He thought, *I'll go to the first landing today and then come down. I can sleep in my bedroom and try it again tomorrow.* When he got to the first landing, he was trembling, but he didn't go back, after all. Five steps up was another landing, and then four steps to the attic. He would go to the next landing.

There was no gas to light here. On the third step, in the near darkness, he put the tip of the stick too close to the edge of the tread, and when he swung the bad leg up, the stick slipped. He went down hard on his left side, twisting as he went, wrenching his left shoulder, and then crashing down the stairs to the landing below. He hit his head on one of the steps and he lay there, dazed.

Atkins came pounding up from below. 'Good on you,' he said when he saw Denton.

Rupert came behind Atkins and stared.

'I think I've hurt myself.'

'Well, sit up, let's have a look at you.'

'What the hell's the good? Jesus Christ, I can't even climb the stairs!'

Atkins helped him sit up against the wall, then went down and got an oil lamp and looked at Denton's head, then had him work his shoulder. 'No real harm done, I think, Colonel.'

'All right, help me down to my bed.'

Atkins held the lamp up. He looked into Denton's eyes. 'I think you better try it again, Colonel.'

'And fall again!'

'You know what they say—get back on the horse or stop riding. Be that much harder the next time if you don't do it now.' Atkins bent and put a hand under Denton's arm and helped him up, then put the stick in his hand. 'You slipped in the dark, that's all. We'll fix that.' He went up the stairs with the lamp.

For seconds, Denton hated Atkins. Then he recognized that Atkins was taking a risk for him—if he fell again and hurt himself, it would be Atkins's fault.

'All right. Just don't laugh.'

Six minutes later, weak, panting, he sat on the top step with the darkness of the attic behind him. He grinned at Atkins. 'All right—now how do I get down?'

'You stay up there. I'll brew us up some tea. Going on four, anyway—breakfast soon. I'll bring it up.' He looked back from the landing. 'Take some exercise while you're about it.'

After that, he was able to labour down the front stairs and so outdoors, and he began to walk in the streets again. First to the Lamb and back, then down to Guilford Street, then to Russell Square, always with a pistol in his pocket and Cohan, borrowed from Janet Striker, behind him. One day he dragged himself up to the attic again and rowed in the contraption, which had to have its springs set at the weakest so he could move the oars. It was the kind of exercise he wanted, but getting up there wore him out.

She was living in a hotel again, waiting for the work on her house to be finished. Many afternoons, they sat together in the long room. One day she said, 'I've been reading your Henry James.'

'*My* Henry James.'

'He seems to me sometimes very right about women. You don't like him? Or you do like him, what does that shake of the head mean?'

'We're very different.'

'Denton, say what you mean.'

Denton moved uncomfortably. 'People call him a genius. I'm not a genius.' He didn't want to say anything else, but she was waiting. 'He can do a lot of things that I can't.'

'And you can do things that he can't?'

Again, he was uncomfortable. He said, 'One, maybe.' He started to go back to his book, raised his eyes to her. 'I can deal with the life most people know.' He had let his own book fall on his crossed legs; he raised it, lowered his eyes to it, and again raised them to say, 'His characters never have to worry about making a living, unless they're bad and want the money that the good ones have. I'll admit, this frees James to be high-minded about moral decisions, but he just doesn't understand that for most of the world, making a living is the great reality. And the interest— the drama, the excitement, whatever you call it—comes from the struggle to survive *and* to make moral decisions. And the farther down the income ladder you climb, the harder the decisions are.'

'Like Cohan, who wouldn't take a place with the Jewish madam.'

'Yes, just like that.' He settled the book again and looked down and started to read.

She said, 'Where do writers get their ideas from?'

He chuckled. 'That's just what James and I talked about. From everywhere.'

'From people they know?'

'Sometimes.'

'I don't want you ever to write about me. Even if we...' She left it hanging. He knew she meant *If we go our separate ways,* and he didn't say that if they did, that would be exactly when he'd be likely to write about her. The truth was, he was wondering if he would ever write again; his mind was empty, as if Jarrold's bullets had gone through his brain and not his back.

He carried the manuscript of the new book down to the publishers himself. He had pretty well forgotten it while he was in the nursing home, certainly had had no desire to work on it. Once home, he had stared at the pile of typed sheets and felt vaguely repelled by it, but he had at last begun to read. The type-writer had done the final copy; still, it had to be gone through once more. Reading it after so long was actually helpful; the months away freshened his eye.

'It's damned good,' he said to Diapason Lang.

'It's *months* late.'

'I suppose I should have put a clause in my contract about being shot.'

'Oh, my dear fellow—' Lang looked anguished. 'I didn't mean it that way. It's only—Gwen's so particular—'

'He got the insurer's money for the motor car.'

'Oh, yes. Yes, he did.' Lang looked at the pile of paper, craned his neck to read the title page, read the title, *The Love*

Child, and murmured, glancing at his picture of the maiden being visited by the nightmare, 'Title's a bit risqué.' He peeled back the top sheet as if to make sure the rest of the pages weren't blank. 'When can we expect the next one?'.

'What next one?'

'We always look forward to your next one! And, of course, there's the, ah, clause in the contract.' He seemed to want Denton to help him say what had to be said. 'The clause that we are to be offered your next book.'

'You *have* my next book.' Lang looked startled. 'This one is the replacement for the one I couldn't write a year ago. The Transylvania book was therefore the "next book".' He smiled, because he'd been thinking about it. 'The Transylvania book was written under a letter agreement, you'll remember, that made no mention of a next book.'

Lang stared at him, said that it couldn't be so, said that they didn't do things that way, said excuse me and hurried out of the office and came back, his pale face almost pink, with the letter agreement. 'Well, yes,' he said, 'of course we didn't mention a next book, but—' He looked hopeful. 'It was understood as a gentleman's agreement.'

Denton had brought with him the letters from other publishers that he'd been getting since he'd returned in September. He began to drop them on Lang's desk. 'Longwin and Barnes—Low—Hildesheim—Henry Strath—Osgood—' They piled on the desk like blown leaves. 'They all want my next book.'

'They can't have it.' Lang's voice was a whisper.

'Lang, maybe being shot in the back has made me testy. I like you personally. But I want more money.'

Lang winced. 'There isn't any more money.'

'Five hundred guineas a book in advance against a ten per cent royalty.'

'Oh, no, no—'

'Or perhaps I ought to hire one of these agents that keep pestering me.'

'Oh, don't do that!' Lang's desiccated face looked to be near tears. 'They're not gentlemen!'

Denton heard a heavy footstep in the corridor and then the impressive bulk of Wilfred Gweneth himself filled the doorway. 'What's this, then? Ah, Denton—' Gweneth seemed quite jolly, as if the motor car had never existed. They shook hands. Denton was sure that in fact Lang had sent for Gweneth while he was out of the office.

Gweneth looked at Lang. 'Anything amiss?'

'Mr Denton—our friend and valued author, Mr Denton—ah—'

'Wants more money,' Denton said.

Gweneth smiled. 'Ah.'

'You got your money back for the motor car. The Transylvania book has made you a pot. I've delivered the new novel. I want more for my next.' He didn't say he didn't have an idea for a next in his head—not a hint.

Gweneth picked up one of the letters from the desk, read it, picked up another, then another. Lang whispered, 'He's talking about an agent.'

Gweneth smiled and shook his head, as if the vagaries of authors were beyond understanding. 'How much?' he said.

Denton told him. 'There's nothing about a next book in the letter agreement.'

'I know.' Gweneth laughed and showed his back teeth. He lifted Denton's new book as if weighing it, apparently judged it sufficiently heavy. 'Let's say pounds not guineas, ten per cent royalty, but the old terms on the Empire and we'll forget about the next-book clause!' He pointed a hand at Lang. 'Draw up a contract that meets the new terms. We don't want him going to a wretched bunch of thieves like Longwin's.' Gweneth hooked a hand through Denton's arm. 'Lunch? I want to hear about your being shot. Is there a book in it, do you think—? Perhaps something that might touch on spiritualism—a moment when you saw beings in white robes all about you, a magical light, music—? Do you like fresh-caught salmon?'

At the end of April, Janet Striker handed him a pasteboard box.
In it was a folded something of grey wool with blue trim. When
he laid it out on his bed, he stared at it and tried to guess what it
was and what he was supposed to do with it. The sleeves came, he
thought, about to the elbows, the trousers to just below the knee.
There was a little hat to match, rather like the caps that Eton
boys wore. Surely they weren't some sort of pyjamas she thought
he would wear?

'Unhhh—' he said.

'It's a rowing costume.' She was undressing, was wearing an
only slightly frilly thing that came halfway down her thighs and
had garters to attach to her stockings. 'Can't you tell that?'

'You're distracting me.'

'You hate it, don't you.'

'In the attic, it'll be fine.'

'You're not going to wear it in the attic! You're going to wear
it at Hammersmith. I've bought you a season ticket for a rowing
boat. You'll wear it on the Thames!'

He stared at it. She began to unfasten her stockings. He said,
'I know I told you I'd do anything for you, but—' She looked up,
bent forward, a foot on the divan, pulling off a stocking. He said,
'Of course I'll wear it. It's just the thing.'

The likely death of Erasmus Himple caused a brief sensation.
Journalists came to interview Denton and were turned away. A
French detective came with a translator and went over everything
that Denton and Janet Striker knew and left without comment.

Denton sat late one evening with her and let the room go
almost dark before he lit a lamp. He said, 'It grieves me that
they've got away with it.'

'They?'

'There had to be two of them. One man alone couldn't have murdered Heseltine. You can make a man lie down in a bathtub, maybe, but you can't hold both his arms and slash his wrists for him. He'll fight you. From Munro's description, Heseltine didn't fight and didn't splash blood around. That means he was unconscious when his wrists were slashed, already in the bath or there'd have been blood all over his flat. One small man couldn't have dragged him to the bathroom and got him into the tub, even if he was unconscious.'

'You still think Mary and her brother are different people.'

'It's the explanation that takes care of the most questions.'

'You think a small man and a small woman could have moved Heseltine?'

'Oh, yes.' He stretched out both his legs and slowly raised the right one to put it over his left ankle. 'I need to think. I've missed things.'

Lady Emmeline's legal people got in touch with Sir Francis Brudenell, his solicitor. They were offering to pay his medical expenses in return for his signing a paper absolving Lady Emmeline and her son of all responsibility. 'This, of course,' Sir Francis wrote, 'is nonsense. They are clearly terrified that we will sue. We should most certainly win, as there is no question of his having shot you or of her negligence in controlling him. However, the law is slow, and publicity could be an embarrassment to you, as it is my understanding that the shooting took place immediately after your egress from a premises less well-respected than many. It is my recommendation that I make them a counter-offer to settle the matter out of court for, let us say, your medical expenses plus ten thousand pounds. We shall settle for five. It will hardly matter to Lady Emmeline, as she owns a good deal of central Portsmouth. Of course, in case there is permanent damage from the bullets, we shall make the matter conditional on full recovery.'

It gave Denton something new to think about. With five thousand pounds, he could electrify his house, perhaps put in central heating, buy a motor car and still have enough to put away—a previously impossible luxury. On the other hand, he believed that he should earn whatever money he got. After two days, he scribbled a note: 'Go ahead.'

He made lists. He compared dates. He reconstructed everything that had happened, dated it, made a chart of the what and the when, with the events down one side in chronological order, from his opening Mary Thomason's letter through to the finding of the bones in Normandy. He tried to make a graph, or perhaps it was a map, of who had been in various places at various times, but it was too complicated and at the same time too empty: he didn't know enough. After several days of it, sitting sulkily and looking at the papers he had stuck up with pins on his bedroom wall, he said, 'Somebody's lied to us.'

'Who?'

He chewed on a thumbnail. 'I mean to find that out.' He stared at the papers; she moved about the room, picked up a book, sat to read. He said, 'I've been thinking about those dreams. After I was shot.' He chewed on the thumbnail. 'I was afraid.'

'But you know that.'

'But not afraid the way I thought. It isn't any of that elaborate allegory the doctor was trying to build; it was fear of— It's something about the woman. The doctor was sure it was fear of death. Well, of course—all fear is fear of death, I suppose. But this was about—I don't think the one with the shotgun was a man—'

'It was Mary Thomason.'

He nodded.

'A while ago, you thought that "they" would try again.'

'I think that's over. If they ever meant to. I wonder a little that they didn't try to move Himple's body after they shot me, but it was probably just too much—too risky. And they thought I'd die.'

'They've given up?'

He studied his charts. 'I hope that they don't care about me any more. As soon as the news about finding the body hit the newspapers, there was no longer any reason. When the police couldn't find them, they knew they'd won.'

'So you're safe.'

'Unless we find something that sets them going again.' He got up and limped around the room. He stood in front of one of his papers, arms folded. 'I'm going to ask Munro to let me see Struther Jarrold.'

'Why?'

'Because I think he knows who Mary Thomason is.'

The Hobhouse Prison for the Criminally Insane was on the edge of Exmoor, facing a landscape that would have been bleak on the best of days. In a thunderstorm, it was dramatic and dismal. He'd asked Janet Striker if she wanted to come with him, but she'd shuddered and said she'd been inside such a place too long to ever want to see one again. When he said it was supposed to be a model of progressive institutionalization, she had said there was no such thing.

The building was grey stone, with square towers at each corner and a steepled central one for the entrance. Surrounded by a high stone wall, it was inescapably a prison; whatever was modern or progressive about it had to be inside. Munro, seeing it in the distance, said it looked like a cotton mill. 'Not that a cotton mill wouldn't be just the thing for Jarrold and his ilk—never done a day's work in his life. His mum's got him a private cell that's furnished like a bedroom, with bookshelves and carpets and easy chairs. Everything bolted to the floor, of course, and nothing dangling about he could hang himself with. Still, it beats ten hours a day bent over a power loom.'

'That's the court's idea of punishment?'

'He isn't being punished—no trial yet. He's being kept isolated for society's sake.'

Their carriage turned in at a gateway and stopped while Munro identified himself, and then they were waved in and passed under the steeple and into a vast courtyard where barred windows stared down into half an acre of gravel. Around the entire yard at ground level, porches with heavy wire from floor to ceiling held men who gaped, then shouted and gestured at the carriage while they twisted their fingers into the wire mesh.

'Newest thing,' Munro growled. 'No trees or flowers to distract the demented brain.' He looked at the porches. 'Hell with fresh air,' he said.

Jarrold's cell was on the third floor. They waited in an interview room, very spare, a double table down the middle with a chest-high partition and a few oak straight chairs. The sounds of a prison made their way through the walls: incoherent voices, metal banging on metal, footfalls and the clang of doors, and here and there the screams and laughter of the insane.

They heard Jarrold before they saw him—the metallic scuffing of a chain on stone floors, the jingle of his manacles. Influential mother or not, he was put into chains to move out of his cell, and he came in bowed by the weight of them. Two warders in dark uniforms nudged him along to a chair on the other side of the partition from them, and it was only when Jarrold was seated and had clanked his ankle chains into some sort of comfortable position that he looked up at his visitors. When he saw Denton, his scowling face was replaced with a knowing, childish grin, as if they shared a secret.

Jarrold, he had been told, never spoke. Since he had fired the two bullets into Denton and shouted those few words, he had been silent, even with his attorneys and his mother. 'Utterly withdrawn into a world of his own,' the chief physician's report had said. Denton wondered.

'Please ask your questions, gentlemen,' the more senior of the warders said. 'We have to remain present. We think he hears what's said to him, but—he don't respond.'

Jarrold's face, after that knowing smile, had fallen back into its scowl, and now he looked at his hands, limp in his lap.

Denton remained standing. He took the drawing of Mary Thomason from an inner pocket and unfolded it, looking at it to make sure it was the right side up, and then he leaned quickly forward and held it against Jarrold's side of the partition. One of the warders started forward, saying, 'Sir—' and Denton said, 'Albert!'

Jarrold's head lifted; his eyes found the paper. His mouth opened. He began to scream.

'I never told! Astoreth—Astoreth—I never told! I never did—Astore-e-e-th-!' His body spasmed and his back arched as he went into a seizure.

❀ ❀ ❀

Denton was silent all the way back in the train. He'd told Munro he wanted to think and he wanted to talk to Janet Striker; Munro was welcome to come home with him, but he'd have to wait until then.

'You knew he was going to do that, didn't you! Dammit, Denton, that was a cheap courtroom trick. And what did you get out of it? All that way so you could—'

Denton held up a hand and said nothing. At Lamb's Conduit Street, they climbed his stairs and sat silently while Atkins went for Mrs Striker. As soon as she was in the room, Denton told her what had happened.

'Mary Thomason is Astoreth? But that's impossible. Jarrold painted "Astoreth" on my wall months ago, when there was no way that—' She looked at Munro. 'Has he explained this to you?'

'He hasn't explained to me why I spent a day going to Devon and getting nothing out of it. Don't be cute, Denton—spill it and let me get back to New Scotland Yard.'

'I don't have much to spill yet. Yes, Mary Thomason is Astoreth. That's what I had to know before I could know anything else.'

'Why?'

'Because it means she's alive and she isn't missing, and because it means that she's the one who told Jarrold to shoot me.'

Munro was sitting with his head tilted slightly back, his eyes half-closed, looking at Denton. 'You're spinning a tale.'

'Why would Jarrold shoot me? Because his obsession with me had got out of hand? Yes, of course—that was something that was easy for her to play on. But why the very morning that Heseltine and I came back from France? Coincidence? I'd have said yes, if it hadn't been for Heseltine's death.'

'It was suicide.'

'No, it was murder. I respect you, Munro, and I like you, and you're a good cop because you're cautious. But now it's time to jump. One, we need to show the drawings to the old man who's supposed to be the gateman at Albany Court, and we need to show them to every man and boy who lives in the Albany. Then, when they identify at least one of them, you need to get Heseltine exhumed.'

'Like hell—excuse me, Mrs Striker.'

'I think he'll show signs of some means of putting him out, probably a knock on the head. Munro, you don't get a man to lie down in a bathtub so you can cut his wrists without a struggle!' Munro hadn't moved. If anything, his eyes had narrowed even more. 'The coroner didn't present evidence of a blow to the head, did he?'

'Because there wasn't any.'

'Because he didn't look for any. Exhumation, Munro.' When the detective was still unconvinced, Denton leaned towards him and said, 'If people at the Albany recognize the drawings, what other next move do you have?'

Janet Striker was working a cigarette out of a shagreen case. 'Denton, it's fanciful that Mary Thomason and Jarrold knew each other. You knew of Mary Thomason only because that letter reached you by way of Heseltine—the sheerest chance. You said that she wrote the letter to frighten Wenzli or Geddys—maybe both. It wasn't supposed to reach you, but Heseltine found it and sent it on. Nothing to do with Jarrold! Jarrold was a poor sick man who got obsessed with you because of your books. There's no connection with Mary Thomason!'

'Not then, no.'

'When?'

He moved uncomfortably, trying to get the bad leg into another position. 'It's why I made all those lists. The question is, when did Mary—or her brother—see Struther Jarrold as opportunity? Because they're opportunists, rather impressively so. But there's another question that maybe comes first: when did they learn that I was asking about them?' He glanced at Munro, then back at her. She was smoking now. He put out a hand for one of her cigarettes. 'That's when it started—when they learned I was asking questions: that's when they took notice of me. So who told them? There are several candidates—people we asked about Mary Thomason, I mean. The office people at the Slade, but I think that's unlikely. Mrs Durnquess. Geddys, the picture dealer. Much later, the other artist, Wenzli; Mrs Evans, Himple's housekeeper; and his valet, Brown. I think they can be discounted because it was too late—the opportunity to exploit Jarrold must have come earlier to have worked. Mary Thomason must have needed time to work on Jarrold.'

Munro shook his head. 'Brown's clean, anyway. I liked the idea of Brown—disgruntled valet, left behind in England, nurses a grudge against Himple and Crum—but it won't wash. He's stupid, but he isn't criminal. Once a week, he goes to the studio to "do the pictures", which I think is what housemaids call dusting. He sent on the bills and letters to the poste restante boxes; they were still there when the French police went looking. He's taken a job evenings in a pub—never misses a day. We all *wanted* Brown to have done the dirty, but he didn't. Too many people vouch for him.'

'Well,' Janet Striker said, '*somebody* told them about Denton.'

Denton made a negative grunting sound. 'That sounds pretty cold-blooded. Passed a message, more likely—something innocent like "Send me a picture postcard of the beach if anybody asks about me." This was way back last September, remember. Himple was already dead—had been dead since at least the first week of September. Arthur Crum was travelling, presumably as

Himple, forging demands on the letter of credit, forging reports about where they were going next, and then disappearing. He—they—had got off scot-free. Until the message comes that I'm asking questions.' Abruptly, Denton laughed. 'But what must they have thought when they first learned I was asking questions? Me! When they were the ones who had used me as the bugbear to scare Wenzli! I wonder if they ever learned somehow that it was their own letter that got me going. My God—do you suppose they saw the horror of it?'

Janet stirred. 'At any rate, you were asking questions, and somehow they found out—horror or no horror.'

'Then—I can show you the sequence in my charts—Jarrold savages your rooms and paints "Astoreth" on the wall. At that time, Astoreth exists only in his mind. Mary Thomason hasn't yet thought of becoming his Astoreth. His attack on your rooms makes the newspapers with lip-licking mention of Jarrold's possible involvement in the incident behind my house. My name is mentioned, Jarrold's is trumpeted, and at least the cheap papers do follow-ups that manage to hint at his obsession with me. And they all mention Astoreth and imply that Jarrold is dotty. So Mary Thomason or Arthur Crum needed only to read the papers to see the possibilities of Struther Jarrold. Not as a certainty, but as a possibility. These people are seducers, both of them—Mary Thomason with Geddys and with the other painter, Wenzli; Crum with Himple. They're like confidence men, able to play on their victims' wants and needs, able to manoeuvre their victims into *wanting* to do things for them. Mary got Wenzli to almost give her the painting, the "little Wesselons"; Crum got Himple to make him his valet, to take him to France—to be his lover, I suppose. So I think they decided to have a look at Struther Jarrold and the situation at his mother's country house, and I think that what they found was that the security was laughable and a woman as talented as Mary Thomason could con that poor, sick brain into believing she was his demon and wanting to do anything she told him to do. So that if I got closer, they had a weapon.'

Munro had put an elbow on his chair arm, and his head on that hand. He looked bored and sleepy, but Denton knew he was as alert as a cat. 'And she didn't tell him to do anything until you went to France?'

'Why would she have? I hadn't learned anything new in weeks. Not anything serious, anyway. I was writing a book; I had other things on my mind.' He glanced at Janet, got a cool look from her through the cigarette smoke. 'What's more important, they must have been as much in the dark about me as I was about them. That's why Guillam and the private detectives were a godsend to them, because that way they at least knew when I was getting warmer, as we used to say in the kids' game. But I think that except for the detectives' reports they couldn't keep track of what I was doing. It's also why I think they never went after Janet—they lost her after she moved out of her rooms in Bethnal Green. It must have made them nervous, maybe frantic, and they did a frantic thing when they got hard information about my going with Heseltine to France—they tried to kill me, and they did kill him. It was the kind of mistake you make when you're confused and panicked. Even though, as it turned out, finding Himple's body didn't help us find them.'

'Thanks to the incompetence of the CID,' Munro growled.

'You know I don't believe that.'

Munro took his head off his hand and studied his fingers. 'We tried to pick up that trunk at Biggleswade. It had been collected.'

Denton was surprised. 'When?'

Munro glanced at a notebook. 'Ninth of October.'

Janet said, 'Not too long after I put it back.'

'As apparently Mary Thomason's still with us,' Munro said, 'why didn't she pick up her trunk before?'

'You're sure it was she who picked it up?'

'Not sure of anything. Clerk said a young woman; he thought the drawing "might have been her" but wasn't sure.' He turned to Denton. 'But I want to hear what you think—why didn't she pick up the trunk as soon as she could after it was sent?'

'Maybe that's exactly what she did. It depends, doesn't it, on where she was and what she was doing between writing me the note in early August and picking up the trunk in October. And once she knew that Himple was dead, she had to disappear, because she was too connected to Himple—her face was in the *Lazarus*; her brother was the man who went to Normandy with Himple. She couldn't go back to work for Geddys, couldn't go back to the Slade, couldn't go back to modelling and flirting with Wenzli. I suppose she was quite right in thinking that the trunk wasn't going anywhere. And there was nothing in it worth a damn, anyway.'

'Except the drawing,' Janet Striker said. She was involved in handing a cigarette to Munro, who had been seduced by their smoke. 'If she made the little drawings in the corners—but then she didn't, did she! The bit from the *Lazarus* and the sketch of the baths were about Arthur Crum, not her.' She smiled and took out another cigarette for herself. 'Which might suggest to some that they were the same person.'

The remark hung in the room like the sonority of a bell. Denton knew he had caught his breath; he thought Munro had, too. Janet's smile, faintly wicked, persisted. At last, Munro grunted and said, 'I wondered when somebody would get to that.'

'By God, Munro, you mean the idea doesn't disgust you? Janet's been pushing it for days. I thought you'd have a fit.'

'Even at New Scotland Yard, we old fogies are now and then able to tell a hack from a handsaw.' Munro ground out his cigarette. 'I have to think of them as two people, brother and sister, Mary and Arthur. But, yes, I can see a version of the tale where they're the same person.' He pulled himself out of his chair, rose to his full height, like a bear on its hind legs. 'I'm not saying you two are right. Not even saying I'm convinced that your ideas hold together. But I will say, it's always a treat to hear you talk. Makes you understand the power of the storyteller in olden days of yore. Ring for my hat and coat, will you?'

'You still don't believe us?'

'Just the opposite—I do. That's what's got me worried.'

On a balmy, breezy day, Denton and Janet Striker took a cab to Fitzroy Street. She said, 'Are we starting here because it's the likeliest?'

'Or the safest; I don't know.'

They gave their names again to the harassed Irish maid and were shown into the same cluttered room, where the same plump woman sat in what looked to be the same clothes. She was shocked by the very idea that she might not have told them the entire truth. 'The police have been here!' she said. Her laces fluttered. 'Do you think I would dare to lie to the police?'

'We thought you might have forgotten something.'

'Do you think I am senile? Do you think me incompetent? You are very insulting. Please to ring the bell and tell the maid to show you out.'

Denton bowed, winked at Janet Striker and limped out of the crowded, stuffy room.

When they had been standing in the central hall for more than a minute, the Irish maid appeared from somewhere below. Her sleeves were rolled up again, and sweat had stained her blouse. Pushing back loose coils of hair, she said, 'I'm mangling. It's hot work.'

Denton held up a shilling. She reached for it and he said, closing his fingers over the coin, 'Do you remember we talked about Mary Thomason?'

'Oh, that again.'

'You remember.'

'Of course I do.'

He held her eyes. Her look was what so-so novelists called 'bold', meaning she didn't flinch. He said, 'When Mary Thomason left, did she give you a way to get in touch with her?'

The bold look wavered. 'Why would she?'

'She might have wanted to know when somebody came asking after her.'

'Well, what if she did?'

'How did you let her know after we were here asking?'

The young woman hesitated, wiped her forehead with the back of her hand, and settled back on her spine and looked straight at him. 'She left me a card with a stamp to post to her— what of it?'

'You didn't tell us that when we were here before.'

'You didn't ast me.'

'Did you tell the police?'

She snorted. 'The English polis can go suck eggs for all of me.'

He held out the coin. When she took it, he said, 'Which of them came back—Mary Thomason, or her brother?' He had caught her fingers and held them as they held the shilling.

The girl's voice fell almost to a whisper. 'How'd you know somebody come back?'

'Which?'

'Her.'

'She wanted to know who'd been here?'

'Yeah. Just that.'

'You had our names?'

'Your cards, yeah. I give them to her.' She flared up. 'Where's the harm, then? She was a poor lone thing like me; she had somebody meaning to hurt her! She give me a sixpence—be like a sovereign to you! She was a sweet, harmless little thing that wanted to know who was after her!'

'So she left you a stamped card to send to her. What was the address on the card?'

'You think I can read?' She made a contemptuous, snorting sound in the back of her nose. 'I grew up in a house no better than a pigsty that was a dozen miles from the nearest school— you think the old folks sent me there? I was needed to home! Reading's for you fine English people.'

'Did you send her a card or anything after Mrs Striker was here the other day?'

'She left me oney the one card. It was oney the once!'

'And after we leave here today—are you going to tell her somehow?'

'I ain't, I ain't, I got better things to do! I ain't seen her in half a year and I got no more cards with stamps to them! Now leave me be.'

She started back for the stairs, but Denton caught her arm and held her. She was frightened, but she was angry; he thought that if he spoke one wrong word, she'd punch him. 'If Mary Thomason or her brother comes back again, Hannah, you have to tell me. I'm going to give you a card. If either of them comes back, you take the card to Mrs Durnquess and have her read my address to you. Mary and her brother are involved in some very bad business. You don't want to help them.' He let her go and gave her one of his cards.

When they were out on the street, Janet Striker said, 'I hope you don't believe she'll do what you told her to.'

'No. She thinks Mary's a victim, and she'll side with her. Still, it was worth a try.'

Walking down Fitzroy Street, Janet said, 'You thought all along she was the one?'

'Since I thought there had to be somebody, yes. She seemed the likeliest. I'd rather it was Geddys—I don't like him, and I like her—but I'll take what I can get.'

'You going to tell Munro?'

'Mmm. Maybe. Not yet.'

She squeezed his arm. He told her he wanted to walk, to help his recovery; they went on down Charlotte Street. The bad leg dragged and had to be favoured, with much use of the walking stick, but he got around well on it now, not as fast as he used to but well enough. At Oxford Street, she suggested they stroll along past the shops. 'If you're not too tired.'

'Being tired isn't the problem; it's being *slow*.' They turned into Oxford Street. 'You have shopping to do?'

'I come to places like this to look. To see what I'm not missing, perhaps. Mrs Cohan is making curtains at the moment; I'm shopping for ideas.'

'Which you won't buy?'

'She knows the remnant houses in the East End. We'll go there when I know what I want. She has fantastic taste. One of her places has bolts of old Liberty silks and cashmeres, magnificent things that are out of fashion. I intend to surround myself with it.'

The shop windows were full of coronation goods, the coronation itself still almost two months off. They saw coronation chocolates, coronation cakes, the Coronation Tea Set with Spirit Lamp and Kettle, coronation platters and plates and bone china cups with portraits of the new king and queen. A coronation corset was being advertised.

'The Socialists say that the coronation is a trick, a very large piece of advertising for capitalism and the Empire,' she said.

'What do you know about the Socialists?'

'I go to the Reading Room. I read about everything! Because I know nothing, Denton—nothing! I'm as ignorant as that Irish girl, except I can write a ladylike hand.'

'Atkins has got himself into the truss business. They're going to call it the Coronation Model if they can get it ready in time.'

They stopped at a window where a portrait of the king was displayed on a carved easel and surrounded with velour draperies. She said, 'A fairly common type in a whorehouse.'

'Kings?'

'Fat men with stinking cigar breath and plenty of money to pay people to do things that humiliate them.'

'You don't have respect for your new sovereign?'

'None.'

They turned back at Oxford Circus. She said, 'What would you think of my attending University College?'

'If it's what you want to do.'

'I'm so ignorant. Truly, I don't know anything. I might even take a degree. Would you mind?'

'If you became learned? Of course not. A degree in what?'

She hesitated as if she feared his answer. 'Economics,' she said. 'I so like having money.' They both started laughing.

CHAPTER

24

April turned into May, May into June. Heseltine had been dead six months, Erasmus Himple even longer. Mary Thomason and Arthur Crum or whoever they were had vanished.

The Boer War stumbled to an end. Janet Striker moved into her house, with the Cohans to take care of her. Atkins's vegetable garden produced baby lettuces and early peas and threatened courgettes. Denton rowed on the river every other day from a boathouse above Hammersmith Bridge. The first time, he had worn old trousers and a shirt without a collar but had been surprised to see that most of the men who were serious about it wore some costume of the sort Janet Striker had given him. They seemed unembarrassed by the mid-calf trousers and the collarless shirts, even by the little caps. They looked distinctly silly to him, but he had long since resigned himself to a culture in which the well-off wore different kinds of clothes for every activity and didn't feel ridiculous in them. Thereafter, he carried his rowing clothes in a little satchel, changed in the boathouse with the rest and rowed in what he called 'my funny duds'. Warmer weather proved their value: he sweated buckets—so much so that he had to buy two more outfits.

Usually, he rowed downriver, now and then as far as Battersea, then back up against the current, with or against the tide; if he felt strong, he went on past Hammersmith as far as Mortlake before turning back. He loved the pull of the oars, the feeling of power returning in his shoulders. He could lift a hundred pounds again, although only a few lifts without a rest as yet; he had gained back more than twenty of the lost pounds; when he walked, the bad leg had to be favoured but he put the stick aside; he rarely looked behind him any more, although he went on carrying the Colt in the street until the weather got too warm for heavy fabrics and overcoats, and then he carried the derringer, which was easier to hide in light clothes.

The bad leg seemed better when he rowed, delivering force to push the sliding seat back. The boat was not a rowing shell but a kind of long skiff, double-ended, narrow, the interior an intricate crossing of narrow planks and ribs every two inches, the whole thing varnished to a warm, glowing brown. He found himself holding his own with other rowers, knew that his long-postponed urge to row had been correct.

The coronation had been scheduled for 26 June. The city was brilliant with bunting; the newspapers were burbling with patriotism; a kind of hysteria had gripped people of all classes—the Socialists were right: the selling power of the coronation was enormous. Even the sweatshop workers saved to buy a Britannia-ware coronation spoon. There hadn't been a coronation, after all, in sixty-some years.

On 24 June, the king had an attack of appendicitis. The coronation was put off.

The Bohemian Girl

As Denton passed through the city on what should have been the great day, he got a sense of vaguely nasty resentment. It was as if a child's treat had been denied. The marketing of the crown had created a huge appetite whose denial led to tantrums. There seemed to be an unusual amount of bickering in the underground station. Men whose uniformly black business clothes had been brightened by patriotic colour in the buttonhole were funereal again. People scowled. Although it was the most beautiful day so far of a beautiful summer, the only comment Denton overheard was 'What a day!' It was not meant happily.

Changed into his ridiculous costume, he stood on the wooden ramp that sloped down to the water, momentarily leaning on the long, spoon-bladed oars. The water glittered. It was still hardly eight o'clock; the sun was not yet hot, and a soft breeze was blowing upstream, bringing with it what he thought was a smell of the sea. 'What is so rare as a day in June?' he muttered, then reminded himself that an American had written that.

He glanced around him, the habit still there, looking for the shadow that never grew solid—Jarrold was still in the institution in Devon, would always be so. The derringer had been left in the valise; a pistol out on the river seemed absurd. Standing in the sun in that glorious weather, he thought, *I'm still afraid*. He shook the idea off. There was no reason for anybody to follow him now. He was out of it—it was all a police matter now, and already an old one, at that.

The case was open, but Mary Thomason and Arthur Crum were gone. The old man at the Albany gate thought he might have seen somebody who looked like the drawings of Crum, but he couldn't tell them more than that. Munro had got an exhumation order, despite Heseltine's father's anguish; the local coroner had found damage to the back of the skull 'consistent with a blow or a fall'. But the trail, as Munro had said, was dead cold.

The boat, as always when he first got into it, felt like an uneasy eggshell, yet when he was seated it was secure enough that he could rock his hips and feel no loss of balance. He started downriver slowly, the incoming tide only a ripple against his bow.

What am I really afraid of?

Working his shoulders, he increased his power without upping his tempo; after turning around at Battersea, he raised the beat, his legs working, the boat seeming to fly over the water. On he went upstream, past Putney and Hammersmith and then, feeling glorious and strong and exultant in the day, past Mortlake.

There was bunting on houses and boats along the bank. It had been meant to be a holiday; some people were apparently going to make it one, anyway. A steam launch chugged past, flags flying, heading for Hampton Court; other rowing boats, always recalling water insects, darted back and forth. He went on up the river, his beat slower now, making himself a tourist looking at houses and boats and people, seeing himself as part of the spectacle.

Up past the little village of Strand-on-the-Green. He had been there—why?—of course, to visit the valet, Brown. He looked over his shoulder, searching out Brown's house, which he remembered for its steep roof and bright blue trim. And, yes, there it was, a low concrete wall meant to keep the river out separating its back garden from the tidal mud, a flagpole flying the Union Jack; in the garden, flowers along each side, multi-coloured, pastel, the stuff of art. And as if called up by that idea, on the green of the little lawn, a woman in a white dress, sitting at an easel.

He came even with the house and went on, meaning to turn around at Kew, and he saw the woman only as a woman— white gown, straw hat, long hair—and then in an instant he saw everything, so startled that he caught a crab with his left oar and almost flipped the boat. Had she noticed? No; she was looking the other way.

He was rowing hard again, sweating, the sweat stinging his eyes. He turned almost too fast at Kew Bridge, backing with one oar, the gunwale coming within an inch of the water, and then he was pulling downriver again and moving to his right, bringing the boat in closer to the stairs that pierced the concrete dyke. He had picked out the high dormer of Brown's house with its blue-trimmed window, the flagpole and the flag, and he kept his eyes on them until he was right at the shore and beached the boat at the foot of a flight of stairs. He got out clumsily, his bad leg trailing.

The mud was sticky and smelled bad. He grabbed the bow and pulled the boat up the gently sloping bank and tied it off in a ring set in the stone. For no other reason than vanity, he tossed the absurd little hat into the boat. He patted a pocket for the derringer and then remembered that it, too, was back at Hammersmith.

No matter.

Nothing mattered—only this: to climb these stairs, and cross this lawn and then the next and then to approach the woman who was painting at the easel in Brown's back garden. He never took his eyes from her; she was looking partly upriver, must have seen him as part of her scene as he had rowed up. A bit of moving, anonymous colour.

He stepped over a clump of tall summer flowers and pulled his bad leg after and said, loud enough for her to hear, 'Miss Mary Thomason, I think.'

Her head whirled.

'Or is it Arthur Crum?'

She screamed and got up so fast the easel swayed and fell on the bright green grass. Lifting her white skirts, she ran, crying, 'Ralph! Ralph, help me!' Her yellow straw hat came off and drifted to the grass.

Denton cursed the leg and the bullet wounds. He moved as fast as he could, a man walking like a pair of compasses, huge strides, stiff. He could hear her screaming the name Ralph. She went through a doorway. The top half was mullioned glass; he could see her after she closed it, a terrified face, hands working frantically.

He didn't try to be polite. His momentum carried him to within a few feet of the door, his weight coming on his right leg, which was clumsy but would carry it, and, as an extension of his long stride, he raised his good leg and kicked the door open and almost fell through it as his right leg lost its balance.

'Ralph! Kill him—kill him—'

Through the door, he saw her within two yards of him and reached out. He was late in seeing motion to his right and behind him; too late, he turned, his right arm up, and caught an iron poker just above the elbow as it slammed down where his head was meant to be. The arm went dead, pain shooting to the shoulder. He saw the poker raised again. The face of Brown the valet was dark red, the eyes wide open with hatred. Denton forced himself in tight against the man and felt the poker swing behind him; he smashed his forehead into Brown's face. Blood spurted. Denton had his left hand twisted into the man's shirt then, pulling him close and using his head again to batter him, then kneeing him in the groin and hearing him howl. Denton swung him to his right and flung him into a wall. The valet collapsed down it to a sitting position. He put his hands in front of him.

Denton picked the poker up in his left hand. Brown's eyes pleaded: *No more.* Denton hit him backhanded with the iron poker. The sound was like a hammer hitting a post.

The woman screamed. She turned and ran for a flight of stairs and up them. Denton followed as fast he could, reaching the bottom of the stairs only as a door slammed on the floor above. He started up, found it hard going without his stick, and he threw the poker aside and used a banister to pull himself up with his right hand. It was like rowing one-handed, the muscles bunching in his back, the blow on the upper arm aching.

At the top, a corridor ran the length of the small house, a door on each side. He saw but didn't register the prettiness of it—rag rugs on the floor, watercolours on the walls, fresh flowers. His attention was on the closed door on his left. He tried the handle; it turned, but the door wouldn't open. He pushed, felt a slight movement and heard the sound of scraping. She had pushed something against it from the other side.

He couldn't kick this one open, and he couldn't easily push it with his shoulder. Instead, he put his back against the door and turned the knob with his left hand. It was like pushing the sliding seat in the boat.

The door moved; the scraping sound grated. The opening widened—six inches, a foot, almost enough room for him to go through—and he saw her face, demonic, pale, and the razor that gleamed in an arc and missed his face as he recoiled but slashed down his left arm. He fell back into the hall, almost going down the stairs. The door slammed again.

Blood was running down his arm and dripping on the rag rug. The unconnected thought that she had made the rugs herself came into his mind. She had built herself a nest, he thought. He was tearing off the shirt of his silly outfit and wrapping it around his arm, then pulling it tight and holding the end with his left hand so it wouldn't unwind.

He pushed the door again. It swung open and banged against the dresser that had been pushed against it. Holding his bleeding arm above his head, Denton nudged the door with his hip, alert for the razor, waiting for her to attack again.

The room was empty. Like the hall it was pretty. On the far wall above a double bed was the 'little Wesselons'.

The dormer window was open.

He pushed the dresser out of the way and looked around the room for her, even bending and lifting the girlish flounce to look under the bed. She was clever enough to hide and let him think she'd gone out of the window, but she wasn't in the room.

The dormer was high, six feet wide; the window was a tall double casement that swung from the middle post. Both leaves were open. If he went out of the wrong window, she might be able to come back in the other and escape him before he knew where she was.

He closed the door and pushed the dresser against it again to slow her if she came back in. His blood dripped on the floor and he raised the arm over his head again.

He went out of the right-hand window. When he looked down the pitch of the roof to the eave, vertigo staggered him. His old fear of heights. He closed his eyes, shook his head; then, not looking at the ground, he went out, left leg first, pulling the other after, peering around the corner of the dormer for her and pulling his head back in case the razor swung.

She was most of the way up the roof, heading for the peak. She was sitting, boosting herself upon her buttocks, keeping her feet and hands on the slates. She, too, was afraid of the height, he thought. When she saw him, she began to move faster. Above her and at the edge of the roof to her right was a chimney; she seemed to be making for it. Maybe there was a way down there; he didn't think so, rather that she was going for the chimney because it was solid and seemed to offer support. If she could get down the other side of the roof, however, she could probably drop to the front garden; the house was higher at the back than the front because of the drop to the river.

'You can't make it!' he shouted.

She moved herself up again. He saw the razor flash in her hand.

'Give it up!'

He started up the roof. He went on his fingertips and the balls of his feet, the light rubber shoes he wore for rowing a help. She screamed, screamed again. He was aware of voices below them and understood how it must look to anybody who could see them—a half-naked man chasing a woman.

'Come down from there, you monster!' a woman's voice shouted, the sound thinned by distance.

Mary Thomason screamed again. She had almost reached the chimney. And then what?

Denton pushed himself harder. He forgot the bad leg. He looked at nothing but the woman in the white dress. Straightening, he went up on the diagonal faster than she was moving, and when she reached the chimney, he was only three yards behind. He put his right foot over the peak of the roof and balanced there, a foot on each side. She looked down towards the ground at the front of the house. Several people were down there, foreshortened, shouting.

'Leave that poor girl alone! The police are coming!' One of them blew a police whistle.

She scrambled upright, using the chimney to support her. With her back to it and the razor at her side where they couldn't see it from below, she faced him. Denton moved closer. He raised his arm over his head because of the bleeding.

'Give it up. It's over.'

She was very like the drawing. Not quite pretty, but arresting. The breeze stirred her hair. He said, 'Give it up. You think you're a nasty piece of work, but I'm nastier. I'll kill you if I have to.'

They were fixed on each other as if they were the only people in the world. They were, in that shared concentration, like lovers. The Thames, the day, the glory of the summer, didn't exist. He looked at her and she looked at him, and for a moment he saw her face soften and he felt for her something that was beyond sympathy, almost an identification, a sharing of self, as if in the instant of violence that was coming they were the same. He held out the bloody left arm with the hand open. 'Give it to me. It's over.'

Then her face changed to the demonic one he had glimpsed through the door, and she swung the razor at him. He flung up his arm and caught it on the part that was wrapped in the shirt. It slashed down; he felt its bite again and grabbed her wrist. He raised it high, as if they were doing some country dance, drawing her off the chimney, and she tried to pull away. His other hand was balled into a fist, and he hesitated an instant because she was a woman, because her female face was so near his own. Then the razor's blade cut into his palm as his slippery hand lost its grip and she turned in the air in front of him, one foot on a slate and one foot in the air, and then she was gone and he heard the thud of her body on the flagstones beside the house.

And then he felt his own vertigo, and he collapsed against the chimney, hugging it as if he had been thrown against it by a wave.

'Man or woman?'

'Man.' Munro grinned. 'Relieved?' He set down a mug of tea for Denton.

'I was about ninety-eight parts in a hundred sure. But I thought—If she was a woman—'

'Well, he wasn't. How's that arm?'

'Hurts like hell. Nice lot of stitches.'

'You lost a good lot of blood. Feeling queasy?'

'I've been told to take Extract of Meat and Malt Wine. I think I'll stay with Mrs Cohan's soup. The tea's a godsend for now.' They were in a borrowed office in Brentford Infirmary. The local constabulary had first arrested Denton and brought him there in handcuffs to be sewn up. It had taken three hours to sort out what had happened, the actual sorting-out being done only when New Scotland Yard had been brought in. More time had passed while somebody figured out that what had happened at Strand-on-the-Green was part of a case Munro was already working on.

Munro put his hands in his trouser pockets and stared out of the window. 'He's dead. I'm sorry about that—I'd like to see the bastard in the dock.' He looked at Denton. 'I've got a dozen witnesses that will swear they saw you push a woman off that roof.'

'I'm sure. But I didn't.'

'I've read your statement. Funny, what people see.'

'How's Brown?'

'Head's too broken for us to take a statement. Concussion. Maybe by tomorrow. You didn't have to try to kill him, too, you know.'

'I didn't want him behind me while I went after the woman.'

'His nose was mashed flat against his face, he has two broken ribs, and he fractured a finger, apparently trying to protect himself from the poker. Can't you ever go easy on them?'

'I told you, I didn't want him behind me.'

Munro stared out of the window, then shook his head. '*Did* you push the woman? The man?'

'I lost my grip on her wrist. She was off balance.'

'I wouldn't blame you if you had. He was an ugly piece of work. Cutting the head off Himple, killing Heseltine—the painting that came from Heseltine's flat pretty well cinches that one. You're always right.'

'Like hell.'

Munro grinned at him, then became serious again. 'You think he was insane?'

'Anybody who commits murder is insane, isn't he?'

'I meant, playing at being a woman.'

Denton said nothing, then, 'She was sane. Maybe he wasn't.'

'They were the same person, Denton!'

Denton shrugged again. He felt light-headed, detached.

Munro said, 'We're digging up Brown's garden to look for Himple's head.'

'Yes, you should do that. Although I don't think you'll find it.'

Munro grunted. 'No. I suppose it's somewhere like the middle of the Channel.'

'Or in an abandoned privy in Paris.'

'She wasn't here until last week—we've asked the neighbours. Why the hell do you think she came back *here*?'

'They wanted to be together, I suppose.'

Munro gave a snort of contempt. 'Queer sort of being together—murdering folk. You think it was always the two of them?'

'I didn't until I saw her in the garden. Yes, I think it was always the two of them—before anything else. Maybe Crum met Himple first at the Baths, but then when he met Brown—funny, how people pair off.' He gave a grim smile. 'There's a novel in that.' He moved the arm painfully to another position, then sipped the tea. 'Think you'll ever know who Arthur Crum really was?'

'Mr Nobody from Nowhere. Some little chap who thought he'd found himself a clever way off the factory floor.'

'And it got away from him?'

Munro shrugged. He sighed and opened the door. 'Well, you can go. Although I think I'm letting the most dangerous man in London walk.' Denton got up and strode to the door. Munro said, 'Speaking of walk—'

'What?'

'*Look* at you.'

Denton looked where Munro was pointing, at his right leg. He wasn't limping. He didn't have a stick.

'Where's the bad leg, then?'

'I guess she took it over the roof with her.'

Janet Striker was waiting for him at the infirmary gate. She hurried him into a waiting cab and made him lie back into a nest of pillows she'd put there. 'Don't ever let anybody tell you that money isn't important,' she said. 'I bought these for you to lie on and they're going in the dustbin as soon as we get you home. But worth every penny!'

'I'm not an invalid.'

'You bled like a pig, I was told. You should be feeling weak and ill.'

'I'm not a pig.'

'No, you're a man, and a fairly good specimen of one.' She kissed him. 'Tell me everything, including how you got your leg back.'

As they rode, he went through it all. 'Finally,' he said when he had told her everything, 'I felt sorry for her. Not sorry, perhaps, but—sorrow.'

'And then you could walk.'

'It was going up the roof. I had to and I did. I've been letting it rule me, giving in to it. Being an invalid meant I'd never have to risk killing her.'

'Is that what it was about—not killing her?'

'Being afraid to kill her? No, more like being afraid I'd get to the moment and find I *wanted* to kill her.'

'Because I told you all men hate women.'

He was silent.

'And you found you didn't.' Janet held his good hand. 'Does it make a difference that he wasn't a woman?'

'She was a woman when she went off that roof. I know in my soul I didn't want her to go off, and I'm satisfied.'

They were silent for a long way, and then they talked of trivial things like the cancelled coronation. He said, 'Atkins, at least, is delighted. The pneumatic truss wasn't ready, and now they've got at least a couple of months to get it right.' Just before they reached his house, he said, 'You had it figured. I wouldn't accept that the woman and the brother were the same.'

'Well, the evidence was thin.'

He remembered the dreams. 'It was the rags. I couldn't—'

She put a finger on his lips. 'It doesn't matter. You did what you set out to do—you found the woman who asked for your help.'

'And found that I was the one who was going to hurt her.' He shook his head. 'She didn't really ask for my help at all, but— I wonder if she was thinking about her letter when we were up on that roof.'

She came behind him up the stairs as if she might need to push, but he made it well enough, light-headed, weak. Atkins appeared with a bottle of the Army and Navy Stores' Extract of Meat and Malt Wine. That, and more tea, and a chop from the Lamb, gave Denton the illusion of feeling normal. A false euphoria came over him; he didn't recognize it as the giddiness of blood loss. As they ate, he talked about the future, an idea for a new book that had leapt into his head while he was on the roof, some sort of travel they could do together. He was opening his mail at the same time, over-excited, hands trembling. He hooted.

'Jarrold's sainted ma has instructed her lawyers to offer me seven thousand pounds and medical expenses!' He cackled happily. 'Sergeant!' When an answer came up the dumb-waiter shaft, he shouted, 'We're getting electric in the house! And heat! And a proper modern ice-box!' He turned back to Janet Striker. 'I'm going to buy a motor car. Where would you like to go?'

'University College.'

'Ah, I'd hoped Constantinople by way of Athens.'

She laughed, shook her head.

He shouted, 'Sergeant! Want to motor to—?'

'No,' came the hollow answer, 'and neither does Rupert.'

343

He put the letter down. He looked at her. 'Well, I'll pretend that your house is Constantinople. Your bed, most certainly.'

'Some of the time, anyway.'

'There'll always be the door in the garden wall, you mean.'

'But with a lock.'

'And you'll have the key.'

'I'll have the key.'

'Oh—well—' He leaned back, then suddenly sat up and said, 'Dammit! I left my boat tied up by the river!' He jumped up too quickly, felt the room start to go black and collapsed back into his cushions. He grinned at her foolishly. 'Maybe I'll leave that for tomorrow.'

ABOUT THE AUTHOR

Kenneth Cameron is the author of one previous novel featuring Denton, *The Frightened Man,* as well as of plays staged in Britain and the US, and the award-winning *Africa on Film: Beyond Black and White.* He lives part of the year in northern New York State and part in the southern US.

Praise for Elle Spencer

Waiting for You

"I laughed, I cried, I fanned my face (hot, sexy ... ...ncer is becoming one of my favorite writers!"—*... ...arian, Ponca City Library (Oklahoma)*

"This book is so much fun to read. The di ... funny... This is definitely recommended: lovely la... ...chemistry, great supporting cast and high fun factor in the wri... *·Best Lesfic Reviews*

"I do have to give it to Spencer: she is really, really good at writing chemistry between romantic leads...This is a book that has just about everything, comedy, feelings, sexy scenes, a great supporting cast and past lives. Fans of rom coms or dramadies will love this."—*Colleen Corgel, Librarian, Queens Public Library*

"I've come to count on Spencer to take me away from whatever drama is going on in the world to a place where sharp, attractive women will entertain me with their wit and warmth."—*Lesbian Review*

"I love the books Elle Spencer writes. Ever since her first novel, *Casting Lacey*, I have gravitated to everything she has written. BIG FAN! Spencer does a great job with this book, the story reels you in and holds you captive chapter after chapter."—*Romantic Reader Blog*

30 Dates in 30 Days

"As usual with Spencer, the characters are wonderfully layered and flawed, [and] the chemistry is out of this world."—*Jude in the Stars*

"Spencer imbues the story with some great humour and witty banter that brings the characters to life, and the romance works wonderfully. I really enjoyed this one—it hit all the right notes for me and left me with a bit of an aw, shucks smile on my face when I finished."—*C-Spot Reviews*

"Ms. Spencer knows how to build the tension so thick that you could cut it with a proverbial knife. The intimate scenes are really hot... Overall, a clever, funny and light romance with great chemistry and a superb cast."—*LezReviewBooks*

By the Author

Casting Lacey

Unforgettable

The Road to Madison

30 Dates in 30 Days

Waiting for You

The Holiday Treatment

Hot Ice
(with Aurora Rey and Erin Zak)

THE HOLIDAY TREATMENT

by

Elle Spencer

2020

THE HOLIDAY TREATMENT

ISBN 13: 978-1-63555-660-5

This Trade Paperback Original Is Published By
Bold Strokes Books, Inc.
P.O. Box 249
Valley Falls, NY 12185

First Edition: November 2020

CREDITS
Editor: Barbara Ann Wright
Production Design: Stacia Seaman
Cover Design by Tammy Seidick

Acknowledgments

As always, a huge thanks to Rad, Sandy, and the entire Bold Strokes team for all they do. I consider myself extremely lucky to be a part of the BSB family.

To my editor, Barbara Ann Wright, thank you for always laughing along with me and for (so far) never telling me I need more emotion on the page.

Thanks to all my publishing friends who inspire and encourage me. You have my respect and admiration.

To my team—FJ, Poppy, Bear, Edward, and Peanut, keep up the good work. Your bonuses are in the mail.

Paula, I'm grateful every day that you're my AMAZEBALLS bff. I wouldn't want to do this writing thing or life without your love, support, guidance, and awesome sense of humor.

To my wife, Nikki, who happens to love cheesy holiday romance movies, you are my reason for everything. You and me, baby. Forever.

And to the readers, thank you from the bottom of my heart for continuing to come on these adventures with me. Hope you enjoy this one.

For Nikki

CHAPTER ONE

With all of the Christmas props and decorations the Wifetime Channel had in storage, Holly thought the yearly office party would be more festive. It wasn't much more than a few tables with deli trays from Gelson's or some other fancy LA grocery store. The makeshift bar featured a few random bottles on the desk in an unused cubicle. Holly glanced at it and rolled her eyes. This party featured the world's most overpriced turkey platter, but the wine still came from Trader Joe's.

Most people wore jeans and sweaters and not even ugly Christmas sweaters. Sure, a few people were dressed up. Only because, like her, they had plans after. It wasn't that Wifetime couldn't afford to do better. It wasn't that no one wanted to be there. These people lived and breathed Christmas year-round. The last thing most of them wanted to do was fight the never-ending Westwood traffic on the Saturday night before Christmas just to swap crappy gifts in the stupid Secret Santa thing.

Holly wandered away from the sad little bar and stopped at the winter wonderland of Lucille's cubicle. Obviously, Lucille was a rare exception to the staff's anti-holiday spirit. She was the mildly bossy office manager who'd been at the network since it was founded. Or as the network president was fond of saying, "She saw Louis B. Mayer come up in the business." Whenever he made some version of the joke, he'd give Lucille or some other innocent bystander an obnoxious slap on the back. Lucille would give a look of mild disapproval, which was to say Lucille would give a look that was pretty much the same look she had all the time, the holidays being the one exception. Holly tried to stay on her good side because something about the way Lucille would look over her reading glasses at her when she was displeased made Holly feel like she was a disappointment to her own grandmother.

Christmas was Lucille's time to shine. She made up for the lack of everyone else's enthusiasm by decorating every available square inch of her cubicle in all things Christmas.

Promo postcards from some of the bigger Wifetime Christmas movies decorated the outside of her cubicle. They included fan favorites like the fantasy adventure *Sleighing the Dragon* and *Christmas & Coco*, which could have been about high fashion but was actually about two dogs conspiring to bring their owners together. And then of course, there was *The Wedding Claus*. That was the one where, due to arcane corporate bylaws, Nick Claus Jr. wasn't allowed to take over the family business until he found a wife. Because that seemed perfectly healthy and normal.

Holly was sad to see that her personal favorite was not represented. *Ho Ho Hope* was about a woman who'd lost the spirit of Christmas only to find it again with the help of a handsome stranger whose car had broken down. Due to some kind of holiday miracle, the network's standards and practices department had failed to anticipate that including a woman's name and "ho" in the title would provide years of internet jokes.

The real action happened inside the cubicle. Lucille had

fastened tiny garlands and little twinkling lights to the framed photos of her grandkids. Every greeting card she'd received sat proudly on the top shelf with a collection of miniature snow globes. Holly looked a little closer and noticed that all of Lucille's pencils had Christmas themed erasers. Little trees and wreaths and elves sat atop every pencil.

"The attention to detail," Holly whispered to herself.

There was an Elf on the Shelf, of course. Or two. Or three. With a quick scan of the cubicle, Holly counted five little elves, one of which dangled by the leg from a desk drawer. Holly was sure that had been an oversight and that Lucille wasn't one of those people who enjoyed posing their elves in precarious or pornographic positions. She wasn't that macabre. Not when elves were involved. She also lacked the immature sense of humor required to think that two elves 69ing would be funny. Holly laughed under her breath when she thought about poor Lucille's reaction if she walked into her cubicle only to discover that all of her elves were getting it on.

"Hudson, where's your Christmas spirit?"

Holly turned and threw a hand over her eyes. While Lucille genuinely embraced the holidays, her boss, Brian, did so with an in-your-face sense of irony. "My God, Bri, do you really need an outfit that turns on?" He'd taken a strand of big, multicolored bulbs and wrapped it around his neck several times like a winter scarf. They blinked at her aggressively, or at least that was how Holly felt. What the hell was powering those things? She was curious but not enough to ask.

Brian handed her a cup of eggnog. "Made this just for you. I call it office party in a cup. Now, get out there and mingle. The higher-ups want to congratulate you with a firm handshake and possibly a new contract."

Holly pulled her sunglasses out of her purse and put them on. "Seriously. You could direct traffic with those lights."

With a roll of his eyes, he reached behind his back and turned off whatever was powering the lights. "How can someone who writes the most magical Christmas scripts be such a scrooge?"

"I am not a scrooge. Just because I don't feel the need to dress like Santa threw up on me—"

"Ouch." He tapped his chest. "That gets me right here, Hudson. And everyone knows you hate the holidays. Please, Ebenezer's more likely to plant one on the Grinch under the camel toe than you are to find the holiday spirit."

She laughed. "Pretty sure you mean the mistletoe."

"See? Look at you throwing Christmas lingo around. I bet you feel better already."

"Uh-huh. And here I thought I'd hidden my disdain for all things Christmas." She sniffed the drink. He had definitely spiked it. A lot.

"Well, you haven't. Seriously, though, you need to up your game for the next hour. I've kept your secret, but these guys expect their celebrated writer to have a bit of spirit. This humbug horseshit won't fly."

Holly adjusted her sunglasses and folded her arms. "What if I kept the shades on?"

"Then you'll just seem weird. Spirit, Hudson." He pointed to his light-up choker. "Don't make me turn up these lights."

"Fine." She tucked the sunglasses back in her purse. "Did you tell them I'll only write another script if it's a gay Christmas movie?" She took a sip of the eggnog and almost choked on it. "Damn, Brian. Are you trying to get me so drunk I'll sign anything?"

He took the drink and set it on Lucille's desk. "You gotta let go of this gay Christmas stuff, Holls. It ain't gonna happen. Not on this network. Or have you forgotten who you work for? *Wifetime* ring a bell? An audience of straight women who send their kids to school and pine for their favorite soaps? Wives, Holls. Wives. The kind with husbands."

She knew who her audience was. Or at least who the higher-ups thought her audience was. With all the money and time they spent on market research and dissecting the ratings, she thought they'd realize their audience went a little beyond some straight lady in the suburbs named Heather.

Obviously, they also had any number of viewers named Jennifer as well.

Okay, so it was true that the network catered to a certain demographic. She also knew that plenty of people who didn't fit into Wifetime's idea of a target audience loved holiday romances. And that included most of Holly's friends. The subject of a gay Christmas movie came up every year, usually starting around October. It wasn't rocket science. People wanted to see love stories that resembled their lives. If their lives involved hotshot lawyers whose cars broke down in small towns just days before the big Christmas pageant. And until then, they'd keep watching what was offered.

Holly wondered if maybe that was part of the problem. "It's shortsighted," she said. "And the network name is so ridiculous, I can hardly say it out loud."

He took a piece of silver tinsel off Lucille's mini tree and threw it at her. It wafted through the air and landed on her shoulder. He took several more pieces and tossed them her way. "Now we're getting somewhere."

She lowered her voice to a loud whisper. "What the hell are you doing? That's Lucille's special tree. We'll both end up like that elf hanging from her drawer."

"Just work with me, Holls. You'll thank me later." He had already grabbed Lucille's tape dispenser and wrapped a piece of tape around the string of an ornament. He pressed it onto Holly's sweater. He did the same with a few more ornaments, randomly placing one on her shoulder and another on her arm. His level of concentration made her want to laugh out loud, but she stayed still while he added a few more, then scrutinized his work. One ornament had to be moved slightly higher. A bit more tinsel seemed necessary. This time, it was strategically placed, not just thrown in her general direction.

"Oh. This one," he said.

"That ornament has a hook. You are not...oh my God, you just hooked me." He had hooked the ornament onto her sweater where a name badge would go, and before he could utter the word he famously overused, Holly put her hand over his mouth. "Don't say *voilà*. You did not just create a masterpiece."

He clutched his chest. "You're breaking my candy cane heart. Just one voilà?"

It was his thing to cap off everything he did with that one word. He'd probably said it after he'd dumped five shots of rum into her drink earlier. Seeing as it was the season of giving, she shrugged and motioned for him to go on. "If you must."

"*Voilà.*" He leaned in and kissed her cheek. "Now, behave out there. You don't want to be a story editor forever, do you?"

"Hey. Don't take away the job that actually has benefits. I'll keep writing at night. That's when I have my best ideas anyway."

"Well, as long as we get the very best of your mediocrity all day, what more can a guy ask for?" He gave her a grin. "I gotta go mingle. Find me later and let me know how it goes."

She squinted as he walked away. "Yeah, I'm sure I'll have no trouble finding the guy who thought dressing up as Clark Griswold's front porch was a good idea."

"Good one," he shouted over his shoulder. "Sign on for another *Evermore*, Holls. And don't bring up the gay thing."

With a heavy sigh, she picked up her drink and took a sip. It was pretty much straight rum with a dash of eggnog, but she held on to it. She'd probably need it later.

She had written five holiday scripts for the Wifetime Channel, a series based on the fictional world of Evermore, Vermont. Series weren't the norm for the Christmas division, but they'd made an exception due to the popularity of the first movie. That meant there were some recurring roles for some of the actors, including the man who had become her best friend at the network, Griffin Taylor.

The *Evermore* series followed the love lives of the city's mayor and his five sons. This year, it was Griffin's turn to be the main love interest, and he'd pretty much killed it. Holly made a mental note to bring him back something cool from Hawaii.

She'd fulfilled her five-script contract and had promised herself she wouldn't sign a contract to write anything else unless it included a gay character. And not as a wacky sidekick. A *main* character. And for romance, that only meant one thing. Two women or two men would kiss under the mistletoe and then fade to black.

Griffin grabbed her from behind as she walked into the office party. She knew it was him from the sweet smell. Because who else would have drowned themselves in sugar cookie body spray?

"My God, woman," he whispered. "Have you no shame? Lucille's sick grandson made that gingerbread man hanging from your left nipple."

"Wha…" She scanned her chest for a gingerbread man but found none. She spun around and poked him in the chest. "You asshole. I about had a heart attack."

"Gotcha," he said with a laugh, then gestured up and down her body. "You get an F for effort."

"Give Brian the F. He's the one who decorated me."

He took the cup from her and gave it a whiff. "Yep. Brian made this too." He downed it in two gulps and shivered. "God, that's awful."

She gave him the once-over. "Griff, what the hell are you wearing?"

"I think it's a toy soldier outfit, but I'm going for a princely look. Or a young king." He straightened his shoulders. "I hear there's a new Prince of Rolexia being written, and I want the lead."

"Rolexia? Are you being serious with that name?"

"If I get the part…"

"You'll buy that Rolex you've been eyeing. Got it." She tilted her head. "Maybe that could be my gay movie. Two princes from competing lands fall madly in love on Christmas Eve."

He gasped. "I thought you wanted to write a lesbian script, but I'm so in. Will you make his love interest the Prince of LandRovia? I really want one of those too."

She leaned in and whispered, "Big boss at two o'clock. I'd tell you to put your gay away, but I think that's impossible given what you're wearing."

"Funny. Good thing I drank that awful concoction for you, or you'd be downright hilarious right now." He gave her a wink and caught the attention of his costar, Trudy Banks. "See you at the real party later. I expect you to give me the first waltz because that's what princes do. They waltz."

"Yeah, okay. I'll run right down to the mercantile and get me a dance card. Maybe they'll sell me a coy attitude too. And bloomers. And uncomfortable shoes."

Griffin glanced at her leather boots. "Now, that would be a step up. Beauty before comfort, Miss Hudson. And now, I must mingle with my fellow Rolexians."

Holly lifted her foot. The boots were cute, but she had to admit, the heel was decidedly low by LA standards. "Hey, these are classics. All the best lesbians wear them." He had moved on. She shrugged and scanned the room for the man who would no doubt reject her gay Christmas movie proposal for the umpteenth time. She found him standing awfully close to his latest assistant, but that was no surprise. Holly picked up her pace when she realized Lucille was headed her way. She knew she'd get an earful later, but for now, Lucille would never be so rude as to interrupt a conversation with the head of programming to accuse Holly of theft or cubicle vandalism or just generally ruining Christmas.

"Mr. Cruz." Holly offered her hand. "Sorry to interrupt. I just wanted to say hi."

His assistant whispered something in his ear and walked away. His eyes stayed locked on her ass. "Holly. Good to see you again." When he finally decided to tear his eyes away, he furrowed his brow at the festive shitstorm Brian had taped to her purple sweater. And no, she hadn't even bothered to wear red or green. He cleared his throat. "Anyway, let's firm up another contract before you go to…Hawaii, is it?"

How the hell did he know where she was going for Christmas? And then she remembered that everyone knew she went to the same place every year. A blush crept up her chest as she wondered if absolutely everyone also knew that she went there alone. Yep, Holly Hudson, successful writer of Christmas romances, spent the holiday as far away from snow and mistletoe as she possibly could. Oh, and she couldn't forget the *alone* part.

"Yes," she said. "Hawaii."

Mr. Cruz stopped scanning the room over Holly's head and took a sip of his drink. "It's weird."

"What's weird?"

"You, going to Hawaii alone."

Okay. Apparently, everyone did know about that detail. Where was Brian's eggnog when she needed it? "I just like to get away for the holidays. That's all."

"Well, like I said, it's weird. No one does that unless they're a diehard surfer. Are you a diehard surfer?" He didn't wait for an answer. "I don't think so."

What. An. Asshole. "Maybe I go there to pick up chicks, just like the diehard surfer dudes do."

"Ha. Good one, Holly Hobby. You just made me laugh on the inside."

Theodore Cruz, Senior VP of Programming and all-around arrogant jerk, knew perfectly well that Holly was gay. Despite the network's insistence that no gay people on Earth watched TV movies, Holly wasn't in the closet. Far from it. But Cruz was the kind of guy who remained convinced that all women were interested in him.

She took a deep breath and said, "Mr. Cruz, before we talk contracts, I was wondering if you'd given any more thought to letting me write a gay Christmas movie."

He guffawed but she kept her eyes on him. He did a double take at her and probably realized she wouldn't let this go until he gave her an answer. "You're like a dog with a bone, but as I've said before, our audience isn't ready."

"I think our audience deserves a little more credit than that," she said. "The vast majority of Americans are in favor of gay marriage. Love is love. And people who watch romances know it." He abruptly turned and went to the buffet table. She followed. "Mr. Cruz, I really think I could write a gay storyline that the whole world would love, including our core audience."

"What are you going to do? Make the mayor of Evermore's youngest son gay?"

She hadn't thought of that. It wasn't a terrible idea, but she was hoping to do a stand-alone movie. "That wasn't what I had in mind, but—"

"You need to finish the *Evermore* series. Have young whatever-his-name-is come back from college excited about his future. That is, until his father, the mayor, tells him he's responsible for keeping the family legacy-slash-business going."

"But I really think—"

He put up a finger. "Don't interrupt me, I'm on a roll." He tapped that same finger against the rather deep dent in his chin. "Youngest son is disappointed, of course. He had big plans for his life outside of Evermore. He's angry at his older brothers for shirking their responsibility." He sighed. "And then he meets the new girl in town. Her name is Cherry Stone."

"Cherry?" Was he kidding with this shit? His earnest stare told her he was dead serious.

"Ha. I'm brilliant. And I just saved you a lot of work." He stuffed a miniature quiche in his mouth and chewed with a grin so big, he barely kept the food from falling out. Once he had sufficiently chewed, swallowed, and downed an entire cup of Christmas punch, he added, "Is it hard knowing that virtually anyone could do your job?"

She held back her anger. Blowing up at Mr. Cruz in front of everyone she worked with wouldn't serve her well in the long run. In the short run, she'd probably be their hero, right up until she was let go due to budget cuts. That didn't mean she couldn't tactfully counter the statement. "So can I have a gay storyline if I write it into *Evermore*?"

"Did I say that? I didn't say that. *Cherry* Stone, not Harry Stone." He laughed at his stupid joke as he stuffed another pastry into his mouth. "Our audience wants clean entertainment."

"Being gay isn't dirty," she said.

"To some people, it is." He grabbed another pastry and put it in her hand. "Have one of these. They're delicious. And sign a contract before you leave town. For *Evermore*. The youngest *straight* son. Got it?"

She gave him a barely noticeable nod. When he turned his back, she opened her fingers and let the pastry drop into the trash bin. Mr. Clean Programming would come on to his assistant in his office before the night was over. She was sure of it.

Griffin came back out of nowhere with wide eyes and a thumb pointing behind him. He mouthed the words, "Your crush is here."

She peered over his shoulder and ducked back down. "Shit. Don't move. She can't see me like this."

"Oh, you mean because of all the tinsel caught up in your hair? I wholeheartedly agree, but does she even know you exist?"

"We met briefly. I spilled my coffee. It wasn't pretty." Holly smoothed her hair. A few strands of tinsel fell to the floor. Leave it to Griffin to exaggerate the situation again.

"She looks amazing," he said. "Are you sure she's gay?"

"What's that supposed to mean? Gay women can't be beautiful?"

"No, what I meant was..." He glanced back. "I know your soft little heart, babe. It would break in two if you asked her out and she got offended or something."

"Are you speaking from experience, Griff? That fancy exec with the slicked-back hair break your soft little heart?"

He rolled his eyes and turned back. "You don't have to get all nasty about it, but yes, I've been where you are. My God, just look at her. Is that Chanel she's wearing?"

Holly put her hands on his shoulders and raised her head

barely enough to get another look. "If you're trying to tell me that Meredith Drake is out of my league, I already know that, but thanks for the vote of confidence."

She stilled and swallowed hard. Word around the water cooler was that the new development executive was indeed gay. And tall and gorgeous. Dark, short hair swept perfectly across her forehead. With a smile that could blow someone's bra off. *Socks, Holls. Not bra.* She bit her bottom lip and let out a tiny squeak.

He turned slightly and whispered, "Did you just squeak?"

"She's too gorgeous for words. And she digs women. If you were me, you'd squeak too."

"She's like a brunette version of Claire Underwood. Let's hope she's not as evil."

"Evil or not, I'd call her Madame President all day long."

Griffin turned back around so they were face-to-face. "I've never seen you drool over a woman quite like this. How deep in are you?"

"What do you mean?"

"Holls, it's fine to have a crush," he said. "I have a new one at least twice a week. But you're Skipper, and she's Barbie. They don't hook up."

"That's because Skipper was Barbie's sister, you freak. And maybe Barbie didn't hook up with Midge in your Barbie condo, but she did in mine. Countless times. And unlike you, I got rid of my Barbie condo before high school."

He sighed. "Haters gonna hate, but I know you're just jealous I still have mine."

"Well, now that you mention it, you've never once invited me over to play with it."

"Because it's a collector's item."

She got up on her tiptoes again. "Cruz is headed her way. Oh my God, he's bound to make an ass of himself." She cupped her hands around her mouth and whispered, "She's gay, Cruz. Nothing for you there. Just walk away."

Griffin glanced over his shoulder. "You know what? I'm an asshole. Ignore everything I just said and go over there and offer her a glass of punch. This is your chance. Remember in that movie you made me watch where the bride and the photographer have a moment by the punchbowl?"

She hid her face behind him. "I can't."

"Why not?"

"Because for all of my big talk, I don't want to risk things getting messy at work. And besides, I left my Chanel suit at home."

Another voice called, "Holly?"

She turned and found Lucille bearing down on her. "Oh. Lucille."

"You have my husband on your chest."

Holly could've killed Griffin for not telling her. She gently pulled the tiny framed photo of Mr. Lucille from her sweater and with a sheepish grin, placed it in Lucille's hand. "Sorry about that. I wish you both a very happy holiday." She turned back to Griffin and said, "See you at the neighbors' party later?"

He reached for her hand. "I'm sorry."

She backed away. "It's fine. You were right. I'll see you later." And with that, she bolted from the room before Griffin or anyone else could stop her.

Chapter Two

The yearly Neighbors' Christmas Party was already in full swing by the time Holly got home. Holidays or not, this was one party she wouldn't miss. With two bottles of wine and a hostess gift tucked under her arm, she walked across the courtyard of her small apartment complex.

Built in the 1930s, what the Spanish-style building lacked in amenities, it usually made up for in charm. Sure, Holly would have liked to be able to blow-dry her hair without knocking the power out, but she really couldn't complain. Who didn't love arched walkways and subway tile?

She considered herself lucky to find the place when she'd first moved to LA fifteen years ago. For weeks, she'd looked at tiny apartments that were way outside her price range. When she found anything remotely clean and at least semi-free of odor, she had to compete against a dozen other applicants who were also vying for the chance to live in such luxury. Then she heard that a friend of a friend of a friend was giving up his acting dreams in LA to pursue his tech startup dreams in San Francisco. And the rest was history.

Of course, paying for it back then was another matter entirely. It was at the tippy-top end of her budget. The only reason it worked out at all was because it had no parking and sat next to a fast-food chain, making the ever-present smell of fried chicken one of the building's hallmarks. It was situated in an otherwise residential part of the La Brea neighborhood, just a few blocks from non-fried chicken restaurants and stores. Home was about six miles from work, but she'd quickly learned Angelinos didn't speak in distance; they spoke in time. So home was about an hour from work. Except on Thursdays. Or when it rained. Or if there was a protest at the federal building. Holly had briefly considered taking up cycling.

She loved the building and the people so much that when the owner of her unit had decided to sell, she'd jumped at the chance to buy it. In the eight years she'd owned it, she'd made a few renovations, like pulling up the old carpet that someone had installed over beautiful Mexican tiles. But for the most part, she'd wanted to keep the old charm of the place.

She climbed the stairs to the second floor. It was Desiree's turn to host, which meant a few things would happen. For one, old Christmas albums would play on a vintage turntable all night. Most of them were compilation albums that were sold in Goodyear tire stores back in the 60s and 70s. *The Great Songs of Christmas*, sung by legends like Bing Crosby, Steve Lawrence and Eydie Gormé.

Holly paused at the top of the steps and listened to the muffled sounds coming from behind Desiree's door. "Dinah Shore," she exclaimed. One of her mom's favorites. Well, Christmas music, period, was her mom's favorite.

"Twenty bucks says it's Doris Day. What's on your ass?"

Holly turned and found her neighbor, Ty, waiting a few steps down where he was at eye level with her crotch. "Don't be a creeper, Ty. God. And you'll lose that bet."

"I can't really go anywhere, Holls. You're in the way."

He wasn't a creeper at all. Quite the opposite. A shy guy with a kind heart. And the only reason she knew that was because she'd taken the time to get to know him. Well, that and because she was a lesbian. Poor Ty had zero game when it came to the ladies. He kept his sweet face covered in a full, reddish-brown beard and was rarely seen without a baseball cap, beanie, or one of a seemingly endless assortment of dorky vintage hats. Except for tonight.

"Your hair," she said with a tilt of her head.

"What about it?"

"I can see it."

He rolled his eyes. "I went to the barber. Please don't make a big deal of it."

He sure had. His curly, unkempt hair was a lot shorter. And styled, no less. "Ty, your hair is gorgeous. Why do you hide it under a cap all the time? I figured you had some sort of weird bald spot and were making up for it with the beard."

"My eyes are sensitive to the sun."

"Oh." She wasn't sure if he was being serious or not. "Wait. I call bullshit."

He shrugged. "Fine. I'm a hat guy. I like hats. But I can't wear them when I go home for Christmas, or that's all my mom will talk about, how if I'd just stop wearing hats and Hawaiian shirts and socks with pinup girls on them, I'd find a nice girl, blah, blah, blah."

If her hands weren't full, Holly would've gestured wildly or grabbed his shoulders and said *listen to your mother*. "There are so many things I could say right now, but I can't talk without my hands. It's a thing."

His eyes widened as if this was some big revelation. "I wish that worked with my mom, but she could turn a request to clean my room into a twenty-minute-long speech while holding two laundry baskets full of dirty clothes for effect."

"A laundry basket full of Hawaiian shirts and socks with pinup girls on them?"

"No. That didn't start until college. Really, though, what's on your ass?"

"It's an ornament. A stupid work thing." She turned back around to find their neighbor Gwen had joined Ty on the ass-level stair below hers. "Okay. Everyone can stop looking at my ass now. Eyes up here, people." She made a weird gesture with her entire body, as if she were pointing at her own eyes with it. "You too, Gwen," she added when she saw her neighbor staring at her chest.

Gwen stood there with her mouth hanging open. "Is this some sort of anti-Christmas protest you have going on?"

Holly thought she'd removed all of the ornaments before she left work. Apparently, she'd missed a few and would have to apologize profusely to Lucille when she went back to work in January.

"I could just pull that off for you," Ty said. "But you have to consent to letting me—"

"Don't you dare touch my ass, Tyler Jones." How one of Lucille's ornaments had managed a long migration south for the winter, Holly wasn't sure, but once her hands were free, she'd take care of it herself, thank you very much. "Okay, guys, just listen."

She was just about to explain how her boss Brian was an idiot when ornaments were involved, and oh by the way, it was swell working at Homophobivision when she noticed Gwen's enhanced cleavage. How had she missed the entire drama of boob surgery? Gwen had been talking about it for months, but to make such a big decision without informing the neighbors so they could bring her soup and doughnuts didn't make any sense. Or maybe Holly was the only one who hadn't been told? She would try to hide her hurt feelings if that was the case.

"Gwen, your..." Again, she needed her hands. She

gestured with her chin. "They look great. Don't they look great, Ty?"

He put up his hands. "Hey, you said eyes up here, so my eyes are up here."

Gwen flashed a camera-ready smile and let out her trademark Louisiana drawl. "Then how d'ya know what she's talkin' about, darlin'?" She was an actress by trade, and she'd reached that stage in life where she was being cast as the mother of the love interest, not the love interest herself. Her confidence had waned, and she was looking for every way possible to get back to her glory days when she was the prettiest woman in the room. If only she knew how beautiful she still was.

It was the plight of a woman to be too hard on herself when it came to her looks. Gwen was a gorgeous forty-nine-year old woman with a luscious pinup girl figure that she would never be able to appreciate until it was gone. Okay, so maybe Holly had formed a slight crush on her neighbor when she'd first moved into the complex. There was a fifteen-year age gap, but Holly had never been concerned with age. If she found a woman attractive, why should age matter? In reality, though, Gwen was just a good friend and the first one Holly had made when she'd arrived in LA. It had taken her a few weeks to get over being enamored of the whole starlet thing. They'd quickly discovered an easy friendship. Gwen had introduced Holly to LA, or more specifically, the business side of LA. She'd even introduced Holly to her first boss, which eventually led to her job at Wifetime.

As for Holly, she played the part of supportive friend. She was the perfect antidote to the constant critiques Gwen experienced. For every jerk who told Gwen she was too old, too young, too fat, too thin or any of the other industry standard BS, Holly was there to lift her friend right back up. She also delivered the occasional shot of tough love whenever Gwen fell into the trap of thinking Hollywood was real.

So yeah, it would have been fine if Gwen had wanted to keep the surgery private, but she should have told Holly. And Holly was mad at herself for being so focused on work and the movie no one wanted to make that she hadn't even noticed her friend recovering from surgery. How was that even possible?

"They look great, Gwen." Holly did her best to mask whatever feelings she had. Now wasn't the time. "I just wish I'd been there to help you."

Ty climbed the final steps and scooted past her. "I don't know anything about anything looking great," he mumbled. Then he took a quick glance at Gwen and swung his head away so fast, both Gwen and Holly had to hold in their laughter.

"Honey, I don't need your help stuffing my own bra," Gwen said. "I've been doing it all by myself since I was twelve."

Holly looked at Gwen's ample cleavage. No Kleenex in the world could do that. "But how?"

"I didn't get the surgery. I wanted to get a feel for something bigger before I took the plunge, so I ordered these fancy gel inserts that push everything *way* up."

"Oh," Holly said with a sigh of relief. "You really don't need anything bigger. I mean, in my humble opinion."

"Well, now, seeing as you are my own personal expert on the loveliness of ladies, I s'pose I'd best keep that in mind." She winked.

Holly wanted to say something charming in return, but she chose to turn bright red instead. Her five-minute crush may have been a thing of the past, but she still had a way of turning into a total dope when beautiful women flirted with her.

It turned out Holly wasn't the only one auditioning for the

lead in *50 Shades of Red*. Ty appeared to be dying a slow and painful death, having reached his physical limit of boob talk with beautiful women. He cleared his throat and pointed at Desiree's door. "I'm just gonna..."

"Right. Go," Gwen said. "If I wanted to discuss my breast augmentation with you, I would've brought a six-pack of beer and some of those Slim Jim sausages."

"I'm a vegetarian, Gwen. You know that," he said over his shoulder.

Once he was out of earshot, Gwen stepped a little closer to Holly and said, "Is it just me, or does Ty look unusually handsome tonight?"

Holly took another look while Ty waited for Desiree to answer her door. "No hat of any kind. Not even a beanie hanging out of his back pocket. A crisp button-up shirt tucked into clean jeans. Loafers instead of flip-flops. You're right. He's workin' it tonight."

"Well, I can see that. The question is, who's all this fancy dressin' for? Does our boy have an actual date later?"

"I don't know." Holly turned to her. "You did know he's a vegetarian, right?"

"Of course I knew that. Why the good Lord saw fit to house him in the shadow of a KFC, I'll never know. And furthermore, Miss Smartypants, I also happen to know that the boy drinks herbal tea and some truly vile concoction called kombucha, not beer. What kind of man drinks that?"

"One that dresses like a slob but is more evolved than all of us combined?"

"Yes, well, between you, me, and this here stucco"—she tapped on the exterior wall of Desiree's apartment—"that part is kind of sexy." She paused. "In a dating your best friend's son sort of way."

Holly scoffed. "Oh, please. Age is just a number. Besides,

you're not *scandalously* older than him. Just old enough to teach him a thing or two."

Gwen put a hand on her hip. "Okay, first of all, I'm not going to fuck that young man in there. Honey, you and I both know I'd probably break him in more ways than one. And second, can we please focus on my breasts here? Because I need you to be honest. Does it look like I'm trying too hard? I don't want to look like one of those Hollywood housewives where everything is puffy-pouty-poofy, and if I smile too hard, my face will split in two and shoot collagen all over the poor camera guy."

Holly stood motionless. "Wow. That's…descriptive."

"Damnit," Gwen said. "It's too much, isn't it?" She pulled what looked like raw chicken filets out of her bra and tucked them in her purse.

Her breasts were perfect without them. Just enough. Her nipples had hardened and were visible through the festive silver blouse she'd worn for the party. Holly's mouth went dry. "You don't need anything, Gwen. Just your confidence back."

"Aw, that's sweet. I wish every casting agent was a desperate lesbian who knows how to gaze at an old has-been's tits."

"That's impressive," Holly said. "You managed to insult both of us in one sentence. And to be clear, I'm not desperate. I'm just picky about who I…fu-date."

"Who you fu-date? Is that how you lesbians do it? Sounds fun." Gwen took her by the arm and walked her to Desiree's door. "Which brings up a question. Do lesbians judge each other the way men judge women?"

"What do you mean?"

"I mean, being judged as too easy if you get down and dirty on the first date. Are there looser girls, as my mama would call them? You know, the ones everyone looks down on but not so much that they wouldn't partake in a bit of fun if given the opportunity?"

Holly laughed. "I wish I knew. Unfortunately, I don't live in *The L Word.* I'm too busy with work and writing to know what's going on with other people's sex lives."

Gwen lifted her eyebrows. "So what I'm hearing is, we're your only friends? In all of LA, you haven't managed to expand your social circle beyond your apartment complex?"

"Okay, so first you imply that I'm desperate, and now I have no one in my life except you and...Desiree! Hi. Merry Christmas."

Desiree stood at her open door and clasped her hands. "Oh, you two could be mother and daughter."

Holly tried not to laugh. Gwen put on a fake smile and whispered, "If you value your life, you won't agree with her."

Holly leaned in and whispered back, "Does it help that I have a thing for older women?"

"Fuck you, hon. Also, there's a Milk Dud stuck to your ass." Gwen gave her a wink and turned her attention to Desiree. "Hello, darling Dez. You're looking as classy as ever."

A Milk Dud? Holly juggled her purse and the two bottles of wine while trying not to let Desiree's gift slip out from under her arm.

"Can I help a lady in distress?" Griffin stepped up next to her, still dressed in his toy soldier suit but smelling a bit more like spiced rum than warm sugar cookie this time.

"Yeah. Get the Milk Dud off my ass, please."

He raised an eyebrow as he leaned back for a look. "Ah, madam, I think you are mistaken. In my rather humble opinion—"

"Griff! Just get the damn thing off me before Desiree physically removes my pants and washes them in her bathroom sink."

"That sounds like a story that needs to be told."

"There's no story. It's what old ladies do. They handwash shit."

He tapped his chin. "It's complicated, Holls. I can't just flick it away because it's not a Milk Dud. It appears to be a Reese's Peanut Butter Cup, or at least what's left of one. What I really need is a scraper of some sort."

"Don't be such a wuss. Just take your thumbnail and push it off. Or take this stuff from my hands so I can do it."

He took the gift and bottles of wine and stood in front of her, blocking Desiree's view. "I'll give you some privacy during the procedure," he whispered over his shoulder.

Holly reached behind and patted her butt until she found it. Problem was, those idiots didn't know their candy. It was clearly a turtle of the chocolate, caramel, and nut variety. How in the holy hell had she managed to get a turtle stuck to her ass?

She racked her brain. Any turtles at home? No. In her office? No. And then she remembered the box that had gone around the table during her two o'clock meeting in the conference room. Had she sat on someone's turtle and worn it the *entire afternoon*? She was half surprised Cruz McCreepy hadn't noticed it and offered to remove it during their conversation. But really, in all of the time Brian spent scrutinizing her outfit at the office party, he'd failed to detect that?

"Oh God," she whispered to herself. "The office party." Had Meredith seen it? Holly spent about two seconds being extra mortified that her crush might have noticed the candy on her ass before she realized how silly she was being. Meredith Drake didn't even know she existed and certainly wasn't checking out her ass. Besides, was it really any more embarrassing than having Lucille's ornaments taped to her sweater? This was one time she was glad Meredith had never really noticed her.

"Is everything all right, honey?" Sweet Desiree, who only stood about five feet tall and had the sweetest demeanor of anyone who had ever worked in Hollywood, easily maneuvered around Griffin. "We're waiting on you," she said.

Desiree had just celebrated her eighty-third birthday. In her prime, she'd been a very successful makeup artist. Holly had never seen her without lipstick. She wore every shade, depending on her outfit. Tonight, it was red to match her festive sweater.

Holly tossed the turtle in a nearby trash can and gave Desiree a smile. "Everything's fine, Dez. Let's do this."

❖

Desiree had told Holly that she rarely dated the same man for more than a couple of months. She said her time on this earth was short and men got lazy if you expressed any sort of commitment. She wanted a steady stream of *wooing*, as she put it. Fancy dinners, dancing, the symphony, and opera. Of course, she couldn't drive anymore and neither could most of her dates, but Desiree found a way around that particular problem.

Holly thought back to a conversation they'd had in the courtyard a few weeks earlier. *Have you ever tried this Uber, dear? Courting has never been so easy. You just push a button, and the car shows up. Now if only the driver would arrive with potential dates for me to consider. It would save so much time.* That was when Desiree's enthusiasm for the possibilities of ride sharing took an unfortunate turn. *Oh, Holly dear. If it were that easy, maybe you could even find someone.*

An eighty-three-year-old's love life was more exciting

than Holly's. She took little comfort in the fact that this particular eighty-three-year old's love life was more exciting than just about everyone's.

Desiree's current man of the hour, a gentleman named Thad who wore a tweed suit and one of the thinnest mustaches Holly had ever seen, took her hand and kissed it when they were introduced. "Ah, the queen of Christmas romance. I've heard so much about you from Desiree," he said. "In fact, we plan to watch your newest movie on Christmas Eve."

Christmas Eve? Desiree didn't spend Christmas Eve with her boyfriends. For years, she'd volunteered at the local homeless shelter, serving dinner to those in need. Afterward, she always attended mass at St. Agatha's, a Catholic church that was best known for its Sunday morning gospel mass. She never wavered from those plans, as far as Holly knew. She couldn't wait to get Desiree alone so she could find out more about this Thad fellow.

"Is this what I think it is?" Desiree shook the hostess gift as if it would make a sound.

"If you think it's the 1966 *Great Songs of Christmas Volume Six* vinyl LP featuring Steve Lawrence and Eydie Gormé, then, yes. Yes, it is," Holly said.

Desiree beamed with delight. "Oh, you do know how to get an old woman going, don't you?"

Gwen snorted behind a freshly poured glass of Chablis. Of course, she hadn't offered to hold one of the bottles when Holly was trying to balance them on the stairs, but once inside, Gwen had already started in on one of them. "I do." Holly said. "Just ask Gwen over there."

Gwen gave her a smirk that Holly read as showing appreciation for her quick comeback even though she loathed doing so. Holly returned the wink she'd given her earlier. Messing with Gwen was always a good time.

"I see the turtle is gone," Ty said behind her.

"Hey, at least you got it right. Gwen thought it was a Milk Dud, and Griffin thought it was a peanut butter cup."

"Amateurs," he said. "Also, I was eye to eye with it, so I had an advantage."

"Eye to eye with my ass or the turtle? Never mind." She grabbed the bottle of beer from his hand and took a long swig. The sooner she got tipsy, the better.

❖

Griffin had taken off his toy soldier jacket and unbuttoned his shirt during charades. Holly couldn't blame him. Desiree's apartment was always too warm for the average person. She noticed Gwen was enjoying the view, so she leaned in and said, "Griffin is gay."

He was new to the complex and still in the getting-to-know-you phase with Gwen. When a condo had gone up for sale the previous year, Holly told him to jump on it because she knew he'd fit right in. And she was right. Desiree adored him and treated him like a grandson.

"I know that young hunk of a man is gay," Gwen said. "Doesn't mean I can't enjoy the view." She gave Holly a side-eye and said, "I still haven't nailed down your type, but I will."

"Still don't have a type."

"Everyone has a type," Gwen replied with certainty.

"Are you telling me that your type is a sweet gay guy who's half your age?"

"No, my type is male, under forty, nice abs, good head of hair. Your turn."

Holly found beauty in every type of woman. A dapper suit could be just as enticing as a sexy dress. As for her own look, she leaned more toward the feminine side. She liked pretty dresses and sexy underwear. At work, she kept it simple. Jeans, mostly. If it got chilly, she went for oversized sweaters because it was basically like wearing a blanket to work, and she was all about the cozy factor. Even then, her bra and panties nearly always matched. Not that anyone ever saw them. But she knew, and that was what mattered.

She'd once made the mistake of pointing out an attractive butch girl to Gwen in a restaurant. Since they'd had numerous discussions about the appeal of various celebrities, along with a particularly bookish barista at their local coffee shop, Gwen had mistakenly taken the interest in the butch girl to mean Holly might be interested in virtually anyone. This had opened a floodgate of proposed blind dates until she told Gwen to take off the matchmaker hat and just be her friend.

"Honestly, Gwen, at this point, I just want to find someone who has their feet firmly planted on the ground, knows who they are, and can be loyal and trustworthy. Is that too much to ask?"

"Only if you want a nice rack too."

"You are truly awful."

"Look, what you want, we all want that, kiddo. Finding those traits in a body you want to cuddle up to for the rest of your life is the tough part."

"Don't I know it."

Griffin was in a sweat when Thad finally guessed his mess of a charade. It said more about Thad's charades prowess than Griff's acting, considering the latter's efforts consisted mostly of marching and swimming motions. How that related to the movie *All That Jazz* was anybody's guess.

Holly leaned in and whispered, "What do you think of Thad?"

"Handsome. Charming. Perfect for Dez if he's not some sort of swindler who plans to drain all of her bank accounts."

Holly gaped at the reply. "Could you be any more cynical? Dez seems happy. Let her be happy."

"I'm the cynical one? Take a look in the mirror, hon. You're wearing purple to a Christmas party, and unless you've suddenly taken an interest in crocheting, I'd say someone took pity on you and slapped a few of their own ornaments on your sweater."

Holly hadn't noticed the tiny crocheted wreath that hung just under her left breast. She really should've taken a quick look in the mirror when she'd rushed into her apartment and grabbed the gift for Desiree. She stood firm under Gwen's scrutiny but without a single good retort in her head. Finally, she blurted, "It was a turtle stuck to my ass, not a Milk Dud."

The room went silent, and everyone turned to them. "Oh, don't mind us," Gwen said. "Holly was just telling me about her crazy weekend with *another* one-night stand. She's such a freak, this one. I mean, who takes a turtle to bed?"

"It must be a lesbian thing," Thad said. "I understand they use very interesting techniques when consummating their love."

He spoke with such fantastic diction, Holly assumed he must've attended the school of I Don't Use Contractions When I Speak, now defunct because even the highest of high society debutantes enjoyed a good contraction now and then. Not that Thad appeared to be high society. He probably got in on a scholarship.

"Yeah, no turtles are ever involved, Thad. Just beavers. Oh, and if you can't find a willing beaver, there are many other options on Amazon." Holly smiled at him mischievously.

"Really?" he said. "I never would've guessed a beaver."

But somehow a turtle made sense to him? Griffin got behind Ty and buried his face in his back. He obviously needed support to stay upright since he was silently laughing so hard.

Ty stood still, hands in pockets and a grin that indicated he was amused but also slightly embarrassed.

Holly could tell Gwen was formulating some sort of insulting response. Sweet Desiree, who was no prude, whispered something in Thad's ear. Gwen leaned in and said, "I'm an Amazon Prime member myself."

Holly gave Gwen a side-eye. "What? No insult? No condescending remark about lesbians and their tools?"

"Hey, we all gotta do what we gotta do."

Thad chuckled once he was in on the joke. Holly wished she could've heard Desiree's explanation. *You see, dear Thad, in less sophisticated circles, a vagina is sometimes referred to as a beaver.*

Gwen held up her glass. "We have a Christmas movie to write, don't we? Come on, people, let's do this."

Thad rubbed his hands together in delight. "I feel honored to be here, Ms. Hudson. The *Evermore* series is my favorite, and when Desiree said she knew the writer, well, I just had to meet you."

Gwen motioned up and down Holly's body. "She's usually more put together than this, Thad."

"Definitely not at her best tonight," Ty added.

With a sympathetic tone, Desiree said, "Maybe I chose the wrong moment to introduce you two. It should feel magical when an artist meets one of their fans."

With a huff, Holly said, "Oh, come on. You guys act like I'm a walking Charlie Brown Christmas tree or something."

"That's what you remind me of," Gwen shouted. She wrapped an arm around Holly. "But remember what happens once that poor little tree gets all spruced up? All the ladies suddenly take an interest."

"I literally hate you right now. You know that, right?"

"Aw, come on." She guided Holly toward a chair. "We

have a surprise for you, kiddo. Have a seat over there, and I'll get you a glass of wine."

Holly sat on one of the dining room chairs they'd pulled in from the kitchen. Gwen handed her a glass of wine and proceeded to blindfold her. "How am I supposed to drink wine while blindfolded?"

"*Feel* your way," Gwen said. "Just don't spill it on Desiree's expensive rug."

"Yeah, thanks." Holly found the edge of the glass with her finger and brought it to her mouth. She took a good long sip so she'd only have to do it once, then asked, "Is this a sex thing? Like a group orgy?" She could hear them rummaging around, but no one answered. "If I take this blindfold off and you all are naked, that would be…"

"Awkward," Ty said.

"Awesome," Griffin added.

"Life-changing," Thad said with a sense of wonder in his voice.

Gwen chimed in. "Not what we planned, but I'm in."

"Oh, not on my Persian rug," Desiree said. "It's from the set of the 1975 film *If Love Was Made of Money*. One of my favorites."

Holly heard a noise that sounded like a tarp was being shaken out. She felt a slight breeze and heard it settle on to the floor. "Oh," Desiree said. "What a great idea, Griffin. I knew you were a smart boy."

Holly felt a twinge of nervousness. She loved her friends, but they weren't the most refined lot. Nor were they particularly trustworthy when it came to a joke. What was supposed to happen on a tarp in the middle of Desiree's living room with Christmas music playing in the background? And what in the hell made Gwen think Holly would want to be stuck here blindfolded while they plotted out God knew what? Finally, the blindfold was pulled from her eyes. Holly let out a sigh of relief. Yes, there was a tarp on the floor, but everyone appeared to be appropriate enough. "Thank God," she said. "You're all still dressed."

"My, oh my. You were hoping for something different?" Gwen slung the scarf she'd used as a blindfold over her shoulder. "Who could've known that our little writer of sweet, tame Christmas movies would have such a big-ass naughty streak?"

"It's always the quiet ones," Thad said under his breath.

Holly put a finger in the air. "Okay, number one, since when am I quiet?" A second finger punctuated her next statement. "And number two, I was relieved that you weren't all naked. *Relieved*, Gwen. Not disappointed."

Ty started in. "Holly, we know we usually play spin the bottle to help you develop storylines, but this time we're doing it a little bit differently."

For the past several years, once everyone was sufficiently tipsy, Holly's neighbors had made a game of holiday romance writing. They'd spin the bottle to reveal the locations, characters, and key plot points of "Holly's Next Movie." By the end, they'd have a ridiculous plot outlined. Last year's involved a recently single New Yorker who got stuck in a small town with his dog because the main road was wiped out. If boy had met girl at that point, it would have been a pretty serviceable setup, but of course, that wasn't the end of it. Not by a long shot. In *Scout Saves Christmas*, the main character, Lance, was the only one who could hear his dog talk. Meanwhile, he was forced to direct the town Christmas pageant in order to show Santa that Hickory Farms—yes, that was what they'd named it—really did still have Christmas spirit. Along the way, Lance fell in love with a schoolteacher with a talking cat. Holly couldn't remember if it was last year's movie or the year before, but a minor sledding accident might also have been involved.

"Ty, I feel like you might be using the word 'help' a bit loosely," Holly said.

"Exactly. And yes, we've noticed that our ideas rarely make it onscreen."

Holly snorted. "Or put another way, they never do."

"Right. Yes. That's what we noticed. And we thought perhaps a change of scenery would do us all some good." Ty looked over at Griffin and gave a nod.

Griffin Taylor, Professional Actor, took his cue. He stood next to an easel that had a blank piece of poster board attached to it and flashed his award-winning, cosmetically straightened, professionally whitened grin. "Holly Hudson, we're about to blow your mind, and you'll never have to work another day in your life because what we're about to give you will be watched by millions and adored for years to come." He pulled the blank piece of poster board away and revealed the next one, which said *Holly's Next Christmas Movie (working title)*.

"It'll be like *A Christmas Story* with the leg lamp," Gwen said. "You know, the kid who gets left home alone?"

Ty snorted. "You could call it *Lonely Christmas with a Leg Lamp*."

Holly put up a finger again, then realized she probably did that much too often and instead, tried for a casual scratch on her head. "Two different movies, Gwen, but I think I get your point. It'll be a classic."

Thad chimed in. "If you want a classic, you really should consider writing something similar to that Jimmy Stewart movie *It's a Wonderful Life*."

Holly eyed them with suspicion. "And you're going to help me write this classic? Because that's gone so well in the past?"

"We sure are." Griffin flipped the tarp over and shook it high into the air.

As it floated back down to earth, Holly tilted her head to one side. "Is that Twister?"

Desiree cupped her hand around her mouth and said, "Better than an orgy."

"Though in my experience, it could lead to one," Griffin said with a sly grin in Ty's direction.

Great. Now Holly had to worry about both Gwen and Griffin taking advantage of innocent, inexperienced Ty. Holly didn't know for sure that he was so innocent, but everything about him kind of screamed virgin. She'd have a talk with Griffin later.

In the meantime, everyone looked so pleased with themselves, Holly felt it was necessary to show a little bit of enthusiasm. "I can't wait to watch you all contort yourselves on my behalf."

"Oh no, dear. You'll be the one on the mat," Desiree said with a somewhat disturbing look of glee on her face.

Holly stood. "Oh, no. I'm not going to…in front of all of you…just…put my ass up in the air. I mean, haven't I been humiliated enough for one day with candy on my ass and these damned ornaments hanging from my sweater?"

Griffin wrapped his arm around her and said, "Don't worry, hon. We're in this together. And if it happens that all my sexy neighbors collapse on top of me, so be it."

Thad leaned over to Desiree and said, "I haven't been to a party with this much promise since 1978."

"Okay, so here are the rules, Hollister."

"Not my name, Ken Griffey Junior."

"Her real name is Hol—"

Holly put up her hand. "No, Dez. Just because you saw

my driver's license once doesn't mean you get to tell everyone the name my dear parents blessed me with."

"Well, it's such a fun name for a girl who grew up in Christmas Town, USA," Desiree said. "And I only saw your license because you were pulled over for speeding."

"Okay, moving on," Griffin said. "Here are the rules. Green dots are for main characters. Blue dots are for locations. Red dots are for points of conflict. Yellow dots are for time period. We've all put our ideas in. Desiree and Thad will be in charge of calling out the colors, and we're going to shortcut this by having all four of us put one hand and one foot on two different colors. Then, whoever gets to the color Dez calls out first gets their choice read." Griffin kicked off his shoes and rubbed his hands together. "Here we go, kids. May the most limber person win."

"Spin the bottle is so much easier." Holly stepped up to the mat and crouched so she could put her hand on a dot. "Also, shouldn't we be high right now? Otherwise, aren't we just a bunch of insane adults playing Twister?"

Gwen didn't bother crouching. She bent her body in half, ass in the air. "It's always the weak ones who don't want to play the game." She had a decided advantage thanks to a brief yet life-altering affair with a yogi. The relationship had died out in record time, but Gwen's passion for yoga had been ignited.

Ty and Griffin took their places, and Desiree called out, "Left foot, green."

"Ty got there first," Thad said. He consulted a clipboard. "His choice for main character number one is a woman who lives with her grandfather."

"Nice choice, but you should've taken your socks…off." Holly had barely gotten the words out when Ty's foot slipped out from under him. "Well, crap. Ty's out."

"Right hand, blue."

"Damnit." Holly's hand went down right on top of Griffin's.

"Well, deck the halls," Griffin exclaimed. "It sounds like someone's getting into this."

Gwen's body was fully contorted, but she twisted toward Griffin with ease. "Griffin, dear. Surely by now you know how competitive young Holly Jolly Christmas is."

"Have I mentioned that I hate you all?"

They responded as a group. "Yes!"

"If I may." Thad cleared his throat as if he was about to introduce the queen of England to parliament. "Griffin's location of choice is a farmhouse in New Hampshire."

"Oh, come on," Gwen said. "You're making it too easy on her. My choice was the International Space Station where an actress in her thirties who just happens to look a lot like me plays an astronaut who's looking for love on all the wrong planets."

"Thirties, huh? Your arms are shaking, old lady. You won't last another move." Hard as Holly tried to smack talk the competition, she knew perfectly well no one was going to outlast Gwen.

"Stop staring at my cleavage, little girl. You can't handle a woman like me."

Holly grinned. "Not gonna work, Mama. You're outta here."

Desiree threw a hand over her heart and sighed. "Oh, I can't wait to see who lives in that farmhouse."

"A woman who lives with her grandfather," Ty said. "That was my choice, remember?"

"Okay, but can't she live with her grandfather on the space station?"

"She could have if you'd been faster." Holly tried to give Gwen a kick, but she couldn't quite reach, and she just ended up bucking into the air. "Keep rolling, people. Gwen won't last much longer." Holly wouldn't either, but she was determined to be the last player standing.

"Left foot, yellow," Desiree shouted. "Oh, miracle of all miracles, Holly won."

What had gotten into Desiree? She wasn't usually one for such blatant sarcasm. Holly muttered under her breath, "I *was* going to choose you, Dez, but—"

"No buts, honey. For the time period, I choose the 1940s."

"1940s," Gwen cried. "My God, just kill me now. Why not the goddamned Civil War if you want merriment mixed with mass killing?"

"It was a very compelling period in our history," Desiree said. "Men were off fighting in a war, and women were at work in all manner of factories. Our country was united. Everyone was working hard for the same goal. It's the perfect backdrop for a lovely Christmas movie."

"On the upside, I could wear a military uniform," Griffin said. He was the most contorted of the bunch, with a hand in one corner and one foot at the top of the mat and another foot in the opposite corner. "They could give me a Purple Heart at the Christmas tree lighting ceremony in the town square." He fell to his knees. "Okay, I'm done. It's up to you ladies."

Holly's strength was waning. She fell to her knees and rolled onto her back. "Okay, Mama. You win."

Ty smiled down on her. "She beat you," he said in a deadpan voice. "Your humiliation is complete."

Gwen also collapsed onto her back and turned to Holly. "Just so you know, I'm never letting this win go. I'll bring it up every chance I get. I'll start so many sentences with 'Hey, remember that time I beat your young ass?' that you'll want to kill me in a dark alley, but that's okay because I have this win to cling to. Forever."

Holly couldn't help but smile because even with all of their sassy banter and Gwen's sharp tongue, Gwen was a forever friend. In fact, Holly hoped she'd have all of these people in her life for a very long time. They were a quirky bunch, but they were steady and loyal. Even Thad seemed to have a good sense of humor and a kind heart. She'd have to make a point to get to know him better.

"If no one has any objections," Thad said, "I'd like to choose the other main character."

"Go ahead," Holly said. "Just don't make him too complicated. Women like simple men."

"I wasn't thinking of a man at all. I'd like her to be a lady veteran returning home from the war. Sorry, Griffin. That means you'll have to be cast as the war hero's jealous brother who can't stand to watch his sister getting all the attention. And if that's not hard enough on you, your sister is going to win the heart of the farmer's daughter as well."

Holly sat up. "Thad, you're evil in such a good way."

"Damn right," Griffin said. "He just took away my Purple Heart. And do you really see me playing the loser brother who outs his gay sister to the whole town?"

"This story is getting sadder by the minute," Gwen said. "How could you possibly fix all this so the family can celebrate the birth of Christ together?"

"It's true," Griffin said. "Wifetime is not in the business of bringing the bummer to Christmas."

"Or diversity and inclusion," Gwen said. "In fact, I'm amazed they hire gay people at all."

"Oh, that's what's so silly about the whole thing," Desiree

said. "The gays have always comprised a good share of the creative talent in this town. They can't ignore that fact."

Holly sighed. "They don't. We're half the damn staff."

"Yeah, well, a bunch of the company is Jewish too," Griffin added. "But you haven't seen *Eight Nights of Love* on the schedule yet either, have you?"

"Right. That's Wifetime's thing. Half the staff and none of the programming." As much as Holly wanted to exclusively write gay Christmas movies for the rest of her life, watching two women get run out of 1940s New Hampshire for falling in love with each other wouldn't be a good time for anyone. "Sorry, folks. I know you had high hopes for this twisted game of Twister, but hey, at least we all got to see some asses in the air and some boobs dragging on the floor. I'm kidding, Gwen. Your boobs did not drag on the floor."

"No, but they did drag across my face a few times," Ty said jokingly.

Gwen stood. "Don't say it like you hated it, cowboy. Now, who needs another drink after the most depressing game of Twister anyone ever did play?"

Every hand in the room went up.

Desiree kept her hand up. "May I say something first? I think Holly would write the most beautiful love story with our selections, but really, we don't have to wait for that, and we don't have to wait for Christmas Eve to watch the latest *Evermore*. Let's watch it tonight in the company of our dear friend and amazing screenwriter, Holly Hudson."

Gwen raised a hand in the air. "I second that emotion."

Ty got up and put his shoes on. "I have the best organic popcorn down in my apartment. Don't start without me."

It surprised Holly when no one balked at the idea. She knew Griffin wouldn't because he loved watching himself onscreen, but she expected some sort of snide remark from Ty or Gwen. She got up and put on her shoes too. "I have some big floor pillows. Don't start without me, either." Once she was out of the apartment, she let the huge grin she'd been holding back come out in full force.

❖

After the movie, a few more drinks, and a terrible group rendition of several Christmas carols, the hugs good-bye started. With so much booze in them, those hugs quickly turned into slow dances. Holly lifted her head off Griffin's shoulder and said, "When I get back from Hawaii, will you marry me and have my babies?"

He kissed her forehead. "Only if I can wear this toy soldier outfit to our wedding, and we build a life-size Barbie condo where the back of the house is all glass and looks out on the ocean. Oh, but it's a hard no on the baby thing. I can't risk losing my figure."

Gwen sway-walked her way over to them and put out her hand. "My turn. I have to say Feliz Navidad in Hawaiian." She pulled Holly into the traditional dance position and actually started to do a weird version of the mamba.

"Whoa. Are you going to say it with your lips or your hips? G, I'm too drunk to move this fast...oh God. Don't spin me."

"Don't be so flat-footed," Gwen said. "I learned this dance in the 90s, and I've still got it."

It was Holly's good fortune that Gwen let go and decided to freestyle the hell out of whatever dance that was. She didn't seem to care that Andy Williams was still crooning in the background.

Ty walked up to Holly and offered his hand. "I promise to say it with my lips, not my hips."

"Oh, thank God." He seemed to be slightly soberer than Holly was, so she took his hand. "This is where we dance like we're two scared teenagers and barely move back and forth, okay?"

"You had me at scared teenager. I learned that dance in the late 2000-teens, and I still got it."

"Yeah, you're killing it." Holly rested her head on his shoulder. "And now, I'm going to kill the drunk thirty-something who can't hang like she used to dance."

"What time is your flight?"

She opened her eyes. "Oh, fuck. I have to catch a plane tomorrow, don't I?"

"Today technically." He slowed his sway and pulled back. "It's 2:30."

"Silent Night" ended abruptly. It was probably a good thing since it had successfully lulled Holly into a state of sleeping while standing. She lifted her head and gave Ty a hug. "I should go pack." She paused for a second. "Are you going to say it?" She turned and looked at everyone else. "Does anyone in this room actually know how to say Merry Christmas in Hawaiian?"

Desiree stepped up to Holly and took her hands. "*Mele Kalikimaka*, Holly. And safe travels." Holly leaned down and let Desiree kiss her cheek. She was sure to have a lipstick mark, but she didn't care. These were her people. Her best friends. And she loved every one of them as if they were family.

CHAPTER THREE

Holly stopped dead in her tracks. "Be cool," she whispered to herself. She turned around oh so casually, hoping she wouldn't be spotted. *Don't be daft. She probably won't even remember you. And stop thinking words like* daft. *You're not British.* Holly took a breath and peeked over her shoulder. Meredith Drake, aka Madame President, had moved through the crowd to the luggage carousel. Madame President was the new nickname Holly had recently conferred upon her crush, resulting from a fantasy involving a certain desk in the Oval Office. Holly had never lacked creativity.

How the hell had Holly been on the same flight to Honolulu with her and hadn't even known it? It seemed wholly unfair. It also seemed like her fantasy should've taken place on Air Force One.

Meredith had probably been in first class, which explained why she looked so well rested. Her short brown hair lacked the typical flattening on the back of the head that usually happened on a long flight. It had a slight wave to it. No frizz. A pretty shine, and Holly was sure that if Meredith jumped up and down, her hair would have a natural, hairspray-free bounce to it, which meant it was being held in place with nothing but God's love. Of course it was.

Holly lowered her gaze to Meredith's off-white linen pants, loose except for the part that hugged her backside perfectly. She wore a fitted, navy-blue T-shirt that made Holly pray she would turn around, and a gray cashmere scarf that had probably kept her cozy on the flight.

Holly, on the other hand, felt like a hungover, crumpled piece of Kleenex due to the one too many glasses of wine she'd had the night before. She hadn't worn her nice track pants. Nope, not Holly. She was in sweatpants and a hooded sweatshirt that said Nantucket and had a drawing of a whale on it. To say she was a bit worse for wear would have been an understatement. It didn't help that she'd been stuck next to a guy who'd snored his way through the entire flight.

No matter. She had a plan. She'd hold back and leave her luggage on the carousel until Meredith got hers and left. Then everything would be fine. Holly moved through the crowd but kept her eye on Meredith. She imagined any number of surveillance scenarios. Going around the corner and secretly watching from a mirror. Cutting two peepholes out of a newspaper. A drone, but that wasn't really viable inside the airport.

Holly really wasn't a creep. She was just prone to vivid daydreams. It had gotten her in trouble plenty growing up, but it had served her well in her professional life. She allowed herself a brief moment of glee thinking about that time Miss "Not Ms., Not Mrs., Miss" Winchell had told her she'd never amount to anything if she couldn't learn to "cut out the dagnab stargazing and just focus." She wondered if Miss Winchell was harassing any future screenwriters in this year's class.

And that was when the worst luggage disaster the Daniel K. Inouye International Airport had ever seen, happened. Okay, so maybe it wasn't the worst. Sadly, it wasn't even a movie-worthy explosion of bras and panties. More like a steady spill as the zipper on Meredith's suitcase gave up on its only job in this world. Granted, the suitcase appeared to be stuffed beyond capacity.

Meredith had managed to pull it off the carousel along with most of her clothing. Unfortunately, a set of light pink panties and a matching bra that still had the tags on had exceeded her reach and were about to be viewed by everyone on the flight.

When a young boy was shushed by his mother after he shouted, "Look, Mommy. Are those your panties?" Holly decided to make a run for it. She pushed her way through the throng of tired passengers who were crammed up against the carousel. "Excuse me. Sorry. Excuse me." With a lunge, she grabbed the bra and panties, managing to travel a few feet on the carousel for good measure. She pushed herself back up and threw her hand in the air. "Got them."

The strangers, apparently not appreciative of the athletic prowess she'd just demonstrated, stared at her. A teenager with major attitude gave her a slow clap. And to make things worse, her chivalrous gesture had gone unnoticed by Meredith, who'd managed to get her belongings on a cart and was headed toward the door. Holly quickly recognized the near miss for the blessing it was. While her instinct had been to play the panty-saving superhero, in reality, she looked like an ass standing there holding Meredith's lacy pink bra and panty set. She glanced at the tag. Neiman Marcus. Of course. Holly let the lingerie drop to her side. Funny how many of her Meredith fantasies involved bra and panty sets, yet never quite like this.

She turned back toward the luggage carousel. *Time to get back to your table for one, Holly. At least then, when you make an ass of yourself, an airport full of people won't be around to see it.* She watched as her bag disappeared onto the back side of the carousel. She'd have to wait there until it circled around again.

"Excuse me?" a voice came from behind her. "I believe those belong to me."

Holly cringed and delivered a silent prayer: *Sweet Jesus, please take me. Please take me. Please take me.* Nothing. She felt compelled to clarify: *Jesus, please take me. Now.* Nope. Holly would have to turn around and face Meredith Drake. She manufactured a smile and turned. "Well, howdy," she said with a bit too much enthusiasm and way too much howdy.

The corners of Meredith's mouth curled up slightly. Her eyebrows arched. Then she grinned. "Holly Hudson. What a surprise."

"I, I have your um…" Holly stammered and held up the lingerie. At precisely that moment, her grandmother spoke to her from the grave and gifted her with the perfect word. "You know, your unmentionables." At least it would have been the perfect word in 1938.

"Since you're displaying my underwear in the middle of baggage claim, I think it's probably okay if you call them by name."

"Right. Of course. Your panties." *Oh God. Why? Why? Why?* Holly shoved them at her. "Here you go."

By that point, Meredith looked beyond amused, clearly trying to keep her grin contained. "Thank you, Holly. I must admit, my day started off pretty horribly. And it didn't help to have my things paraded for the whole flight to see." Her smile widened. "But seeing you risk life and limb, or at least a very public trip around the carousel, really put things in perspective for me."

"Oh sure, yeah. I'm here to help." Holly gave a stupid at-your-service bow and then capped the whole nightmare off by saying, "Besides, it could have been worse. You could have had a vibrator in there." *Because oh my fucking God, this isn't bad enough.*

"Right. Well, I suppose it's a good thing my carry-on didn't spill then."

Holly blinked approximately four hundred and twelve times and wondered if she'd heard that right.

"I'm joking, Holly."

"Right. Yes. Of course. I didn't know you joked, I mean, of course you joke. Is it hot in here? And it's muggy. Isn't it muggy?" She went to pull her hoodie over her head. "Ow. Ow." The claw clip that held her hair up in a messy bun had somehow gotten caught on the hoodie, and she was sure she'd just lost a chunk of hair and possibly shown off her oldest, most comfortable sports bra to the entire airport because her T-shirt had decided to make the trip too. So that was that. She'd have to quit her job and leave LA so she'd never run into Meredith Drake ever again.

That was how Holly rolled when it came to communicating with beautiful women. She'd forget how to form coherent sentences, and then, whatever did come out was something akin to Yoda speak. She was surprised "you could've had a vibrator in there" hadn't come out as "a vibrator you could've had in there, hmm? *Yes*."

She managed to remove both the clip and the hoodie only to find Meredith staring at her as if she was just this side of flying over a cuckoo's nest. "I was hot. Like, super hot."

"So you mentioned."

Holly waved a hand in front of her face. "Couldn't take another second of that hoodie. Has that ever happened to you? Like, you just have to rip your clothes off?"

In a deadpan tone, Meredith said, "Not in the airport."

Stupid, you are, Holly Hudson. Best to just get started on that plan to leave LA.

"Do you know where the taxi stand is? Or should I take

an Uber? I was supposed to be traveling with my sister, and she's the one who knows Honolulu like the back of her hand."

Holly got behind Meredith's cart and gave it a good push. "Follow me." Once they got outside, she realized it had rained, and there were puddles everywhere. No wonder it felt so muggy. "Watch out for the—"

But it was too late. Madame President had stepped right into a puddle and mumbled, "Fuck me," under her breath. In an effort to shake the water from her expensive looking slip-on loafer, she ended up kicking it off. It landed smack in the middle of the puddle.

"I got it." Holly picked up the shoe and wiped it with her hoodie. She noticed Meredith's expression had changed. She looked like she was about to cry. "Bad day, huh?"

"You have no idea." Meredith took her shoe and put it back on, then ran a hand through her hair. "Bad day doesn't even come close."

"Yeah, holiday travel can be the worst." Holly got behind the cart again and pushed it toward the cab stand. "Everyone is going somewhere they don't want to be, i.e., their parents' house, with Aunt Leona in the twin bed next to you sawing redwoods all night while you stare at the same ceiling you spent your entire childhood staring at, and you can't believe you're back there, you know? Back under your parents' thumb for three solid days with no escape plan, and the only viable option is to closet-drink and eat yourself sick so you can actually claim to be sick and then get a room of your own because Aunt Leona's immune system isn't so good." She parked the cart at the end of the queue. Meredith didn't seem to be listening, so she backed away and said, "Anyway, take care."

Holly would never forget the moment she'd first laid

eyes on Meredith Drake. Any card-carrying lesbian would have had a visceral reaction to the tall, brown-eyed beauty. Except she must've been wearing heels that day because Holly remembered having to look up to her as they'd shaken hands and subsequently spilled a bit of coffee on herself.

In her loafers, Meredith was only slightly taller. The fancy suit she'd worn on the day they'd met had been smokin' hot, but the linen pants and T-shirt allowed Holly to truly appreciate her athletic physique. No doubt the woman took her Pilates seriously.

Holly turned to walk away when Meredith said, "Could my day get any worse?"

Holly wasn't sure if the question was directed at her, but she turned back and said, "Oh, definitely. I could've been a man chasing after you with your panties and bra, saying, hey, lady. You left your sexy lingerie behind. And by the way, can I get your number?"

"Okay, that would be worse." Meredith flashed her a smile. "Thank you, for saving me from that *particular* embarrassment."

"No problem. Hey, can I get your number?" Meredith's smile faded, causing Holly to put up her hands. "Totally kidding."

"Good one. You got me."

"Right," Holly said. "I'm a jokester. I make stupid jokes all the time, in fact. One right after the other, they just spill out, so really, you have nothing to be embarrassed about because I'm the hold-my-beer girl."

Meredith raised an eyebrow. "Hold my beer?"

"Yeah. You know, if someone does something really stupid, I always manage to up the ante."

"Like what happened just now with the…" Meredith circled her own head with her finger.

Holly covered her face with her hands and groaned, then dragged them down her cheeks and said, "Did you by any chance see my bra? It's my airplane bra. And my Sunday bra. And sometimes my Monday bra if the thought of going back to work is too much for me, and I just need, you know, something soft wrapped around me."

"Everything in the trunk?" the cab driver grumbled, taking Meredith's attention away. Probably just in time since Holly's inner thoughts sometimes turned into outer thoughts, and to say that she would have loved to know what it felt like to have Meredith's soft legs wrapped around her would be a huge hold my beer moment with only one participant—Holly, upping the ante on herself—it was time to walk away.

There weren't many people who stopped Holly cold in her tracks the way Meredith Drake did. Sure, LA was full of beautiful women in all shapes and sizes. But the thing about Meredith Drake? Well, she exuded not just one of Holly's weaknesses, but two: power and attitude. In fact, if Holly wasn't so averse to pain, she'd probably let a woman like Meredith throw her up against a wall and dominate her. Tie her to a bed and blindfold her. Maybe pull her hair a little. Possibly the candle thing if she asked nicely. They'd need a safe word. S'more. S'more would be their safe word. Except that would never work because things could go downhill whenever someone simply wanted more.

She decided then and there that their safe word would be no. It was straightforward and to the point. Also, she really never should've watched that damned shades of gray movie.

And now, she just needed to walk away before she turned bright red due to her scandalous thoughts. "Okay, then. I should catch up with my family. Because who comes to Hawaii alone?" *Stop talking, Holls. She couldn't care less who you are or are not here with, so just be on your way.*

"Holly?"

She stopped and turned back around. "Yes?"

"Merry Christmas."

Holly rarely returned the sentiment anymore. It had long ago lost its meaning after she'd heard her parents use the phrase practically year-round. She preferred something simple like, "Yeah, you too," which came out of her mouth a little too fast given how sincere Meredith seemed to be. Meredith had said merry Christmas, but her eyes were saying so much more. Thank you? Wish I could give you my number? Okay, so not that last one, but Holly could dream, right? She could also say, "I mean, merry Christmas to you too. And a happy new year. And whatever comes next."

"Um, Valentine's Day?"

"Yes," Holly exclaimed. "Happy Valentine's Day. I'll send you some chocolates. Or flowers? Which do you prefer? Tasty or smelly?" She slapped a hand to her forehead. "Crap, that sounded gross. Never mind. I'll work it out. You just go on and enjoy Hawaii, okay? Get lei'd and all that. I mean, you know, the flower kind. L-E-I."

The car door closed before Holly got that last part out. So that meant that the last thing Holly Hudson ever said to Meredith Drake was to get laid. Freaking fabulous.

❖

On her way down to the hotel swimming pool, Holly received the dreaded phone call she got every year from her mother telling her it wasn't too late to hop on a plane so she could spend Christmas with them. Except it was too late. And even if it wasn't, that was not where she wanted to be. She tried not to make a habit of answering her phone in crowded elevators, but delaying this one would only make things worse. "Hey, Mom. I'm on my way down to the pool, can I—"

"Glad to hear the plane didn't crash."

"Right. Sorry. I forgot to text last night." An older woman turned and gave her a motherly glare. "All is well, Mom. No need to worry," Holly added in her best cheery voice.

"All is not well, Holiday. You're spending Christmas on a beach. Again. Alone. Again. Without your parents. Again."

Another scowl from the elderly woman caused Holly to turn her back to everyone. She put her large sunglasses on even though it was too late to go incognito. No doubt she'd run into the older woman everywhere she went over the next few days. Plenty of time for lots of scowls at the bad daughter. Maybe a change of subject would help. "How's Dad? How's the store? Busy as ever?"

"You mean your brokenhearted father? Oh, he's fine. Just fine. Thanks for asking. I'll let him know you care."

Holly put on her floppy beach hat. "I do care, Mom. Tell him I said hi." The elevator stopped again. Holly tucked her head down and cupped her hand around the phone. "Will you do that for me, Mom?" She heard her mom's sniffles. "Oh God. No, don't start crying."

"Coconuts."

"What?"

Had she heard right? "Mom? Did you say coconuts?" She meant to turn the volume up on her phone but her finger slipped, and she accidentally put it on speaker. Her mother's voice blared through the elevator.

"Any idea how hard it is knowing that you hate Christmas so much you'd rather drink out of coconuts with little umbrellas than your grandmother's special Christmas punchbowl? Come home, Holiday. Your family—"

In a panic, Holly hit the End Call button. Silence filled the elevator. She didn't dare turn back around to face the strangers who'd heard her mother's rant. Mentioning the punchbowl was a new low for her mom. She usually kept her guilt trips a little lighter. Things like it being Holly's job to put the angel on the tree, and no one could replace her. Or how the gingerbread cookies were never quite as good when she wasn't there to decorate them. Her mom had taken it to a whole other level with the punchbowl comment. Holly leaned forward and pressed her forehead against the wall. She'd stay like that until the world's longest elevator ride came to an end.

Traditions loomed large in the Hudson house. Grandmother Hudson had a silver punchbowl that had been passed down to her by her grandmother. It came out of storage once a year on Christmas Eve and was placed on the table with almost religious reverence. The same fruity punch recipe had been used for generations, and it was the only drink ever served from the bowl. Holly likened it to a warm sangria of sorts, but she didn't know what all was in it. It had been handed down with the punchbowl, and tradition held that only the inheritor could know the recipe.

Grandmother Hudson had passed away the previous year. She'd left the punchbowl to Holly, and along with the recipe, it was still in a box in her parents' attic. As much as she knew they'd want to get it out and use it for Christmas, they never would. It was Holly's responsibility to continue the legacy of the Christmas punchbowl. A task she wanted nothing to do with.

When the elevator dinged, Holly turned back around. The car had emptied except for one great pair of legs. She lifted the brim of her floppy hat and saw Meredith standing there holding the door open. Great. Perfect. Just great. Had she, along with everyone else, heard the entire conversation with her mother?

"After you," Meredith said. She had a smirk on her face. A smirk that said, yeah, so about that phone call with your mom.

Shit, shit, shit. Not only had Meredith possibly, no, most likely, as in totally definitely, heard Holly's conversation with her mother, but by the looks of her sheer white swimsuit cover-up, she seemed to be headed in the same direction as Holly. "Oh God," Holly whispered. She wanted to pull the brim of her hat over her face. She wanted to disappear. "Thanks, but I think I forgot something in my room. My aunt! I forgot my aunt in the room. And my uncle. He's there too. Oh, and my brother. It's just my parents who couldn't join us this year. Every other year, of course, but this year they couldn't make it."

"All of you stay in the same room?"

"We're super close-knit," Holly said. "You know those tight family bonds. Families who sleep together, stay together." She should shut up now. The idiot factor was hitting max capacity.

Meredith took her hand from the door and let it close behind them. "What floor?"

"Sixteen." It was another lie. Why couldn't she speak truth to power or whatever the hell that saying was? Why was practically every word that came from her mouth an unnecessary skid off the road of reality?

Of course, there wasn't even a number sixteen for Meredith to push, so she stood there with her finger at the ready while she stared Holly down.

"Eleven," Holly said.

"Are you sure?"

"I don't know why I said sixteen. I always stay on eleven. Same room every year. Unless of course, that room has a plumbing issue, in which case, I was moved to twelve one year. Better than being under the plumbing problem, right?"

Meredith tilted her head. "Don't you mean, *we*?"

Holly decided enough was enough. Any explanation would just lead to another lie. She wasn't sure if she could even come back from the lies she'd already told. She would have to get a table for four everywhere she went in case she ran into Meredith. Then tell her that everyone in the family except for Holly was a fast eater, and she was just finishing up. Yes, because that made so much sense.

"I knew it was kismet," Meredith said.

Holly raised her head but didn't reply.

"A panties flying everywhere kismet shitshow, but still, I knew I'd run into you again."

She'd move to a different hotel. Holly would just pack up and have the relaxing, quiet, solo Christmas break she'd been looking forward to. She didn't need the elegance and quiet of the fancy hotel she'd been going to ever since the first *Evermore* came out. An out-of-the-way resort with the best seafood she'd ever eaten? And those plush robes? And honestly, with the bicycles and the paddle board yoga class? Nope. She didn't need any of it. She could just spend the rest of the week at the Best Western on Waikiki. Surely there had to be one. No more humiliating run-ins with the hottest executive the Wifetime Channel had ever employed. Then, maybe one day, a very long time from now, they'd pass each other in the hall again, and Meredith would ask about the family, and Holly could lie again. Problem solved.

The elevator doors opened, and Holly made a run for it. "Good to see you again," she said in the cheeriest voice she could muster.

"I rented a cabana by the pool for the day," Meredith said. "Get your shit together and join me later?"

Holly stopped but didn't turn around. Get her *shit* together? She was pretty sure Meredith wasn't referring to the human beings she'd claimed to have forgotten. She turned around and was about to decline because she'd be too busy packing and moving to another hotel when Meredith said, "You'd be doing me a big favor. I mean, how silly will I look sitting in there all alone?"

Holly gestured with her thumb. "I have to get—"

"Bring them with you. There's plenty of room for everyone." Meredith shrugged. "Or you could tell them you met someone."

Time seemed to stand still. Holly waited for Meredith to clarify the same way Holly would, with a quick lie like, *I mean, a friend. You found a friend.* But that obviously wasn't Meredith Drake's style. No, her style was to keep steady eye contact while the elevator filled up with steam due to her sexiness. Power. Attitude. Holly didn't have a chance.

"Yeah, okay." Her voice seemed weak and unsure compared to Meredith's. How could a woman like that possibly be attracted to her?

❖

Holly walked past the row of cabanas that dotted the enormous round pool. Each was a large, tented bed with curtains on each side. They faced the pool, and each had their front drapes tied to the posts that made up the cabana's frame. Holly knew from that time she'd gone to a friend's bachelorette party in Vegas that they probably ran six hundred dollars for half a day, not including the food and beverage minimum. They were nice.

She walked past a few more that had lounge chairs for sunning and shaded sofas for relaxing. Those were more permanent structures with flat-screen TVs, ceiling fans, and mini fridges. Holly glanced into one and saw a man at a laptop talking loudly into a speaker phone. A bored-looking kid sat next to him playing video games. Holly wondered why they even bothered.

Most of the land on either side of the pool extended to gardens and walking paths. The hotel loomed large with its two hundred or so lanai rooms that overlooked the water. On the south side, a strip of land separated the pool from the ocean. That was where Holly discovered that there were cabanas, and then there were *cabanas*.

Cabana twenty-five had a gate that opened onto a patio. Behind that was a small building with French doors. It looked more like a guest house. The front side faced the pool. The back side, which Holly could see through the windows, faced the ocean.

Meredith stepped through the doors with two glasses of champagne. "I'm so glad you could make it." Holly took her glass, and Meredith tapped it with hers and said, "Here's to leaving all of the bullshit behind."

Holly couldn't help but wonder if by *bullshit*, Meredith meant Holly's big fat family lie. The fact that Meredith had two glasses—and only two glasses—at the ready certainly suggested she already knew. Should Holly just cop to it? Just tell the damned truth, that she hated Christmas and everything related to it? Hated red and green as a color combination. Hated pine-scented candles and pine cone wreaths and mistletoe. Let's not forget tree-lighting ceremonies, fruitcake and eggnog. And secret Santas. Ugh. Oh, and Christmas carolers. What were you even supposed to do when they came to the door? Should you join in? Were you supposed to tip? It was so awkward. She hated all of it. And she hadn't spent Christmas with her parents since her junior year of college. She clinked their glasses together. "I can drink to that."

Meredith seemed to scrutinize her after taking a sip of champagne. Her intense brown eyes wandered down Holly's body and back up again. When their eyes met, Holly couldn't hold her gaze. She turned away and said, "You really scored with this cabana. Can't imagine it was easy to come by this time of year." She took a breath and willed herself to be cool this time. No lies. "Seems like a Christmas haven to me."

"How so?"

Holly took another sip of champagne and turned back around. "Well, you're staying in a great hotel on the beach. Sand, champagne, a ginormous tropical fruit plate." Holly stuck a toothpick in a small piece of papaya and popped it in her mouth. "What more do you need?"

Meredith furrowed her brow. "Are you being serious? Holly Hudson, the queen of all things Christmas, thinks *this* is what it's all about?" She made a big sweeping motion with her hand, almost knocking over a bottle of champagne. "And is your name really Holiday? Again, sorry. I overheard your mom."

Holly somehow managed to catch the tilting bottle before it fell. Remarkably, she didn't fall, or spill it, or lose her bikini top in the process. That was a very good sign indeed. She topped off her glass and said, "Yes. And yes. But the only people who get to call me Holiday are my parents. So don't even think about it, Mer. Can I call you Mer?"

"No, you may not."

"That's fair."

Meredith tilted her head. "I can't seem to wrap my head around it. I mean, your *Evermore* series has upped the ante on cheesy Christmas movies. I've seen the numbers. You're changing the industry. And yet, your mother said you hate Christmas so much you won't even go home."

This was where it always started. How could Holly Hudson be so anti-Christmas? She moved to a chair, sat back, and crossed her legs. "Should I be flattered that you googled me after I saved your sexy undies from the circle of shame, aka the luggage carousel at the airport?"

Meredith sat on the arm of the sofa. "No. You should be flattered that your name came up in a development meeting. That's where I first heard about you."

"Oh, I see. So you haven't actually seen the *Evermore* series, and you have no idea what it's about."

Meredith set her glass on an end table and clasped her hands together. "Why do I feel like I'm being punished for giving you a compliment?"

It was a power move for Meredith to stay on the arm of the sofa where she sat taller than Holly. That was fine. It gave Holly a nice view of those long legs. Of course, that didn't stop her anger from flaring up. Sure, Meredith had given her a compliment. A compliment frosted in judgment. "Because you heard my name and you thought you'd throw out a few facts to impress me, but the truth is, you know nothing about me."

"Maybe your aunt and uncle could fill me in on the details." Meredith smirked. "Never mind. I know you lied to me about being here with your family, which is your prerogative. I just wonder why you felt it was necessary."

"You said it yourself. How could Holly Hudson possibly hate all things Christmas? And when people find out, they decide I'm some sort of fraud and look at me like I'm crazy. Kind of like you're doing right now." Holly leaned forward. It wouldn't make her sit taller than Meredith, but maybe she'd look more serious because as usual, she was tired of this particular topic. "Besides, from where I sit, it looks like Merry, Merry Meredith is here in paradise to escape Christmas too."

Unfortunately, Meredith didn't seem the least bit fazed. In fact, she leaned in a little bit and said, "So I guess we're not going to join the children on the mezzanine this afternoon for the gingerbread house building contest? I was really looking forward to that."

"You were looking forward to competing with children? Sorry, but you're on your own there."

"I'm a competitive person who happens to make a damn good gingerbread house. It's all in the frostcicles."

"Frostcicles?" Holly wasn't sure that was even a word.

"Join me and I'll show you."

Holly waved it off. "Eh, you don't need me and my grinchiness weighing you down."

"You're right," Meredith said with a shrug. "I have this whole thing in the bag, but I'd prefer to not show up alone."

"You mean because it's a children's event? Yeah, probably not a good look for a Hollywood executive right now, is it?"

Meredith stiffened. "That's not what I meant at all, but forget I asked. Consider yourself off the hook for all of it. In fact, you can leave right now if you like."

Her hard stare told Holly she was dead serious. It was probably for the best since Holly was sure to continue down the Path of Humiliation until she fell off the cliff of You Can't Come Back from This One. She grabbed her beach bag and headed for the door but stopped before she opened it. "I'm sorry, Meredith. I really didn't mean to insinuate—"

A young woman dressed in a crisp white uniform opened the door. "Oh perfect. The bride is here. Congratulations." She burst into the cabana followed by a stream of people brimming with the well-starched enthusiasm of event staff. One guy held at least two dozen white and gold balloons. He let the whole bunch go at once, and they drifted to the ceiling. The ribbons hung just low enough to tickle everyone's noses.

"Meredith, what the hell is going on?" Holly whispered not all that quietly. But Meredith just shrugged, smiled, and sipped her champagne.

Food and gifts were brought in. Bouquets of flowers. A very expensive looking cake that had the words *Congratulations Sheffield and Chelsea* expertly frosted on the side. Holly had no idea someone could write such perfect calligraphy with frosting. Maybe she could write that into her next screenplay. Calligrapher turned baker falls for blah, blah, blah.

But Holly had bigger things to think about, such as how to keep the nice woman from putting a sash on her that said *Bride*. "Oh, I'm not…okay, then." There was no arguing. That sash was flung over her head with lighting speed, followed by several white leis. Holly searched for Meredith through the curtain of balloon ribbons and hotel staff. "Um…Meredith?" Another lei was draped around her neck. "Okay, I'm probably good with just the ten, but thank you. They're stunning."

The woman put a full glass of champagne in her hand and said, "We'll be back to check on you later. Enjoy your bachelorette party, Ms. Drake."

Meredith thanked everyone and closed the cabana door. When she turned, Holly said, "Look, you're super hot and all, but you're moving way too fast for me."

For the first time, Meredith laughed out loud. A real laugh. Holly loved hearing it.

"It was too late to cancel all of this." She pushed some of the balloons aside and stepped toward Holly. "Here, let me help you."

"Yeah, I couldn't possibly get this glass to my lips with all of these leis in the way, and something tells me I need to get really drunk before I walk down the aisle."

Meredith took the glass. "I think the bride is supposed to take a lei from her neck and put one on each of her bridesmaids with a kiss on the cheek. Or something like that. I don't remember for sure."

"Oh. Okay. Well, it might be bad karma to not do that. Where can I find a bridesmaid?"

Meredith pulled up a chair. "Holly, meet Chairy Hollahan, your maid of honor."

Holly took a lei from her neck and hung it on the back of the chair. "Hi, Chairy. Sorry about that sitting on you thing." She rounded the table, putting a lei on each chair. She still had two left so she put one around Meredith's neck. "Who the hell is Chelsea?"

"My idiot sister."

"Oh, you mean because she was going to marry someone named Sheffield?"

Meredith laughed. There it was again. That hearty laugh that warmed Holly's insides. "I'm really glad you're here," Meredith said. "Please don't leave."

Holly gestured with her head at the table full of food. "Mind if I dig in?"

Meredith went to the table and picked up a plate. "Here, let me fill a plate for the bride."

"Don't forget I'm eating for six."

"Right. Seven of everything in case one of you wants seconds." Meredith gave her a wink. An actual wink. And Holly swooned.

❖

Holly stretched out on the beachside lounge chair and rubbed circles on her very full tummy. "That last piece of cake was a mistake."

"Piece? As I recall, you took a fork and ate all of Sheffield and part of Chelsea." Meredith stretched out on the lounge chair next to her.

"I was sick of looking at his name. It had to go." They'd put on their sunglasses, so Holly felt safe taking a good look at Meredith and decided she looked like a movie star lying there with her face to the sun and a glass of champagne in hand. She had one knee up, which caused her cover-up to slide up her thigh. Holly resisted the urge to let out a slow whistle, but damn, what fun she would have nibbling on that inner thigh. Holly's ogling was interrupted by Meredith chuckling. "What's so funny?"

"It's a ridiculous thought, but I was just considering if the fact that we just devoured the weight of a midsized poodle in front of each other means we're bonded for life."

"I don't think that's a thing," Holly said. "There's your standard poodle and your miniature poodle, and if you like to carry your dog in your purse, there's the toy poodle."

Meredith lifted her glasses and gave her a side-eye. "Okay, poodle expert. I thought you were going to say that bonding for life while gorging wasn't a thing."

"Oh no. That is definitely a thing. I ate your sister and supposed-to-be future brother-in-law," Holly said. "With abandon. We're either bonded for life or sworn enemies. But right now, I'm like a snake that just ate a small antelope. Totally defenseless. Can't move until that antelope has been digested. Bones and all. So please don't try to get your revenge right now."

Meredith lowered her sunglasses and laid her head back.

"Gluttony and pointless conversations. That usually only happens when I smoke too much weed."

"Oh, that's just a typical Friday night for me."

"And who do you have these pointless conversations with?"

"Just some friends from my apartment building."

"No big dates on Friday night?"

"I've been in a dating desert for months now."

"How many months exactly?"

"Sixty-three."

"That's hard to believe."

"How so?"

"Well, because…" Meredith trailed off. "Never mind. I'll just put my big foot in my mouth."

Holly leaned up so she could examine the foot. "Looks like a normal-sized foot to me." She tilted her head. "But what's that big bump on your toe, and does it make it hard to wear shoes?"

Meredith threw both feet in the air. "What bump? Where?"

Holly fell back on the lounge in a fit of laughter. "Oh my God, the look of panic on your face."

Meredith shook her head. "You're something else, Holly Hudson."

"I'm just messing with you, Mer. Can I call you Mer?"

"Still a hard no on that one."

Holly rolled onto her side. "Sorry. I think I'm drunk on cake and champagne."

"And canapés and petit fours and don't forget the very expensive caviar that my dear sister with commitment issues requested."

"When did you find out she was bailing?"

"When half of first class failed to board."

Holly was aghast. "Whoa. Hold up. You didn't know until yesterday?"

"Yeah, she texted me. Apparently, she was so busy informing all of her twelve-year-old bridesmaids, so they could make plans to spend the holidays with their families, that she forgot to actually tell me."

Holly let that sink in for a moment. "Meredith?"

"Yeah?"

"Is it just me or did Sheffield totally dodge a bullet here?"

Meredith laughed again. "You know, Holly, I'll say it again. I'm really glad you're here."

"Me too, Mer-Bear."

"And that would be a nope. Multiple nopes, in fact."

"Okay. Seriously, though. I'm so sorry she left you high and dry like this. I mean, she missed out on one helluva bachelorette party."

"It's not the money," Meredith said. "It's the immaturity. The lack of knowing what you really want in life. Getting everyone on board and then abandoning ship as if no one matters but yourself." Meredith turned onto her side as well. "I would never leave a person hanging the way my sister left poor Sheffield. And a hundred bucks says she'll change her mind, and we'll have to go through all of this again."

Holly waved it off and said, "Nah, just tell her she had her chance. The caviar wedding will have to be lunch at a taco truck near the courthouse."

"Oh my God, you're brilliant. I'm absolutely going to tell her that exact thing. And I'll offer to buy those tacos. All they can eat." Meredith threw a fist in the air. "Yes!"

So this was what relaxed Meredith looked like. And with both of them lying on their sides, it felt sort of intimate, the way it would if they were lying in bed together.

Meredith lifted her glasses. "What's that big smile for?"

Holly resisted the urge to look away and blow off the question with some sort of inconsequential reply. Instead, she held Meredith's gaze and said, "You're kind of adorable, you know that?"

"That's a word not many people use to describe me. Driven. Determined. Ambitious."

"I would say you're layered." Holly's gaze wandered down Meredith's body. "Take your toes for instance. What is that shade of pink called?"

Meredith lifted her foot. "It's called Baby, Take a Vow. It's my neutral go-to pink."

"See? Both the color and the fact that you know the name of the color screams 'I'm a softy.' And on top of that, I bet those people don't know about your gingerbread house-making skills."

"And I'd like to keep it that way," Meredith said. "So what will it take for you to keep my deep, dark secrets, Ms. Hudson?"

"You keep mine, and I'll keep yours." Holly offered her fist. "Let's bump on it." She cringed on the inside. *Let's bump?*

With a sly grin, Meredith bumped her fist. "Deal."

Chapter Four

Holly hadn't made any promises regarding the gingerbread house competition. She'd planned to walk off some of her gluttony on the beach, maybe put some words to paper, then take a long hot bath before dinner. Of course, that assumed she'd ever eat again, a possibility that remained up in the air at that particular moment. Her plans were never set in stone when she was in Hawaii. They didn't need to be since she didn't have anyone else to worry about.

She'd flirted with Meredith more than once. She was either so bad at it that Meredith hadn't noticed, or she'd purposely ignored the flirtatious banter. She didn't think she'd taken it too far, even though she was kind of tipsy. They both were. She didn't say anything inappropriate like *hey, hottie, come and sit on my lap, would ya?* Or *give me your finger and let me slather caviar all over it and slowly lick it off.* A caviar dipped nipple would have been better anyway. Holly entertained that thought as the elevator made its way down to the mezzanine where the gingerbread fiasco was to take place and about which, again, Holly remained noncommittal.

Meredith Drake up close and personal? Would Holly even survive such an event? Maybe the strong attraction was why she'd eaten practically everything in sight. Nerves did that to her. She'd eat and talk too fast and eventually, usually without fail, never have a second date. Gwen would point out that the dates nearly always called and that Holly was the one who ghosted them. She'd say, "The only way to get over a fear of horses is to actually climb on top of one and ride her." Whatever, Gwen.

It wasn't a problem if Holly was just kind of, sort of attracted to a woman. She could look them in the eye while cutting a perfectly proportioned piece of steak, slide it into her mouth like a porn star, and moan the words *have you ever tasted anything as perfect as this steak?* Then cut another piece and hand feed it to her date. When the stakes were low, Holly was a regular old Don Juan. Relatively speaking anyway.

She'd managed pretty well with Meredith. She'd kept her cool and made jokes. But Meredith would never see the smooth, sexy side of Holly. Not in a million years could she be that cool with someone who made her heart beat so fast.

The elevator doors opened onto the mezzanine. Holly looked around and whispered, "Of course." The hotel staff had set up tables around the large Christmas tree for the contest, so all the guests could look on while children of all ages decorated some premade gingerbread houses. That was smart. The problem—and this was something Holly had seen time and again—was getting the walls to carry the weight of an overly frosted roof.

As with most kids who grew up in Christmas Cove, Vermont, Holly knew a thing or two about gingerbread houses. She even had a few blue ribbons in a box somewhere to prove it. That was a lie. There was no way her mother had them in a box. They were probably still tacked to the bulletin board in her childhood bedroom, right next to the dried-up crown of holly she'd gotten at the Little Miss Christmas pageant her mother put on every year.

Holly weaved through the crowd and stopped when she saw Meredith sitting in a chair on the sidelines, sipping a martini. Why wasn't Ms. Frostcicles participating when there were a few extra chairs and several houses that hadn't yet been claimed? "Well, shoot," she whispered.

With a big sigh, Holly went over and bent down next to her. "I can't blame you for sitting this one out. I mean, look at the frostcicles on that kid's roofline. He's unbeatable, if you ask me."

Meredith set her martini down and leaned forward. "I'd put that kid out of business in no time flat." She shrugged. "But it'd be weird."

"I find that surprising. A strong successful woman such as yourself shouldn't give two hoots what anyone thinks."

"Maybe I'm not that strong. Maybe I'm just faking it."

"Are you?"

"Everyone has their weaknesses. The trick is to never let the wrong people see them."

"Sage advice," Holly said with a firm nod. "But no one you know is here, so it's not like you're letting the wrong people see your softer side."

Meredith pulled back and turned. "Is that what this is? My softer side?"

"Vulnerable side. Whatever you want to call it." Holly stood and waited.

Meredith took a deep breath. "So I guess I should march over there with my head held high and my eye on the prize."

"What is the prize?"

Meredith stood and set her half-full glass on a waiter's tray as he walked by. "Doesn't matter. It's the winning that matters."

"And if you don't win?"

"You cannot be serious."

Holly envisioned the photo op. A bunch of disgruntled kids surrounding a winner twice their height with her trophy held high above her head. She held in her giggle. "Right. The winning. Here's to Meredith Drake, queen of the gingerbread houses, taking home that prize."

Meredith's expression seemed hopeful. "Join me?"

Not on any planet in any galaxy could Holly turn Meredith down when she'd shown this side of herself. "Or miss out on schooling these little know-it-alls in the fine art of gingerbread house decorating? I am so in."

They sat side by side at an empty table. Holly could tell Meredith had just showered. She smelled delicious, and the ends of her hair were still damp. Holly resisted the urge to lean over and breathe her in. Maybe wrap her arm around her waist and whisper something like *can I have you for dessert later?* That was what smooth Holly would do.

"Are you sure you're okay with this? We might be here a while," Meredith said.

"I'll survive. Besides, there's a need-to-know situation building up inside me."

"You're wondering if I'm really that good." Meredith spread her interlocked fingers out as if she was cracking her knuckles. "Sit back and watch the master."

Holly laughed. "Master. Right. Now this I've got to see."

Meredith gave her a steady stare. "Unless you'd prefer to do one of your own, Ms. Hudson."

It wasn't exactly a double-dog dare. Except Holly knew it totally was. She maintained the eye contact. "You should probably know, this is not my first gingerbread house."

"*Oh*, I'm shaking in my flip-flops."

"Okay, smartypants. If I win, I get to call you Mer."

Meredith grinned. "Absolutely, but fair is fair. If I win, you know what I get to call you."

"I assure you, it won't come to that."

"That's an awful lot of confidence for someone who was being dragged around a luggage carousel less than twenty-four hours ago."

It turned out that Holly was exceptionally good at multitasking. As she watched Meredith organize her supplies with precision, she spent a good portion of time imagining all of the other things Meredith could possibly be good at. Things like the deft use of her tongue while slow dancing. The thought made the butterflies in her stomach stir because in her mind, she could hear the sounds of moist lips touching and soft moans of pleasure.

Even as Holly focused on decorating her own house, her eyes kept drifting over to Meredith's nimble fingers. She imagined them dancing over her body with the same skill and grace the gingerbread house was receiving. She also imagined Meredith's long, slender fingers dancing inside her and the sounds that would evoke. The gasps for air, the breathy moans with every push. Whatever incoherent things Holly would cry out when she climaxed.

She wiped her brow, squeezed her legs together to ease the ache, and tried to focus on the task at hand. This was definitely different from all of her other gingerbread house competitions. Of course, most of those had taken place before she'd realized she was gay.

Meredith looked at her and said, "Everything okay?"

Holly gave her a weak smile. "All good over here. Just figuring out my game plan."

Meredith gave her a nod. "I appreciate your professionalism."

Holly bit her lip and focused on the task at hand. If Meredith only knew just how unprofessional she could be.

❖

It had been two hours of bliss that Holly would never admit to anyone. The seriousness with which they'd both eventually taken to the task was unparalleled. The concentration, the cute words of satisfaction Meredith whispered to herself when she finished a task. And the end result? Well, it was indeed impressive, frostcicles and all.

Back in Christmas Cove, Meredith's house would have been an easy fourth place, maybe third if one of the town's usual frontrunners had a disappointing showing.

"Okay, there's no way my roof could have held all that weight," Meredith said.

Holly had used the walls of an extra house to cut out the shape of Santa's sleigh. She'd perched it on the snow-covered roof next to the chimney. The feet from a chocolate Santa stuck out of the chimney. Holly didn't look up from the mountain she was creating with the extra roof. After dotting her mountain with trees, and adding plenty of fresh snow, she just needed to smooth out trails to complete the look of her ski-in/ski-out lodge. She shook her head. "Amateurs."

"I'm just saying, all pre-made houses are not created equal, and you clearly got a superior one."

Holly looked up. "My source materials are no different than yours." She pointed at her house. "As you can see, I've used these candy canes to approximate post-and-beam construction and do the job of a load-bearing wall."

"It's possible I've underestimated you."

Holly grinned. "I appreciate your admitting that, Mer. It means a lot."

Once they'd awarded the prizes, Holly leaned in and

lowered her voice. "Your house is meticulous. Too bad they were so ageist they wouldn't even include us in the competition."

"We would've taken gold and silver."

"I think you mean silver"—Holly gestured toward Meredith's house before pointing at her own—"and gold."

Meredith gave her a side-eye. "I feel like I've been hustled."

"Oh, you absolutely have been."

With a careful hand, Meredith picked up her gingerbread house.

"Where are you taking that?" Holly looked around. "Everyone's leaving theirs here for the display. We can't deny them the opportunity to see our quality work."

"Oh, no. This is going to my room so I can have at least one Christmas decoration in there."

"And also so you can admire it up close?"

Meredith smirked as they headed for the elevators. "No one will appreciate the fine details the way I will. Call it a Christmas gift to myself." She paused. "Thank you, by the way."

"For what?"

"For joining me."

With hesitation in her voice, Holly said, "You kind of have a thing about showing up alone, don't you?"

"I have a thing about spending the most family-oriented holiday of the year alone. Damn my sister and her flakiness. If I did that to our parents, they'd cut me out of their will, but not Chelsea. She's the baby of the family, which means her slack line could span the Grand Canyon."

"I'm going to guess that what you really don't like is being seen as someone who's lonely."

"Strangers taking pity on me and inviting me to sit at their table because no one should be alone on Christmas Eve? Yeah. Just kill me now."

"I come here every year. I always figured people saw me as self-assured and independent."

"Keep telling yourself that, Holiday."

Holly imagined what her parents would do if they saw a woman like Meredith dining alone on Christmas Eve. It would never cross their minds that a person would choose quiet over chaos. Surely, something bad must've happened. A family tragedy. A divorced mother having just dropped off her kids at the other parent's home for a night of festivities they couldn't share in.

She thought about a scene she'd written into a movie where a lonely widower sat in the town diner. Without a miracle, the diner was sure to go into bankruptcy thanks to the big chain restaurant that had moved in across the street, but that wasn't the point. The lonely widower ordered two slices of pumpkin pie, one for himself and one for his dead wife. Holly's mom had called bawling the night the movie premiered when she'd seen the slow zoom on the piece of pie sitting across from the widower, untouched. It was fair to say her mother had a low tolerance for holiday loneliness. In fact, the scene had been inspired by something she'd seen as a kid.

Holly always felt so embarrassed when her parents would approach total strangers after having assumed the worst. Rarely did the people join them at their table. And the man who'd inspired Holly's scene? The one Holly's mom had thought for sure was a lonely widower? Well, he'd perked right up when his wife showed up a few minutes late with shopping bags full of Christmas gifts for their nine grandchildren.

Of course, Holly and Meredith weren't in the same boat. Meredith wanted to be with her loved ones and seemed sad that she wasn't. Holly loved her parents, but she'd lost the desire to be anywhere near her hometown at this time of year. For the record, she had invited them to Hawaii in the past, but they always turned her down. She pushed the up button on the elevator and said, "If you saw someone who seemed to be all alone on Christmas Eve, would you approach them?"

"I don't know. I guess it would depend on the situation. And maybe it would depend on the person."

Holly pointed at herself. "Me. If you saw me eating alone, what would you do? Would you assume the worst like my parents always did when they saw someone alone, or would you consider other options? Such as, I'm a perfectly normal human being with a full life who just happens to prefer being alone on Christmas?"

Meredith tilted her head. "So this hatred for all things Christmas runs fairly deep, huh?"

Holly gave her a gentle nudge and said, "Hey, I just spent two hours decorating my Holly Hudson ass off, so no judgment, okay?"

Meredith grinned. "It's nice."

"What is?"

"The Holly Hudson ass." The elevator doors opened, and Meredith stepped in. "Going up?"

"Actually, I thought I'd take a walk on the beach before dinner."

"I'm going to pour myself a glass of wine and send pics of this masterpiece to my mother. She'll love it."

"I'm sorry you don't get to be at home with your family." The doors started to close, but Holly reached a hand out to stop them. "But I'm glad you're here."

"You're sorry, and you're glad?" Meredith smiled. "You know what, Holly? So am I. Enjoy the beach."

The doors closed, and Holly stood there, replaying Meredith's words in her mind. There was no questioning the fact that Meredith had just flirted with her. Holly walked out of the hotel sporting a grin the size of the White House Christmas tree because, of course, everything in her childhood had been compared to the size of the White House Christmas tree.

❖

"I'll be right there." Holly wrapped her wet hair in a towel and threw on her fluffy pink robe. She looked through the peephole and took a step back.

"It's me. Meredith."

"Hey," Holly shouted through the door. "I was just—"

"Getting ready to join me for dinner?"

Holly opened the door. "Getting out of the shower." She gave Meredith a lightning fast once over and said, "Wow, you look amazing."

"Thank you," Meredith said. "Christmas Eve has always been a dressy event in my world, though I will most likely be surrounded by tropical shirts and dresses tonight. Hmm. I hadn't thought of that until just now. Do you think I'll look too out of place?"

Holly folded her arms across her chest and acted like she was seriously considering the question. "You could be right. I mean, who wears a satin smoking jacket on Christmas Eve?"

Meredith started to protest. Holly put up a hand. "Wait. I was just teasing you. This is quite possibly the hottest Christmas outfit I've ever seen on a woman." She took a step closer. There were tiny sprigs of holly embroidered on the black jacket that tied at the waist with a velvet cord. The forest green cigarette pants and matching velvet loafers looked so runway worthy, Holly briefly considered telling Meredith she'd picked the wrong profession and should move to New York posthaste to model for Dolce & Gabbana.

Holly couldn't tell if there was a blouse or a camisole under the jacket. If there was, it was low-cut because all she could see was bare chest. She huffed and said, "The ugly Christmas sweater fad can bite me if this is the alternative."

"Does that mean you'll join me for dinner?"

Holly folded her arms again. "That depends. Is this because you feel sorry for me? Or because I'm your only option? Or because you're playing a grown-up Cindy Lou Who, and you've made it your mission to see my heart triple in size?"

"Or maybe, just maybe, I had a great time with you today, and I'd very much like it to continue over dinner." Meredith held up two white leis made of small white and red flowers. "Would you care to join me?"

Well, shit. There it was. Holly's heart tripled in size. She raised an eyebrow. "So you're saying this might have happened whether it was Christmas Eve or not? You asking me out on a date because that's what you're doing, right?"

"I can see you're someone who likes to have clarity in her life."

"I just don't want to misunderstand the situation," Holly said.

Meredith seemed to consider it for a moment and said, "How about if I go change into comfy clothes and join you in your suite. We'll order room service, and you'll know without a doubt that I simply want to spend some time with you tonight."

She hadn't scoffed at the mention of it being a real date. Hadn't even flinched. Holly wanted to jump up and down and scream *I'm the luckiest lesbian this side of the White House*

Christmas tree, but she managed to keep her cool. She looked Meredith up and down again and said, "That's a nice idea, but if you think I'm going to let that hot jacket go to waste, well, you just don't know me very well." She closed the door and immediately opened it again. "I'll meet you in the lobby in fifteen minutes."

❖

Holly found Meredith waiting by the Christmas tree with the leis in hand. She put one over Holly's head, then Holly did the same for her. Meredith leaned in and kissed her cheek ever so lightly and said, "You look gorgeous. Love the dress."

Holly hadn't brought much in the way of dressy clothes, but she always packed a little black dress and heels just in case she needed them. After five holidays in Hawaii, this was the first time she'd needed them. She smiled a little, thinking how appalled her mother would be that she wore black on Christmas Eve. She'd blown her hair straight and put on some light makeup. She didn't need much since she'd gotten a bit of color at the pool.

Meredith put her hand on Holly's back and pointed. "We're this way. Are you a fan of spiked eggnog, or would a non-Christmassy drink suit your tastes better tonight? A piña colada maybe?"

"What, no wassail? Or hot chocolate with a candy cane straw?"

"I'm sure that, given the right incentive, I could make that happen for you," Meredith said.

They were headed in the direction of the more formal restaurant that had a high glass ceiling for all of the lush greenery that grew on the periphery. Holly loved to have breakfast in that particular room because it felt so tropical. As they entered, she gaped and said, "Oh my God, climate change is real."

Meredith tilted her head. "Okay, so someone got a little bit overzealous with the flocking."

Every plant, tree, and shrub had been not just lightly dusted, but doused in fake snow. "They flocked the fuck out of everything," Holly said. "It looks like the invasion of the abominable palms. Any second now, I expect them to start coming alive and eating the little children." The music stopped abruptly, and Holly turned to Meredith. "That might be their cue. We should run."

Meredith grabbed her by the waist. It wasn't necessary because she wasn't actually going anywhere besides lesbian heaven now that those warm hands had found their way to her body. In fact, she stilled under the touch, determined to remember everything about this moment when Meredith touched her while the opening salvo to Nat King Cole's 1961 version of "The Christmas Song" floated through the air, and a small boy stood at their feet and stared with fascination. Maybe that part she'd leave out, but the feeling Meredith's hands had just evoked in her was something she'd never forget.

"I find you so charming," Meredith said. "Even when you use profanities in front of children."

"Sorry," she whispered. "I usually save my swear words for more appropriate situations like zombies surrounding the city or, you know, great sex."

Meredith didn't break their physical contact, but she did drop one hand and turn so they both faced the room. She moved her other hand to Holly's lower back and leaned in to say, "It's okay. I'm sure he's heard much worse."

It felt as if her hand was burning a hole through Holly's dress and would soon find bare skin. When that happened, Holly would surely burst into a hot flame of sexual desire, and everyone in the room would know how long it had been since a woman had touched her with such strong intention. And yes, she was sure that Meredith had intended to provoke a feeling with that touch.

Holly might as well have considered the night over at that point because soon, she'd talk too much. Probably with her mouth full of candied yams and cranberry sauce. And there would be no kiss good night or even future plans made. Unless she could somehow keep her shit together.

She spotted the kid who'd taken first place in the gingerbread house contest sitting with his parents. He even had the blue ribbon pinned to his little chest. Yes, he would be the perfect distraction from the fingers that were now lightly caressing her back. "Oh, wow," she said. "Look who's here. What was his name? Standish or something? Do you think he's related to Sheffield?"

Meredith's eyes narrowed when she found him in the crowd. "He's sporting that same smarmy smirk that screams *I own this fucking world*. They're probably distant cousins."

The host stopped short, then cleared his throat. "Your table is ready, Ms. Drake."

"Thank you." Meredith leaned in as they followed him to the table and whispered, "It seemed to me like the appropriate situation for a swear word."

"Totally was," Holly whispered back. "Perfect f-word placement in a sentence. Well done."

They were seated at a small table for two near the windows. Outside, the palm trees that lined the beach were wrapped in beautiful white lights, which made up for the flocked monsters from hell. One of the reasons Holly loved staying at this particular hotel was because they never went too overboard with the Christmas decorations. If she had to define it, she'd call what they'd done in the past "Christmas

Suggestive." What had caused the pendulum to swing so far in the other direction, she hadn't a clue. A staffing change maybe? An all too eager volunteer from accounts payable or maybe the events department who claimed to have experience with flocking? It was anyone's guess.

What appeared to be a rather expensive bottle of champagne was chilling in an ice bucket by their table. That would ease Holly's desire to carry on a pointless conversation while stuffing her face with whole Maine lobster dressed up like Santa Claus. She was exaggerating, of course. It was really just a tiny Santa hat sitting atop the head of the lobster that had just been served to their dining neighbors on the left. "Oh God," Holly said under her breath. "It just keeps getting worse." She tried for a casual head nod in Mr. Lobster Claus's direction.

Meredith raised her glass and said, "Holly Hudson, I'm going to make you love Christmas again."

"Ha. Am I supposed to toast to that?"

"Don't leave me hanging."

"Those are some big words, Ms. Drake. Maybe too big. Even for you."

Meredith reached across the table and clinked her glass against Holly's. "I think you'll learn that it's not wise to underestimate me."

Holly kept her eyes on Meredith while she took a sip, then set her glass down. This woman had no idea just how deeply Holly's hatred for Christmas ran. But what the hell? It might be fun to watch her try to make her love it again. Especially if it involved flocking with a U. And minus an L. And also an O. And maybe Holly could get her mind out of the gutter too.

❖

They left the creepy world of climate change behind, along with their shoes, which had been tucked under a hedge while they walked along the beach. Meredith untied the cord on her jacket. "I want to feel the breeze on my skin." She took it off, hooked it in her finger and threw it over her shoulder. She glanced at Holly and said, "I wish it was chilly out here so I could wrap my jacket around your shoulders."

The shy look on her face told Holly that she maybe didn't mean to say those last words out loud. Holly knew the feeling. She took Meredith's arm and said, "I wish I could make a woman swoon the way you just did, but I'm not that smooth."

Meredith smiled. "I don't think the world sees you the way you see yourself. At least, I don't."

"Oh, please. I've had to stumble and mumble and bumble my way through every promising date I've ever been on." Holly made a circle with her thumb and finger. "This much mojo is what I have."

"And you think I have that?"

"Case in point, you just removed your freaking jacket exactly how the most interesting man in the world would do it. He'd be like, I don't usually wear a smoking jacket on the beach, but when I do, I make sure time stops when I take it off." Holly glanced at the red satin camisole that clung to Meredith's breasts. "Also, I was dying to know if you had anything on underneath it, so maybe that's why time stopped."

"And what if I hadn't? What if I'd been naked from the waist up? Would you pretend it was normal? Try to cover me up? Or would you assume I was someone who'd spent too much time in Europe?"

"I would've said 'Merry Christmas to you, Holly Hudson, because it would seem that champagne makes this woman take her clothes off.' And then I would've covered you up so we didn't get arrested."

"See? That's the perfect answer for someone like me. I want to know that you find me attractive, but I also want to know that you're a sensible, responsible person."

"Oh, I'm so both," Holly said. "Totally one hundred percent both. Gay as the day is long, and I always volunteer to be the designated driver."

Meredith looked above them. "Where's the mistletoe when a girl needs it?"

Holly didn't have a funny retort. She stopped and turned to Meredith. "Why do you ask?"

"I was thinking that maybe a kiss under the mistletoe would hasten me reaching my goal."

"Ah, the goal," Holly said. "Well, you should know that I'd probably say anything to get a kiss right now, including how much I love Christmas."

"Don't say it until you mean it."

Holly offered her hand and said, "Deal."

Meredith stepped closer. "I think we can do better than a handshake, don't you?" She reached into her pocket and pulled out a tiny piece of mistletoe. "I actually came prepared. Well, what I mean is, I stole this off a display in the lobby. I'm not even sure if it's mistletoe or just some random greenery."

Holly glanced down. "Um, Meredith?"

"Hmm?"

"I think that's poison ivy." Meredith dropped the sprig and shook her hand as if it had been burned. Holly doubled over in laughter. "Gotcha."

Meredith smirked and shook her head. "Holly Hudson, you are such a little shit."

Holly bent down and picked up the sprig, twirling it between her fingers. "If anyone should know what this is, it's me."

How many times had she held a piece of mistletoe above

her head and imagined kissing a beautiful girl with long brown hair? Too many to count. Meredith's hair wasn't long, and she didn't look like a Disney princess, thank God. She was better than anything Holly could've imagined, so she held the mistletoe high above her head and said, "It's the real thing."

Meredith dropped her jacket in the sand and took Holly's face in her hands. Their lips touched and then touched again, and it felt like a dream. Because first kisses like this didn't happen in Holly's world. They were usually awkward and not at all movie worthy. But this kiss felt like it could and should go on way after the credits had rolled. Long after all of the popcorn had been swept up and the doors locked.

Holly dropped the mistletoe and found Meredith's waist. She needed to hold on so this moment wouldn't slip through her fingers. She needed to never stop kissing Meredith Drake's soft, supple lips. Never stop feeling like this was absolutely meant to be. Kismet. Or Kissmet, as the case might be.

Meredith was the first to pull away. She caressed Holly's cheek and ran her finger over her bottom lip, then took that same lip into her mouth again. And this time, Holly's knees almost buckled when she felt Meredith's warm tongue touch hers. She gripped Meredith's blouse with both hands and tried to hold back, but a moan escaped her throat. A moan that gave away just how turned on she was.

Meredith ran her fingers through Holly's hair with one hand and wrapped the other one around her waist. She pulled her close and deepened the kiss even more. Holly held on tightly. Their breasts were touching, and Meredith's hand had slipped a little lower on Holly's back. She so desperately wanted Meredith to go even lower. She wanted to feel that hand cup her ass and squeeze it.

Meredith pulled away from the kiss just long enough to take a breath and whisper, "My God."

Holly opened her eyes. "You just jumped way ahead in your quest." She leaned in and lightly ran her tongue over Meredith's bottom lip. "Best Christmas Eve kiss ever."

And then, it all ended when a child screamed somewhere close by. They both turned and saw that the little girl was safe with her parents and just excited that a wave had washed over her feet.

Holly also wanted to run through the sand, screaming out her joy, but she kept it to a contented sigh. Meredith abruptly picked up her jacket and said, "We should head back and see if our shoes are still there."

"Yeah, okay." Holly couldn't have cared less about her shoes. She wanted to stay right where she was in Meredith's arms. Just stand there and kiss and gaze at one another until the sun came up. It was obvious Meredith didn't feel the same way. Had Holly been so lost in the hottest kiss known to womankind that she hadn't noticed if Meredith felt the same way?

Holly didn't need to overthink it, but of course, she would. For days on end probably. But then Meredith took her hand and interlocked their fingers and didn't let go until they needed to put their shoes on. That eased her mind and made her feel all kinds of giddy inside.

Holly stepped into the elevator first. She leaned against the wall and watched Meredith push the elevator button. She ran her finger along her bottom lip because if all she got tonight was that one incredibly steamy kiss on the beach, she wanted to remember the feeling forever. Her long hair had fallen forward, and she was so lost in the memory of that kiss, she didn't see it coming. She'd lost her focus for a second. Stepped out of the moment. Thank God she looked up in time to see it. Because to miss the way Meredith's eyes grazed over her body as she said the words, "Would it be presumptuous of me to wish for so much more tonight?" would have been to miss out on one of the most romantic and sexiest moments of Holly's life.

She tried to keep her cool. Told herself to breathe and come up with a sexy, flirty reply. Her mind went blank, but her body lit up. Damnit, she needed all of that hot blood to head north, not south. If she couldn't speak actual words, she'd have to use her mouth in a different way. She smiled, bit her bottom lip and with a slight shake of her head, whispered, "God, no."

Meredith seemed to like that answer. She smiled and held the elevator door when it opened. "Give me ten minutes, and then come to my room. I'll order more champagne."

Holy shit. Something was really going to happen between them. Holly waited until the doors closed before she ran full speed to her room. She freshened up while she tried to decide if she should change clothes. If things carried over into the morning, she didn't really want to have to put her dress and heels back on at the crack of dawn. Then again, she'd never done a walk of shame before. Maybe it would be fun to have that little scenario under her belt. Sex hair. Smeared makeup. The scent of Meredith Drake clinging to her lips. A slow saunter down the hallway in a wrinkled dress that told the world Meredith had just slid down Holly's chimney wearing thigh high boots and crotchless panties. Not that she had either of those on hand, but fuck yes, she'd stay dressed up.

Holly got to Meredith's door and gave it a light knock. "Not housekeeping. You can keep your clothes off." The door opened and so did Holly's mouth. "Holy fifty shades of Mrs. Claus."

Meredith opened the door a little wider. "It was supposed to be a funny gift for Chelsea's honeymoon, but I figured it wouldn't hurt to up the ante on my Christmas campaign a bit."

"I was just...in my bathroom...imagining...I just."

Meredith closed the door and leaned against it. "I guess it's a good sign that you're not making any sense right now." She tilted her head. "It is, right?"

Holly wanted to cry tears of gratitude and joy. The risqué Santa outfit Meredith had on was made mostly of red fishnet, with tiny patches of velvet covering certain areas and a long zipper from crotch to neck. It was quite possibly the sexiest thing she'd ever seen.

The candy-cane-covered strip of leather belted around Meredith's waist made her look like a Christmas superhero. Maybe she threw candy canes that exploded in the bad guys' faces with a minty-fresh, poisonous mist. She could star in a movie called *Christmas Domination*, along with sequels one, two, three, and four and possibly a prequel.

"You look…my God, what did I do to deserve this?"

"You've been rescuing me since I got off the plane." Meredith pushed off the door and sauntered across the room the way only a dominatrix superhero could.

"Right," Holly said. "The panty debacle. Yeah, I guess you owed me one for that."

"And then there was the bachelorette party at the pool where you kindly pretended to be my sister." Meredith took the champagne bottle out of the bucket and filled two glasses.

"Well, you paid me back for that with a champagne and finger food feast."

"And the gingerbread house competition," Meredith said. "Which I very much enjoyed and wouldn't have participated in if you hadn't been there." She gave Holly a glass and said, "Cheers."

"You should've won. Well, silver at least. Those ageist judges robbed you of that first-place ribbon. Standish's house looked like an elf frat house, for Christ's sake."

Meredith's eyes grazed over Holly's body. "And then

tonight, you wore that amazing dress to dinner, which complimented my festive jacket perfectly."

"We were the best dressed couple there, if I do say so myself." Holly cringed at what she'd just said. "I mean, not a couple per se, just..." She decided to stop talking and take a large gulp of champagne.

"And on top of all of that, I haven't stopped smiling since we kissed on the beach."

Holly narrowed her eyes. "So if I'm reading between the lines correctly, what you're really saying is that I, Holly Hudson, saved Meredith Drake's Christmas."

"If you wrote the script, that would be a perfect title. *Holly Saves Christmas.*"

"I like it. So how does it end?"

Meredith took a step closer. "I'm not sure. But I think I know what happens in the second act."

"Will it involve little candy canes and wet lips?"

Meredith slid a candy cane out of its holder and dipped it in her champagne before running her tongue over it and sucking it into her mouth. She slid it back out and said, "You're the writer. You tell me."

Holly's mind reeled with the possibilities. She took the candy cane from Meredith's hand and put the wet end in her mouth. Was this really happening? Candy canes being sucked in such a seductive way that the room seemed to have less air to breathe than it did a minute ago? And Meredith standing so close, Holly could see the faint smile lines around her eyes?

If they kept this up, Holly would fall hard on a Christmas Eve spent in Hawaii, that much she knew. What she didn't know was what to do next. The kiss on the beach had ended much too quickly. She needed those soft lips again. She needed to feel that playful tongue in her mouth. She needed to kiss Meredith Drake for at least an hour.

She also needed to stay upright, so said kiss could not buckle her knees just yet. She needed to enjoy the moment. No stumbling. No mumbling. Just full words and complete sentences. Eyes wide open. Except, not wide open because that would be weird while kissing.

"Can I just…"

"Just what?" Meredith took the candy cane back and sucked on it where Holly's mouth had just been.

So much for complete sentences. Holly tried again. "I just want to look at you for a minute. You're so…I can't really put it into words." She wanted to say sappy things like *you're a Christmas miracle and a dream come true*, which Meredith kind of was, given Holly's bathroom fantasy a few minutes ago.

"I actually feel quite silly right now," Meredith said. "This is more Chelsea's thing than mine. I just thought it might be a fun surprise."

"It is," Holly said with wide eyes and a big nod. "Do you have any idea how stunning you are? I don't know Chelsea, but I find it hard to believe she'd rock this outfit the way you are."

Meredith's eyes lit up. "It would kill my sister to hear you say that. Could you repeat that for me while I record it? Where's my phone?"

Holly took Meredith's glass and set both of them down. "I'll repeat it to her face if you'd like." She stood close and put a finger under Meredith's chin. "I'm going to kiss you now because I can't wait another second."

Meredith tilted her head and whispered, "That's the best news I've had all week."

Peppermint had never tasted quite that good before. Their kisses were soft and gentle, much like they'd been on the beach, but when Meredith's hands fell to Holly's sides and she gripped her dress as if she were going to pull it up, everything changed. Sparks flew and butterflies fluttered and tongues collided, and Holly knew it wouldn't be long before she got her first look at Meredith's incredible body. Her first taste of her soft neck. Her first time touching a hardened nipple. Taking it into her mouth. Rolling it around on her tongue.

It might have just been a thank-you from Meredith. In lieu of a thank-you card, let's fuck, sort of thing, but Holly felt determined to make sure she'd get seconds. Maybe even thirds if she could keep the sun from coming up too soon. There was no way once would be enough.

It wasn't until Holly pulled away from the kiss that she heard the Christmas music playing in the background. "I Heard the Bells on Christmas Day" took on a whole new meaning. With a feather light touch, she caressed Meredith's bare shoulder, then leaned in and kissed it. "You're so soft. So beautiful. So sexy." She worked her way up Meredith's neck to her ear and whispered, "So fucking sexy."

Meredith moved her head, giving Holly better access to her neck. "You have no idea how sexy you look in that dress, but that doesn't mean I won't take it off you."

Holly stilled and set her gaze on Meredith's beautiful brown eyes. She needed to know this was real and that her words were sincere. Sure, she'd caught the eye of a few desirable women over the years, but they'd never told her she was sexy. Cute. Adorable. Kissable. Those were the words they'd use to describe her. But Ms. Smoking Jacket slash Ms. Sex on Wheels in a Santa Suit had just described her as sexy with a capital X.

"Am I going too fast?" Meredith said. "I didn't mean to assume."

Holly shook her head. "No, it's not that. It's just that there are moments in life that you want to remember forever, you know? Like inner Polaroids. You may not have a tangible photo, but you have the memory burned into your brain."

Meredith ran her finger down Holly's chest to her cleavage and said, "Burn me into your brain, Holly Hudson."

Holly leaned into her ear and said, "You already are."

Those words seemed to give Meredith all the permission she needed because before Holly knew what was happening, Meredith had taken Holly's bottom lip between her teeth and pulled her dress up. She sucked on Holly's lip while she slid her fingers under her panties and squeezed her ass.

Holly lost the ability to think or worry or speak. That was probably a good thing. She moaned into Meredith's mouth, and it felt as if all of the blood had left her brain, and any second now, she'd crash to the floor.

But that didn't happen because Ms. Super Claus held her close and kissed her like she'd never been kissed before. She was kneading her ass, and her tongue was caressing her lips and her mouth, and Meredith Drake would surely make love to her tonight. Holly's eyes popped open at the thought. She couldn't call it that. It wasn't making love. It was having sex. Fucking.

Meredith stepped behind Holly and unzipped her dress. She placed a light kiss on her shoulder and followed it with a much firmer kiss that sent chills through Holly's body. She pushed the dress off Holly's shoulders, and it fell to the floor. Soft fingers explored her back and arms. Meredith gently moved Holly's hair out of the way and kissed her neck. "You're perfect, Holly. Just perfect."

Holly stood there in her bra and panties, savoring every second. Meredith worked her way back around so they were face-to-face. She stroked Holly's side and seemed to be taking in every detail. Finally, she looked Holly in the eye. "Thank you for standing here while I admire all of you." Her eyes fell to Holly's breasts. Thank God she'd worn her good bra. "I love undressing a woman. It's so sensual. So intimate."

Holly tried to control her breathing, but her body was so hyped up, she found it difficult to take in air. She said a silent prayer to Father Christmas to not let her pass out. "I want you so much, I can barely breathe." She took Meredith's face and kissed her with all of the pent-up passion, all of the raw lust, all of the desire she'd felt for her over the last couple of days—it all came out in that kiss. And Meredith accepted it all and let it be known with a long moan that the feeling was mutual.

Holly managed to unzip Meredith's sexy Santa outfit while maintaining the kiss. The only problem was, she desperately wanted to see what she'd just uncovered, so she gave Meredith's bottom lip a little bite and said, "My turn. I have to look at you."

Meredith stilled while Holly slid the outfit off her shoulders. Holly was a breast girl. She loved everything about them. Feeling the weight of them in her hand. Running her tongue over a hardened nipple. In fact, she'd long ago decided that one of the softest places in the world was a woman's side-boob.

Meredith's breasts did not disappoint. Holly brushed her thumb along the side of Meredith's breast while she held it. Yes, it was most definitely the softest place on a woman's body. She looked Meredith in the eye and said with wonder, "Can I live in this moment forever?"

Meredith lifted Holly's other hand to her mouth and kissed it. "You say the nicest things."

Holly's mouth watered with desire. The plump lips that caressed her hand needed kissing again, but so did the hardened nipple she was circling with her thumb. And so did some other places, aka Meredith's entire body. "I'm just...I'm lost in you right now," she said. She placed a soft kiss on Meredith's neck.

"Lost in your scent, which you'll have to write down for me so I can buy it and drown myself in it. Lost in your body." Holly brushed Meredith's hair off her forehead. "Lost in you." The Santa outfit hadn't fallen to the floor. It sat on Meredith's hips, only partially unzipped. She took hold of the zipper and said, "May I?"

"I'm yours tonight," Meredith whispered. "And I hope you're mine."

In every sense of the word, Holly wanted to say, but all she could do was slowly nod.

"Good. Then I can't wait another second." Meredith pushed Holly's bra straps off her shoulders. Her eyes flicked from one breast to the other before she said, "Thank God all of my plans for this trip fell apart."

Holly cried out in pleasure when Meredith's tongue swiped her breast. She'd always loved the feeling of that first lick, followed by little nibbles and sucks. Meredith switched to the other breast, and Holly had to look. She needed to see Meredith flick her tongue against her nipple. Watch her lips take a nipple in and not let go. But the watching didn't last long. Holly threw her head back and said, "My God, that feels good." She held Meredith's head and kept her there, sure that just this would make her come if Meredith kept it up.

But Meredith seemed to have other plans. She knelt in front of Holly and worked her way down, kissing and giving her abdomen little love bites as she went. Each time her lips and tongue found a new spot, Holly felt it in her core. The closer she got to her panties and the tighter she gripped her hips, the more Holly felt as if she was coming undone in a way that had never happened before. She wanted Meredith to do whatever she pleased with her. Own her. And make Holly come so hard in her arms, the neighbors would get jealous. Possibly the entire hotel.

Holly felt her panties being pushed down as Meredith worked her way back up with more soft, teasing kisses. Their tongues met again, and Meredith's hands landed firmly on Holly's backside. She kneaded both cheeks and murmured what sounded like appreciation into Holly's mouth.

Holly pulled back and said, "You really like my ass."

"I've been admiring this ass since the airport." Meredith grabbed both cheeks and pulled Holly in so their pelvises were touching. "And I can't wait to get you on your knees," she added.

Holly's tummy did a major flip-flop. If she remembered correctly—and truth be told, it had been a very long time—being on her knees was one of her favorite positions. It appeared Meredith Drake was ambitious in and out of the office. "I want that too," Holly said. She unzipped Meredith's outfit all the way and pushed it down her legs. She helped her step out of it and got her first glimpse of her entire body. Her desire to grab Meredith by the hips and force her tongue through the wet folds and devour her clit warred with her desire to let Meredith have what she wanted. What they both wanted.

Holly turned away and knelt on the floor. If her level of arousal was high before, after being face-to-face with Meredith's shaved center, it had shot through the roof. Meredith moved behind her and knelt, too. She reached around to massage Holly's breasts. Holly covered Meredith's hands with her own and leaned back against her. Meredith's bare breasts pressed into her back. Her warm breath tickled her ear. Her fingers rolled Holly's nipples between them.

Was this really happening? Holly's eyes popped open when Meredith's hand slid down her stomach and her middle finger barely grazed Holly's clit. Her hips bucked involuntarily. She reached up and put her hand on the back of Meredith's head, then turned and flicked her tongue against her lips. Meredith's tongue flicked back at hers, then delved into Holly's mouth. She gasped as bolts of electricity shot through her body.

Holly started to feel like she was in another world where gravity didn't exist. It wouldn't have surprised her one bit if she opened her eyes and found herself floating near the ceiling. Her clit burned hot under Meredith's finger. Her shoulder was sure to be bruised by a love bite. And just when her world was about to explode, Meredith stopped what she was doing and urged Holly onto her hands and knees. "Oh God, yes," she whispered.

Meredith nipped and sucked on Holly's ass cheek and said, "Took the words right out of my mouth." She entered Holly with one finger and then two while her other hand sat firmly on Holly's lower back. "You're fucking gorgeous, Holly." She reached down and urged Holly's legs open.

Holly gladly accommodated her. With every push, she felt a little explosion inside her, because not only did the hot, sexy, powerhouse of a woman behind her know how to fuck, Holly knew that *this* was the moment she wanted to stay in forever. The moment where she gave Meredith all of her. Heart, mind, body, and soul.

Her nails dug into the carpet. Her back arched. Her hips bucked uncontrollably. "Oh God," she said with almost every breath as the orgasm built inside her. "Fuck, I'm coming. Oh God."

She came with a force that would've brought her to her knees if she wasn't already there. As she tried to catch her breath, she got up on her knees again and fell back into Meredith's arms. "Well," Meredith said. "Howdy to you too."

Holly let out a laugh and pushed herself off. "Really? You couldn't let me bask for like two seconds before you brought that up?"

"What? Bad timing?" Meredith stood to help Holly up off the floor. She led her to the bed and pulled the covers back. "I'll get us some water," she said.

Holly got under the sheets. Did she really just have sex with…her mind went blank when Meredith sauntered back to the bed like the runway model she was and offered a bottle of water. Yes. Fucking yes, she'd just had sex with her!

In an instant, Holly went from wanting to cry, then laugh, then desperately wanting to jump on the bed in celebration, but instead, she reached for the water the gorgeous woman standing in front of her offered. She took a long sip and said, "Thanks."

Meredith grinned. "For which part?" She slid under the covers and pushed Holly onto her back, then lay on top of her.

Holly spread her legs open and let Meredith settle in against her. "Well, dinner was pretty great."

"Mmm-hmm." Meredith kissed Holly's cheek and whispered in her ear. "What else?"

"Then there's the sexy jacket you wore tonight. I was very appreciative of that."

Meredith ground their pelvises together. "What else?"

Holly groaned and wrapped her legs around Meredith. "You'll get me worked up again if you keep doing that."

"Then I'll keep doing it."

Holly grabbed Meredith's ass and let their hips move in unison. "Did fucking me turn you on?"

"You have no idea." Meredith threw her head back. "Oh God, you feel good."

Holly moved her palms in circles over Meredith's nipples. "It felt so good having you inside me." She urged Meredith onto her back and got on top of her, then continued grinding against her. Meredith grabbed her face and kissed her deeply. Intimately. It felt different than the other kisses.

When they stopped for air, Meredith said, "Fuck me. Hard."

Holly didn't hesitate to fulfill the request. She slid to the side so she had access and pushed into Meredith with a level of force she hoped would send her tumbling toward an orgasm she'd never forget.

Meredith gasped, then cried out her pleasure. "Oh God, yes," she said, over and over. She gripped Holly's shoulder with one hand and dug her fingernails into her back with the other. Her hips jerked with every push, and when Holly thought she'd had enough, she pulled out of Meredith and focused her attention a little bit higher. With her middle finger, she circled Meredith's clit and dipped her tongue into her mouth. Meredith raised her head and deepened the kiss.

Meredith pulled away and put her hand on Holly's cheek. "Best Christmas ever?" she asked.

It was by far the best Christmas of Holly's adult life. Only one thing could make it better, so she increased the pressure on Meredith's clit and said, "Right after you come."

"I'm so close," Meredith said in between gasps for air. She sank her teeth into Holly's shoulder, and with a muffled scream, she came in her arms. And life, as Holly knew it, was over. Because *this* was the moment she would cling to forever, the moment when Holly knew she was in big trouble. Because there was a very real possibility that she could, and probably would, fall in love with Meredith Drake.

Chapter Five

Holly woke up to an empty bed. She got up and stretched, then threw on a fluffy robe and poured a cup of coffee from the room service tray. The gingerbread house caught her eye, so she went and examined it up close. It was turned slightly so the front door faced the hotel room door. It must've been some sort of gingerbread feng shui.

She gripped the warm cup with both hands and got lost in the tiny details Meredith had added to the windows. It really was an excellent piece of work, at least for anyone outside of the North Pole or its sister city, Christmas Cove. How Meredith had managed to make it look like a light was on inside the gingerbread house mystified her. "Impressive," she said under her breath.

"What was that?" Meredith shouted from the bathroom.

"Nothing. Just...I fucking love Christmas," Holly shouted. "Now that naked women are involved," she mumbled under her breath.

"I asked you not to say it until you mean it, remember?" Meredith leaned against the bedroom door. Her robe didn't have the hotel logo embroidered on the chest like Holly's. No, her robe was a caramel colored silk number that left very little to the imagination. Of course, Holly didn't need to imagine anything. She'd run her fingers over a taut stomach and down a soft leg the night before. She'd dipped into all of the sweetness. Sucked it off her finger. Let it linger on her lips.

Had it really happened? All of those words whispered in her ear that had made it very clear the desire was real for both of them? It felt like the only thing that kept Holly connected to this world when she'd climaxed the second time was the grip her fingers had on Meredith's silky dark hair.

"Oh, but I do mean it," Holly said. "You didn't just deck the halls, you went window to the wall. Roasted my chestnuts."

Meredith laughed. "Well, I know I had a holly jolly Christmas. See what I did there?"

"We harkened the herald angels. Several times."

Meredith stepped closer and caressed Holly's cheek with the back of her hand. She softened her tone and said, "Best. Christmas. Eve. Ever."

Holly's mouth went dry. There was so much she wanted to say, but would it be too much? Too fast? They barely knew each other. Besides, Meredith's statement wasn't a declaration of love. She'd simply let Holly know that she'd enjoyed last night. *Be cool, Holls.* She took Meredith's hand and placed a soft kiss on her palm. "I've never made love on Christmas Eve before." She decided to leave it as a blank statement with nothing particular implied. Except she'd used those two words: made love. She should've said she'd never had sex on Christmas Eve before. *Damnit, Holls.*

"That was a first for me too," Meredith said.

Holly wrapped her arms around Meredith's waist. "Should we blame it on the mistletoe? The magic of Christmas? Your hot body in that pornographic Santa suit?"

"Blame it on my lingerie spilling out of my suitcase at the

airport and me realizing it was that sexy writer with the very nice backside who rescued the very set I'm currently wearing."

Holly gaped. "Really? The pink lacy set?" With one finger, she pushed Meredith's robe aside just enough to expose the lacy trim. "I don't want this to sound too over-the-top, but this is literally the best Christmas I've ever had in my whole entire life. Including the year I got a retro typewriter and felt like Patricia Highsmith when she wrote *The Price of Salt*."

Meredith laughed. "How is that not over-the-top? Holly Hudson, the great writer of Christmas movies, just declared—"

Holly put her hand over Meredith's mouth. "Okay, you're right. Way too over-the-top. How about, this is the best Christmas *sex* I've ever had in my whole life?"

"Does that mean I've met my goal? Is Holly Hudson now a lover of Christmas?"

Holly tapped her chin. "Hmm. I might need a little more convincing. Lose the robe and we'll talk. Or not talk."

Meredith took the coffee from Holly and set it on the table next to the gingerbread house. "I need to hear the bells on Christmas day again. Can you help me with that?"

"O come, all ye faithful." Holly slapped her forehead. "Sorry, that was the first song that came to mind."

Meredith untied Holly's robe and opened it. "Seems apropos." She kissed Holly's neck and nibbled on her earlobe.

Holly took a quick breath. "You're getting me all turned on again." Meredith hummed her approval against Holly's ear. It sent chills through her entire body. She steadied herself by putting her hands on Meredith's shoulders as she worked her way down to Holly's chest. "Oh, God," she whispered as Meredith wrapped her lips around a taut nipple. She moved to the other one and gave it some attention. Holly's chest heaved. Her lips went dry. She opened her eyes in time to see Meredith fall to her knees. When she looked up at Holly, the dark, lustful expression on her face made her intentions clear. She dipped her head and found Holly's clit with her tongue.

Holly threw her head back. Could she stay upright long enough to climax, or would her knees really buckle this time? She had a strong need to touch her own breast, so she slid the robe off her shoulders and squeezed her own nipples, matching the pressure Meredith's tongue had on her clit.

Holly opened her eyes when that magical tongue stopped. She lowered her gaze and said, "Please, don't stop."

Meredith's eyes were focused on Holly's hands. "I had to. Because you touching yourself is one of the sexiest things I've ever witnessed. And let's just say, you're making it hard to concentrate."

This seemed like Holly's chance to get herself on the naughty list. She slid her index finger into her mouth and made sure it was good and wet before she ran it down her own body and across Meredith's bottom lip.

Meredith took it into her mouth and sucked it clean. Holly's tummy did a somersault. When Meredith released her finger, Holly slid it into her folds and whimpered when she made contact with her clit. Meredith lifted her gaze and said, "Give me that finger again."

Holly circled her clit a few more times before she gave in to the request. Meredith sucked it clean again and got up off her knees. She grabbed Holly's face and kissed her so hard, it made her feel dizzy. Meredith released her lips, and Holly stood there in a daze with her eyes closed.

"Holly."

Meredith saying her name in that sexy bedroom voice had to be one of the best sounds Holly would ever hear. She opened her eyes and said, "Say my name like that again, and I might melt in your arms."

"I just wanted to wish you a Merry Christmas."

Holly's smile morphed into a huge grin. "Merry indeed."

❖

Meredith turned in Holly's arms so they were face-to-face. She looked so sated and beyond sexy with her messy hair and lazy smile. "Am I just dreaming, or is it almost noon on Christmas Day, and I'm in bed with a hot lady who has moves I didn't know were even a thing?"

"Your moves are pretty good too." Meredith mimicked Holly by putting her finger in her mouth and slowly pulling it out. Holly blushed and buried her face in her pillow. "Hey," Meredith said. "Don't get shy now. The day is young."

Holly snuggled in closer and breathed in Meredith's scent. To Holly, the scent had become both erotic and comforting. Sexy and familiar. She wondered if it was the same for Meredith. Was she imagining an entire life together the way Holly was? No, it was silly of her to think that way. This was a hookup like any other hookup.

Not that Holly had hookups. But if she did...Except it wasn't. Because the kiss Meredith just placed on Holly's forehead told her there was more to it for both of them. It was soft and lingering, and Holly could've sworn that Meredith just breathed her in too.

It would feel so natural to say the words *I love you*, in this moment where silence filled the air. To pull the sheet back and memorize every curve, every freckle and mole. Holly put her hand on Meredith's hip. The same hip that had so expertly moved against her the night before. She wanted to own that hip. Touch it every day. Worship it with her lips. Declare today to be National Meredith's Hips Day. National I Want to Love This Woman for the Rest of My Life Day.

"Tell me one of your dreams," Meredith said, pulling Holly from her thoughts.

"What do you mean?"

Meredith lifted Holly's chin so they were eye to eye. "A dream you have. Personal or professional. It doesn't matter."

"Hmm. Are you planning to make them all come true? Because I'd be so down with that."

"I'm just trying to get to know you better." Meredith took Holly's hand and interlocked their fingers. She brought them to her lips and kissed them. "I know your body, but I don't know what's going on in that very creative brain of yours."

"Naughty, vulgar things," Holly said. Because jokes were so much easier than the truth. "You could make a porno with all I've got going on up there," she added.

"Has it been a while?"

Holly scoffed at the question. "How do you define a while?"

"Hey, I'm not here to judge," Meredith said. She tapped Holly's nose. "But I sense that it's been a while since you let someone in."

"Are you referring to my vagina or my heart?"

Meredith raised an eyebrow. "Have I conquered both?"

Holly raised an eyebrow too. "Conquer is a big word. We hardly know each other."

"I don't think that's how the world works," Meredith said. "The heart can be conquered in a matter of minutes. Seconds, even, when the right person enters your line of sight."

Holly didn't dare ask if that was what Meredith was feeling now when the answer could be so devastating. She decided to answer the first question. "My biggest dream right now is to write a gay Christmas movie and have it air on the Wifetime Network. But every time I bring it up, I get shot down because in Mr. Cruz's opinion, it's too soon. It's been too soon for five years now."

"It's not," Meredith said.

Holly perked up. "Right? It's time, straight people. Let's do this. Give the gays a little Christmas joy, for God's sake. I mean, this is what I've been working toward, and if I can't make it happen, the *Evermore* series and basically my entire career will have been for nothing."

"So this is your ambition. Not to win an Oscar or write a smash hit feature." Meredith leaned up on her elbow. "If you hate everything Christmas, why is this so important to you?"

Why was it so important? Holly could easily cast it all aside and find something different to write about. She loved suspense thrillers. Maybe she could write those. But was this dream of hers so unreachable? Were people still so cruel that they'd deny the gay community a simple, sweet Christmas tale they could relate to? Something to make what was already a really tough time of year for a lot of gay folks a little bit easier to bear? Out of hundreds of straight Christmas romances, could there not be even one well-written and well-produced gay love story?

"I want it for my community," Holly said. "And there's no one better suited to give it to them than me."

"Then write it," Meredith said. "Have it ready to go because that moment will come, Holly. Wifetime might be way behind the rest of the world, but they'll be forced to catch up eventually, and I'd be happy to join you in that effort."

Having an ally like Meredith could make a world of difference. Holly felt a sudden sense of excitement about her job that had been missing for some time. "The truth is, I've already written it," she said. "And I happen to think it's by far the best screenplay I've ever written. It has all of the elements that the target audience loves so much but with two women."

"I'd love to read it sometime."

Holly shook her head. "It's my secret baby. I haven't let anyone read it. And no one at the network will see it until they prove to me that they're dead serious about being more inclusive."

"That's smart, I guess." Meredith ran her finger along Holly's hairline. "But this is me we're talking about."

"Does that mean I should trust you?"

Meredith furrowed her brow. "I hope you know you can."

If Holly didn't think she could trust Meredith, she never would've been so adventurous in bed the night before. Letting someone take her from behind definitely wasn't her go-to position on a first date. What would it hurt to let Meredith see more of her? "The story," she said. "It's what I always wanted for myself but never had. The small-town Christmas fairy tale where everyone, even the two young lesbians, get to celebrate their newfound love in front of the entire town and live happily ever after. They don't have to run away from everything and everyone they love just so they can live in peace and safety. They stay right where they are. Where they belong. Together."

"Ah," Meredith said. "Is this why you hate Christmas so much? Because you couldn't have it when you were young?"

Holly shook her head. "No. Christmas was all I knew. My hometown is Christmas Cove, Vermont, also known as the Christmasiest town in America. Years ago, the city council got super high and voted to turn the town into a year-round winter wonderland. Every street was renamed with a Christmas word or phrase. Every storefront was remodeled to look like the town's vision of the North Pole. And for my entire life, my parents have played a huge role in keeping the town alive and thriving. They literally play Santa and Mrs. Claus in the annual pageant."

Meredith laughed. "You are making that up."

"I am not. Okay, maybe the part about them being high. But everything else is true. The town needed to turn its financial prospects around, especially in winter. I didn't realize how crazy it was until I went away to college. Seriously, there's a working reindeer farm. So, yeah, I'd say Christmas is in their blood."

Meredith smiled. "I think it's in your blood too, Holly. Your history with Christmas must be what makes your movies so good."

"I grew up thinking I was of North Polish descent," Holly said.

Meredith's jaw dropped. "*No.*" She rolled onto her back and held her stomach while she giggled.

"It was my dad's favorite joke, but for the longest time, I believed it. I thought there were Polish people and North Polish people."

"And let's not forget the South Polish."

"Also known as Antarcticans."

"Okay, back to reality," Meredith said. "So you had to get out of Christmas Cove."

"Big time. It was all I knew, but I couldn't stay there. Once I knew I was gay, I had to find another way to make my crazy childhood work for me, so after college, I moved out here and worked my way up at Wifetime until I had enough confidence to submit a script. Writing Christmas is easy for me. It's what I know, my first language, in a way. But living in a small town with almost as many churches as people? Not so much." Holly lowered her gaze. "Most small towns in rural USA aren't exactly gay friendly places to live, and my little town was no exception."

Meredith's expression sobered. She nudged Holly and said, "Roll over. I need to spoon you right now." She wrapped her arms around Holly and peppered her neck with soft kisses. "We're going to get your unabashedly gay, impossibly happy, covered in snow and mistletoe movie made. Believe it, okay?"

With the memory of their first kiss and everything that followed so fresh in her mind, Holly felt like maybe anything was possible. The word *Believe* had been on display in her parents' home for as long as she could remember. Her mom had taken an old piece of barnwood, cut it to about three feet in length, painted it red, and painted *Believe* on it in white lettering. It hung over their fireplace year-round and was often pointed to when Holly would question her parents about the validity of this or that thing. She'd sit on the floor and squeeze her eyes shut and say the word three times out loud, just like her mom told her to do, as if that would make everything true. Sometimes, it made her feel better. Sometimes, it just confused her even more.

For whatever reason, Meredith saying that word just once felt more powerful than all of those times her mother had said it put together. It wasn't magical. It didn't require a wink and a nod. Holly kept her eyes wide open and said, "I believe you."

"Merry fucking Christmas," someone shouted. Meredith shot up, and Holly dove under the covers.

"Chelsea," Meredith said. "You scared the shit out of us." She pulled the sheet over her breasts and leaned back against the headboard. It created a tenting effect under the covers, which gave Holly a perfect view of Meredith's naked body. She'd enjoy it for the few remaining seconds she had left, sure that she'd soon be kicked out.

"Who's us, Mer? Oh, I see. You found a Christmas plaything. Well, get her dressed because we have a lot to talk about."

Holly blew Meredith's pussy a kiss good-bye and popped her head out. "Hi," she said in a cheery voice. "I'm Holly."

Chelsea plopped down into a chair. "You're in my bed, Holly, and I'm running on fumes here, so what say we put that trashy little Christmas stripper outfit back on and skedaddle right on out of here? Oh, and if you see the maid in the hallway, tell her my bedding needs to be changed, would you?"

Meredith threw the covers back and went into the bathroom. "You didn't show up, Chelsea. Therefore, the suite I gifted to you and Sheffield is no longer yours."

"Have you been doing Pilates again, Mer? Damn, your ass is tight." Chelsea looked at Holly. "Are you still here, babe? Because this party is over."

"Well," Holly said. "I don't do Pilates, so my ass isn't quite as tight as Mer's, so if you don't mind." She made a circling motion with her finger.

Chelsea scoffed. "You want me to turn around? Are you fucking kidding me right now? I'm sure half of Hawaii has already seen your mediocre ass." She dug through her purse. "You want me to pay for it too? Fine. Here's a twenty. Now, please go before I call security."

To Holly, Chelsea looked like a strung-out, blond version of Meredith, though she probably cleaned up really well. Her leather pants and faux fur coat made Holly think that traveling to Hawaii had been a last-minute decision, possibly made in a drunken stupor.

Meredith came out of the bathroom and put up a hand to Holly. "Stay where you are. It's my rude sister who needs to leave."

"Can't you see I'm a basket case right now, Mer?" Holly gave Chelsea a big nod. Chelsea pointed at her and said, "No input from the bimbo gallery, please."

"Chelsea, stop," Meredith said. "Number one, Holly is a work colleague. Number two, it was me who had that outfit on last night, but it was originally intended to be a silly gift for your honeymoon night."

Holly raised a hand. "May I comment on just how good Mer's Pilates ass looked in said outfit?"

Chelsea stared Holly down while she seemed to process the new information. "No one calls her Mer except family."

"Oh," Holly said. She looked at Meredith. "Sorry. I didn't realize it was a family thing."

Meredith shook her head. "Chelsea's messing with you. She's the only one who calls me that, even though she knows I don't love it."

"It reminds her of a horse," Chelsea said with a smug grin. "And damnit, I wish I could've seen you trying to be all sexy in that Christmas porn thing." She held her stomach and snort-laughed. "Mer doesn't have a sexy bone in her whole body, unless you consider those stuffy suits she wears to be sexy."

"Oh, I do," Holly said. "And you may not know this because you're straight, and you like dudes named Sheffield, but your sister is every lesbian's wet dream."

"Is that so? Then why is she always paying for it?"

Meredith visibly bristled at the rude question. "You know, Chels, when you say things like that out loud, someone within hearing range might just believe it. Do you really want people thinking that your sister frequently picks up prostitutes?"

"Fine. I'm just giving you shit anyway." Chelsea stood and dropped her purse. "Seriously, you two are giving me a headache, so please get the fuck out of my honeymoon suite."

"Is the wedding back on?" Holly asked. "Because we had your bachelorette party without you, and it was lit. Like, champagne and caviar lit."

Chelsea ignored the comment. "Mer, if you don't get your

work-sex colleague out of here right now, I'm going to blow a gasket labeled, my life as I know it is ruined, and I really want to kill someone right now, so why not Holly What's-her-name?"

"Okay, that's enough. I get that you're hurting, Chelsea, but that doesn't give you the right to say horrible things to someone you don't even know." Meredith handed Holly a towel. "I'll collect your clothes and bring them to you in the bathroom."

"No, let me," Chelsea said. She picked up Holly's dress and tossed it to her. "That should take about five seconds to put back on."

Holly got out of bed with the towel wrapped around herself. She grabbed her shoes and purse and said, "I can change in my room." She went to the door and didn't look back, even though she heard Meredith call her name.

❖

Holly waved Meredith over to her table in the coffee shop a block from the hotel. She sat down with a big sigh. "Thanks for seeing me again. I thought after that terrible encounter with my sister, you might decide it wasn't worth it."

"She's a hot mess."

"And she interrupted the lovely moment we were having."

"There were lots of lovely moments this morning," Holly said in a teasing tone.

"And last night."

"It's still my best Christmas ever."

"I'm so glad you still feel that way." Meredith lowered her gaze. "You're right about Chelsea. She's a hot mess, and no one back home wanted to deal with it, so she hopped on a plane thinking her big sister would take care of her until she got her shit together. Unfortunately, it's going to cut into our time together."

Holly put up her hands. "Hey, that woman is out for blood. I plan to stay as far away from her as possible."

"Chelsea lashes out when she's hurting. She's not much for self-reflection," Meredith said. "She hasn't told me anything yet, but I get the feeling Sheffield is the one to blame. Not that he called off the wedding, but maybe she found out something about him in the last week. I just assumed it was Chelsea's doing because she can be so flighty at times, but I think he really hurt her."

Holly reached for Meredith's hand. "Then you should be there for her."

"Maybe we could do lunch back home sometime. Or dinner. Or just champagne and caviar. I'm up for anything, really."

"Mmm, I like that last one," Holly teased. Meredith paused for a moment. Holly could tell she had something on her mind. "What is it?"

Meredith tightened her grip on Holly's hand. "It felt very special being with you," she said. "And the truth is, I'm up for more than those things I just mentioned. I'd really like to date you, Holly. Assuming that my family hasn't completely turned you off."

Holly jumped out of her seat a little faster than she would've liked, but at least she didn't let out the big whoop she'd managed to hold in. She offered her hand, and Meredith stood. "I'd like that too." She wrapped her arms around Meredith and breathed in her scent. It would have to suffice until they saw each other again. "I loved every second of our Christmas together. It's one I'll never forget."

Meredith kissed Holly's cheek. Her lips lingered there, and she whispered, "Neither will I." She backed away a few steps, then turned for the door. Before she walked out, she stopped and said, "How much do you love Christmas, Holiday Hudson?"

Holly smiled. "Only my family calls me that."

Meredith blew her a kiss and left.

Chapter Six

Even though her eyes were closed, Holly could feel Gwen staring at her. "Stop staring, G."

"Didn't you get enough sun in Hawaii? And by the way, where's my captive audience when I need her?"

"She's still in Hawaii. Getting more sun."

Gwen gave Holly's lounge chair a light kick. "You never lie out by this hole in the ground the management likes to call a swimming pool. What's wrong with you? Where's High Anxiety Holly when I need her?"

She laughed. "They should give that name to a Barbie doll. She'd sell like crazy."

"Yeah, and one of her accessories could be a chocolate turtle that easily attaches to her ass with Velcro."

"And a laptop that conveniently tucks under her arm."

"And moveable arms that go like this when she talks."

"Nice try, but I'm not opening my eyes," Holly said. "Not even so I can witness your unflattering impression of me. Oh, and she'll need to wear a vintage T-shirt that says *I got lei'd in Hawaii*."

Gwen gasped. "You did not."

"Fine. Can we talk about your Barbie doll now?"

"Oh, you mean Geriatric Gwen with the shriveled-up knees and saggy ass?"

"Aw. Come on now, G. You're way too hard on yourself." Holly put her hand out. "Let me touch those knees and see just how shriveled up they are."

Gwen flicked her hand away. "They're covered in Vaseline right now."

"How about your ass then?" Holly aimlessly poked her hand around. "Or is that covered in Vaseline too?"

"You're not usually this fresh. Did something really happen in Hawaii, or are you just messing with me?"

Holly flung her arms out and let them hang off to the side. "Look at me. I'm lying here like a rag doll in a bathing suit cover-up that doesn't even cover up very much. That never happens unless I've had earth-shattering sex."

"Which would explain why I've never seen you in a bathing suit, let alone a crocheted cover-up, or whatever the hell that is. Now, spill."

"You first," Holly said.

"Oh, come on. I'm on my second glass of wine at eleven thirty a.m. That should tell you all you need to know about my holiday."

Holly lifted her head and lowered her sunglasses. "No hookup behind the jazz club with a washed-out soap star on New Year's Eve?"

"That happened once. Let it go."

Holly pushed her sunglasses back up and closed her eyes. "I will if you will."

"I can't," Gwen said. "It was the best sex behind a dumpster I've ever had. Plus, he called me a star fuck, and any actress who tells you she doesn't like being called a star fuck is lying to you. Now, spill, damnit. Tell me about this little rendezvous with Hipster Crunch Heather who spent her last five hundred bucks getting to Honolulu. Should I expect to see an old, rusted out Chevy Nova with Wyoming plates and a dream catcher hanging from the rearview mirror in the parking lot soon?"

"Wow, G. I had no idea you thought so highly of me. Or are you just trying to make yourself feel better about the dumpster sex?"

Griffin walked up with Ty right behind him. "Who told you I had dumpster sex? Damnit, I knew that guy's big mouth would get me in trouble one day."

Ty sat at the umbrella-covered table and pulled his long board shorts up around his thighs. "I had dumpster sex once, but I think my date was referring to the quality of the sex, not the location."

Both Gwen and Holly lowered their sunglasses and at the same time said, "You've had sex?"

Ty leaned back and closed his eyes. "What can I say? Women find my masculine scent attractive. Right, Gwen?"

Holly whipped her head around to Gwen. "Did you two… oh my God, I can't deal right now."

"I told him to use some extra deodorant," Gwen said. "He thought I was flirting."

"If you didn't want some of this, you wouldn't care what I smell like." Ty lifted an arm and took a whiff. "Mmm…I smell like full-bearded manly swagger now."

"You smell like misogyny and musk," Holly said. "Not a good combo."

Ty lifted his arm again. "Really? It took me twenty minutes to pick this scent."

"Sorry to interrupt this armpit hair raising conversation," Gwen said. "But we have bigger things to talk about. Holly said she got laid in Hawaii, and I'm pretty sure she's not referring to the traditional floral necklace."

"Names," Griffin said. "I want names, or it didn't happen."

"Okay, but I swear to God, this stays between us, or I will personally see to it that you are incapable of any future sex acts, dumpster or otherwise."

"What the hell, Holls?" Griffin seemed surprised by her intensity. "Did you bone a politician or something?"

Ty put his head in his hands. "Oh, God. No, no, no. Holly's so desperate she slept with Tulsi—"

"You stop that right now," Gwen said. "Put that vile thought right back where it came from." She turned back to Holly. "Now, why all the secrecy about whoever put the 'ho' in 'Holly'? Did you finally have your own star fuck?"

"First of all, no. To all of that. And Ty, that's just disgusting. Now all of you, promise."

Eager to be let in on the news, they all agreed to keep it to themselves. Pinkie swears and all.

"Her name," Holly paused to drag out the suspense, "is Meredith Freaking Drake."

"No. Way." Griffin stood up so fast, his chair fell over behind him. "I can't believe you met someone with the same name as your work crush."

"Did I not just use the middle name Freaking? It's her, Griff." She folded her arms across her chest. "And now, we'll wait for Gwen to type that name into the Google machine and see what it spits out."

Ty reached for his phone. "What is this woman's name again?"

Gwen raised what looked like a shiny new rose gold Apple watch to her mouth and said, "Siri, who is Meredith Drake?"

"According to Wikipedia, Meredith Drake is an American film producer and studio executive who currently works as the head of development for the Wifetime Network. Prior to joining Wifetime, Drake produced four films, including the acclaimed *The Diary*, which was nominated for…"

Gwen turned the speaker off and lowered her hand but didn't say anything. Ty put his hand to his chest and said, "Well, I for one am proud of our little chocolate turtle smasher."

Griffin put his hands together in a dramatic prayer stance. "You guys have no idea how gorgeous this Meredith woman is. You walk by her in the hall, and you feel like you're on the runway, returning to the changing room while she gets a standing ovation." He clutched his chest and blinked back what looked like real tears. Once he pulled himself together, he said, "And somehow, that magnificent woman noticed our little Holly Bell Hudson."

"Not my name."

"Well, it should be," he said. "Your parents dropped the ball on that one."

Holly lowered her sunglasses and turned to Gwen. "Cat got your tongue, G?"

"I'm processing."

Holly grinned. "I understand. It's a lot to take in. I mean, it took me a minute to get used to the idea too, but once I did, all clothes were off." She let out a little squeal and kicked her feet. "I still can't believe it happened."

"I never would've put you two together," Griffin said. "Not in a million years."

"Okay, pull yourself together, Griff. I'm not exactly the beast to her beauty," Holly said.

Gwen set her wineglass down and leaned forward. "Okay, I'm done processing. Here are my thoughts."

"On two glasses of wine for breakfast? I can't wait," Holly said.

"Oh," Ty said. "That's when all of the big, important words come out. Words like deo-dor-ant."

Gwen put up her hand. "Shut up, Ty. This is important. This is Holly's heart we're talking about. And I fear it's about to be broken."

Holly sat up and wrapped her arms around her knees. "Why do you say that?"

"Because if I'm not mistaken, you're envisioning a future with her right now."

"With Meredith? So what if I am?"

"Holly Bear, I know a thing or two about vacation flings." She leaned over and put her hand on Holly's knee. "Sun, sand, fruity cocktails, and not a care in the world. And now, it's back to reality for both of you. Hell, is she even single?"

Holly put up her hands. "Okay, enough with the Holly Bear and Holly Bell shit. I'm not some small-town girl who decided to date way out of her league. And my life isn't G-rated like the movies I write. I'm a big girl, and I can handle a woman like Meredith Drake, okay?"

They all found a way to look otherwise occupied, no doubt so they wouldn't have to agree with her. Gwen's fingernails were suddenly of great interest. Holly lay back down and closed her eyes. She wouldn't let these dimwits ruin her last day off. She screamed when she felt hands all over her. "No! No tickling."

"We're just messing with you," Griffin said.

"Yeah, we know you can handle a real woman," Ty added.

"We're happy for you, hon. Maybe a little jealous too, but we're truly happy for you."

Holly reached out and hit all of their hands. "Thanks, guys."

❖

Holly was about to avail herself of a rather tasty looking lemon bar Desiree had made for her when Brian walked into her office and plopped down in a chair. "Give me one of those cookies, and I'll fill you in on the big news."

Holly slammed the lid down on the tin box. "They're lemon bars, not cookies. And these are special. My favorite. Probably the best thing I'll taste all week, so forgive me if I don't think your news is worth losing one of these babies."

Brian tilted his head. "You seem different, Holls. What's up?"

Oh, this was ridiculous. It couldn't possibly be true that someone could actually tell that you'd had sex for the first time in a while, could it? Not just sex, fantastic, mind-blowing sex. "Don't try to sweet-talk your way to one of my lemon bars by telling me I look radiant or rosy cheeked or some other bullshit."

He folded his arms across his chest. "I wouldn't dare say something like that. But yeah, someone got lucky over the holiday break."

She tried to suppress a smile, but it didn't work. She opened the tin and slid it across her desk. "Fine. Have one if you must."

He took a big bite out of a lemon bar. "I think your news is bigger than mine. Epic, in fact. Should we have a Holly is no longer a virgin party? I could hire a few strippers."

Holly gave him a few seconds to bask in his virgin joke before she asked, "Why is everyone so interested in my love life?"

"Because we've all been waiting for you to find that special girl who makes your heart go ba boom. Ba boom. Ba boom." He tapped his chest with every *ba boom* and grinned like he'd just been told he was the funniest man in the world.

She waved a hand. "Okay, enough with the fucking ba

booms, Bri. And for your information, I haven't been a virgin since Meagan Butterworth got some courage after the college orientation pep rally."

Lucille stepped into the small office and closed the door behind her. "I couldn't help but overhear."

Brian grabbed the tin and offered it to her. "Have a lemon bar, Lu. We were just about to get to the good part."

She sat in the chair next to Brian. "Don't mind if I do." She grabbed a pen off Holly's desk. "First, I need to write down that name, so I can look her up on Facebook. Meagan Butterworth, you say?"

Holly threw her hands in the air. "Seriously! Why is everyone so interested in my love life?"

"Like I mentioned before, it's because you haven't had one," Brian said. "So spill. Who is she? How did you meet her? When do *we* get to meet her? Tell us or I'll start ba booming again."

She leaned back in her chair. "Okay, look. I know you two are doing the parent thing since mine are so far away, but I'm going to keep this under wraps until I know where it's going, okay?"

They looked at each other and shrugged. "Okay," Brian said. "What I came to tell you is that Cruz has been fired over reports of sexual misconduct."

Holly's eyes widened. "Mr. Cherry Stone got canned?"

"Mr. who? No, I said Cruz got canned."

"Sorry," Holly said. "It's just a name he suggested I use for a character, so in my head, I think of him as Mr. Cherry Stone now."

"Oh, dear," Lucille said. "That's an awful name for a main character, and truth be told, I never liked the man. He won't be missed by me."

"Also, am I the only one that finds it the least bit ironic

that you grilled me about my sex life and *then* told me about Cruz?"

Brian appeared to give that some thought. "Okay, that's a good point. Sorry about that." He waited for a moment and then continued. "You wanna know the best part? It'll kill Cruz when he finds out who replaced him. Turns out he has zero gaydar and he just couldn't quite understand why Ms. Drake wasn't impressed by his pectoral muscles that he'd been working so hard on."

"Huh," Lucille said. "I thought he'd started buying smaller dress shirts."

Holly felt like the ceiling had opened up and rays of sun were pouring into her somewhat dreary office. Also, were there angels singing, or was that just in her head? "Hallelujah," she said under her breath.

This was a game changer. With Meredith in charge, there would be diversity and rainbows and gay everything. Gay commercials and gay content and more gay actors. They'd rival Bravo in their gayness. "Halle-fucking-lujah," she said.

"I wouldn't have put it quite that way," Lucille took a lemon bar and headed for the door. "But I second that emotion."

Holly had to find Meredith. This was probably why they'd only exchanged a few short texts since Hawaii. It made sense that Meredith would be busy with negotiations and everything else that went with a big promotion. Not to mention dealing with that hot mess of a sister of hers.

Holly power walked down the hall to Cruz's office. It was completely empty. She got on her phone and ordered a big bouquet of flowers to be delivered to Meredith while she made the short hike to the building that housed the executive offices of Wifetime. Since she wasn't sure exactly which office Meredith was in, she glanced at the name on every door as she went past. Too excited to think straight, when she finally found it, she burst through her door and said, "When were you going to tell me?"

Meredith stood. The two gentlemen who looked like lawyers stayed in their seats. Holly's face was already heated from the fast-paced walk she'd just made, but she was sure she'd just turned a dark shade of beet red. And Meredith looked less than pleased with the interruption. Holly took a step back. "So sorry to interrupt."

She closed the door and berated herself for not knocking first. The door flew open behind her, and the two men brushed past her but not before giving her a glare. She stuck her head in, and Meredith waved her into the office. Holly wanted to rush into her arms and congratulate her with a spray of kisses all over her face, but she held back.

Was she beaming from head to toe? Grinning like a love-stricken fool? Holly was sure both of those things were happening. Her smile faded when she realized Meredith didn't look at all happy to see her. "I'm sorry," she said. "I should've knocked."

Meredith's expression softened. "Is everything all right?"

"Yeah, I just heard the news about your promotion and ran straight here. I've missed you. How's Chelsea?"

"She and Sheffield are trying to work things out." Meredith gestured toward a chair. "Please sit."

Holly thought it strange that Meredith sat back down behind her desk. No hug? No *I missed you too*? She sat and said, "Maybe I should be the one to ask if everything is okay."

"It's a complicated situation I'm walking into with this promotion. I need to get it right."

"You will," Holly said. "Are you kidding me? You'll be replacing an idiot. A moron who thought all women were here for his harassment, be it sexual or otherwise. No one will miss him, and everyone will embrace you just like I want to do right now."

"Don't say that." Meredith leaned on her desk and ran her fingers through her hair.

On closer inspection, Holly noticed how stressed she looked. "Mer, what's wrong?"

"I told you, it's complicated. With the Cruz thing, there will need to be some damage control. New rules put in place. Rules that I not only have to enforce but also will have to adhere to."

"Oh. Okay. Yeah, sure. Of course." Holly looked around the office and back at Meredith. "Um, what does that mean?"

Meredith clasped her hands and furrowed her brow. "I was going to come and find you so I could break it to you myself. You see, the higher-ups want to make a very big proactive statement with Cruz's firing. It's going to break in the *Times* in the next few days. They want to get in front of it, you know? They're taking initiative and creating new codes of conduct. No-tolerance policies. Things they should have done a long time ago, frankly. None of this bodes well for you and me, Holly."

Holly's heart sank. "That sounds rather ominous."

"What happened in Hawaii needs to remain between us. I can't date an employee. Any employee. But especially the best writer on staff. My head would be on a platter so fast, my name wouldn't even make it into the Cruz press release."

"But—"

"No buts, Holly. I have to set the example. It wasn't just Cruz who chose to treat women poorly. There were other complaints that the CEO ignored, and now it's come back to bite them in the ass. Hard."

"But—"

"But what?" Meredith said. "The rules will be posted, and we will have to adhere to them or risk being fired. As an executive with direct reports, this is literally in my contract."

Holly felt like she was looking at a stranger. Meredith's tight tone, her unforgiving gaze, the way her jaw seemed to clench, relax and clench again. None of it felt familiar. "Look, I know you must be under a lot of stress right now—"

"You have no idea."

"Right. And I get that, I really do, but I'm the girl from Hawaii, remember? The same girl who couldn't wait to get back so she could see you again. But I'm not sure who I'm looking at right now."

"You're looking at the new president of the holiday division. It was all very unexpected, and I haven't had a chance to call you. I'm sorry about that."

Holly didn't like that answer. Meredith could've texted with the news; she could've left a short voice mail. Connecting with Holly obviously wasn't a priority. "Yeah, for a moment there, it seemed like a good thing. We'd see each other every day, we'd gay up the joint, and we'd see if there was more to us than just Hawaii." She stood. "But I guess you didn't tell them that we were already dating, so therefore, we should be grandfathered in."

"I didn't think that would sit well with them given the circumstances I was being promoted under, and beyond that, we never said we were dating, so I might've been opening up a big can of worms for nothing. Holly, don't leave like this. We still have to work together."

Holly stopped at the door. "And we will. Because believe it or not, you're not the only one who knows how to put their job first."

❖

"So to make a long story short, I will never have Meredith Drake's pussy in my mouth again." Holly glanced over to see if Gwen was actually listening to her sob story or if her mind had wandered off to other topics such as boob lifts and tummy tucks.

"You get me into your bed, and all you can do is blow your nose and cry and talk about another woman's pussy. I feel like I'm on the worst date ever."

Holly rolled her eyes. "I didn't get you into bed. You insinuated yourself into my personal living space and proceeded to spill wine on my best sheets while telling me I told you so."

"Well, I don't usually drink in bed," Gwen said. "But this story is so fucking sad. And what was I supposed to do, ignore the wailing coming from your apartment? I'm not a monster, you know."

"Wailing? If anything, it was a light sniffle. And I can't wait to hear your version of this story from Desiree. Something about how I just needed a little bit of sexual healing, and since you've had a few lesbian encounters over the decades, you stepped up to the plate."

"Ouch, sweetie. You couldn't just say years? And it was me or Desiree who was heading down here tonight. You're just lucky I was willing to take one for the team, or you'd be brushing face powder and red lipstick smears off your sheets."

Holly grabbed the last tissue out of the box on the nightstand and threw it across the room. "Why do you always run out of things you need right when you need them?"

"I say that about wine all the time. I should just give in and start drinking that boxed crap." She offered Holly her shirt sleeve. "This is an old T-shirt. Should I take it off so you can blow your nose on it?"

Holly glanced at the shirt. "What the hell is Battle of the Network Stars 1976?"

"Only the greatest shitshow on television. I was, of course, a child at the time, so the important thing is that I can still fit into this shirt."

"Barely. It's so tight, I can see your outie belly button."

Gwen did a slow shake of her head. "I know you want me to examine my very normal belly button right now because you're just that childish, but I'm on to you, asshole."

Holly sat up so she could blow her nose. "At least Desiree would've held me close to her rosewater-scented bosom and tried to comfort me with gentle, sympathetic words." She threw her last tissue on the pile at the side of the bed and flopped back on her pillow.

"Aw. Get in here and let Mama kiss the boo-boo away."

Holly cuddled in close and wrapped her arm around Gwen's waist. "Did you just call yourself Mama?"

"I assumed that since you're wearing a onesie, you wanted some mama-daughter roleplay."

Holly slapped a hand over her eyes. "Gwen, there's a big difference between footie pajamas and a onesie."

"I'm sure there is. And maybe one day I'll let you explain the difference to someone who cares, but right now, close your eyes, and let's sleep off this tragic thing you call a life."

"You always know just what to say, G. Even when you're drunk and slurring your words, I'm like, wow, she is so smart."

"And now you can add good in bed to all of the things that I am. And do me a favor. Mention that fact to Ty, would you? I mean, not because I'd ever sleep with him. But I do enjoy knowing he has his little fantasies about me."

"He'll know by tomorrow morning that you're a top-notch snuggler with soft, natural feeling boobs."

"And he'd be at my door in two seconds flat."

"Totally." She settled back into Gwen's arms. She wasn't too proud to say this was exactly what she needed. Gwen was the furthest thing from a mother figure, and her bedside manner was atrocious, but Holly wasn't sure her own mother would be much better. She'd somehow find a way to make it Holly's fault that yet another relationship hadn't worked out. At least Gwen hadn't gone there yet.

A moment passed before Gwen said, "Every time I've cried over a man, I always came away from it believing one thing: I'd rather have those long, tearful moments of my life back than give one more second of it to him. Don't let this Drake woman steal another second of your joy because if she can't see that you're worth a little risk, then she's blind."

Holly smiled. "You realize I'm not asleep, and this isn't a soap opera, right? I can hear every nice thing you're saying."

"Okay, fine. If this woman can't see what a hot mess you are, then she's blind, and you two deserve each other. Better?"

"Much better."

"On a more serious note, when you were telling us about her, I knew I'd seen that look before. Remember the girl with the funny name who took your heart and hurled it against a brick wall?"

Holly lifted her head. "Haven?"

"Yes. Heart Hurler Haven. The Barbie doll with the bad attitude and stalker tendencies. Not a big seller in the suburbs."

"Where do you get this shit from? Haven dumped me when she found out I worked for Wifetime. She may have been super intense, but she wasn't a stalker. Besides, she wasn't really my type."

"Hmm," Gwen said with a tap of her chin. "I see a correlation here. Maybe it's your job that's keeping you from finding everlasting love."

"Or maybe the thing I write about doesn't actually exist, and Evermore is just a bullshit town where everyone needs therapy or a good slap upside the head, depending on which generation you're from."

"Okay, now I'm depressed too."

"I think what you're supposed to say right now is 'it *does* exist, honey. You just have to let it find you. Stay open to the possibilities life has to offer.'"

"Omg. You just quoted yourself, didn't you? That line was in the second *Evermore*."

Holly buried her face in Gwen's chest. "Shut up."

"Holly Bear, you don't actually believe the stuff you write, do you? The whole reason the world watches that channel is because they don't have that kind of love in their lives. It's not real, but we all long for it."

"You're the worst mom in the history of ever, G."

Gwen patted Holly's head. "You're right. I'm a self-absorbed, vain actress. Right up there with Joan Crawford, minus the great eyebrows and big checking account."

Holly gave her side a squeeze. "But you're a great friend, and I'm lucky to have you."

"Aw. I'd kiss your forehead, but I'm scared you'd look up at the wrong time, and our lips would lock in an unfortunate, but oh-so-hot kiss."

"How is anything a surprise in your life when you go around predicting all of it? Also, I'm not moving my head, so go for it."

Gwen gave Holly a light kiss on the forehead. "Thanks for not making it awkward."

"You're welcome. Now, go into a heavy wine snore. That'll lull me to sleep."

Gwen sighed and rested her cheek on Holly's head. "It's like you know me and love me anyway."

"Ditto, G. Ditto."

CHAPTER SEVEN

With every lap around the rooftop track at work, Holly became more lost in memories of Hawaii. It had been a few weeks, but she could still see Meredith's dark eyes roaming her naked body. Feel her fingers caressing her breast. She could hear that sexy voice telling her what she needed. *More.* She needed more of Holly. *Deeper. Go deeper, Holly.*

"I heard you come up here when you need to work something out."

Holly stopped jogging and turned. Meredith stood there, hands in her pockets, her short hair swirling around her face in the light breeze. In the three weeks since Meredith had moved into her new office, Holly had avoided going anywhere near it. Why torture herself with glimpses of that beautiful face? All she wanted to do was keep her head down, not cause any trouble, and heal her broken heart. The problem was, their new boss was never very far from her thoughts. Longest three weeks of her life.

Holly wiped her brow with the back of her hand and said, "Work something out or just work out?"

"Maybe I misunderstood Lucille," Meredith said.

Holly would have to let Lucille know that she needed to be a bit more discreet and not announce to the whole freaking world that Holly Hudson was not feeling like herself today. "What's up?"

"I'd hoped we could still work together," Meredith said. "But it seems like you're avoiding me."

"Just staying in my lane. Wouldn't want to rock the sexual harassment cart." Holly grabbed her water bottle off the bench and took a sip. Meredith got closer. Too close for Holly's liking. She took a step back. "What do you need, Meredith? Is it something for work, because otherwise, I don't think we have anything to talk about."

Meredith took another step toward her. "You have to understand that I was promoted under difficult circumstances. All eyes will be on me. It wouldn't look good for me to be involved with one of my subordinates."

"Yeah, I understood that the first time you said it. What happened between us just happened. Wrong place, wrong time. End of story."

"It doesn't have to be the end of our story," Meredith said. "We can still work together. We can still work on that dream of yours." Holly tried to walk away, but Meredith stood in her way. "I don't want you to think this is easy for me. Hawaii was special for me too."

"I never said it was special. It was sex." Holly expected her to let go and back away, but she didn't move.

"Say that while you're looking me in the eye."

It reminded Holly of the little mind games Gwen played with Ty. It stroked her ego to know that he fantasized about her, so she'd give him little bread-crumb-sized offerings to keep him interested. Close but not too close. Flirty but not too flirty.

In fact, when Holly really thought about it, Gwen wanted the same thing from her. She wanted to be desired by everyone who couldn't actually have her. Maybe Meredith needed the same thing, but Holly would be damned if she'd give it to her. She headed for the door. "Let me know if you need something work related."

"I do, actually." Meredith tucked her hands back in her pockets. "You haven't signed the *Evermore* contract."

"You know my feelings on that front. I'll only write it if I can make the youngest son gay."

Once again, Meredith removed the distance between them and stood practically toe to toe with her. "Will you at least come to my office so we can discuss it further?"

Oh God, why didn't Meredith back the hell up so Holly wouldn't have to breathe her in? Or at least get downwind from her. She managed to keep her game face on. Just barely. "It's not up for discussion. I won't write another straight Christmas movie."

Meredith didn't move, although her eyes did wander down to Holly's chest. "You haven't even heard my offer."

She really should've backed away by now. Surely, she was breaking some rule of conduct by encroaching on Holly's personal space. And the way her eyes kept moving southward to Holly's tight workout top seemed highly inappropriate under the new rules. "Careful, Mer. I can feel the sexual harassment cart wobbling."

Okay, so maybe she said those words in the sexiest voice she could muster because why the hell not? There was no winning here, so they might as well both suffer.

Meredith straightened under Holly's intense gaze. But she didn't take a step back. How interesting. Holly decided not to move either. She couldn't help herself. She had to take in every feature. Her eyes tracked down Meredith's neck where she'd placed kisses on her way to a delicious collarbone. And even lower than that, to her freckled chest. A pearl button on Meredith's silky blouse stopped her from going any further, but she could see in her mind's eye those pert breasts that begged for attention. She imagined that they probably burned under her stare, along with other parts of Meredith's body.

How long could they stand like this, having imaginary sex? Because the look on Meredith's face and the way her cheeks had gone pink told Holly that something was definitely going on behind those gorgeous eyes. Meredith wanted her. And that knowledge made all the difference. Holly didn't have to pine alone. She didn't have to be Meredith's cast-aside lover. She could be herself and tease Meredith relentlessly if she wanted to. And she did want to.

Holly leaned in and whispered, "Why are you standing so close, boss?"

Meredith finally took a step back. Holly thought she would turn to leave, but it turned out Meredith needed to pace.

"I didn't know you were a pacer," Holly said.

"You talk with your hands when you're excited, and I pace."

Holly bristled at Meredith's arm flailing interpretation of her. No one ever got it right. It wasn't random. Each movement had a purpose. Why didn't they understand that? Had they never heard of body language before? Holly decided she'd give Meredith some good old-fashioned body language and put her hands on her hips. Everyone knew that one meant shut up or your life as you knew it was over. Well, the mom version anyway. Holly just wanted to exude some confidence when she said, "I thought you liked my hands."

Meredith stopped pacing. Holly could tell she was holding something back. She took a breath and said, "Give me a straight *Evermore*, and I'll give you your gay movie. Wouldn't you rather see two women kiss under the mistletoe?"

Holly gaped at Meredith's overconfidence. "Just like that, huh? With a snap of your fingers, you'll just make it a reality?"

"It won't be quite that easy, but I told you before that you shouldn't underestimate me."

"Ah," Holly said with a nod. "The whole I'm going to make Holly Hudson love Christmas again thing. And how did that work out for you?"

"Not as well as I had hoped. Since there was an embarrassing costume involved that I will never live down."

"Hot. It was...hot." It was slow in coming, but a smile appeared on Meredith's face. Holly tried to suppress her own smile and pointed a finger at Meredith. "No. You're not allowed to make me smile, or laugh, or—"

With a quick few steps, Meredith moved in and grabbed her shoulders. "Just listen for a minute, okay?"

Holly nodded. "Okay."

"I'd like to be president of this company one day, and I'd like you to still be here when it happens. I think that together, we could make a big difference. And while we have to give up some things, I think the end result will be worth it."

Holly thought that was kind of like saying *yeah, you were okay in bed, but I have my career to think of. I have people to impress, and they won't be impressed by you.* It felt like another punch to the gut.

Could Holly really put her career first too? That was all she'd ever done, but the truth was, she'd quit her job that very day if it meant having a chance to date Meredith. Meredith, who was still standing so close it wouldn't take much to lean in and kiss her. Or maybe whisper something sexy in her ear. So Holly did just that. She leaned in and whispered, "It wasn't just sex. It was everything."

She backed away, but Meredith didn't move. Holly got to the door and turned for another look. Meredith still hadn't moved. Was she stunned? Angry? Turned on? Unfortunately, the expression on her face didn't give anything away.

❖

Brian popped his head into Holly's office, a habit she'd tried to break him of since it sent her through the roof every time. This time, it was a slow pop and an even slower retreat. As his eyes disappeared behind the wall, she said, "It's an improvement. Also, slightly creepy."

He stepped into her office and plopped into a chair. "Happy Valentine's Day. What did you get for me?"

She tossed a heart-shaped cookie across her desk. "Lucille sends her love."

He bit off half of it and said, "Any plans tonight?"

She furrowed her brow. "With the way you eat, you really should have your own YouTube channel."

He gasped. "Do I get my own Ken doll too? Mukbang Brian. Oh my God, life would be complete."

She leaned back in her chair and narrowed her eyes at him. "Have you told everyone about High Anxiety Holly? That was between you, me, and my friend Gwen."

"Right. Gwen. So when are you going to set me up with her?"

"I'd really like to keep her as my friend, so never with a capital 'N.'"

She glanced up and saw Meredith standing in her doorway, looking as hot as ever, of course. Why couldn't she show up one day in something ill-fitting and not her color? Maybe something that made everyone google words like *chartreuse* and *puce*. But no, she'd chosen a classic navy pants and red sweater ensemble. "Where's your yacht?"

Meredith furrowed her brow. "Pardon me?"

Brian glanced over his shoulder. "Oh hey, boss. Heading to the Hamptons later?"

"Brian, shut up." For some reason, it bothered Holly that he joined in on the teasing, even if Meredith did look dressed for a polo match or whatever the hell people did in the Hamptons. Never mind that they were on the West Coast. Maybe Santa Barbara or Ojai was a better choice. "Did we have a meeting?" Holly looked at her desk calendar. "Nope. I got nothing."

"I was hoping for a meeting of the minds," Meredith said. "Brian, could you give me a minute with Holly?"

He stood. "Sure. I got what I came here for." He brushed his fingers clean and pointed at Holly. "I want to meet Gwen. Make it happen."

Meredith sat where he'd just been and glanced around the small office. There wasn't much to see, but Holly found herself looking around as well. She had bulletin boards covered in sticky notes. A cat calendar, even though she didn't own a cat, but Lucille thought she should. A small bookshelf with all kinds of crap on it. She grabbed a pen and scribbled on a sticky note, *clean off shelf.*

They hadn't talked much in person since the roof conversation. She'd seen Meredith in a few group meetings and said a quick hello. And they'd communicated via email about the last *Evermore* script, which Holly had been working on. Other than that, there hadn't been a reason to make contact. Holly figured that if Meredith wanted to see her, she'd make up a reason, and maybe that was what this was.

"Who does Brian want to meet?"

The question surprised her since it was a personal one. She hadn't expected Meredith to show any interest in her personal life. "Oh, just a friend of mine. Never gonna happen. They'd rip each other apart with their cynical scissor tongues." Meredith gave her a questioning look. "They're both super sarcastic, and the entire date would be spent trying to one-up each other on the retort scale. You know, like that old-fashioned carnival game where the first person to hit the thing hard enough with a hammer to ring the bell wins? Only, it wouldn't be a bell, it would be complete annihilation of feelings. They'd take it too far, is what I'm saying." She sighed. "Which is just a long-ass way of saying they know too much about me, and the two shall never meet and compare notes."

"Ah. And yet, I know so little about you," Meredith said.

"I guess it depends on what the definition of 'know' is." Holly used finger quotes.

Meredith laughed. "I guess you're right."

Holly focused on the script in front of her for a moment. She loved that she could make Meredith laugh, but it also made her feel a sense of sadness that they hadn't had the chance to really get to know each other. She took a deep breath and made eye contact again. "So what's up, boss lady?"

Meredith leaned back in the chair and clasped her hands together. "I have a dinner reservation at seven."

Holly did love those hands so much. Her tummy did a flip-flop when her brain betrayed her and took her back to a certain bed in a certain hotel, when those fingers were pushed deep inside her over and over again. She tried to shake loose the memory but not before she heard herself cry out when she came with those fingers still inside her.

"Holly?"

"What? Wait. What?" Holly grabbed her glass and gulped down the cold water, which helped her brain to catch up. She slammed the glass back down and said, "You have a dinner reservation in LA on Valentine's Day? You must know people." She glanced at her watch. "And you should get going. Traffic will be a nightmare."

"It's just down the street," Meredith said. "That new place called Ford's."

"Oh. Very posh. Very this month. Of course, if there's one thing I know about you, it's that you know how to make a girl feel special."

Meredith leaned forward. "There won't be a special outfit this time."

"Really? No Valentine superhero who goes around saving the hearts of the good men and women of LA? I could get the costume department to whip something up for you. Maybe black fishnet with strategically placed pink velvet triangles and thigh high boots? What do you think, Mer?"

She smirked. "I think my date would probably love it, but it's not the Playboy Mansion I'm taking her to, so no on that one."

Holly shrugged. "Fine. It wouldn't be the first good idea you've shot down." She put up a finger. "Quick question. Why aren't you correcting me when I call you Mer?"

"I'll tell you if you'll join me tonight."

Holly took that same finger and pointed it at herself. "Me?"

"Yes, Holly. You."

She shook her head. "No. It's Valentine's Day. You can't ask a girl out and expect her not to read into that. Besides, I'm kinda used to you dressing up for me, and since there won't be a special outfit, I can't possibly know how to act."

Meredith grinned. "Was that a yes?"

Holly leaned forward and rested her elbows on the desk. "Why now? Did the higher-ups change the rules?"

"No, the rules haven't changed, and you should know that I can't really offer you anything beyond dinner."

Holly considered it for a moment. If she said yes, they'd probably have a great time while eating great food. If she said no, nothing would change. They'd avoid each other as best they could, which sucked on every level. Why hadn't she already accepted the offer? What was she waiting for? "I've missed you too," she said.

"Don't put words in my mouth." Meredith stood and went to the window that looked out on nothing of interest. "This might be the worst idea I've ever had, but you're the only person I want to spend the evening with." She turned, and with her arms folded protectively over her chest, she said, "I guess I should've asked if you're seeing someone else."

"So it's not random that it's Valentine's Day?"

"My intention is not random, no. But as I said—"

"You can't promise anything beyond dinner. Don't worry, I heard that loud and clear."

Meredith turned to leave. "You should say no because I have no idea what I'm doing."

Holly jumped to her feet. "It's a big fat yes, Meredith. And I have no idea what I'm doing either, but I'm not going to let you walk out of my office and go have dinner alone while I drink half a bottle of wine and watch *Sleepless in Seattle* in my footie pajamas. It's Valentine's Day, and even if that means absolutely nothing tomorrow, it means everything tonight."

Meredith lifted an eyebrow. "Footie pajamas?"

"That's all you heard of my big climactic speech?"

She grinned. "It stood out, but I heard everything." She went out the door and popped her head back in. "Meet me there at seven. And Holly? You should write that big climactic speech into a script."

Holly waited until Meredith was out of earshot before she said, "I already have."

❖

"You're dumping me on Valentine's Day?" Gwen threw a sweater back at Holly. "And stop throwing your secondhand store wardrobe at me."

Holly turned away from her closet and put her hands on her hips. "Number one, we didn't have any big plans, and number two, it's not my fault you chose to sit right in the line of fire. Now, get off my bed and help me figure out what to wear."

"No. Not until you tell me who you're dumping me for."

"Oh, good grief. All we were going to do was watch old romantic movies with Desiree while we stuffed our faces with chicken wings and way too much chocolate, none of which was going to possibly, maybe end up in great sex with a beautiful woman."

"What am I, that tin of old chopped liver in the back of the pantry that no one wants to eat?"

"Call Ty, Gwen. Maybe he likes expired chopped liver."

"Okay, fuck you. And if you want help with your outfit tonight, which you desperately need by the look of things, you'll name her right now, and it better not start with Meredith and end with Drake."

Holly pushed a pile of sweaters off the bed and sat. "It starts with Meredith and ends with Drake." She leaned over and put her face in her hands. "Oh God, what am I doing?"

Gwen draped an arm over her. "Well, sunshine, it would seem you're thinking with your heart and not your head. Fitting for Valentine's Day."

Holly sat back up. "You're right. I am. How stupid is it of me to hope we'll have sex tonight? Like that will somehow make it all a little less painful that she doesn't see me as someone worth fighting for."

Gwen stood and offered her hand. "I'll help you look sexy as hell tonight if you promise not to have sex of any kind with her. She doesn't deserve you."

Holly took her hand. "Deal."

Gwen led her out of the bedroom and into the living room. "We don't have much time, so get your shit together and meet me by my car in five. This requires a run to my favorite boutique."

Gwen shut the door, and Holly threw her hands in the air. "Why is everyone always telling me to get my shit together?"

❖

Holly was five minutes late due to an Uber driver who insisted on following all rules, such as not putting two wheels up on the sidewalk to circumvent an accident. She hated being late after Meredith took the initiative with what she hoped was a special Valentine's dinner. She rushed through the front door and spotted the hostess station to the right, "Hi. I'm meeting Meredith Drake. Is she here already?"

"Right this way." Holly followed the hostess, who would no doubt have her own breakout television series next fall. She was just biding her time. Getting by on this hostess job and probably sharing a one-bedroom apartment with two messy dudes who never cleaned up after themselves. Boy, would they be sorry when she signed a big contract and never spoke to them again.

It looked like someone had spent a large fortune to renovate what used to be a run-down steak house, if Holly remembered correctly. Back in the day, it was enough to put up a few framed photos of the celebrities who regularly dined at your restaurant. To attract any attention now, you had to hire a celebrity chef and decorate the place the way an A-lister would decorate their own home.

Ford's was what Holly imagined Gwen Stefani's home looked like, with the large chandeliers and shiny black patent leather booths with hot pink trim. Hopefully, they'd spent as much money on the chef as they had on the gold leaf ceiling.

Meredith was chatting with a man sitting at the table next to theirs. Holly hoped she wouldn't have to make small talk with him through the entire meal. After a trip to Gwen's favorite boutique, followed by a blowout at the Dry Bar, and then the uber slow Uber driver, Holly felt a bit frazzled. She also felt like she could eat twelve appetizers if they were all as small as the tiny three bean salad she just walked by. There were literally three beans placed ever so carefully in the center of the plate. Was someone kidding with this?

Meredith laughed at something the man said. They both spotted Holly at the same time. He leaned over and said something. She gave him a nod and got up.

"Sorry, I'm a bit late," Holly said.

Meredith took her elbow and leaned in. Holly expected a kiss on the cheek, but Meredith whispered, "HR is here," then pulled back and said a bit more loudly, "Happy Galentine's Day, BFF."

Oh. So this was how Meredith planned to play it? Holly took a quick glance around. She couldn't see anyone she recognized from HR, but she put up an open palm. "Put it right here, BFF. And don't miss like you usually do." Meredith went to give her a high five but found only air when Holly pulled her hand away. "You'd think for someone who was the president of holiday programming at the Wifetime network that you'd be smart enough to stop falling for that." Holly slugged her playfully on the shoulder as if she had done it a thousand times before.

Meredith cleared her throat and turned to the gentleman sitting next to them. "Holly, this is Ken Ensign. Wifetime hired his PR firm to handle the fallout from the Cruz situation."

"Oh." Holly offered her hand. "Pleased to meet you, Ken. Holly Hudson."

"Holly Hudson? My wife makes the kids and me watch the *Evermore* series every year. She's a big fan."

Holly turned to the woman sitting across from Ken. She looked too young to have kids over two. That and the way she shook her head almost imperceptibly told Holly that she should just move on. "Well, great. That's great. How was the bean salad? I was actually eyeing that on the way in. It looks delicious."

The woman offered Holly her plate. "I could only eat two of the beans. Would you like to have the third? I'd hate to see it go to waste."

The lima bean and green bean were gone. Only the white bean remained.

Sure, they were the biggest beans Holly had ever seen, but this chef had taken his deconstruction of the classic three bean salad everyone's grandma served at the family barbecue to a ridiculous level of stupidity.

Holly was joking when she said the salad looked delicious, but she took the plate because all bets were off ever since Meredith used the word Galentine. "Don't mind if I do." She sat at their table and popped the white bean in her mouth. It tasted vinegary and so delicious, she just had to moan her satisfaction. "God, that was good. I may have peaked early. Where's dessert?"

Meredith put two fingers on the base of a champagne glass the waiter had poured for Holly and slid it out of her reach. "Are you okay?" she asked.

Holly leaned in and whispered, "If you want to keep those valuable fingers you have on my glass, you'll slide it back here and order some goddamned food. Pronto." She straightened back up and gave Ken a polite smile. She gave Meredith the same smile and raised her glass. "I'd like to make a toast." Meredith's eyes widened. "Come on, Mer. You're here. You're single. You might meet someone tonight. Get a little tipsy with me." She turned toward Ken and his secretary of two minutes, well, maybe five, and leaned in to clink their glasses. "Hit me, kids. This one is being a party pooper."

Ken raised his glass. "She's probably sick of me giving her advice all day long, and then boom, we're sitting near each other for dinner."

"What kind of advice, Ken?" Holly shouldn't have asked, but this night was going to shit anyway.

"Well, I help companies who've been mired in scandal to come out of it not only unscathed but elevated." He said that last word with a wink. "She's handling it like a rock star." He reached across the table and caressed his date's arm. "And Katrina here really likes her too."

It was said with such thick sexual innuendo, there was no mistaking his intent. Holly almost snorted champagne out of her nose. She turned away and coughed into her napkin. When she recovered, Meredith was getting out of her seat.

"Going somewhere?" Holly asked.

"It's time for us to go."

"But I'm starving. I need food and drink. Lots of it."

Meredith offered her hand. "We'll find someplace else to eat."

"On Valentine's Day? Without a reservation?"

"I'll take you to a drive-thru."

Holly reluctantly pulled herself off the chair. "I want In-N-Out."

Meredith turned to Ken. "Thank you for the champagne. Have a lovely evening."

"Was it something I said?" He got up. "Meredith?"

She ignored him and urged Holly to walk in front of her by pushing her along. Holly swatted her hand away. "Stop rushing me. These damned heels aren't the easiest things to walk in."

They got out onto the street, and Meredith with the long legs decided to walk full speed ahead. "Hey, slow down," Holly said.

Meredith stopped, shook her head at the sky, and then yelled, "I can't believe that just happened. Women truly aren't safe anywhere they go. There's always a hidden agenda." She threw her hands in the air and starting walking even faster.

Holly caught up and led her to a dark spot between two buildings. "You need to calm down. Everyone has a camera these days, remember? You don't want to show up on You-Tube as the crazy woman who had a meltdown in front of Ford's."

Meredith leaned against the building and covered her face with her hands. Holly moved in closer and softened her tone. "Hey, now. What do you say we find a cab and—" Meredith pulled Holly into her arms and held on so tightly, it almost took her breath away. She steadied herself and put a hand on Meredith's head. "It's okay," she whispered.

Meredith sighed. "It's not just about them. I've missed you. You said it to me, and I didn't say it back. It was so hard to not say it back, but I'm saying it now. I've really, really missed you, like crazy missed you, and when you walked in tonight looking so gorgeous, all I wanted to do was greet you the way I would if you were my date, but instead, I said all of that stuff about us being friends for that asshole's benefit."

"Oh. You mean the asshole that just insinuated he'd like you to join his little party?"

Meredith scoffed. "What about me says that I'd be into a threesome with those two?"

Holly shrugged. "Well, you do have an air about you."

"What the hell does that mean?"

"Wealthy single lesbian who spends a lot of time alone in her high-rise apartment on Wilshire seeks a straight couple for sexual exploration."

"That's not me. What the hell, Holly?"

"I know it's not you, but your outfit screams it in the highest octave."

"My yachting outfit, as you put it? Well, fine. I'll take it off."

Holly stilled and waited with anticipation.

"What are you looking at?"

"You said you were going to take your clothes off…okay, fine, I'll turn around, but it's not like I haven't seen it. Or tasted it. Or fucked it, for that matter."

There were several seconds of silence before Meredith said, "Were you trying to kill me with that silver dress tonight?"

"Are you looking at my ass when you're supposed to be de-frocking?" Holly had to smile. Gwen had said her ass looked pretty slammin' in the form-fitting dress. She wanted to go with something whimsical in pink or red, considering the holiday, but Gwen said that would be too obvious. Holly would have to thank her with a bottle of her favorite merlot.

"Answer the question," Meredith said.

Holly turned back around. "I didn't want to kill you. Maybe just make it a little harder for you to talk business all night."

"Your hair looks amazing. Have I said that out loud yet?"

Holly shook her head. "No, but when would you have?"

"I should've said it the second you walked up to the table. You look absolutely stunning tonight." She moved closer. "I'm so sorry I ripped us out of that restaurant. I should've handled it differently."

"You can make up for it by taking your clothes off."

She laughed. "I'm not going to take my clothes off in the street. Is there some other way I could salvage the evening for us?"

"Do you karaoke?"

Meredith put her hands over her eyes. "Okay, something besides—"

"I was kidding," Holly said. "I mean, I'm totally dressed for it, but Whitney would probably be very disappointed by my rendition of 'I Will Always Love You.' And Dolly? Well, she'd be downright heartbroken."

"I don't know much about karaoke, but who would choose to perform that song when everyone knows Whitney is the only person in the world who can hit those notes?"

Holly's hand creeped up into the air. "Worst night of my life."

"Worse than tonight?"

"What do you mean? I'm having a blast standing in this alley having a pointless conversation with you." She motioned toward a dumpster. "Wanna cap it off with some pointless dumpster sex?"

Meredith looked down the alley with wide, questioning eyes. Holly decided to let her off the hook and took her arm. "I'm kidding again. Sort of. But the truth is, I wouldn't have the strength for vertical sex until I get a burger in my belly, so let's hit the diner around the corner. I'm sure there are some seats at the counter."

Meredith bent her elbow and put her hand on Holly's. "They have great milkshakes."

"And the best fries this side of the Rocky Mountains." Holly glanced at her as they walked and wondered if it felt as good to her as it did to Holly to be touching again. She leaned in and said, "Ken's an asshole, but he has great taste."

Meredith squeezed her hand. "I'm the one with great taste."

❖

When Gwen opened her door, Holly held up the note she'd found attached to her own door. "Are you okay, G? What's the emergency?" She walked in and found Griffin, Ty, and Desiree sitting in Gwen's living room. There were three heart-shaped boxes of chocolate sitting on the coffee table. Two had been opened and were half-eaten.

"What did I tell you?" Gwen said to them. "Did I work a miracle with this one or what?"

Griffin stood and clasped his hands together. "If I had a dream girl, you'd be it. Turn around. I need to see what that dress does to your ass."

Holly furrowed her brow. "No. Okay, fine." She held her arms out and turned in a circle.

Ty let out a low whistle. "If I was attracted to anxiety-ridden genius lesbians, I'd fight Meredith for you, but my type is older and well, straighter."

"How old are we talking?" Desiree asked.

Ty winked at her. "Break up with Thad, and it's on."

Desiree threw her head back and laughed. "Oh, how you do amuse me, Ty."

Griffin grabbed the unopened box of chocolates and handed it to Holly. "Happy Valentine's Day, love." He kissed her cheek and took a step back. "I don't think she had sex tonight, guys. Her hair looks too good."

"Agreed," Gwen said. "I'm proud of you, Holls."

"Well, it wasn't for lack of trying. I even suggested we have pointless dumpster sex."

"Honey, that isn't something you suggest," Gwen said. "It's something that just happens when you're too drunk or high to care."

"Seriously," Griffin said. "Even gay men don't do that sober, and we don't give a shit where we have sex."

Holly kicked her heels off and plopped into a chair. "Great. She probably thinks I have a trash kink or something." She ripped the plastic off the box of chocolates and hoped the one she chose had caramel in it. "Damnit," she said. "Anyone want half of an orange crème? No takers?" She tossed it onto the table. "That's okay. I'll just try again."

Gwen sat in a chair and wrapped her arms around her legs. "Before you stuff another one in your mouth, I demand details."

"Yeah, I'm on pins and needles here," Ty said. "I love stories that don't involve two hot chicks getting it on. What was she wearing?"

Desiree patted Ty's knee. "Enough with the sarcasm. Some of us want to hear the story even if there isn't a big climax at the end. In fact, it'll be a lot like the stories you tell, and we all listen to those with bated breath."

Griffin, who was sitting on the floor, rolled onto his side in a fit of laughter. Gwen stayed slightly more contained by not falling out of her chair. Holly put her purse in front of her face and giggled because Desiree was so right. A good storyteller Ty was not. But since storytelling was Holly's jam, she decided to lean in.

"It was a typical Valentine's," she said in her best storytelling voice. "Happy couples of all ages were dressed up, and most had ordered a nice bottle of champagne to celebrate their love, so imagine Holly's surprise when there was a bottle on ice by Meredith's table."

She eyed her friends. They all stared back at her like anxious five-year-olds. Talk about owning the room. This story would be fun to tell.

A few minutes later, Griffin said, "So you didn't even kiss good night?"

"Oh," Holly said. "How could I forget that part?"

Gwen narrowed her eyes. "You better not tell me you had safe hair sex."

"Didn't know that was a thing but good to know. And Meredith did give me a soft peck on my cheek that, in hindsight, I'm so good with. I mean, in the moment, I wanted more, but we still have to work together under those stupid rules."

"Be grateful for those stupid rules," Desiree said. "Back in my day, sexual harassment didn't have a name, it just was. And, boy, could it be brutal when you caught the eye of a superior. It was almost impossible to keep his hands off you and also keep your job."

Holly gave her a nod. "You know what, Dez? You're right. I should respect Meredith's desire to be a good example, and maybe one day, when things have calmed down a bit, we can revisit the idea of dating each other."

"Wow," Gwen said. "Our little girl done growed up right in front of our eyes, and all it took was a slinky dress and a good hair day."

Holly tilted her head and opened her chocolates again. "And a chocolate covered caramel, if I can find one."

❖

Holly looked both ways before she leaned into Meredith's office and whispered, "I had a great time last night."

Meredith put her pen down and waved Holly in. "It was a strange but highly enjoyable evening."

"Haven't all of our encounters been strange?"

Meredith waved her hand. "Oh God. We don't have to go through them again, do we?"

"Nah, that's not why I'm here." Holly sat with her legs crossed and one elbow on her knee. She'd told herself to avoid lengthy eye contact. Physical contact was, of course, out of the question. No hug hello or good-bye. She'd stay on her side of the desk and hoped Meredith would do the same.

There wasn't even a hint of the nautical look from the previous night. Meredith had ditched the Hamptons for New York City business chic. The creamy silk blouse with round pearl buttons looked expensive. So did the black velvet belt with the large gold buckle that Holly could only see the top of over the desk. She resisted the urge to ask Meredith to stand and slowly turn in a circle. That would completely defeat the purpose of her visit. Meredith needed to stay fully dressed in Holly's brain. She didn't need to close her office door and lean against it while she unbuttoned that silky blouse. And Holly definitely didn't need to push herself against Meredith and pull that tight black skirt up her thighs. And Holly's tongue? Well, it definitely needed to *not* lick that soft neck only to find itself deep inside Meredith's warm, wet mouth.

Meredith pushed her hair behind her ears and clasped her hands in front of her. How long could Holly stare at that face, those lips, before it got weird? A minute? Two minutes? Turned out fifteen seconds was the maximum time allotted before both of them turned away. "Sorry," Holly said. "I really did come here to tell you something and also give you something."

Meredith's expression changed to a look of worry. "Sounds serious."

"It is. I mean, I'm taking it seriously now, this thing about not sleeping with your boss." She glanced behind her to make sure no one was in the hallway listening. "Sorry. I didn't mean to say that so loudly." She made eye contact again, and in a lower tone, she said, "I wish I could read your mind."

"Ha. That wouldn't help our situation."

"Okay, look. I know you're trying to be the consummate professional, and I respect that, but could you give me something? Anything?"

Meredith glanced toward her office door. "Holly, I—"

"It's okay," Holly said, interrupting. "Forget I said that. I don't want to be like Cruz or that jackass from last night. I want you to know that I respect your decision to keep your work life and private life separate. In fact, I admire you for it, and so will everyone who works here."

"That's good to hear." Meredith picked up her pen and jotted something on a notepad. "You said you have something you want to give me?"

Holly assumed the jotting of illegible words was purely a way for Meredith to distract herself from what was going on between them. Holly wished she'd brought a pen and notebook too. But she had nothing. "I do have something, but I'll need your personal email address. I want this to stay private for now."

"Color me intrigued."

"I hope you still think so once you read it."

Meredith's eyes lit up. "Your gay Christmas script?"

"Do you really think you can get it approved?"

Meredith stood. "One way or another, I'll get it done."

Holly took that as her cue to leave. "Right. I've taken up enough of your time." She stood, but Meredith had closed her office door. She kept her hand on the knob and turned.

"Thank you for understanding the awkward position I'm in. It certainly isn't my first choice."

"Oh yeah? What would your first choice be?"

Meredith's grip on the knob seemed to tighten. She shook her head and whispered, "I wish I could. But I can't."

"I know," Holly said. "Sorry. That was out of line. Text your email address and I'll send the script from home tonight."

Meredith opened the door and raised her voice so everyone could hear. "Thank you, Holly. It was good to see you."

What was it about the way Meredith said her name? It wasn't as if she pronounced it differently from everyone else. But every time she heard it come out of Meredith's mouth, Holly felt it in her core, and her mind went blank. "You can call me Holiday," she blurted. "I mean, you can call me anything, really. Holly, Holiday, Holls, that crazy chick you—" She stopped herself from rambling when she remembered where she was. "I'll just be on my way now."

"Probably for the best."

Holly gave her a nod. She knew Meredith was purposely being cold, but hearing her say it was for the best stung a bit. Holly told herself if they ran into each other, great. But Holly wouldn't seek her out again.

CHAPTER EIGHT

Griffin opened Holly's front door. "You are an angel."

"Griff, you can't just whoosh into my apartment without knocking. What if I'd been naked?"

"You're never naked, Holls. In fact, you're usually overdressed for the weather."

"So I like a cozy hoodie. Who in this world doesn't?" She closed her laptop and set it on the coffee table.

"Who in the world leaves their door unlocked in LA? Seriously, Holls. You're not in Christmas Cove anymore."

She stood and went into the kitchen. "I have four locks on that door, so don't lecture me on how to survive in LA. Your usual?"

"No. We need to go out and celebrate. Dinner is on me tonight."

She stepped back into the living room. "This is why my door was unlocked. I knew you'd get the new *Evermore* script today. I also knew you'd be thrilled that your character gets plenty of air time."

He rushed over and threw his arms around her. "You have no idea how happy this makes me. And how happy it'll make my churchgoing mother to see me with my beautiful television wife and a baby on the way."

"Question. How did you get away with having a Barbie condo when you were young?"

"Well, I explained to my mother that G.I. Joe couldn't ask Barbie to marry him if he had no place for her to live. And of course, she'd need her own Jeep. Army green isn't her best color."

She offered her fist. "Well played, my friend."

A hard knock on the door made them both jump and grab on to each other. He let go first. "Sorry about that. I'll get it."

"I'm not expecting anyone. Put on the chain before you open it."

"Oh, now you're concerned about your safety?"

"No, I can hold my own, but after the way you just jumped into my arms?"

In a loud whisper, he said, "I thought a bomb had gone off, okay? Who knocks that loud?" He put the chain on the door and opened it a crack, then slammed it shut. "It's her," he whispered. "Hashtag hot boss. Hashtag you look like hell." He motioned for her to smooth her hair down and straighten her clothes.

"Oh for God's sake, Griff. You just slammed the door in her face. Open it." She casually lifted a hand and smoothed her hair down. It was fine, and her jeans and T-shirt were fine too.

He opened the door and said, "Hi. Please come in." His enthusiasm was so over-the-top, she wanted to give him a kick in the butt.

Meredith didn't step into the apartment. "Griffin. I'm looking for Holly. Do I have the right apartment?"

"You're in the right place." He gave Holly a wink. "Rain check on that dinner?"

"Absolutely," she said. "And you're buying."

Once he was out the door, Meredith stepped in. Holly

swallowed hard because Meredith's jeans were fitted and sitting low on her hips with a cool leather belt and a tight tee tucked in. Griffin obviously didn't know the first thing about lesbians. Hashtag twinsies.

"Hey," Holly said. "You're pretty much the last person I expected to knock on my door."

"I know. I should've called first."

Holly couldn't imagine what could be so urgent that an email or text wouldn't suffice. "It's okay. What's up?"

"*Evermore* has been cast. Everyone's excited to get going on production. It'll be a big hit." She seemed nervous or stressed. Something was wrong.

"That's good to hear. Thirsty?"

Meredith gave her a firm nod. "Just some water would be great."

Holly grabbed a bottled water out of the fridge and took one for herself. Meredith hadn't moved from the middle of the living room. Holly handed her the bottle, and she took a long sip. "You didn't come here just to tell me about *Evermore*, did you?"

Meredith set the bottle on the table and shook her head. "No."

"Is something wrong?"

"I saw you today in the cafeteria. I didn't stop and say hello, but I watched you while you ate a salad and read a book at the same time."

"I multitask well," Holly said. "You should see me eat breakfast and put on makeup while driving in bumper-to-bumper traffic."

Meredith smiled. That was a good sign. But maybe she wasn't there just to praise Holly. Maybe she was there to tell her she had to let her go. To fire her. That was what had Holly's tummy tied up in knots. She was waiting for the hard blow.

"Sorry," Holly said. "I didn't mean to interrupt." She shoved her hands into her back pockets to stop from fidgeting.

"I came to see you because nothing I'm about to say would be even remotely appropriate for the workplace." She looked at the ceiling and sighed. "God, I'm so stupid."

Holly took a step closer. The way Meredith's hands were shaking made her want to grab them and give her some reassurance that everything would be okay. She wanted some sort of physical contact. Anything. Because to see someone she loved in distress and not do anything about it wasn't an option. And she realized in that moment that her feelings for Meredith hadn't diminished one bit. Not that she thought they had. She played it safe by putting a hand on Meredith's arm instead of her waist, which was where she really wanted it to be. "Tell me," she said.

"I want you. I wanted you on Valentine's Day and every day since. And every time I see you in the hall or the cafeteria, I have to stop and stare."

Holly let go. "Please don't tell me you came all this way to say all that only to then list the reasons why you can't have exactly what you want."

"I didn't. I came to ask you if you'd be willing to engage in a secret love affair with me."

"Secret?"

Meredith nodded. "I know it's asking a lot."

"I came out of the closet a long time ago. Don't ask me to go back in."

"I'm not asking you for that. I'm asking you for discretion. I'm asking you to help me keep my job and the respect of everyone under me."

"You're asking me to let you have your cake and eat it too." She turned away. She needed a moment to think.

Did any of that really matter? Did she care if she couldn't shout from the rooftop that she was dating Meredith Drake? Sure, it would feel amazing to say that out loud, but was it a dealbreaker if she couldn't?

"Holly, should I leave?"

She turned back around. "Why didn't you think of this sooner? It kills me when I see you but can't touch you. It's like the worst kind of torture. Okay, waterboarding would probably be worse, but—"

Meredith rushed over and covered her mouth with one hand. "Holls, normally, I love your rambling, but right now, I need to know if that was a yes."

Holly smiled at the use of her nickname. "Yes, Mer. That's a yes."

Their lips collided, and Holly's heart, along with her body, melted in Meredith's arms. This was where she belonged. Kissing those lips and feeling those hands roam her body. Hearing Meredith's breathing intensify. Feeling the heat build between them. And knowing that whatever happened next would feel so perfect and right that Holly would probably find it difficult to keep the tears at bay.

Meredith's hand slid under her T-shirt. She kneaded Holly's breast through her bra. It wasn't enough. Holly needed to yank her shirt and bra off so she could feel Meredith's lips and tongue caress her breast. "Touch me," she said. *"Touch me everywhere."*

"Holly!"

Her eyes shot open. She lifted her head off her desk and shouted, "What?" Brian stood in her doorway, laughing. "Damnit, Brian. I was just getting to the good part."

"The part where you win the lotto? Yeah, I have that dream too." He sat and took a cookie from Holly's lunch.

"Yes, I was about to win the lottery. What do you need? Never mind, I'm on my lunch break. Figure it out yourself."

He put up his hands. "Whoa. I didn't mean to wake the beast. Just tell me if you've mentioned my name to your actress friend. I have tickets to a hockey game, and I need a date."

"She doesn't like hockey. Or any sport. She likes expensive jewelry and hanging out at rodeos."

"I think you just offended every spur-wearing cowboy in America, Holls." He stood. "But sport or not, I think I'll stick with hockey pucks and avoid the cow pies." He put up a hand and waved as he walked away. "Thanks for the cookie."

"Yeah, I didn't actually give you my only cookie," she shouted.

The part about Gwen liking expensive jewelry was true. The rodeo part was a stroke of genius. Now maybe he would leave her alone about Gwen. She cleaned up her lunch and went into the restroom. She took a good look in the mirror while she washed her hands. Wait. Was she having a good hair day? How did she not know that her hair was lying so perfectly on her shoulders? The short nap looked good on her too. She couldn't let all of this bright-eyed bushy-tailedness go to waste. She also couldn't visit Meredith's office without unbuttoning one more button on her blouse.

It had been weeks since their last conversation. Holly had kept her word to herself by staying as far away as possible. If only that had helped take her mind off what they'd shared together in Hawaii. If only it had made the damned sex dreams go away.

Holly peeked into Meredith's office, then walked in and shut the door. "Oh, good. You're alone."

Meredith looked up from her laptop and smiled, but that smile quickly faded. "Is everything okay?"

"I just had a very vivid dream."

Meredith stood. "Okay. Come in. Sit down."

Holly stayed where she was by the door in case she needed a quick exit. "Also, I've been avoiding you."

Meredith shut her laptop. "I noticed." She didn't seem angry, but Holly thought she saw a look of pain shoot across Meredith's face. Had the distance been hard for her too? If so, she certainly hadn't done anything about it.

"Anyway, about this dream," Holly said. "You asked me to have a secret affair with you."

"Oh." Meredith stared at Holly for a few seconds, then slowly rounded her desk and stopped a few feet away. "When this promotion happened, it crossed my mind to keep seeing you that way, in secret, but a very long time ago, I did that to someone else. The reasons were different, but it hurt her, and eventually, she grew to hate me. I don't want you to hate me, Holly. This isn't easy for me either. But I do want us to at least be friends. I want us to work together, not avoid each other."

Holly lifted her chin. "Good. Because who the hell do you think you are expecting me to be your dirty little secret?"

Meredith smiled. "Can we get back to the part where it was just a dream?"

Holly folded her arms across her chest. "This isn't funny. You're taking up too much space in my head. I need closure. And why do you have to smell so damned good? You should stop wearing perfume."

Meredith pursed her lips as if trying not to laugh, but her shaking shoulders gave away her amusement. "I've missed you."

Holly shook her head. "Not helping." She closed her eyes and took in a deep breath. Even from a few feet away, Meredith's scent took her right back to Hawaii. Right back to that damned velvet jacket and the sexy Christmas costume and Meredith writhing naked on the bed, her nipples so hard and her pussy so wet and her voice begging for more.

Holly opened her eyes again. "I need closure," she said. "I need you to tell me that you ended us not because of what happened with Cruz or the new rules. I need you to tell me you ended it because you just weren't that into me. Then maybe I can move on and stop dreaming about you and wishing—" She stopped and lowered her gaze. She'd said too much. Or not enough. She had no idea if she'd even have a job when she walked back out of that office.

Meredith went back to her desk, scribbled something on a sticky note, and stood in front of Holly, closer than she'd been before. "I can't give you what you want, but maybe we could continue this conversation in private."

Holly took the paper. "Is this your home address?"

"It is."

Holly's melancholy mood lifted slightly. Meredith hadn't blown her completely off. That had to be a good sign. "Promise you won't answer the door in a sexy Easter bunny outfit?"

Meredith laughed. "I think that would defeat the purpose of showing you what I do on a typical Friday night. It's really quite boring, but maybe that's what we need since every time we've been together up until this point has been a crazy whirlwind of—"

Holly put up a finger. "Wait. I've got this. Humiliation, gluttony, and hot sex?"

Meredith put up her hand for a high five. "Bingo. A night of pizza and back-to-back *Dateline* episodes should counteract that, don't you think?"

"Oh, you're a *Dateline* girl? You'd fit right in with my friends at the complex where I live. They're huge Keith Morrison fans."

"His voice," Meredith said with a sigh. "Somehow, it makes murder and mayhem feel like a bedtime story."

Holly felt like she could smile again. Maybe they could be friends, and all of the other feelings would eventually fade away. She turned to leave and stopped at the door. "You should know, I'm one of those weirdos who likes pineapple on her pizza."

Meredith grinned. "Hawaiian pizza. How apropos."

"See you Friday night, then." Holly left the office and practically skipped down the hallway. This fell somewhere between complete avoidance and having hot sex on Meredith's desk, but she'd take it.

❖

"I thought we weren't going to do this." Holly dropped her purse on the floor and turned her head to the side to give Meredith better access. "Oh my God, your tongue. I need it in my mouth. Give me your tongue, Meredith. Let me suck on it. Let me make love to your tongue. Let me have babies with your tongue."

Holly opened her eyes. Once she got her bearings, she shook her fists at the ceiling. "Why, God? Why do I have to dream about her every damn night?"

She knew it wasn't God's fault she couldn't control her thoughts, but maybe he could help out with the cheesy dialogue. Because if she ever actually verbalized that she wanted to have babies with Meredith's tongue, well, she'd just have to leave the country. Maybe the continent. Siberia would work. No one would find her there and remind her of that time she said those words out loud. Maybe she should cancel tonight. Call in sick.

Her phone buzzed. She put it to her ear and said, "You're up early."

"I can feel your apprehension vibrating through the walls." Holly loved it when Gwen didn't try to tone down her Southern drawl. Something about it was soothing, even if the words weren't.

"Did you leave the batteries in your vibrator again? What did I tell you about that, G?"

Gwen huffed into the phone. "I've worn the damn thing out, hint, hint."

"Yeah, no. I'm not ever in this lifetime buying you a sex toy, so just get that thought out of your head."

"I will if you'll stop telling yourself you're not good enough for that woman. She invited you to her house for *Dateline*. Any *Dateline* addict would tell you that you don't invite just anyone into your Friday nights, willy-nilly. There's a reverence to it. People must respect the *Dateline*."

"I just dreamt that I told her I wanted to have babies with her tongue. How can I go tonight with that kind of shitty dialogue in my head?"

"You can't. Cancel it right now. My God, Holls. What kind of sick—"

"Okay, fine. It was just a dream. I'm going."

"That's better. Now, open your front door. I have the perfect thing for you to wear."

Holly grumbled as she got out of bed. "I can't look like I'm trying too hard. This isn't Valentine's Day." She opened the door and gaped. "What the hell, G? You want me to wear a pantsuit to *Dateline*? I'm not Hillary Fucking Clinton."

"It isn't that kind of pantsuit. It's sexy, and lesbians love sexy pantsuits."

"Um, I don't know where you're getting your 'what lesbians love' information from, but that's not a thing."

"I took a poll. It's a thing. At least it is for the lesbian at my hair salon. She was all over this."

Holly's eyes shuddered closed. "You just pointed at your vagina, G. So I guess that means you wore this pantsuit into the hair salon just so you could take a poll of one?"

"Don't freak out. I was wearing panties."

"Oh, that's good to know. I feel so much better now." She blocked the doorway when Gwen tried to enter. "Don't bring your slutty pantsuit into my apartment. I'm wearing jeans tonight."

Gwen sighed. "Well, at least make sure they're the ones that hug your ass. You've gotta give her something to lust after."

"That's not the point of tonight. We're going to try to be friends who do normal stuff like you and Dez and your special *Dateline* martinis with the cocktail onion, which I've never understood. Martinis were made for olives."

"Just make sure you roll that little onion around on your tongue while she's looking at you. That'll get her going."

"Right. Roll an onion, of all things, on my tongue, which I've never done before, so it'll probably fall out of my mouth."

Gwen waved her off. "Okay, just stop. You obviously weren't made for the onion roll, but trust me, it works." She brushed past and went into the kitchen. She took the lid off the trash can and stuffed the pantsuit, hanger and all, in it, then put the lid back on and brushed her hands off. "Okay, so let's talk about how we're going to let your little lesbian light shine tonight."

Holly stood there, stunned. "You just threw away the pantsuit that you wanted me to wear tonight? Oh my God. What did it cost you, all of five bucks at the secondhand store?"

"Well, unlike some folks, I know how to move on from a bad idea. No onion roll and no pantsuit. Got it." She plopped down on the sofa. "We might need wine for my next bad idea, since it involves you taking on a very subtle but sexy Southern lilt."

Holly slapped her hand against her forehead. "I can't even with you right now."

Gwen shot a finger in the air. "Moving on. I didn't think that one would fly anyway."

Holly sat. "I thought you didn't like Meredith. Why are you encouraging me to make something happen tonight? What happened to being proud of me for not sleeping with her on Valentine's Day?"

Gwen leaned forward and put her hand on Holly's knee. "Because I know you haven't been able to let go. You're still pining for her. And while I've watched you date other women, I've never seen you fall this hard. And if she's as great as you say she is, then you should grab the bull by the horns and make it happen. None of this pussyfooting around. Go and get the girl."

❖

Holly's hand shook as she punched Meredith's number into the call box. She willed herself to calm down. It was just pizza and *Dateline*. A starting point to a lasting friendship. No sex would be had. No kissing. No making out on the sofa. No heavy breathing. No licking or grinding. "For God's sake, get a grip," she whispered.

"Holly?"

"Hey. It's me." She glanced down at her hoodie and realized it was the same one she'd gotten tangled up in at the Honolulu airport. She'd purposely dressed down. No makeup, no low-cut blouse. Just leggings, a hoodie, and running shoes. Gwen would be appalled, but Holly felt good about the choices.

Hopefully, Meredith had gotten comfy too, although Holly imagined their ideas of what getting comfy meant were quite different. In Hawaii, it meant bathing suit cover-ups and silky robes. Who knew what it meant in LA?

"Come on up," Meredith said. "Fourth floor, apartment 4B."

Why was Holly so nervous? She'd already had Meredith every which way from Sunday. She knew how it felt to touch her. Kiss her. The door opened, and Holly knew why she was so nervous. Casual Friday night Meredith was a mystery. "I don't really know you," she blurted. "Like, at all." Then she scanned Meredith from head to toe. She'd removed her makeup, her damp hair was combed away from her face, and her feet were bare. Turned out this was a look Holly knew well. The post-sex look.

Luckily, Meredith wasn't wearing a sexy robe. She had on loose shorts and a sweatshirt that was thick enough to hide her lack of a bra for the most part. Holly managed to rip her eyes away from what little she could see.

Meredith opened the door wider. "Come in."

Holly shook her head. "Not until I know more than what I can read on your LinkedIn profile."

Meredith leaned against the door jamb and folded her arms. "Are you freaking out because you had sex with someone you barely know, or is it because you do know me, but you wish you didn't?"

"Well. At least we're acknowledging Hawaii now. It seemed like you'd purged it from your mind. Also, why do you always smell so good? You can't expect me to behave if you smell this good."

Meredith took her hand and pulled her into the apartment. She shut the door and bolted it, then turned. "What do you want to know?"

"Tell me about your first crush. Your first girlfriend. Tell me about the person you had to hide. Was it because you weren't out yet? Is that why? Because pretty much all of us gays beyond the age of thirty have that person in their past."

"I'd be happy to tell you all of that," Meredith said. "I'd be happy to talk about my family, where I grew up, where I went to school, but—" She lowered her gaze.

Holly took a step closer. "But, what?"

"I need a hug first."

"A hug?" The request surprised her. Meredith had been so stoic about her feelings. So professional at all times. Holly opened her arms. "I give great hugs."

"I know," Meredith whispered. She looked as if she was about to cry as she wrapped her arms around Holly's shoulders.

Holly held on tightly and said, "Hey, what's wrong?"

"I've missed you so much. I hate that I've had to keep you at arm's length. I hate that I can't be myself with you anymore." She turned her head slightly and kissed Holly's cheek. "I hate that I know you're so close, but I can't touch you."

Holly tightened her grip around Meredith's waist. "Why didn't you say something? This whole time, I thought it had been easy for you to just walk away from us."

"Far from it." Meredith pulled away from the hug and took a step back. "Sorry, I didn't mean to get all emotional on you."

Holly stood speechless for a moment. She hadn't expected an explosion of feelings from Meredith. Especially not those particular feelings. "You probably didn't mean for my little heart to go pitter-patter again either."

Meredith took a deep breath and put a hand on her hip. "Sorry, I just—"

"Stop apologizing for letting me know how you feel. I need to know what you're feeling. I need to understand because most days I don't." Holly took a step closer. "We have something. I feel it every time you come near me. I feel it in my dreams. I wake up and see your face, and you know what this is?" Holly pointed at herself. "This is honesty. This is what I need from you, Meredith. I need you to tell me everything so I can understand how it is that you can have feelings for me but still let me go."

"The higher cause," Meredith said. "Bringing diversity and inclusion to Wifetime. Changing the work environment so it's safe for every woman. I have the power to make a difference now, and I don't want to jeopardize that. But don't for a second think that it's easy for me. I mean, look at you." Meredith motioned up and down Holly's body. "Even in that hoodie you got all caught up in at the airport, you're absolutely stunning."

Holly's stomach chose that moment to growl so loudly, it caused Meredith to look right at it. "Let's get some pizza in that tummy of yours."

"But wait. You were saying something about me being stunning. Could you expound on that?"

"Ha. Like you haven't heard it before. Make yourself at home while I dish up."

Her apartment was a hundred times nicer than Holly's. Of course, her salary probably was too. The hallway from the door to the kitchen was lined with framed photos. Holly walked by them, stopped, and backtracked. "I see Chelsea and Sheffield finally took the plunge."

"They did," Meredith shouted from the kitchen. "Do you like wine or beer with your pizza?"

"Beer." Meredith's family looked happy. Even after their daughter canceled her expensive Hawaiian wedding, they were there with her on the courthouse steps, their expressions of joy no different from all of the other photos.

Meredith was in the photo too, looking as gorgeous as ever, her arm wrapped around her sister. Looking at the photo, Holly understood why Meredith seemed so distraught in Hawaii when she realized she'd be spending Christmas without them. They were clearly a close-knit family.

"Hope you don't mind that I'll be texting with my dad during *Dateline*. He loves trying to out-predict me, but he's rarely right." She handed Holly a local porter and took a sip of her own. "It's go time. I have the pizza on the coffee table."

Holly followed her into the living room. "Does it have pineapple on it?"

"Would I deny you your favorite pizza topping?"

"Well, you're denying me some slammin' hot sex, so…"

"We're both being denied, so don't act like you're the only sexually frustrated girl in the room, okay?" She sat on the sofa and patted the spot next to her. "Now, sit and eat so your tummy doesn't drown out Keith Morrison." Holly sat, and Meredith threw a blanket over their legs. She grabbed the pizza box off the coffee table and put it on Holly's lap. "You get first pick."

"Oh, that's a mistake," Holly said. "I show no mercy when it comes to getting the biggest slice."

"That's my life motto too." Meredith winked and took a slice. "Here we go. And don't say it's the husband who did it, even though it's usually the husband who did it."

Holly took a slice and closed the box as quietly as she could. This *Dateline* thing was even more serious than she'd thought. She'd have to ask Gwen and Desiree if that seemed normal. Then again, what did either of them know about what was and wasn't normal?

❖

Holly put the four empty beer bottles in the recycling can. "And this wasn't even our worst pig-out session."

"Second worst." Meredith wrapped up the one and only leftover pizza slice and tossed it in the fridge. "I kind of missed the champagne and petit fours."

Holly went to the sink and washed her hands. "This was nice. Thanks for inviting me." She tried to make it sound convincing, but she only half meant it. The other half of her felt frustrated. Would it really be so terrible if people at work found out they'd had a thing? Would the CEO have them both fired? Would Meredith's higher calling really be jeopardized if they started dating? Shouldn't they discuss the possibility of one of them working elsewhere so they could be together? Holly didn't question Meredith's sincerity. She just wondered if it was overkill.

She grabbed the dish towel to dry her hands and turned around to find Meredith staring at her intently. "I should go." She didn't move from her spot and neither did Meredith. They were a few feet away from each other, but Holly felt that intense stare in every ounce of her DNA. It seemed that when either of them let their guard down, and Meredith's armor had surely just dropped through the floor, there was an energy so strong, they both had to hold on to something.

Meredith gripped the marble countertop behind her, and Holly held on to that dish towel, twisting it as if her life depended on it. She couldn't take it anymore, so she tossed it on the counter and said, "Why do you have to be everything I've always wanted? What the hell did I do in my life to deserve this kind of torture?" Anger built inside her as she said those words. "Fuck the higher calling, Meredith. And fuck you for making me sit through fucking *Dateline* when you know how I feel."

Holly pushed her way past. She needed to get out of there

before she really lost her temper or even worse, broke down in tears. She shouldn't have said anything. She should've said thank you and left on a happy note. She should've invited Meredith to watch *Dateline* at her place next week with Gwen and Desiree. They could do this, damnit. They could forget about Hawaii and be friends. Work buddies. But all Holly wanted to do was say it again. Fuck the higher calling.

She felt Meredith's arms wrap around her from behind, stopping her from exiting the uncomfortable, no, miserable scene. Meredith pressed her mouth against her ear and said, "Do you want to know how I feel, Holly? What you do to me? How my body reacts every time we're together?"

There was no escaping the hold Meredith had on her. With a quick twist of her body, she could escape physically. The emotional hold was another story. She tried to will the tears that had welled in her eyes to not fall. "Tell me," she whispered.

Meredith moved her hair out of the way. "You think I don't remember every second we were together?" She ran her finger up Holly's neck and around her ear. "I know where your freckles are. I know how much you love to kiss." She brushed her lips against Holly's ear and whispered, "I could barely focus on the TV with you sitting next to me." She slid a hand under Holly's hoodie and caressed her stomach.

Holly let her head drop back and moaned. Meredith's breath on her ear had caused a heat to build between her legs. She had no idea what was happening or where this would go, but she wanted Meredith to know she was all in. "This is all valuable information. Please keep talking."

"If I keep talking—"

"Will we end up in your bed? Is it soft, this bed? Will I be comfortable while I straddle you?"

Meredith slid her hand under the waistband of Holly's

leggings. Holly gasped and covered that hand with her own. Her hips jutted forward, and her breathing became shallow. She wanted this. She wanted it, and she didn't care what tomorrow would look like. She reached up and pulled Meredith in for a kiss. Their lips met at the same time that Meredith's fingers slid into her panties. She pulled away from the kiss and whispered, "About that bed."

Meredith gently pushed her up against the nearest wall. "There will need to be rules."

"Bedroom rules?" In one swift move, Holly switched their positions and locked Meredith's hands above her head. She eyed those crazy sexy lips. "Okay, rule number one: there are no rules."

Meredith pushed away from the wall and moved her across the narrow hallway to the opposite wall. She pulled Holly's hoodie over her head. "We can't leave a paper trail of texts. Phone calls only. Oh my God. This whole time you had nothing on under this?"

Holly's head hit the wall. She closed her eyes and groaned when Meredith's tongue circled her nipple. "I can agree to that. What else?" She'd probably agree to anything if it meant they could do this again.

Meredith straightened so they were eye to eye. She gripped Holly's hips. "I don't want us to hurt each other. I need to know that you would never put our jobs in jeopardy."

Holly cupped her face. "Are you asking me to have a secret love affair with you?"

Meredith lowered her gaze. "I don't want to—"

"Hey." Holly put a finger under Meredith's chin and gave her a gentle kiss. "Give me your Friday nights. Here, in your apartment, where no one will ever see us. Give me that and a promise that by the end of the year, you'll figure out how we can start dating for real."

Meredith gave her a sly grin. "You. Me. Junk food. *Dateline?*"

"And this bed you speak of?"

Meredith took her hand and led her down the hall. "I believe it was you who spoke of it."

"I just wondered if it was soft."

"Uh-huh."

CHAPTER NINE

Gwen set a bottle of wine on the poolside table. "We're going to get drunk, and you're going to convince me to audition for a fifty-something mother of three the producers describe as a typical Texas mom with big hair and a protective streak for her children the size of a Belgian Blue."

Holly set her iPad on the table. "We don't have to get drunk. You're perfect for that role. Go get it."

Gwen sat and put her feet up on another chair. "I could say the same thing, you know. You've been having a salacious Friday night affair with this Meredith woman for months now. When are you going to tell her to get real about it or you're out?"

"It's real, G. Very real. And it's no longer just Friday night. I don't come home until Sunday afternoon."

"Wow. She gives you almost forty-eight hours of her life now. Forget I said anything."

"It's not like that. Meredith is doing a fantastic job at Wifetime. The last *Evermore* is in post-production. They've optioned my gay Christmas script. We're happy, and when the time is right, we'll go public."

"Hon, we haven't even met her yet. Your best friends this

side of everywhere haven't met your girlfriend of what, five months?"

"Six months and seventeen days."

Gwen did what she always did when she wanted to be heard. She put a hand on Holly's knee. "What would you be telling me right now if the tables were turned?"

Holly groaned. "You've all been talking about me, haven't you?"

"We're concerned."

"Well, maybe it'll comfort you to know that when we started this, I gave Meredith until the end of the year to figure out how we go public and keep our jobs."

"Honey, you're so smitten, I fear you'd stay in this situation for years if she asked. And given that it's almost October, I wouldn't be surprised if she asked for more time."

Gwen wasn't wrong. Holly was deeply in love. Their weekends were what she lived for. It was enough. For now. And even if it wasn't, it was more than she'd ever had with her previous girlfriends. More love. More in common. More sex. More spooning. They managed to pack more of everything into those forty-eight hours.

It was so good, Holly hesitated to rock the boat by asking for something different. Sure, she'd love it if Meredith stayed at her apartment sometimes. She'd love it if she was willing to have dinner at Desiree's and meet her friends. She'd love it if they could take a trip together. Maybe walk the streets of San Francisco hand in hand. Share a romantic dinner someplace expensive and decadent.

Sure, she wanted more. She wanted everyone to know they were a couple. She wanted the world to know Meredith was hers. She'd even imagined what it would feel like to take Meredith back home to Christmas Cove to meet her parents.

She'd feel such a sense of pride as she introduced her to the entire town. The Hudsons' gay daughter had finally found true love, and maybe they'd be happy for her, and maybe they wouldn't. That part didn't matter. Proving to them that she was living her best life was what she desired most.

Holly gave Gwen a side-eye. "Do you really have an audition, or was that just a conversation starter?"

Gwen waved her hand. "Oh, please, honey. I barely opened my mouth, and I had the job. In fact, if I'm not mistaken, it's a Wifetime production."

Holly gasped. "Did you drop my name to get a part?"

Gwen grabbed her stomach and laughed so hard she almost fell off her chair. "Darlin', if I could make a good living by dropping your name, don't you think I would've done it by now?"

Holly turned in the chair and eyed her. "Fess up, lady. Who did you talk to?"

"Griffin might have introduced me to a few people. No one you know."

Holly shot out of the chair. Gwen was trying just a little too hard for a casual tone. "He took you to meet Meredith, didn't he? You two went around me and poked your nose in my business."

"Oh, sit down," Gwen said. "We just happened to walk by her office on our way out of the building."

"Her office isn't on the way out of the building. Goddamnit, Griffin."

"I'm sure you would've found out tomorrow night when you two were doing what lesbians do in bed. She would've said something like, a little to the left, and oh hey, I met your friends today. Yeah, that's better. Stay right there. They were super nice people, and wow, is that Gwen a looker. Is she by any chance a lesbian?"

Holly slapped her hands over her eyes. "Oh my God, you just said *friends*. As in plural friends."

"Dez and Ty would've killed us if we went without them. Ty would've eventually forgiven us, but Dez can hold a grudge like nobody's business. She's still mad at her first boyfriend for not reciprocating in bed."

"Stop talking, G. You and Griffin have ruined everything."

"Oh please. We're just looking out for you."

"That might be true, but I seriously doubt Meredith is going to casually mention your visit while I'm going down on her. She'll probably mention it through the intercom and refuse to let me into her building tomorrow night."

"Why is this such a big deal? We're your friends, for God's sake. We have the right to meet our Holly Bell's girlfriend. And if you're truly concerned that she'd dump you over this, then, baby, you need to move on."

"She's not just gorgeous, G. She's passionate and caring and smart and funny, and I may only secretly get the weekend with her every week, but the way she treats me during those hours makes me feel so loved and so important and special, I really don't want to go back to not knowing what that feels like."

"Then let her do the right thing before the year is out. No extensions."

Holly nodded. "Okay. But you and Griffin are not off the hook. You both owe me an apology. A sincere apology. One you've written out on a piece of paper that I can look at now and again to remind myself why I shouldn't write you both off for good. Got it?"

"Got it. Should we open the bottle of wine now?"

Holly stomped away. "Drink it by yourself, G. I'm out."

❖

Hiding emotions wasn't one of Holly's strong suits. Her mom often told her that she wore her heart on her sleeve. Her dad said she wore it all over her face. So as hard as it was, she'd tried to limit her contact with Meredith at work for fear someone would figure out just how madly in love she was. The struggle was indeed real.

But today, seeing Meredith felt like a necessity. She needed reassurance. Not the kind of reassurance Meredith could give her while they were in bed. She needed it in the light of day when they were both fully clothed and couldn't touch each other. Meredith needed to say it out loud, not just show it with her warm, sexy body.

"Be strong," Holly whispered to herself before she stepped into Meredith's office. "Hey, babe."

Meredith looked up from her laptop and smiled. "This is a nice surprise."

Holly had used the term of endearment in a quiet tone, so no one else could hear. She wasn't sure if she'd get a negative reaction. But it was a risk she was willing to take. Meredith's big smile gave her the courage to say more. "That shirt is a nice surprise. Could you just loosen that top button?"

Meredith gave her a quizzical look. "What's gotten into you?"

"You. Many times."

Meredith's smile widened. "Are you sexually harassing me at work?"

Holly sat. "Do you ever think about it? I mean, knowing I'm just down the hall, do you ever—"

"Yes," Meredith said. "I'm especially fond of the janitorial closet scenario."

"Oh, the one where we get locked in and have to wait for the late-night cleaning crew?"

"And we argue about whose fault it is until one of us admits we're in love with the other person."

Holly went still. She absolutely did not expect to hear those words come from that sexy mouth. She'd wanted to say them so many times. Had almost blurted them out. But she didn't want to push.

"Are we still on for tonight?" Meredith asked. "You're not here to cancel on me, are you?"

Holly shook her head. "No." She tried to swallow the big lump in her throat. Meredith had given her exactly what she needed and then some. "I heard you met some of my friends, and I just wanted to assure you that I didn't put Griffin up to that."

"I didn't think you had." She tilted her head. "Holls, what's wrong?"

"We can talk about it tonight." Holly stood. "I really just wanted to say hi."

Meredith stood and rounded her desk. She shut her office door and kept her hand on the doorknob. "You seem upset about something."

"Upset?" Holly shook her head. "I'm trying not to cry because I think you just told me you're in love with me."

Meredith pulled Holly close. She wrapped her arm around her neck and whispered in her ear, "I'm so in love with you." She kissed her cheek and then her lips. "Now get out of here before I drag you to the janitor's closet."

Holly nodded. "I love you too, by the way."

"Tell me later, when you're deep inside me, and all I can see and hear and breathe is you."

A jolt of heat rushed down Holly's spine. She had to force herself to let go when all she wanted to do was stay right where she was, wrapped up in this moment where doubts didn't exist, and her world made sense. Gwen just needed to mind her own business because Meredith Drake loved Holly Hudson. And one day soon, she'd announce it to the world.

❖

"What do you mean it's too good to be a gay movie? What the hell does that even mean? When you had me rush over here, I thought something was horribly wrong. Too good sounds great." Holly dropped her purse in a chair and put her hands on her hips. That was when she noticed the script for her gay Christmas movie sitting on Meredith's desk. And it had Meredith's writing all over it. Lines crossed out. Words added. Her eyes shuddered closed. "Are you saying what I think you're saying?"

"I wanted you to hear it from me first," Meredith said calmly. "And please, Holls. Keep an open mind."

"First, tell me you're not saying what I think you're saying."

"I can't ignore the success you've had with the *Evermore* series. I had to look at this script with a different pair of eyes."

"You mean a straight pair of eyes."

"Ouch. No, that's not what I'm saying. I think if we broaden its appeal, it will be seen for years to come and no doubt become people's favorite Christmas movie. Because it's just that good. I see it being even bigger than *Evermore*."

"Don't even try to sweet-talk me right now."

"It's not sweet talk. It's business talk."

Holly shook her head. "This can't be real. The woman I love thinks that gays don't deserve the very best content out there? That we should just be happy any gay content gets made at all? We deserve happy stories too. We deserve what was specifically written for us. By me. Our people deserve to watch Lucy and Steffi kiss under the mistletoe."

Meredith put her hands on Holly's shoulders. "The network needs this. With Netflix and Amazon making holiday movies, we'll need another big draw next year, and no one can do that better than you."

"Has it ever occurred to you that this is literally how you compete with the streaming companies? Even if we don't do this, they will." Holly pulled away. "You are literally stomping on my dream here. Does that not mean anything to you, or did you just not believe me when I said I would never write another Christmas movie without gay leads?"

"You don't have to. We'll get another writer to change the names and pronouns. Luckily, the story isn't centered on their sexual orientation, so it won't be that hard."

"Are you serious right now? You'll get another writer to edit out the gay?" Holly tried to control her anger, but she could feel her face flushing and her voice going up. "That was the point, Mer. A sweet, happy romance with main characters who just happen to be two women. No agenda. No preaching. No coming out. Just meeting and falling in love like every other Wifetime holiday movie. Only better."

Meredith straightened her shoulders. "I promise you—"

Holly took a step back. "Your promises mean nothing. And I can't date someone I don't trust."

"It that a threat?"

"You're breaking my heart here. You're tearing it out of my chest and throwing it on the floor." Tears welled up in Holly's eyes.

"Okay, calm down. It's just a script."

"A script you encouraged me to share with the network, even when I didn't want to. You told me to believe. Remember that bullshit? And now, you've just stomped all over it. Please don't tell me to calm down. Yes, it's just a script. To you. To me, it's what I would've given anything to see when I was a kid. It would've given me hope that one day, I'd find my Lucy, and we'd kiss under the mistletoe in the town square, and we'd make snow angels and drink hot chocolate together, and everyone would be happy for us. Our moms and dads, our friends, the bank teller, for God's sake, would be happy for us. But clearly, you don't get it, Meredith. How is that possible when you say that you love me? How could you not know that this would kill me? Kill us?"

"If you'd just drop your pride and realize what another series could do for your career and Griffin's too. What if I promise to give him the lead?"

"Pride? You have the nerve to use that word right now? You don't even have a single rainbow item in your entire house."

"Is that a requirement? I have to fly a rainbow flag to prove, what, that I love being a lesbian? I assumed you, of all people, would know how much I love it."

"You may love the sex and the connection with another woman, but you're not proud of who you are, Meredith. And you're certainly not proud to be with me." Holly grabbed her purse and rushed out of her office.

"Holly. Holly! I'm doing this for both of us."

Holly stopped and turned. "No, you're doing this for yourself. And you're doing it with or without me, aren't you?"

Meredith didn't answer. Holly stared at her for a moment and then shook her head and stepped into the hall. When she was outside, she took her phone out of her pocket and with shaky hands, she sent a text to Griffin. *If you take the straight lead in my gay movie, I will never speak to you again.*

❖

Gwen raised an eyebrow at Holly's single suitcase. "Well, this gives me hope you'll be back sooner than later. Unless you're going to a clothing-optional resort for six weeks."

"Oh God. Don't gross me out, Gwen. I'm going back home where my parents better be wearing long johns and chunky sweaters and big quilted coats."

"So I guess I'll see you next week, then, because there's no way you're going to last more than seventy-two hours in Christmas Hell, Vermont." Gwen looked at her watch. "Especially since we're only four weeks out."

"You're being generous with that number. I give myself twenty-four hours tops. But that'll be my first stop, and we'll see where I end up after that. I just know I can't be here right now, and thank God I had plenty of unused vacation time." Holly checked her phone to see how close her ride to the airport was.

"I'm proud of you for standing up for yourself. I'm sure it wasn't easy, given how you feel about her."

"Damnit, Gwen. I wanted to get out of here without crying." Holly's emotions were still so close to the surface, it wouldn't take much for her to break down again. It wouldn't take much for her to go running back into Meredith's arms either. God, she missed her, and it had only been two days. But this felt like a monumental crack to Holly. Big enough that she couldn't and wouldn't back down. Not when it was so apparent that Meredith didn't take their relationship seriously...both personally and professionally.

Holly was done playing by Meredith's rules, even if it meant she'd have to eventually leave her job at Wifetime.

She just needed time to heal her broken heart before facing Meredith again.

"Geriatric Gwen is going to miss High Anxiety Holly." Gwen wiped a tear from her cheek.

"Geriatric my ass." Holly grabbed Gwen and hugged her. "I will always think of you as Cougar Gwen, the biggest seller in the MILF Barbie line."

"Are you sure we shouldn't have a quickie before you leave? Just once, so I can brag about it when you accept the Academy Award for best screenplay one day?"

"Where's the nearest dumpster?" Holly joked. She wiped the tears from her cheeks too.

"I should be so lucky." Gwen took a packet of tissues out of her purse and stuffed it into Holly's. "Now, go get right with the world and come back strong. We'll be here, waiting for you."

Holly glanced up at Desiree's window, and sure enough, she was there, waving good-bye. "I know I don't have to say it, but take care of Dez."

"We have a date with my new blender this afternoon," Gwen said. "I'm sure there will be a few tears shed for you while Ms. Dez sips the best goddamned daiquiri she has ever tasted in her entire life." Gwen sighed. "I know that statement is a lot to live up to considering her age and lifestyle, but I'm going to give it the old college bartender's try." She reached out and squeezed Holly's arm. "Send her a postcard now and then, okay?"

"I will." Holly blew them both a kiss and waved the driver down. "Oh. Before I forget." She reached into her jeans pocket and pulled out the piece of paper she'd written Brian's phone number on. "I work with this guy, and he's been wanting your phone number for a long time. I was being selfish by keeping you all to myself, but I think you two might hit it off."

Gwen took the paper and scoffed at it. "I don't call men. They call me."

"If you hadn't just offered to give me a farewell fuck, I might actually buy that traditionalist bullshit. Just call the guy. He'll be psyched to hear from you, and who knows, maybe you'll hit it off with someone who's actually a really good guy."

"Oh, hon. You know how attracted I am to losers and boozers. If they ain't broke and smell like whiskey, I don't feel frisky."

Holly hugged her tight. "Call him, G. Let me be proud of you too."

Jokes were keeping the tears away, but it was harder to say good-bye to Gwen than Holly expected. She really was her best friend in all of LA. They gave each other a final wave, and Holly pulled that packet of tissues out of her purse.

CHAPTER TEN

As long as parents kept telling their kids that Santa Claus was real, the town of Christmas Cove's singular purpose—to bring that myth to life—would never change. As the cab driver pulled up to the Victorian-style home where Holly grew up, she noticed the house had been painted recently. Her parents had gone with a darker shade of green than usual. But the gingerbread trim and picket fence were still painted a bright white, and the front door was the same shade of Christmas red it had always been.

Her parents' home was the only remaining house on Main Street that people still lived in. The rest had been turned into Christmas-themed businesses like the Mistletoe Café and Blitzen's Bakery. Her parents' business was housed in a 1960s-era building tucked between the bank and the post office. Hudson's Holiday Shop, along with every other business in town, depended on tourist dollars. So from October first, when the corn mazes around town opened for business, until well into January, the town was hopping with special events. Tourists couldn't get enough of the little Christmas town.

Holly looked at the driver and with a surprising amount of pride in her voice said, "This is the house I grew up in."

The driver's eyes widened. "You grew up in Santa's

house?" He seemed embarrassed by his question and added, "I bring my kids up here every year. Seems like a magical place to grow up."

"It was," she said wistfully. "And looking at it now, I'm not sure why I ever left." Was she seeing it with new eyes, or had she simply matured enough to realize how lucky she had been? She got out of the car and noticed that a candle had been lit in her childhood bedroom window, just as it had been every time she'd come home from college. No doubt her room would smell like sugar cookies and caramel corn, which just so happened to be the scent of her favorite candle. Or it used to be her favorite candle. Holly wasn't sure if that particular blend was still sold at Santa's Mercantile at the end of Main Street. If not, she'd have to put in a special request with the local candlemaker, Mrs. Brown.

The driver put her bags on the curb and said, "Let me be the first to welcome you back home."

"And let me be the second." Her mom opened the gate. "Welcome home, Holiday." She opened her arms for a hug.

Holly fell into her mom's arms. It was a familiar place with the same familiar, comforting scent. Holly used to call her mother Cinna-Mom because she always seemed to smell like a cinnamon roll. She now realized that a cinnamon roll was exactly what Mrs. Claus should smell like.

Unexpected tears filled Holly's eyes. She buried her face in her mom's shoulder. "Sorry for the late notice."

"Don't ever be sorry for coming home, honey." Her mom pulled back and held her by the shoulders. "Your dad's waiting for you inside. Don't be surprised if he sheds a few tears too."

Holly walked up the narrow brick sidewalk, just like she'd done a thousand times before. The old wooden screen door had been replaced with a storm door. Her dad opened it and stepped onto the porch. His hair was whiter, his beard longer.

He had on his old plaid coat. Holly picked up her pace and ran up the steps into her dad's arms. The scent of men's aftershave, pine needles, and hay filled her senses. Rick Hudson smelled like he always did. He smelled like her dad.

It was no surprise that her mom made friends with the driver. Holly expected she'd be sharing a cup of hot chocolate with Oscar at her parents' kitchen table, but her mom surprised Holly when she said, "I haven't seen my daughter in ages, but please stop by when you bring your kids next week. I'll have a special treat waiting for them."

"I will, Mrs. Claus. Thank you, so much." He gave Holly a wave and said, "See you soon."

Holly took it all in for a moment. The clean, crisp air, the lack of honking horns and sirens. Christmas Cove was the antithesis of LA in every way. She turned to her dad and said, "Share a cup of hot chocolate with me?"

Her dad smiled. "It's already heating up on the stove."

❖

Holly's mom squeezed into the small staircase that led upstairs and sat next to Holly on the third step. "We could sit at the table, you know."

"I like it here. Always have."

"It didn't used to be such a tight fit when you were a child. You were such a skinny kid, remember?"

"I believe scrawny was the term everyone used," Holly said.

"Oh, that's right. Scrawny Holiday. I always thought it sounded like a good name for a hit man. You want your significant other snuffed out? I know a guy. Scrawny Holiday. Tell him Sal sent ya."

Holly laughed. "You never told me that."

"It was a joke between your father and me. We'd put on our best gangster accent and give each other reports on your whereabouts. We made each other laugh trying to out-gangster each other."

Holly gaped. "You called me that behind my back?"

"Well, we couldn't very well do it in front of you. That would mean we were terrible parents."

"You weren't terrible parents."

"Sometimes, we wonder where we went wrong. I mean, who would raise a successful screenwriter and not have doubts when you had the potential to make so much more of yourself?"

Holly had to look at her mom to see if she was being serious. Her mom laughed and wrapped an arm around her. "Don't ever forget where you got your sense of humor from. Your dad wouldn't know snark if it bit him in the snark."

Holly's dad rounded the corner and stopped short when he saw them. "Do you know how many photos I've taken of the two of you sitting right there?"

Holly loved the narrow staircase that went from the kitchen up to the second floor. She'd found it a cozy place to read a book or do her homework while her mom made dinner. She felt safe there listening to her mom banging around in the kitchen. It had long since been painted over, but she could still see the faint lines of a heart she'd carved into the paneled wall.

Besides reading and homework, Holly would also sit there and pine for whatever girl she'd fallen head over heels in love with that week. She was pretty sure she'd carved that heart into the wall for the teacher's assistant she had in sixth grade. Everyone called her Miss Stephanie, but Holly privately referred to her as the woman she'd one day marry. On a horse. They'd get married on a horse and ride off into the sunset. Of course, in her fantasies, she wasn't a twelve-year-old kid with long braids.

Her dad came back to the steps with a photo album. "See? Here are my two girls on those very steps. Now, where's my camera?"

His beard had grown so long, it covered the buttons on his red thermal shirt. "How do you stand it, Mom?"

"Stand what?"

"Dad's beard. It's so long and full, it's hard for me to remember what his face looks like."

"As long as I can see his sparkly blue eyes, I'll always know what he looks like."

Holly smiled. Her parents seemed to still be madly in love, just like Mr. and Mrs. Claus should be. She opened the photo album while her mom looked over her shoulder. In the first few stair photos, she was on her mom's lap, then standing by her side, then sitting next to her. In the last photo, Holly sat alone on the step wearing her high school graduation gown. "I've forgotten so much. I barely even remember that day."

Her dad stopped in front of them with his smartphone held high. "Say *candy cane*."

When her dad got a shot he was satisfied with, he went back to his rocking chair and his basketball game. Her mom put an arm around Holly's shoulder and said, "Honey, we don't care why you're here. We're just happy that you are. But I do wonder if someone broke your heart recently."

Holly furrowed her brow. "Why would you say that?"

"Because you have such a big heart, Holiday. Sure, you protect it with your pithy comebacks and cynical attitude, but I know you, and you seem heartbroken to me."

Holly had several pithy comebacks at the ready. How could her mom possibly know her heart when they'd never had a single conversation about her love life? Holly held her share of the blame for that. When she'd first come out, she hadn't felt comfortable talking to her mom about who she was attracted to or even who she'd dated. She realized that she had set the tone. And the limits. Her mom had just followed her lead. Maybe it was time to change that. "You're right," Holly said, her voice cracking. "I was seeing someone in LA, but she betrayed me."

"Oh, honey." Her mom kissed her temple and held her close. "I'm so glad you came home. We all need a refuge from the storm sometimes."

Holly didn't want her mom to get her hopes up by thinking she'd be there long-term. "I don't know how long I'll stay," she said. "This isn't really my home anymore."

"Home is a funny word," her mom said. "It can mean so many things. For me, home is wherever your father is, and it just so happens that we both love our life here in Christmas Cove, so it's home too. Home is also a feeling. A state of being. A warmth in your heart when you hear your child's voice, even if she's telling you she'd rather be surfing than Christmas caroling because at least she took your call and let you hear her voice so you'd know she was okay."

Had Holly told her mom that she actually surfed, and that was why she liked going to Hawaii for Christmas? She'd made so many excuses over the years, she couldn't even remember all of the lies she'd told. "I'm sorry," she said. "You and Dad didn't deserve to be abandoned by your only child just because I couldn't be myself here."

"When you came out, you barely gave us a second to breathe before you'd made up your mind to leave. We were in shock, honey. We had to deal with all of our feelings about that and about you leaving. We had to come to terms with what it meant for all of us."

"It wasn't about you, though. It was about me. How could you possibly expect me to stay in a small town where everything revolves around Christmas, and I was surrounded by only straight couples and their kids coming to see Santa and Mrs. Claus? Where would a young, confused lesbian fit into that picture?"

"We wondered the same thing," her mom said. "That's why we let you go without a fight. What we didn't anticipate is that you'd grow to hate everything we love about our town. We didn't think you'd walk away and never look back."

"I don't hate you and Dad. I just don't belong here."

"Maybe that's true. But I think you belong here right now."

Holly nodded and rested her head on her mom's shoulder. She wouldn't argue that point. Although she would never admit it, home was the first place she'd thought of going after Meredith had shown Holly who she really was. And the strangest part of all was that she didn't question it. She just packed a bag and called HR to tell them she'd be using her vacation time. Only time would tell if it was a good decision or just another blow to her emotional state.

❖

Holly opened the door to her childhood bedroom and wrinkled her nose at how it had been transformed to look like several little elves lived there. "Really, Dad?"

"We rent it out when we can," he said. "Some find the idea of spending the night in Mr. and Mrs. Claus's house appealing and will pay a hefty price to do so."

She turned to him. "How hefty?"

"Five hundred a night. That includes an early breakfast and a hay ride down at the barn."

Holly stepped into the room. Where her queen-sized bed used to be, four twin beds that sat low to the floor were lined up from wall to wall. They looked so cozy with their fluffy feather duvets and crisp white pillowcases, Holly had the urge to crawl into one of them and catch up on some much-needed sleep. On closer inspection, she noticed that there was a name embroidered along the edge of each pillowcase. "Who are Lars, Erik, Elsie, and Britta?"

Her mom stepped into the room. "Santa's elves. They're not here right now, but they come to visit from time to time and help us make toys and bake cookies."

Holly had no idea what to say to that. She moved on to the miniature Christmas tree that sat on a very small desk sitting under the bedroom window. It had the tiniest wrapped gifts under it that Holly had ever seen. They weren't even an inch wide. She bent down to take a closer look at the ornaments on the tree. "What little fingers made these ornaments and fake gifts?"

"Well, Lars and Elsie's, of course," her dad exclaimed.

Holly turned around and in a deadpan voice said, "Of course. What was I thinking?"

She opened the closet door and found tiny elf clothes hanging on tiny hangers, and little shoes placed neatly on the shoe shelf. "You're really selling the myth here, aren't you?"

Her dad wrapped his arm around her shoulder. "Honey, people need the myth. They need something positive to tell their kids. They need the fantasy that will let them escape from their troubles in the real world. Of course, you know all of this since you make a living in much the same way."

He wasn't wrong. She sold the myth too. "This must be the prime time of year for you to book this room. Why don't I sleep in the guest room?"

His eyes widened. "You hate the guest room. It's too drafty for Scrawny, I mean—"

"It's okay, Dad. Mom told me about Scrawny Holiday, everyone's favorite hit man."

Her mom demurred. "I figured she's old enough to be in on the joke now."

Her dad sighed. "I guess you aren't our little girl anymore, but the room is yours if you want it. We can easily cancel whatever reservations have already been made. And I let the elves know we have company."

"Nonsense," Holly said. "Just don't expect me to entertain whatever weirdos book the elf dormitory."

"On Airbnb it's called Hudson's Christmas Haven," her mom said with a wink. "We didn't think that calling it Holly's Old Bedroom would bring in much business."

"I get it," Holly said. "The guest room will be fine."

❖

The next morning, she went down to the kitchen wearing her footie pajamas and fluffy bathrobe. The guest room was probably only a few degrees colder than her old bedroom, due to being on the north side of the house, but she couldn't wait to get a cup of coffee and sit in front of the fireplace.

"Still wearing footie pajamas? I would've expected something far more sophisticated and West Coast. Coffee, dear?"

"What do you imagine women on the West Coast wear to bed, Mom? And yes, please." She sat at the small kitchen table and put a piece of toast on a plate.

"Well, I imagine women on the West Coast probably sleep in as little as possible, given the nice weather, but I also imagine they sleep in fabrics like bamboo and hemp."

"Not this woman." Holly spread butter on the toast and took a big bite.

"It's nice to know some things never change." Her mom

brought a cup of coffee over to the table. "Still like your eggs scrambled?"

"I can make them, Mom. You don't have to do everything."

"They're already made."

"Oh, thank God. I always liked yours better."

"I think for everyone who isn't a chef, food is always better when someone else makes it for you."

Her mom set a plate of eggs on the table and sat. Holly took another bite of toast and waited for the big interrogation. What were her plans for the day? Could she help out with this that or the other thing? Surely, some rugs needed beating, or a driveway needed shoveling.

But her mom just sat there and sipped her coffee. Holly put a spoonful of eggs on her plate and eyed her suspiciously. She'd aged a bit, but she certainly didn't look like a Mrs. Claus. Her dad, on the other hand, totally passed for Santa, right down to his burgeoning potbelly.

"Is there anything I can help you with? It feels weird to be in this house and not have a chore list."

Her mom smiled. "You're an adult, Holiday. Do adult things."

Did she really just say that? And did this mean there wouldn't be any arguments over a silly curfew because otherwise, they'd worry? No putting unwanted food in front of her because they thought she was too skinny? No knocking on the door at seven a.m. because "the world is waiting for you to do something good today, Holiday"?

What was this magical situation? Could she really eat a whole bag of Oreos while binge-watching Netflix all day? "Really? I mean, really? This isn't some kind of trick, is it?"

"A trick? Don't be silly." Her mom got up from the table. "My only request is that you take a walk down Main Street and pop in and say hi. Everyone's excited to see you." She leaned down and kissed Holly's cheek. "But it doesn't have to be today." She went over to the sink and washed her cup. "What's her name? The woman who betrayed you?"

"Meredith. Meredith Drake." Just saying the name brought tears to her eyes. She ached to hear her voice again, but she'd promised herself she wouldn't call or even text. It wouldn't do any good. Meredith had made up her mind and so had Holly.

Her mom turned back around and leaned against the counter. She had a pained expression on her face. "You're in love with her?"

Holly nodded. "Head over heels." She covered her mouth and burst into tears.

Her mom sat back down and took her into her arms. "I'm so sorry, honey. So sorry."

❖

No guilt trips, no chores, not even any errands to run. Holly was free to do whatever she wanted, and first up was a trip to Blitzen's Bakery for a warm sugar cookie. She'd visited some of the most highly rated bakeries in LA, but when it came to sugar cookies, they didn't even come close to Blitzen's version of the classic Christmas treat.

The air was cold, and from the look of the sky, snow was on its way. She could look at her phone to know for sure, but she chose to do it the old-fashioned way, shouting to her dad, "Dad? How's it looking today?"

"High of forty-five. Flurries likely later in the day. I'll be down at the barn giving hay rides."

"Okay. See you later." A high of forty-five meant she didn't need her parka. Just her pea coat would do. She pulled her hair back into a ponytail and wrapped a navy scarf around her neck. She didn't have winter boots, but her suede ankle boots would get her there and back.

The street was busy with shopkeepers adding extra lights and decorations to their storefronts. It was always Christmas all the time, but when Thanksgiving rolled around, they went all out with extra poinsettias and garlands and wreaths. Extra white lights were wrapped around tree branches and lamp posts. There really wasn't a bare spot to be found.

"Holly Hudson?"

She stopped. "Mikey Reynolds? Is that you behind that beard? I almost didn't recognize you." She opened her arms. "How long has it been?"

"Too long, Holiday. Too long. And it's Mike now." He didn't just hug her, he lifted her off the ground. Of course, he had been the center on the high school football team, and his nickname was Ox, which suited him even more now that he looked like Paul Bunyan, plaid shirt and all.

He set her back down. "Wow, it's great to see you. How long are you here for?"

"Not sure yet. It depends on whether or not my parents can keep up this charade they have going where they treat me like the adult that I am, and meanwhile, it's slowly killing them that they can't boss me around."

"Well, your mom always did keep you on your toes. Maybe that's why you went out and made a big success of yourself. Speaking of, now that the *Evermore* series is over, what will you write next? My wife is such a huge fan. She absolutely loves all five of those brothers, and truth be told, she's jealous that we used to pal around."

"Honestly, Mike, I think I might be done with writing Christmas movies." She turned when she heard a loud gasp.

"Say it isn't so, Holly Hudson." Mrs. Brown, the local

candlemaker, stood there with a box full of candles and her mouth hanging open.

"Hi, Mrs. Brown. I was going to pay you a visit. I need my favorite candle."

Mrs. Brown was known for her holiday sweatshirts. Not the silk-screened kind found in the store. No, she made them herself by sewing a Christmas-themed pot holder—yes, the kind found near the stove—to the front of her shirt. Every year, she'd shop the after-Christmas clearance sales, and the following holiday season, boom, that two-dollar pot holder would have its big debut on a red or green Walmart sweatshirt. One year, she even tried to sell them in hopes everyone in town would embrace her amazing idea. The only person other than Mrs. Brown who wore one was her poor husband. Unfortunately, the current version was hidden behind that box of candles.

"Don't you know what it means to this town that one of our daughters wrote the *Evermore* series? That you based it on Christmas Cove? You can't stop now."

"Oh," Holly said. "I didn't realize—"

"If you need ideas, I have plenty. Handsome Mike here could be your inspiration too. Big hunk of a man comes to town with his little daughter and no mama. Sexy candlemaker befriends the daughter and teaches the big hunk of a man how to make candles." She gave them a wide-eyed nod. "Tell me you're not swooning in your boots right now."

"Why, Mrs. Brown," Mike said. "I had no idea you had such strong feelings for me."

"Oh, don't be silly. I was just using you as an example." She moved around them. "Gotta run. Stop in and see me, Holly. We'll get you back on that writing horse again come heck or high water."

Holly looked at Mike. "She sees herself as Demi Moore

to your Patrick Swayze, only with candle making instead of pottery. You know that, right?"

He stroked his beard. "What can I say? All the women in this town love me." He sighed. "Too bad I'm taken."

She gave him a light slug on the arm and laughed. She always loved big cuddly Mike. "Walk with me to Blitzen's?"

"Okay, but you'll have to back me up when I tell my wife that you forced me to eat a sugar cookie and didn't bring one home for her."

"You can solve that little dilemma by bringing one home to her, Mikey."

"Ha. Why didn't I think of that?" They walked in silence for a moment, then he asked, "What about you? Are you taken?"

"Not at the moment."

He furrowed his brow. "Divorced?"

"I'm still gay, Mike."

He leaned in. "News flash. Gay people can get married and divorced now."

"I recently broke up with someone. That's why I'm here. I just needed a change of scenery while I licked my wounds and regrouped."

"Ah." He put his arm around her. "Well, nothing heals the heart like December in Christmas Cove."

"Funny. It was always the hardest month of the year for me once I realized I was gay. I just couldn't envision this town ever accepting me that way, and I was scared shitless that I'd end up being the grumpy old lady who lived in the little house at the end of the street and chased all of the little kids away."

He stopped and turned to her. "When we're done stuffing our faces with all things butter, flour, and frosting, do me a favor and stop by the Misfit Elf. It's where the florist used to be."

❖

Holly stepped inside the Misfit Elf. As with most of the shops in town, the sounds and scents of Christmas permeated the air. A man shouted from the back, "I'll be right there."

"No rush," Holly shouted back.

Most everything on the shelves appeared to be handmade but really nicely handmade, not at all like Mrs. Brown's pot holder sweatshirts. There were beautiful handstitched tablecloths, exquisite ceramic ware, knitted afghans and scarves, and handsewn toys.

Holly picked up a leather strap with sleigh bells attached to it, and for the first time in a very long time, she found herself wanting to purchase some Christmas nostalgia.

"Hello, and happy holidays. I'm Burton, and I'm here to make your wishes come true."

Holly stood there, dumbfounded because before her stood a grown man who looked exactly like Hermey, the misfit elf. Which totally explained the store name. "You even have the blond flip in your hair."

He touched his heavily sprayed hair and seemed to blush. "Only someone who's a big fan of Christmas or over the age of fifty would know that, and you have no idea how much I love it when people get it."

"So you're the owner of the Misfit Elf?"

"I own it with my husband, Paul. Honey, we have a true fan out here."

Paul came out from the back. He was dressed from head to toe in red and green. "She must've mentioned your wave. He gets so excited when people call him Hermey."

Holly's jaw was on the floor. Two gay men lived in Christmas Cove, and on top of that, they owned a store on

Main Street? The city didn't let just anybody open a store. They had to be residents and have something unique and Christmas-y to sell.

"Are you okay? You look like you just saw the abominable snowman," Paul said.

Burton gave him a nudge. "Good one, honey."

"Fine," she said. "I'm fine. So how long have you been open?"

"This will be our second year in Christmas Cove, and everything for sale is handmade by artisans from around the world. Very unique and very good quality."

"We only buy and sell the best," Paul said. "Take that sleigh bell strap you're holding. We get those from a saddlemaker in Colorado, and you won't find another with that particular leatherwork anywhere else. See the little holly leaves he carved along the edges? And on the back, he's branded it with his signature. It'll be a family heirloom if you buy it."

"I'll buy it. It reminds me of the bells my dad used to put on the horses for the hay rides."

Burton's eyes widened. "Santa, I mean, Mr. Hudson? Wait. Are you…?" He clasped his hands over his mouth.

Paul put his arm around Burton's shoulders. "We heard you were coming to town," he said in a reverent tone. "And here you are, standing in our little corner of Christmas. Please forgive us if we cry like when we met Madonna back in 1984."

Burton opened his arms. "May I hug you, Holly Hudson?"

She expected him to give her a crushing hug, but luckily, she could still breathe. "It's nice to meet you both."

Paul shook her hand. "We went to the high school gym and watched the last *Evermore* with the rest of the town. I don't think there was a dry eye in the building when the credits rolled."

"We're kindred spirits," Burton said. "Paul and I love

Christmas the way you love Christmas. Back in Cincinnati, everyone thought we were insane for having our house decorated year-round. That's why we decided to move here. We knew we'd be welcomed with open arms."

"And were you?" Holly asked with hesitation in her voice. She felt like a fraud. She'd lost her love of Christmas years ago, but she didn't have the heart to correct him.

Burton nodded. "We're free to be our gay, happy, Christmas-loving selves here."

She felt stunned. Could it be that the people of Christmas Cove had evolved over the years? "That's so good to hear." She handed the leather strap to Paul. "I'd like to get this."

"Of course. I'll ring it up for you."

❖

Holly felt off-kilter as she walked back home. Everyone who recognized her wanted to chat and take a selfie. She had a bag full of homemade goodies because no one would let her walk out of their store empty-handed. She also received several dinner invitations, including one from the mayor. And no doubt, a pot holder sweatshirt would soon be left on her doorstep along with her favorite candle.

The problem was, it wasn't supposed to be that way. Sure, some people would be glad to see her. Others whom she'd known to be homophobes would avoid her as they'd done in the past. That was what was supposed to happen. The fact that the whole town treated her like some sort of celebrity was so unexpected, Holly felt worn out from all of the attention. She just wanted to go back to her parents' house and take a nap and dream about a woman named Meredith Drake.

She had stayed strong all day. No texts to Meredith. No

calls. Unfortunately, the big gaping hole in her heart couldn't be filled with a bag of Christmas treats. That didn't mean she wouldn't give it a try, though. Probably in the middle of the night. Under the covers in the chilly guest room, she'd mix mint fudge with salty tears and try not to think about the first time Meredith had touched her. Or the first time she'd heard her laugh. And forget about the first kiss. Thinking about that would require more than a little piece of fudge. She'd have to eat an entire tin of homemade caramel corn to get through that. God, she needed a nap.

❖

Holly sat up in bed and brushed cookie crumbs off her chest. She'd been living her dream for the last four days. Binging Netflix on the living room sofa during the day and reading romance novels all night while snacking from her goodie bag. She leaned over and checked the bag. Yep, she'd eaten it all. That meant she'd have to go out in public again unless she could convince her dad to make a treat run for her.

"Holiday?"

"Yeah, Mom?" Holly shouted back.

"Your dad needs your help down at the barn. He said there's a pair of boots for you in the hall closet and don't forget to bring gloves. Oh, and drive his truck down there. It's too cold to walk all that way."

"I knew it wouldn't last forever. It's like they live on a farm where the work never stops," Holly muttered to herself as she pushed back the covers and headed for the shower.

❖

The boots were a brand-new pair of fleece-lined Sorels, much like the ones she used to own. She slid into them and laced them up, then grabbed her parka and gloves.

She had learned to drive her dad's old Chevy truck when she was a teenager. Back then, it was metallic blue, but as with most things in their lives, it now looked like it belonged on a Christmas card. They'd painted it dark green and added wooden slats to the sides. Of course it had a pine bough wreath tied to the grill and garland wrapped around those slats. Holly wouldn't have been surprised if when she honked the horn, it played "Here Comes Santa Claus." She laid on the horn to see, then waved at the car in front of her and yelled, "Sorry. My bad. It's just Santa's kid trying to ruin your day."

She pulled up to the barn and saw her dad hooking up a horse to a wagon full of hay. "Hey, Dad. I heard you needed a hand."

He turned around and waved. "Hi, sweetie. Old George is in bed with a cold. That means I've got two groups and only one driver. Do you remember how to steer a horse?"

"If I can still drive this old stick shift that sticks more than it shifts, I think I can handle a wagon."

"Good girl," he said with a wink.

It wouldn't be too hard. She would follow her dad's wagon down an old farm road and loop back around through a corn field while the customers sang Christmas carols and drank hot chocolate.

One day of this wouldn't be so bad.

Chapter Eleven

Holly pulled the phone away from her ear while Gwen laughed her ass off. "Let me get this straight. For the past three weeks, you've been driving a wagon full of hay bales through a field while drunk tourists sing 'The Twelve Days of Christmas'? All because some guy named George has a cold?"

"Well, if they're drunk, it's because they spike the complimentary hot chocolate, and I have a sign on my wagon that says, *Anything but 'The Twelve Days of Christmas.' It makes Brody anxious, and you don't want him to bolt.*" Holly pulled the phone away again. "Do you have to laugh so damn loud, G? And yes, I do know that my dad is lying about George just so he can spend time with me."

"You couldn't write this shit if you tried, honey. I'm just waiting for the part where your wagon breaks down, and Mikey with the big beard rides up on his blue ox to give you a hand."

"I don't write straight romances anymore, remember?"

"Oh, right. Does Mikey have a sister, and by any chance is her name Paula Bunyan?"

Holly sighed. "Has anyone seen her? Meredith, I mean."

"I know who you mean. Where would we see her?"

"I don't know. Maybe on one of those office tours Griffin is so famous for?"

"No, hon. We haven't seen her. But you're doing good out there, right? Getting along with your parents and making new gay friends and learning a new trade. What do they call that? Equine management?"

"Ha. Ha. Gwen, I can't stop thinking about her. When I'm on the wagon, I go over and over it in my head. Maybe I was too quick to say no. Maybe she's right about another straight series."

"Can you hear yourself? She took the trust you had in her, and along with your dream, she threw it out of the plane at thirty thousand feet. There's no surviving that fall, and you know it. You just need to come to terms with it. Get on that lesbian dating app and meet someone new."

"You're right. I know you're right," Holly said. "And it is going well here with my parents. It's just that I feel like I'm not all here. A part of me is still with Meredith on a Friday night watching *Dateline*." Holly sucked in a breath of air. "God, I love her so much."

"I know, baby. I know. Just hang in there and I promise you that your heart will eventually heal."

Holly wanted to believe her. She wanted to believe that there was someone else out there for her. But in that moment, all she could feel was the same hopelessness she'd felt as a teenager.

❖

Holly opened her bedroom door and found an adorable towheaded boy sitting on the top step. He had a little teddy bear pinned under his arm and couldn't have been older than five or six. Holly sat next to him and wrapped her arms around her knees. "Hi, there. I'm Holly. What's your name?"

"Logan." He held up his teddy bear. "This is Tiger."

Holly shook Tiger's paw. "Nice to meet you. Whose bed are you two going to sleep in tonight?"

"I chose Erik's bed, and my baby sister chose Britta's."

"Oh, good choice. Erik's bed is very comfortable."

"Can you even believe we get to sleep in Santa's house tonight?"

He said it with such a sense of wonder in his gravelly little voice, Holly had to smile. "It's a pretty big deal. Do you think you'll be able to sleep?"

"I'm kinda worried that Erik will be so tired from making toys that he'll need his bed back. And what if Lars comes home and sees my dad in his bed? And my mom in Elsie's? Won't they be mad?"

"Well, that's the thing about Santa's elves. They love sharing everything they have with good kids like you. Now, are you going on the hay ride tonight? You can ride in my wagon if you want, and I'll introduce you to my horse, Brody."

Logan gave her a big nod. "And then we'll go to the big Christmas tree and see Santa?"

"We will. Make sure you wear really warm clothes, okay?"

"I will." Seemingly satisfied with Holly's answers, he went into the bathroom and closed the door.

Holly went downstairs and filled her thermos with coffee and creamer. She turned when she heard her mom giggling behind her. "What's so funny?"

"You're really going to wear it?"

Holly knew that her mom was referring to the pot holder sweatshirt Mrs. Brown had given her, of course. She'd chosen a pot holder that had an old-fashioned horse and carriage on it. Apropos for Christmas Cove's newest hay ride driver. "I've worn worse. You should've seen me at last year's office party. Besides, my only red shirt is in the laundry, and if I were a character in one of my screenplays, I wouldn't be wearing a bright pink turtleneck, which is the only clean thing I have at the moment."

"I don't think you'd be wearing a pot holder sweatshirt that was three sizes too big either," her mom teased. "Will you sit for a minute? It won't take long."

Holly sat next to her at the kitchen table. "I will, but I don't know how we'll have a serious conversation when I know you'll be wondering the whole time if Mrs. Brown meant to leave the loop on the pot holder or if it was an oversight."

Her mom took a closer look. "You know, I've been waiting for years for Mrs. Brown to transition to an oven mitt, just to mix things up a bit."

Holly laughed. "Oh my God, Mom. I hope it happens one day, just for you."

"One can dream." She took a box with a large red bow on it out from under the table.

"I thought we weren't exchanging gifts until Christmas morning," Holly said.

"We'll still have a few guests then, and this is more personal."

"We will?" Holly had no idea she'd have to share their home with strangers on Christmas Day. They'd been so busy the last few weeks, there hadn't been much time to just be a family. There hadn't been much time to think either, which was exactly what she'd needed. No time to think about Meredith Drake and her sexy, well, everything. Nope. Horses, hay, drunk tourists, and pot holder sweatshirts. That was her life now. Holly found herself longing for the days when she was a kid, and it was just the three of them sitting by the fire, watching old Christmas movies and playing games. Had she turned a corner? Was Christmas something she could love again?

It hit her hard that her parents had moved on without her. She had no right to dictate what Christmas should look like in their house now. Maybe having guests had eased the loneliness they must've felt while she was off in Hawaii doing her own thing. She swallowed her disappointment and said, "That's great, Mom. I'm looking forward to it."

Her mom pushed the gift toward her. "It's time you inherited something from your grandfather. Do you remember the sweaters he would bring back from Finland when he went home to visit his parents?"

"Vaguely."

"There was one you loved when you were a toddler. You'd sit on his lap and play with the zipper and run your little finger over the reindeer and say 'Deer! Deer!'"

Holly shook her head. "I don't remember that."

Her mom reached for her hand. "He would be so proud of you, Holiday. And I know he'd love it if you wore his sweater these next few days while you drive the wagon. And besides, nothing says Christmas quite like an authentic Scandinavian sweater."

"I thought nothing said Christmas quite like sewing a pot holder to your shirt." Her mom laughed, and Holly joined in. She leaned down and kissed her mom's hand. "I'd be honored to wear Grandpa's sweater, and in case I haven't said it lately, I love you, Mom."

She stood and pulled Holly into her arms. "I'm so glad you're here. I'm sorry about what brought you here, but I'm so glad you chose to come home."

"Me too." Holly didn't have time for tears, but she buried her face in her mom's shoulder and shed a few anyway. A few for all the time she'd lost with her parents. A few for Meredith.

And a few for herself. Time hadn't healed her broken heart, but her parents' love had stitched it up a bit.

❖

The barn was filled with guests, all huddled around a gas heater, drinking hot chocolate and coffee. Logan ran toward Holly when she walked in. "Hi, Holly."

She bent down and gave him a hug. "Are you ready to ride, Logan?"

"Yep. My dad and baby sister too."

"What about your mom?"

"Dad says she's spending more money. He said she has to meet us at the big tree cause at least that's free."

"A little TMI. But okay then. And good job dressing warm." She pulled his knit cap over his ears and stood back up and put her hands on his shoulders. "It looks like Logan is ready to go. How about everyone else?" They all gave her a big cheer and followed her out the door.

George had taken over for her dad while he'd been playing Santa all week. She gave him a wave and scanned the crowd to make sure everyone was dressed appropriately. They had wool blankets draped over the bales of hay and extras that people could put over their legs, but if they weren't dressed warmly in the first place, they wouldn't enjoy the ride.

Holly proudly wore her grandpa's wool sweater with jeans tucked into her Sorels. She had a white fur hat on and leather gloves. Being the driver, she didn't have the luxury of warming her hands in her pockets. She'd have to put on her parka before they started, but she'd purposely left it off because everyone seemed to want a selfie with their driver, and today, she certainly looked like she'd dressed for Christmas, reindeers and all.

Once everyone was on board, Holly went to her horse. "Hey, boy. You ready?" She rubbed his nose and gave him a carrot from her back pocket. "Slow and easy like we always do."

She climbed on and grabbed her sleigh bells from under her feet and handed them to Logan. "Brody won't go anywhere until he hears these bells ringing. Will you be in charge of that, Logan?"

"Sure." Logan grabbed the bells and shook them as hard as he could.

Holly made a clicking sound, and off they went.

❖

It was dark by the time they pulled up to the Christmas tree in the center of town. There were oohs and ahs from her passengers when they saw how beautiful the tree and all of the lights in town were. Lights were strung across the street from shop to shop and wrapped around trees and lamp posts. Along with the massive tree in the middle of the town square, it was lined with smaller trees covered in twinkling white lights. With the big snow they'd had last night, it truly looked like a Christmas wonderland.

Holly took off her parka and tucked it under her seat on the wagon so she could say a quick hello to her dad. Logan climbed up from the back and stood on the seat. "Can we take a picture with you, Holly? I get to hold the bells."

"Of course." They both turned toward Logan's dad, who was holding up his phone, and Holly said, "Say *candy cane*."

"Candy cane," Logan yelled. His dad gave them a thumbs-up, and Logan handed the bells to Holly. "Thanks for the best day of my whole life."

She felt like her heart would melt. If his nose hadn't been

bright pink and runny, she would've kissed it. Instead, she gave him a big hug. "How about if you keep those bells, Logan, and always remember to ring them every Christmas Eve so Santa will know where you are?"

His eyes lit up. "Really? I can keep them? Really?"

She tousled his hair. "Really."

He wrapped his little arms around her neck and said, "I love Christmas. It's the best thing in the whole world."

She laughed. "You know what, Logan? You're right about that. Christmas is the best thing in the whole world." And yes, those words really had just come out of her mouth. She had indeed turned a corner.

Logan climbed back over the side of the wagon and ran to his dad and little sister. "Look. Holly said I can keep them."

Holly returned the thumbs-up Logan's dad had given them so he'd know Logan really could keep the bells. She turned to climb off the wagon and gasped. "What the…"

"Well, look at this," Gwen said. "She's one of her own Christmas movies come to life."

"Am I dreaming?" Ty rubbed his eyes and opened them again. "Nope, it's real. Holly Hudson drives a wagon now."

Griffin put out his arms. "Here, little lady. Let me catch you."

Holly jumped into his arms and wrapped her legs around him. With a squeal she said, "I can't believe you're here."

She held on while he spun her in circles. "Hello, my love. I'm here to rescue you from this Christmas nightmare, also known as the cutest fucking town I've ever seen."

Holly kissed his cheek and slid down. She ran to Ty and hugged him. He too lifted her off the ground and spun her around in slow motion. "Is this how they do it in the movies? Am I going too slow? What happens next?"

She kissed his cheek. "Put me down now, Ty. I have to kiss the special woman in my life."

"Who, Gwen? Be careful. She started drinking over Nevada."

Holly hit the ground and squealed her way over to Gwen. "I can't believe you're here."

"Oh, hon. We wouldn't miss your big day, even if it meant having to buy this fabulous faux fur coat. How do I look?"

"You look like Christmas. You all look like Christmas." She waved Ty and Griffin over. They'd obviously bought new coats too. Griffin went with a more formal camelhair coat and plaid scarf. Ty had on a black puffer coat and a red scarf and matching beanie. And Gwen's full-length faux mink and fancy leather gloves were too perfect for words. "I've missed you all so much. Group hug."

Griffin nudged her into the middle. They locked arms and held her close. "This is nice," Ty said.

"Stop stroking my fur, Ty."

Holly laughed. She was back with her quirky crew, and she couldn't have been happier. Her eyes popped open when she realized what Gwen had said. "What did you mean about it being my special day?"

Griffin took her by the hand. "You'll know soon enough."

He led her toward the small performance area that the high school choir used for entertaining the crowds with Christmas carols. A crowd had gathered around it, and the mayor was standing on the stage. He leaned into the microphone and said, "Come on up here, Holly."

She had no idea what was going on. She spotted her mom and said, "What's this?"

"Just get up there. You'll see," her mom said, clearly delighted by whatever it was.

Griffin led her to the stairs, and the mayor waved her onto the stage. She had no idea what was about to happen. Had she won something? Maybe her mom had entered her into a drawing of some sort.

She stood next to the mayor and looked out into the crowd. Her crew was right up front, giving her a thumbs-up and blowing kisses. Her parents stood to the side of them, big smiles on their faces. Burton and Paul were there among the other townspeople and tourists. She spotted Mikey and his wife, both giving her a thumbs-up. Logan was on his dad's shoulders, sleigh bells in hand. Holly gave him a little wave and then focused on Gwen. Gwen, with her big faux fur, would help ground Holly since she felt as if she was going to shake right out of her boots. Gwen gave her a wink and a thumbs-up and a tits-up motion. Okay, maybe it was a bad idea to look at Gwen.

She turned toward Mayor Anderson. He gave her a wink and tapped the microphone. "Is this on? Okay, here we go. For those who don't know, this is Holiday Hudson, a daughter of Christmas Cove and the writer of the very successful *Evermore* series on the Wifetime network. All of us in Christmas Cove like to think that Holly gets her inspiration from having grown up in our little piece of Christmas paradise, and we couldn't be prouder of her." He turned to Holly and presented her with a plaque. "Holly, I'm here to announce that the town of Christmas Cove has officially proclaimed December twenty-third to be Holiday Hudson Day." He gave her the plaque and shook her hand while the audience clapped and whistled.

She stood there, speechless. They gave her a day? Was this really happening?

"We also raised funds to get a billboard made that'll be placed just outside of town." The mayor turned to an easel to his right and ripped a sheet off what had to be a smaller version of the billboard. It said, *Welcome to Christmas Cove, childhood home of Holiday Hudson.*

No. This wasn't really happening. Had she hit her head and woken up in her very own Wifetime Christmas movie? She could barely see the crowd through her tears. She wiped her eyes and stood in front of the microphone. "I don't know what to say. This is an incredible honor." She saw Burton and Paul in the audience, holding on to each other. Paul also had his arm around Mrs. Brown, who looked pleased as Christmas punch. "I haven't been around much lately, but when life got a little bit tough for me, all of you welcomed me back with open arms."

Her emotions started to overwhelm her. She covered her mouth to keep her lips from quivering. She took a breath and said, "I'm so proud of our diverse little town. You all work so hard to bring the spirit of Christmas to the world. You inspire me." She covered her mouth again, not sure that she could say much more without totally breaking down.

"You inspire me too."

Holly knew that voice. She looked to her left, and there was Meredith, standing at the end of the stage looking like a sexy Christmas dream in her black wool coat and knee-high leather boots. Holly wiped her eyes again to make sure they weren't deceiving her.

"You've been inspiring me since that fateful day in the Honolulu airport where you did everything you could to help a weary traveler. And after meeting some of the good folks of Christmas Cove, I know exactly where you got your kindhearted spirit from."

Holly glanced at her parents and lowered her gaze. She was so happy to see Meredith, but it didn't really change anything. A few nice words weren't going to fix what had been broken.

"Holly, I took advantage of your kindness, and I'm here to make it right. I'm also here to tell you that nothing is more important to me than you are. And that's why I've been fighting like hell for you and your dream."

Holly raised her head and looked Meredith in the eye. "You have?"

"I have. And you're going to come back to LA, and we're going to make a gay movie together. A big, giant, colossally gay holiday movie.. Together."

"We are?" Holly was dumbfounded. She couldn't put together more than a word or two at a time, it seemed.

With a few more steps, Meredith removed the space between them. "Yes, my love, we are. Because you were right, Holly. We deserve the best love stories. We deserve the happy endings and the mistletoe kisses. And no one can write those stories better than you."

Holly grabbed Meredith and wrapped her arms around her. She thought she heard one of her dad's signature whoop-dee-doos, and she definitely heard one of Gwen's loud whistles. She pulled back and said. "If I'd written this moment, I would've included a kiss. You know, just a lip kiss because there are children watching and Wifetime viewers never need more than a chaste kiss in the last ten seconds to know that everything will be okay."

Meredith put her hand on Holly's cheek. "Would this hand go here?"

Holly nodded. "Perfect. And keep the other one on my waist. Don't let it wander."

"Because of the children."

"Now you're getting it. Lay it on me, woman."

Their lips touched and Holly's heart soared. She heard her sleigh bells ringing and people clapping, and surely, she would soon wake up from this dream. But she didn't really want to because how could life get better than this? And then she felt the tip of Meredith's tongue barely caress her lip and it all came back to her just how much better life could be.

She broke away from the kiss and whispered in Meredith's ear, "You'll pay for that later." She took her by the hand and gave the crowd a wave as they left the stage.

Meredith leaned in and said, "I can't decide which look I like better, the little black dress or this sexy, I drive a wagon in the North Pole look."

"Do you want a ride on my wagon? Because that could be arranged."

"Oh, I'd like several. Maybe hundreds. But first, there are some people who require your attention."

A crowd of young kids were waiting with pens and paper in hand. "Can we get your autograph, Holly?"

These were the same kids she'd gotten to know around town, and now they wanted her autograph? She took one of the pieces of paper. "Sure. But you know I'm still me, right?"

"I want to be just like you," one of the little ones said. "I want to write movies too."

Holly knelt and signed her piece of paper. "Do really well in school, and you can do anything you want." She handed the paper back and stood. She knew there were only two places on earth kids would gather around for the autograph of a celebrated TV Christmas movie writer. One was *Evermore*, and the other was Christmas Cove. Mrs. Brown walked up, breaking Holly from her thoughts. "You don't want an autograph, do you, Mrs. Brown?"

"Oh, heavens no." She got closer and lowered her voice. "I just wondered if your girlfriend would like one of my special sweatshirts."

Holly leaned in and said conspiratorially, "Absolutely. Have you ever tried to make one with an oven mitt?"

Mrs. Brown's eyes lit up. "You're a genius, Holly Hudson. No time to waste." She scurried off to her car.

Holly turned back to Meredith and took a deep breath. "Forgive me. I'm kind of in shock right now." She took Meredith's hand and started walking toward the wagon.

"Happy shock?" Meredith asked.

"Crazy happy. Over the moon happy. My life makes sense again."

"Funny. I was thinking the same thing about my life." Meredith stopped and took her hands. "This living without you business has been hard. Any chance you'd take me up on my offer and come back to LA so we can make the best gay Christmas movie anyone has ever seen?"

"Hurry up," Gwen shouted. "We're not getting any younger."

The crew had made themselves at home in the back of the wagon. Her parents were there too, talking and laughing with her friends. Her dad stood and said, "Come on, Scrawny Holiday. Show 'em what you got."

Her friends gasped like they'd just been given the best present of their entire lives. "Scrawny Holiday?" Griffin changed spots and sat next to Holly's mom. "Do tell, Mrs. Hudson."

"Great," Holly said. "That's just great. Thanks, Dad." She feigned indignation, but really, nothing could've ruined that moment. She turned back to Meredith. "I'll come back if you promise to never call me Scrawny Holiday."

"Not even in bed?" Meredith whispered. "I mean, that's asking a lot."

Holly gave her a nudge. "You're riding shotgun, and if you're lucky, I might even give you the reins." They climbed onto the wagon and Holly looked up at the sky. A light snow had started to fall. "I guess I really did underestimate you, Mer."

"How so?"

"Perfect timing. Just like in the movies." She turned and smiled at Meredith. "I was born for this. Hell yes, we're making that movie together." She tugged on the reins and shouted, "Take us home, Brody."

EPILOGUE

Holly opened her apartment door and announced, "I'm not ready."

Ty's smile faded. "Your grandpa's sweater from last year? Oh, crap. Should I have worn the same plaid shirt from last year too?" He cupped his hand over his mouth and loudly whispered behind him, "Gwen. Get that dead animal you wore last year. Apparently, it's a thing."

Gwen popped her head in. "It's faux fur, and I'm not wearing it." She paused and looked Holly up and down. "Okay, I'll wear it, but once we're inside Desiree's hot apartment, it's coming off."

Holly pulled them both into her apartment and shut the door. "It's not 'repeat last year's wardrobe' night. It's just that I've been too busy with the movie to shop for something festive."

"Oh. Well, that's a relief." He revealed a bottle of champagne he'd been holding behind his back. "I bought the good stuff. Only the best for your big night."

She cringed at the thought of putting anything in her upset stomach. She started to pace in front of her sofa. "You guys, I'm so nervous, I think I'm going to puke."

"Sit down," Gwen commanded.

Holly sat on the sofa and wrapped her arms around her stomach. "What if it bombs?"

"How many times do we have to go over this?" Gwen sat down next to Holly and put an arm around her. "Sweetie, *All the Jingle Ladies* is not going to bomb."

Holly put her head in her hands. "It is, though. I just know it. It's probably going to be the biggest bomb Wifetime has ever seen. They'll stop making gay movies for the next twenty years because of the unmitigated disaster that is *Jingle Ladies*."

"Holls, people are going to love it," Ty said. "Lesbian Twitter has been freaking out for months. They even have a hashtag. Lesflix Christmas."

"Ty, how the hell do you know what's on lesbian Twitter?"

"That's not important." He turned toward Gwen. "What matters is that *Jingle Ladies* has to be better than that crap we watched the other night with the cat that knocked over the Christmas tree and started the house on fire."

"Tragic," Gwen said. "And the fire marshal falling in love with the cat owner? Well, I for one never saw that coming down the pike."

Holly let out a heavy sigh. "Will you please take me seriously? I'm genuinely afraid of failure this time."

"Well, you should've told me that before you cast me as Lucy's meddling mother," Gwen said.

"And me as that extra guy with the cool hat who says nothing but chuckles silently, and may I add movingly, on cue." Ty shrugged. "Welp, there goes my acting career. I'll never work in this town again."

"You're a man," Holly said. "They can fail all over this town and get work the very next day. No one even blinks if a movie written or directed by a man fails, but if it's a woman, she gets eviscerated."

Gwen put her fist in the air. "Preach, sister."

Holly slumped back against the sofa. "Go back to your day job, Ty. This town wasn't made for someone as nice as you."

Gwen glanced at her watch and sat next to Holly. "It wasn't made for someone as nice as you, either, but here you are, a few minutes away from the world premiere of a movie you wrote about two hot, funny, charming yet slightly flawed lesbians who fall in love over a batch of burnt Christmas cookies. So go change out of those pity panties and put on something more appropriate for this occasion. Something that screams *I kick ass all over this town, and it just so happens that I'm fucking Meredith Drake, so basically, all of my dreams came true this year.*"

Leave it to Gwen to speak the truth in the crassest way possible. But she was right. Holly had absolutely nothing to complain about. "You know what, Gwen? You're right. Tactless, but right." She shot up off the sofa and headed to her bedroom. "Hold the party for me."

"Holly?" Ty shouted back. "What should we do, ask Dez to put the TV on pause? Does she even have a DVR? We literally have thirty minutes until showtime."

"I'll be ready," Holly called from down the hall.

Moments later, she stood in front of her full-length mirror. She was overdressed for the weather, but if Desiree's apartment was too hot, she'd take off her grandpa's sweater. The red T-shirt she had on underneath would be festive enough and also tight enough to get a second look from Meredith. She loved it when Meredith did a double take, and it hadn't gone unnoticed that the tighter her shirts were, the more it happened.

If she was going festive, she really should go all in, so she opened her top drawer and took out the white fur hat she'd worn on what was now referred to as Holly Hudson Day in

Christmas Cove. The hat she'd been wearing when Meredith had professed her love in front of the entire town. Not to mention the following evening when Meredith undressed her in that chilly guest room and insisted she keep the hat on. The request for a naked photo was denied, but they did make love that night. Of course, it was a much quieter event than the year before in Hawaii. Holly still wondered if her parents had heard them. But what did it matter when over and over, her parents had expressed how happy they were that she'd found the real thing? True love, as her mother liked to call it.

Holly took the hat over to the mirror and put it on. Now all she needed was a little bit of snow. A light dusting would do. But this was Los Angeles, so Desiree's small, flocked tree was as close as she'd get to actual snow. And wasn't it strange that she actually longed for all of the things she used to avoid at this time of year. Snow falling on a cold, crisp night. Christmas carolers and hay rides with little kids whose eyes were always filled with wonder. Sipping on a mug of hot chocolate while watching *Miracle on 34th Street*. Yes, Holly Hudson had found her Christmas spirit again. Heck, she was practically a walking Wifetime movie. And as Gwen had said, her dreams had indeed come true. She walked back into the living room and pointed at her hat. "This is my 'I have a fucking day named after me' hat. Let's ride, bitches."

Gwen gave Holly a high five as she walked by. "That's more like it."

Holly stopped and scrutinized them a little closer. "Why are you two wearing coats?"

"It was supposed to be a surprise." Gwen motioned with her head at Ty. "Show her before we both die of heat stroke."

Ty didn't just open his jacket like a normal person. Apparently, he thought some sort of striptease was in order, so he unzipped it slightly and pulled it to one side, then the other.

"Oh, for the love of God, Ty." Gwen unzipped her own coat and threw it on the sofa. "First time I've been within ten feet of an oven mitt in years."

Ty took his coat off and said, "I'm quite fond of my snowman pot holder."

Holly gaped at the sight. She had no idea that Mrs. Brown had gifted her friends with their very own special sweatshirts. And they seemed perfect for them too because how could Mrs. Brown have known that Gwen's oven mitt should have a rather chubby version of Mrs. Claus on it? "I think this could be the best day of my life." She opened the door, excited to see what Griffin's would be.

They reached Desiree's door, and Ty stood in front of it with a silly grin on his face and his hand on the doorknob. "I can't let you in until I do this." He leaned in and kissed Holly's cheek, then pulled back and cleared his throat. "I'm damned proud to call you a friend."

Gwen swatted his shoulder. "I didn't get drunk in my apartment just to get sober while we wait for you, Casanova." She looked at Holly and shrugged. "I'm afraid if I kissed you, our lips would never part, so I'll leave it at, yeah, what Ty said." She gave Holly a wink, and Ty opened the door.

Holly hadn't expected a standing ovation. In fact, she hadn't expected most of what she saw as she walked into Desiree's apartment. "Mom? Dad? What are you doing here? Oh my gosh. Is everything okay?"

"Everything is fine, sweetie." Holly's mom stepped forward.

"But what are you doing here? Christmas is only three weeks away," Holly half shouted.

"Honey, we're not *really* Santa and Mrs. Claus. Our absence from Christmas Cove will not ruin Christmas for children everywhere. Don't worry. George is taking care of the hay rides for your dad." She opened her arms for a hug and held on to Holly for a long moment. "Nothing is as important as celebrating this moment with you and Meredith. We're so proud of both of you."

Of course they weren't the *real* Santa and Mrs. Claus, but Holly was pretty sure her parents hadn't ever left Christmas Cove during the holiday season before. She squeezed her mom and then her dad. "Thanks for coming. How's Brody? Does he miss me?"

"I don't know what you did to that horse," her dad said. "He puts up a big fuss every time I hook him up to the wagon."

Holly laughed. "Maybe I gave him one too many apples. He likes Granny Smiths best."

"I'll keep that in mind, honey. And just because we're here for the weekend doesn't mean you get to back out on spending New Year's Eve with us. The town council splurged on some extra-special fireworks this year."

New Year's Eve had always been the last big hurrah for Christmas Cove before everything slowed down. Some years, the fireworks show was a success, and others, well, not so much. "They hired a professional instead of leaving it up to George?"

Her dad tapped his nose with his finger. "Bingo."

"I'll be there too." Griffin handed Holly a glass of champagne. "You're going to teach me how to drive a wagon for my next role. You know, the one Meredith will produce, and I will star in, along with my hunky leading man. Make sure you write him as having three days' worth of scruff on his face. I love scruff more than I love a pair of soft blue eyes, and you know how much I love blue eyes."

Holly held the glass of bubbly up to the light. "Is this the same stuff you bought for last year's Christmas party? I just want to know if I should pencil a headache into my morning schedule."

He clutched his chest. "I wouldn't dream of pouring anything but the best for our guest of honor. It's a forty-dollar brut. You should be fine."

"Forty bucks, Griff?" Holly gave it a sniff. "Are you sure you can afford that when you'll be working for free on this movie where, for some unknown reason, you need to know how to drive a wagon?"

"Free? Remind me to tell you how SAG works some time." He cleared his throat and waved up and down his own body. "Now, how long before you notice that I'm not exactly dressed for this century?"

She gave him a once-over. He looked like he'd just walked off the set of *Seven Brides for Seven Brothers*. "Or the last century. My God, Griff. How far back are we talking?"

"Think *Pride and Prejudice*, only the early American frontier. Oh, and Mr. Darcy is a roughrider who falls for a farm boy, but the farm boy's dad is a total hardass who treats his son badly, so the son steals the family wagon, and then a wheel breaks, and love happens somewhere out on the vast prairie, Robert Redford style. But at Christmas."

She gave him a blank stare. "So pretty much nothing like *Pride and Prejudice*." She patted his chest. "I think it'd be better if I pitched this idea to Meredith."

He lifted an eyebrow. "I get it. You want to make sure she's in a good mood."

"No, I want to make sure it doesn't sound like the bear-meets-twink porno period piece you just tried to sell me. By the way, where's your pot holder sweatshirt? And don't lie and tell me she didn't give you one."

He held up a finger for her to wait and unbuttoned his

shirt. "I feel so seen. So understood. Mrs. Brown gets me, Holls. She really gets me." Griffin was right. An old-fashioned, meticulously embellished toy soldier sat proudly on his chest.

Gwen walked up and put a hand on her hip. "Oh my God, she bedazzled your nutcracker. I guess we know who Mrs. Brown likes best."

Holly covered her mouth to hide her laughter because this was indeed on her top ten list of best days of her life.

Desiree waved her hand in the air. "Welcome, everyone." She stood in front of the TV with Thad by her side. Holly had to smile because it seemed that at the ripe old age of eighty-four, Desiree was finally settling down with one man. Thad was a lucky guy, and he knew it. The cane he leaned on was new, but it went well with his tweed suit and silk bowtie. He had his elbow bent for Desiree and a proud grin on his face. They were happy, and Holly was thrilled for them.

Something at the door caught her attention. Not something. *Someone.* And not just anyone. No, it just happened to be the woman of Holly's dreams walking in. Everyone started clapping as they had for Holly, so she set her glass down and joined in. A sense of pride welled up in her as she watched Meredith make the rounds with hugs for everyone. It was obvious that Holly's parents being there wasn't a surprise to Meredith. She'd probably planned the whole thing.

Once she'd greeted everyone, Meredith stood next to Desiree and said, "Can I have your attention, everyone? We have a special surprise tonight. In fact, set those glasses of champagne down. We have something even better. An old family recipe that Connie was kind enough to share with us."

"The family recipe?" Holly turned to her mom. "I thought that was a secret only I could know."

"Well, it was, honey. But I figured the only way I was ever going to taste that punch again was if I brought it here."

"Your mom really loves that punch," her dad said. "And I really love how much she loves it. Gets her tipsy every time."

Gwen set her champagne glass down. "Well now, that sounds like my kind of punch. Where do I line up for it?"

She, Ty and Griffin scuffled to be at the front of a line they decided to form right in front of Holly's mom. She smiled and said, "Follow me to the dining table."

Everyone gathered around the table. Holly ended up standing directly opposite Meredith, who couldn't seem to stop smiling. Neither could Holly, for that matter.

She'd fallen hard for Meredith in Hawaii, but what she felt for her now was so much more than that. Meredith's love hadn't just washed over her. Over the last year, it had seeped in and filled the empty spots. Covered the gaps that Holly had realized everyone had, even people who were lucky enough to grow up in a town like Christmas Cove.

By the looks of things, her parents had become fond of Meredith as well. The minute she walked in the door her mom's eyes lit up. And her dad gave Meredith a huge hug. Meredith had even charmed her way into their little group. So it was no surprise that she stood there, flanked by Desiree and Thad. Holly's mom gave her a nod. "You do the honors, dear."

"I think Rick would like to say a few words first." Meredith, who stood quite a bit taller than both Desiree and Thad, put her arms around their shoulders and waited.

Holly could see the emotion in her dad's eyes. He was on the verge of getting all choked up, and if that happened, her mascara didn't stand a chance. He put his hands behind his back and rocked on his feet the way he usually did when he had something important to say. "First, I want to say thank you to all of you for being the good friends you are to Holly. Being so far away from home, it's hard not to worry, but I know she has a solid group that she can count on, and that's a relief to both of us." He put his arm around Holly's mom and blinked a few times to clear away the tears.

"Dad." Holly reached for him, even though she was on the other side of the table. Seeing her dad cry had never been an easy thing for her.

"Let me finish, honey." He paused and smiled at her mom while he tried to keep the tears at bay, then took a deep breath and said, "It's a good day for an old dad like me when he gets to see his baby girl's dreams come true. And you all might think I'm talking about the fact that there's a Holly Hudson Day in Christmas Cove. Or that there's a billboard just outside of town that tells everyone they're about to enter the childhood home of my daughter. Or you might think I'm referring to the big Wifetime movie premiere we're about to watch. And all of those things are so special, but I know they wouldn't mean near as much to Holly if she didn't have Meredith to share it all with."

Holly tried to hold it together, but when she felt Meredith's arms wrap around her from behind, tears mixed with happy giggles because no truer words had ever been spoken. And with those words, her dad let her know that they finally understood why she had to leave Christmas Cove all those years ago.

And with that knowledge, Holly could embrace her legacy with the love and care her grandma would've expected of her. Because sitting on that table was an ornate sterling silver punch bowl that had been passed down through four generations of Hudsons who had cherished it. And so would Holly. She kissed Meredith's cheek and whispered, "I'll do the honors." She went to the head of the table, and when she looked around, she saw that there wasn't a dry eye in the room. "Guys?"

"I hate crying in public," Gwen said. "I get swollen in all the wrong places."

Griffin madly waved his hands in front of his face. "Girl, you're looking at the queen of the ugly cry."

"I'm fine," Ty said, dabbing his eyes. "Everything's fine."

"Guys, get your crap together. I have to do a thing," Holly said. Meredith glanced at her watch and motioned for Holly to hurry. "Right. We have a movie to watch, so let me just say, having all of you here tonight to share in this amazing moment with me and Meredith, well, it means the world to both of us." She put her hands on the edge of the punch bowl and turned to her parents. "Mom. Dad. I love you so much. Thank you, for keeping this safe until I was ready for it." She pulled the cover away, and sure enough, it was filled to the rim with the deep red goodness she'd remembered. "You're going to love this, guys. It's the best Christmas punch you'll ever taste."

"Everyone, go find a spot in the living room," Meredith said. "We'll serve the punch."

Holly turned to Meredith and ran her fingers over her velvet collar. "You're really bringing back Hawaii with this smoking jacket."

Meredith took Holly's hand and intertwined their fingers. "And you're really bringing back last Christmas with that hat." She leaned in and whispered, "Will you wear it for me later?"

Holly pictured herself in her parents' guest room a year ago. Naked except for the hat, straddling her. She lowered her gaze since she really didn't need her parents and friends seeing that thought written all over her face. But that was the thing. This unique family of hers loved Meredith too, so hiding her emotions, her love for this woman, wasn't necessary. Okay, so maybe she shouldn't share those dirty thoughts, but she could share her joy. Her happiness. The feeling that her heart might burst wide open.

Holly took Meredith's face in her hands and said loud enough for everyone to hear, "I love you, Meredith Drake.

With all my heart, I love you." And then she kissed her. And with that kiss, she hoped to convey that there was nowhere she'd rather be and no one she'd rather be with.

"Oh damnit," Gwen said. "I just got my face cleaned up and they're at it again."

Ty grabbed the remote and turned the volume down. "Who needs this when we have the live version happening right in front of us?"

Holly took her hat off and tossed it across the room at Ty. "Make room on that sofa. And save us some of that popcorn." She noticed her parents hadn't sat down yet, so she filled two cups with punch and served them first. "Everything okay?"

"Everything's fine," her mom said. Except her mom didn't hide things well. Especially when she was going for casual.

She went back to the table and picked up a tray of punch cups Meredith had poured. "My mom's acting weird."

"She's just excited. It's a big night for them," Meredith whispered.

Holly took the tray and served the punch, all the while eyeing her parents. The punch was getting rave reviews, as expected. Gwen and Desiree were huddled close while they guessed what the ingredients were. That's when she realized that the TV had been put on pause.

"Holly?"

The room went quiet. Holly turned around and found Meredith standing behind her. She expected her to have two more cups of punch in her hands so they could all make a toast. But her hands were tucked into those cute green Christmas pants and she had a very serious look on her face. "Is something wrong?"

Meredith shook her head. "No. Quite the opposite." She took a step forward. "Two years ago, in the Honolulu airport, you, in your adorable, comedic way, rescued my lingerie from certain demise. And the following day, you rescued me again. And the next day too. And every day since."

Those words sounded familiar. Meredith had said something very similar that night one year ago when she showed up out of nowhere in Christmas Cove and walked up on that stage like she owned it. "What are you doing?" Holly whispered.

Meredith reached for her hand. "The last time I wore this jacket, I had one of the best dates of my life. And the last time you wore that sweater, I promised you we would get your movie made. And tonight, I want to ask you on another date. A lifetime of dates."

"Oh my God," Holly whispered. She glanced over at her parents. They both had tears in their eyes. She could hear Gwen sniffling behind her. And possibly Ty. She wiped her own tears away and suppressed the urge to fall into her future wife's arms.

Meredith reached into her pocket and pulled out a beautiful diamond solitaire. "I've been so honored to carry the title of girlfriend. But I want a promotion." She took a deep breath and said, "Holiday Hudson, will you marry me?"

Holly was pretty sure everyone in the room stopped breathing while they waited for her answer. She put her hands on Meredith's cheeks and said, "Have our guests turned blue yet?"

Meredith glanced around the room. "Gwen's about to pass out. They're all kind of frozen in time."

"Huh. I guess I should give you an answer, then." She threw her fists in the air and shouted, "Yes! Yes, yes, yes!"

Everyone cheered and surrounded them in a big group hug, and all Holly could do was laugh and cry at the same time because this was most definitely the best day of her life.

So far.

About the Author

Elle Spencer (http://ellespencerbooks.com) is the author of several best-selling lesbian romances including *Casting Lacey*, a Goldie finalist. She is a hopeless romantic and firm believer in true love, although she knows the path to happily ever after is rarely an easy one—not for Elle and not for her characters.

When she's not writing, Elle loves working on home improvement projects, hiking up tall mountains (not really, but it sounds cool), floating in the pool with a good book, and spending quality time with her pillow in a never-ending quest to prove that napping is the new working.

Elle and her wife live in Southern California.